READERS LOVE
JOHN INMAN

The Boys on the Mountain

"I am so impressed by this author. John Inman has proven time and again that he can write in multiple genres and still entertain, inform, and hold the interests of his audience."

—Joyfully Jay

"This is a very well written horror story by John Inman, and ranks right up there with Stephen King, in my opinion."

—The Novel Approach

"This is the strangest, yet most compelling book I've read in a long time."

—Inked Rainbow Reviews

Willow Man

"…the tone and craft of *Willow Man* is exceptional."

—Prism Book Alliance

"…a terrifying ride that makes you want to clutch tight and never let go of what you hold dear beside you."

—Hearts on Fire

By JOHN INMAN

The Boys on the Mountain
The Second Son
Willow Man

Published by DSP PUBLICATIONS
www.dsppublications.com

THE SECOND SON

JOHN INMAN

DSP PUBLICATIONS

Published by
DSP Publications

5032 Capital Circle SW, Suite 2, PMB# 279, Tallahassee, FL 32305-7886 USA
www.dsppublications.com

This is a work of fiction. Names, characters, places, and incidents either are the product of author imagination or are used fictitiously, and any resemblance to actual persons, living or dead, business establishments, events, or locales is entirely coincidental.

The Second Son
© 2016 John Inman.

Cover Art
© 2016 Paul Richmond.
http://www.paulrichmondstudio.com
Cover content is for illustrative purposes only and any person depicted on the cover is a model.

ISBN: 978-1-63476-572-5
Digital ISBN: 978-1-63476-573-2
Library of Congress Control Number: 2015953081
Published May 2016
v. 1.0

Printed in the United States of America
∞

This paper meets the requirements of
ANSI/NISO Z39.48-1992 (Permanence of Paper).

For Andi—my extraordinary editor, who is always enthusiastic, kind, patient as a saint, and without whom I would be humiliating myself on every page. This one's for you.

Part 1
Flames

CHAPTER ONE
A BEGINNING....

CHARLIE'S DOG, Mac, short for Machismo, had been acting rabbitass weird ever since the earthquake rattled the cabin along about eight o'clock that evening, scaring the holy bejeezus out of both him and the dog and jarring two of Charlie's paintings off the wall before the shaking stopped.

Being a California native transplanted to the Midwest, Charlie was no stranger to earthquakes, but this one had been different. For one thing, what the hell was that eerie glowing light that preceded the tremor by about fifteen seconds, suffusing the cabin in a yellow phosphorescence that looked like something from a fifties horror movie? And for another thing, why had the power gone out, and why was it *still* out, and why, pray tell, was Charlie feeling like maybe he should get around to organizing his life—or at least his candles—so he could find one when he needed it?

It had been cloudy before the earthquake, so with the power off, visibility was zip. Charlie couldn't see his hand before his face, and as he stumbled around in the dark fifteen minutes later, still looking for the goddamn candles, he skinned his shin on the coffee table, then stubbed a toe on the magazine rack before walking smack into the living room wall like some sort of moronic mime. As he stepped backward to get his bearings, he managed to go ass over teakettle after tripping on Mac, who let out a yelp like a piano had fallen on him. The poor dog scuttled off to the other side of the room to get out of harm's way. Charlie picked himself up with a nervous giggle and headed for the bar in the dining room, where even in the dark he *knew* where the Scotch was, by God, and poured a generous portion of it down his throat straight from the bottle.

As he blinked back 80-proof tears, not for the first time in his life, the power came back on.

Charlie and Mac looked at each other for about three ticks, and Charlie was about to apologize for scaring the dog to death, when the shaking started again. Deciding to ride this one out as best he could, Charlie grabbed for the banister that followed the stairs up to the bedroom loft and braced himself while Mac let out a long, eerie yowl from the living room floor, where he had tucked himself under the coffee table, sending shivers up Charlie's arms and making his scalp crawl like maybe he had lice or something.

"Jesus, Mac, don't do that!" he yelled. But by the time he yelled it, the shaking had stopped again. The lights stayed on, thank God, and the night was suddenly silent. Dead silent. No howling insane dog. No crickets. No rattling windows. Nothing.

Charlie let out a sigh of relief, returned the Scotch bottle to the bar (after prying it from his own rigid fingers), and stood there for a moment, waiting for whatever came next. But nothing came. The excitement seemed to be over.

Two minutes later, as Charlie was about to set off in search of a broom (like the candles, he wasn't exactly sure where *that* was either) to sweep up the broken glass from where the two paintings had crashed to the floor, the phone rang.

He figured it was either his ex-wife, Judith, asking for more money, or his ex-lover, Jason, asking for a second chance (which would be a fat one), or a telemarketer asking him to invest his hard-earned money in something he was already pretty sure he could live without. He was wrong on all three counts. It was his agent.

"Hey, Picasso! I sold the—"

"Good," Charlie blithely interrupted. "You know where to send the check." And with that, he hung up.

He suffered guilt pangs for all of five seconds for being so rude to the man, then completely forgot about it. He dug through the broom closet, which seemed the surest place to find a broom, but of course it wasn't there, had probably never been there since the day it was knotted together by some underpaid Taiwanese peasant back in the eighties. Then he remembered the broom was in his studio, where he had plucked most of the straws from its head to use in applying tiny specks of color to one of his canvases since none of his brushes seemed to fit the bill quite so nicely for such delicate work. And because he was in no mood to traipse across the backyard to reach his studio and the stupid broom, which was pretty much bald now anyway, Charlie scraped up the broken glass in a dishtowel and shook it into the trash can on the back porch.

As he stood there, breathing in the night air and waiting for Mac to water the dead grass (the dog had to pee after all the excitement, and who could blame him?), Charlie watched the moon peek out from behind the clouds and illuminate the lake that bordered the back of the property.

The shimmering water seemed a little choppier than usual, probably from the earthquake, but Charlie's small motorboat was still securely tethered to the dock where he had left it, and everything else seemed to be in order. His studio, once a two-car garage before having a thirty-thousand-dollar overhaul, still appeared to be standing. He knew he should be out there right now finishing the paintings he had been commissioned to paint to decorate the outer office of that law firm in the city he could never remember the name of—Swizzle, Pecker, and Jovanovich, or something like that—but he wasn't in the mood. He hated commissions anyway. He only truly enjoyed painting what *he* wanted to paint. Having a pack of overpaid and overpompous lawyer types and their equally pompous wives telling him how his canvas needed to match the blue in the carpeting of their six-million-dollar penthouse suite of law offices made his ass pucker every time he thought about it. As he pondered that, he pulled out Charlie Junior and took a whiz off the back stoop while Mac peed on the flower bed, which Jason had planted before their relationship disintegrated into oblivion and which Charlie had subsequently let wither away with neglect. He didn't own a garden hose, he never knew exactly where Jason had stashed the watering can, and he didn't much care for flowers anyway unless they were rendered in tempera.

He really did need to get his life in order, but Charlie didn't figure it would happen tonight, so he whistled for Mac to follow, and the two of them strode back into the cabin, one zipping his fly and the other wagging his tail. Both were as happy as clams to be in each other's company without the annoying presence of ex-wives or ex-lovers or anybody else to mar the lonely perfection of the evening.

He was settling in before a fire newly lit in the fireplace with the latest Harry Potter book in one hand and a generous dollop of Scotch in the other, in a proper glass this time, when someone knocked at the front door.

Charlie ignored it. So did Mac.

The knock came again, and again Charlie ignored it, but this time Mac set up a wailing yowl that made Charlie's ass pucker once more, and when whoever it was got tired of knocking and decided to jiggle the doorknob instead, Charlie figured he had better answer it before Mac had a stroke and before the person, obviously determined to gain access, opted to jimmy a window and climb on in. Charlie admired persistence, but not when it was directed at him.

With a groan of annoyance, he set the book and the Scotch on the coffee table, told Mac to please shut the hell up before he rang up a taxidermist and had him stuffed and mounted like Trigger, then headed for the door.

Upon opening it, with Mac excitedly hopping around at his feet as eager to see who was out there as Charlie wasn't, Charlie's eyes, previously slit in anger and no small amount of dread, opened considerably wider, and a smile of surprise lit his face.

God knows what he had expected, but it wasn't this.

The young man, who Charlie had never seen before in his life, beamed a smile back at him, apparently unconcerned that he now stood on Charlie's doorstep as naked as the day he was born. To Charlie's practiced eye, he looked damned handsome doing so.

The naked stranger nonchalantly bent to pet the dog, then brushed his long dark hair from his eyes with a strong, brown hand before saying to Charlie, "May I come in?"

CHARLES ALLEN Strickland—Charlie to his friends and exes, and C. A. Strickland to the art world—had sold his first painting at the age of twelve to his mother for the total sum of seventy-five cents and a batch of Toll House cookies. Now, twenty years later, his work commanded a considerably higher price. His last painting, the one his dealer and agent, Edgar Fosse, had phoned him about earlier in the evening, a supine male nude lying in a field of wildflowers, had been listed at nine grand, and judging by the happy lilt to Fosse's voice when he called to tell Charlie the news, it had sold for exactly that. If he ever got around to finishing the triptych—three six-by-twelve-foot panels of the Chicago skyline—for Swoozie, Peahen, and Jackass, or whoever the hell they were, Charlie would be receiving the tidy sum of twelve five.

On the average, Charlie produced about ten canvases a year, five of which he considered worthy of sale, two of which he could never bring himself to part with and kept for his own collection, and three that were just plain crap and were consequently painted over. He wasn't exactly growing rich, but he *was* doing what he most dearly loved to do, and that was a wonderful position for a man to be in.

As his ex-wife and ex-lover had always told him, he could be twice as productive if he simply got his life in order and simplified his messy existence, and Charlie had accepted their advice and dumped them both, first the wife, then the lover, and it did simplify things, but not enough to make him any more productive. It did, however, make his nonproductive hours more enjoyable. His life was still a mess, of course—he couldn't even find a broom or a candle, for Christ's sake. But these were minor inconveniences compared to being nagged and prodded into being something he wasn't and never would be and didn't particularly *want* to be.

Organization, a concept as alien to Charlie as monochromatic art, was low on his list of priorities. His canvases, like his life, were wildly splashed with color and chaos, and as in his life, he refused to paint within the lines. There were no borders in his art and few borders anywhere else in his existence, sexually or otherwise. He enjoyed men and women equally, although lately he was beginning to understand he really needed neither, not on a continual basis, at least. His painting was his passion. The desires of his body were secondary to his need to paint, although sometimes Charlie Junior did raise his head (literally) and protest that decision.

And now, staring at this gorgeous young man with the sweet smile and luscious body standing nude on his doorstep, Charlie could sense Charlie Junior was having second thoughts yet again.

The fact that the stranger had come out of the night like some sort of visiting angel was not lost on Charlie, and while the young man now stared at him with innocently inquisitive eyes, waiting for a response to his question, Charlie could also sense that maybe the kid knew what sort of thoughts were suddenly stampeding through Charlie's mind. Thoughts, shall we say, of a less than an angelic nature.

With an effort of will, Charlie trained his eyes on that innocent, stunning face and tried to limit their wanderings downward as he ushered his visitor inside.

Mac, never particularly good with strangers, was all but slobbering all over himself. He had a sappy grin on his doggy face and his tail was going a mile a minute as the young man stepped over the threshold and crossed the room to stand before the fireplace, hands out, absorbing the heat.

The young man's nudity seemed of little concern to him.

"You're cold," Charlie said. "Let me get you something to put on."

He found his bathrobe on the floor of his bedroom, where he had dropped it earlier after showering the paint from his body, and lugged it to the living room to drape it solicitously over his visitor's shoulders.

The young man shrugged his arms into the sleeves, pulled it snug around his body, and only then turned away from the fire and, much to Charlie's surprise, reached out a warm hand to touch Charlie's cheek and say, "Thank you."

For the first time, Charlie truly studied the face before him. It was a kind face. Heart-stoppingly handsome. Dark warm eyes studied Charlie back with no hint of embarrassment or reserve, as if the young man knew why he was there, even if Charlie did not. Long black lashes any woman in the world would have happily killed for sprang from around deep brown eyes so open and untouched by reticence or doubt. A shock of black hair fell over his wide forehead, swaying across his riveting eyes as the young man once again stooped to give Mac a friendly scratch. Then, absently pushing his hair from his forehead with long, elegant fingers, Charlie's visitor stood upright and settled his shoulders into a comfortable stance. He gazed at Charlie with a slight smile that transformed his sweet face into a thing of utter beauty.

Charlie tore his eyes from that perfect face long enough to gesture to the sofa and say, "Won't you sit?"

"Thank you," the young man said again and, gently nudging Mac aside, stepped around the coffee table and lowered himself to the sofa. The long robe slid open in the front, exposing well-formed legs that were tightly muscled and only sparsely sprinkled with dark hair. He patted the seat beside him and said, "Join me. Please."

As if coming out of a trance, Charlie began to realize how strange this whole scenario truly was, but he plopped himself down beside the stranger nevertheless, and before he could ask the young man where the hell he had come from and what in God's name he was doing there, knocking on his door stark naked in the middle of the night, his visitor said, "You can paint me if you like."

"Uh… thank you," Charlie said. "But how did you know I paint?"

The young man looked around the room at the canvases stacked against every wall and then looked pointedly at Charlie's fingernails, which were permanently splotched with just about every color in the rainbow no matter how hard he tried to clean them, and Charlie realized the young man didn't really have to answer his question, and in fact he didn't. Charlie also realized for the first time that the young man was exactly right. He *did* want to paint him. He wanted to capture that perfect innocence on canvas, if his talents would allow him to do so. He also realized he wouldn't mind capturing the young man on bedsheets either, but perhaps that was moving forward a little too quickly even for him.

He reached out, took a long pull from his glass of Scotch, set the glass carefully back onto the coffee table, and said, "Who the hell are you, anyway? Where did you come from and where are your clothes and how did you find yourself on my doorstep and how did you know I would like to paint you even though I don't know anything else about you? I'm beginning to think maybe I *should* know some of these things since you're sitting in my living room in my bathrobe, and I feel like this is the most natural thing in the world to be doing, but in the back of my mind, I know it isn't. In fact, it's bugshit awkward. Or should be."

"I won't harm you," the visitor said, grinning at Charlie's long speech. "You needn't be afraid of me."

"I'm not," Charlie said, knowing it was true.

Then, as if someone had slipped him a mickey, Charlie felt his eyes grow heavy, and around a barely stifled yawn, he heard himself say, "You can sleep here if you want. I'll get you a blanket. Stay by the fire where it's warm."

"Only if you stay with me," the young man said.

"All right."

Before any of his questions were answered, Charlie stretched his long legs along the length of the sofa and the young man snuggled in alongside him, draped one arm across Charlie's chest, tucked his head into the warmth of Charlie's shoulder, and watched the fire for a moment before allowing his eyes to close.

Together they slept, with Mac snoring softly at their feet, as the fire popped and cracked and eventually died away to embers on the grate.

CHARLIE OPENED his eyes as the morning sun sent its first tentative fingers of light creeping across the living room floor. Flat on his back, he blinked away sleep, wondering for a moment why he wasn't in his bed. Then he remembered his visitor of the night before. With a groan, he twisted his head around to see what he could see. It wasn't much. The fire was long dead. The ice had melted in his unfinished Scotch. Mac was nowhere around. And his houseguest had apparently taken a powder. He recalled how the young man, so beautiful it almost took his breath away, had nestled in beside him to sleep, and for the first time, Charlie began to wonder if maybe he was growing senile or something. Was Alzheimer's known to afflict thirty-two-year-old bisexual artists, or was it simply an incredible lapse of judgment that had allowed him to be mesmerized into accepting the young man, who he didn't know from Adam and who might be a stunningly handsome serial killer for all he knew, into his home, and even *sleeping* with him, for Christ's sake, without learning so much as the young man's name?

Then another thought occurred to him. Maybe it was all a dream. Maybe there had *been* no naked young Adonis standing on his doorstep last night. Maybe it had been a figment of his imagination brought on by too much Scotch and the aftereffects of that bizarre earthquake, if the earthquake wasn't a figment of imagination as well. Charlie twisted his head a little farther around and saw the empty squares of slightly brighter paint on the dining room wall where his two paintings had once resided, and he knew the earthquake, at least, had actually taken place, even if his imaginary visitation had not.

He reached out, still flat on his back, and brought the lukewarm glass of Scotch to his lips, taking a sip as he thought things over. "Blech," he said, making a disgusted face. Funny how Scotch could be so enjoyable in the evening and taste like cat piss at six o'clock in the morning.

"Mac!" he called out.

No answer.

"Gorgeous naked anonymous man!" he tried again.

Still no answer.

He pulled himself to a sitting position and immediately saw his bathrobe neatly draped across the side of the twelve-hundred-dollar armchair Jason had conned him into buying, though it sat about as comfortably as cast-iron lawn furniture. Looked good, though, Jason had continually told him. God, that boy was a pain in the ass.

Charlie tore his mind away from the damn chair, and away from Jason as well, and absorbed the true meaning of that bathrobe hanging there.

He hauled himself to his feet and methodically padded through every room in the house looking for his visitor from the night before, certain now that the young man hadn't been a bit of undigested beef, as old Scrooge was fond of saying, and truly existed. He remembered how the boy, for that was how Charlie truly thought of him, had offered to let Charlie paint him. That simple statement alone implied that the young man intended to hang around awhile, and Charlie found himself hoping he would do exactly that. He felt an undeniable urge to see the boy again. Not because he still held sexual fantasies about him, although he could think of worse ways to while away a little time, but because he wanted to see if the boy was really as beautiful and calm and *otherworldly* as Charlie remembered him being. And he still had about a gazillion unanswered questions he'd like cleared up. Where *had* the boy come from? What was he doing here? And where the hell was he *now*?

The A-frame cabin was empty of any living presence other than his own, all four rooms of it. Upstairs and down. Charlie poked his head out the back door, took in the cool, sun-drenched summer morning, and saw the door leading to his studio hanging open. As he stared at it, Mac appeared from inside the studio and, on seeing Charlie, let out a happy yip and came galloping across the dead lawn to greet him. Charlie gave the hair on the back of Mac's neck an absentminded ruffle and, barefoot, set off across the crunchy stubble of his pathetic lawn and made his way to the studio door.

When he found the young man sitting cross-legged on the floor of the studio, gazing up at the unfinished triptych, which was arranged along three separate easels because of its size and pretty much dominated the whole room, Charlie's heart gave a little twang. The young man was now wearing an old pair of Charlie's jeans and a cable-knit sweater Charlie hadn't seen in a month—had actually been looking for a couple of weeks back but never found. The boy looked considerably better in his clothes than Charlie ever did. Unreasonably, he found himself hoping the boy liked Charlie's work. He also found himself wishing he had brushed his teeth before leaving the cabin, or at least combed his hair. He figured he probably looked like the wreck of the *Hesperus* with his hair poking up in thirty directions and his morning stubble and wrinkled clothes, but then, this wasn't a beauty contest, was it? And even if it had been, Charlie knew he wouldn't have stood a chance next to the perfect specimen of manhood that sat so comfortably on the floor in front of him, gazing with such seeming concentration at the canvases Charlie had been working on for the past two months.

The boy looked as rested as Charlie didn't. Of course, his visitor had probably not consumed a half bottle of Scotch the night before. As

Charlie stared at him, not wanting to interrupt the young man's perusal of his work—which Charlie was rather proud of, in fact—he also felt a twinge of unease to think the boy had been rummaging through his stuff to find something to wear as Charlie lay sawing logs on the living room sofa, but Charlie quickly realized even that didn't bother him much. What bothered him was the way the boy had his head cocked as he studied the paintings, like maybe he was seeing something that shouldn't have been there, or maybe not seeing something that *should* have been there.

"It's Chicago at dawn," Charlie said, rather apologetically, he thought, which irked him. What the hell was he apologizing about?

But the boy smiled as he turned to look at him, and said, "Never apologize for what you do, Charlie. It's wonderful. Your colors breathe life. You brought tension to a static skyline of mortar and glass. I can actually sense people living their lives behind those windows. How do you do that?"

Charlie didn't know what to say, so he said nothing. Silence once again settled over the studio as the boy turned back to the paintings. Charlie found himself crossing the room and squatting down next to him. Together, they stared at the three canvases. Charlie began to see his work through the eyes of the young man next to him, through innocent eyes, something Charlie had not had for a very long time. He was only slightly surprised when the boy laid his hand on his and gave it a gentle squeeze.

"You have a beautiful soul, Charlie."

Charlie had never been convinced he, or anybody *else* for that matter, truly possessed a quantifiable soul, beautiful or otherwise, but the young man had said what he said with such conviction in his voice that Charlie didn't think this the proper time to argue the merits of existentialism versus higher authority, which possession of a soul would certainly dictate. Besides, it was way too early in the morning for such complicated thinking, and he hadn't even brushed his teeth yet, for God's sake.

Charlie turned his head to gaze at the incredible young man next to him, taking in the handsome face, the too-long hair, the clean lines of the tanned throat and shoulders exposed through the stretched-out neck of the battered old sweater and, letting the matter of souls slide for the moment, heard himself say, "What's your name?"

"Joe," the young man said. "My name is Joe."

"I'm Charlie."

"I know."

Mac settled in between them and rested his chin on Joe's leg. With one hand still on Charlie's, Joe slid his other hand along Mac's broad back, and Mac slowly closed his eyes in bliss.

"He likes you," Charlie said.

Joe gave a tiny shrug. "I have a way with animals, I guess." His eyes had not left the canvas.

"Where did you come from, Joe? What are you doing here?"

Again, Joe shrugged. "I'm just here. That's all."

"But where did you come from?"

Joe lifted his hand from Charlie's and swept it across the dawning sky on the canvas. "Where do any of us come from?"

"Well…."

Joe turned, finally, to Charlie and said, "You look hungry. Let's have breakfast. I'll cook."

"Uh… okay."

After easing Mac's head aside, Joe gracefully unfolded his legs and stood, helping Charlie to his feet as well. Together they left the studio, and as they crossed the lawn with Mac at their heels, their bare feet crunching over the dead grass and their shoulders brushing companionably together as they walked, Charlie spotted a bloom in the withered flower bed. One tiny splash of color among the tangle of crisp sepia stems.

"My God," he said, more to himself than to Joe, "it's still alive."

Joe followed Charlie's glance to that one perfect purple blossom, smiled, and said, "It always was."

WHILE JOE puttered at the stove, Charlie sat at the kitchen table, watching him. The boy stood as tall as Charlie, six foot or so, and had the trim body of a long distance runner. Charlie figured Joe was only nineteen or so, certainly not much older than that. As he scrambled eggs and fiddled with a fistful of sausages in a separate skillet, and as he stepped casually across the kitchen to drop slices of bread in the toaster, Charlie was once again mesmerized, not only by the boy's beauty, but by the feline grace of his movements as he set about preparing their breakfast. He seemed to know Charlie's kitchen better than Charlie did. He went right to the butter in the door of the fridge when it was needed, found the salt and pepper shakers over the sink in the little cupboard built into the wall without having to ask Charlie for directions, and hauled plates out of the hutch by the door, taking a moment to admire the willow pattern of the china (a wedding gift from Judith's parents, who were even now probably sticking needles in a voodoo doll of Charlie's effigy for dumping their daughter the way he did, just as Judith was no doubt sticking needles in a voodoo doll of *Jason's* effigy for supplanting her in Charlie's affections, not to mention his bed, before Jason too was evicted). As Joe set the plates on the table, turning them neatly so the willow pattern faced the proper way, Charlie tore his eyes from him and stared out the kitchen window. First, he looked at the one budding flower in the previously dead-as-Caesar flower bed, which he could still see from where he sat, then he looked at the studio, where he thought of his triptych and Joe's reaction to it.

Ordinarily, Charlie didn't much care what people thought of his art pieces so long as there was someone out there willing to pay good money to own one, but the boy's praise had touched him somehow. Charlie had always rather assumed he painted for himself, ignoring critics and admirer's alike, feeling no true pride in his work, only enjoyment of the process. But the way the boy had sat there on the studio floor, taking in the strokes of his paintbrush like a reader takes in the words on a page, made Charlie's heart give another twang. A twang of pride this time. And excitement. He felt an almost uncontrollable urge to step across the room, turn off the damn stove, yank Joe around, and just stare into those deep brown eyes for a minute. He could learn things there, he knew, if only Joe would let him probe deep enough to find them. They were waiting for him, Charlie suspected, those valuable lessons, buried somewhere behind that sweet, handsome face. There was a soul back there somewhere too, Charlie suddenly knew, no longer doubting it for a second. Perhaps Charlie himself had one after all. Joe said he did, and Charlie felt an odd certainty that somehow he would know of such things.

Aside from his first name, Charlie knew absolutely nothing about the young man who was at this very moment scraping eggs onto their plates and buttering toast and flipping sausages from the smoking skillet, serving up their breakfast like it was a truly important thing to be doing. And yet, Charlie began to wonder if he was falling in love with Joe. My God, this wasn't even Charlie Junior's doing, it was Charlie's alone. And it made no sense at all. Charlie might not be the most level-headed man on the planet, but he wasn't a complete imbecile either. For all he knew,

Joe might be a con man, a killer on the run, a stalker of artists, a juvenile delinquent, or a drug-addled hippie, if hippies still existed. But of course he wasn't. Somehow Charlie knew this for a fact, if he knew nothing else, which he most certainly didn't. Still, he did think it was time he learned *something* about this boy, this Joe, who had dropped into his life like an anvil.

Around a mouthful of eggs, which were overcooked to the consistency of clams (the kid was certainly no chef), he said, "Where is your family, Joe?"

Joe was forking up the food on his plate like he hadn't eaten in a week. After downing half a glass of milk, then wiping his lips with a paper napkin, Joe smiled across the table at Charlie and said, "You can finish the triptych today if you start early. It's almost finished now, don't you think? It's lovely the way it is. If you peck around at it too much more, it will lose its spirit. Those people behind the windows will move away."

Charlie blinked. "Did you really see people there or were you just trying to flatter me?"

"Does it matter?"

"I suppose not. Well… yes, now that you mention it. It matters a great deal. I'd like to think you meant what you told me."

Joe tucked a sausage in his mouth, chewed it up, then took a nibble of toast. "I will never lie to you, Charlie."

"Good. I hate being lied to."

"I know."

"So where is your family?" Charlie asked, ignoring the fact that Joe sometimes spoke of him as if he truly knew him, which was impossible.

Joe laughed. "Where do you want them to be?"

"Hell, Joe, I don't know. But you have to come from somewhere. You didn't just fall out of the sky last night, did you?"

"Do people generally fall out of the sky around here?"

"Not that I know of."

"Well, there you go."

Charlie tried again. "What does your father do?"

It was Joe's turn to stare out the kitchen window, and Charlie thought maybe he too was gazing on that one blooming iris at the edge of the yard. "My father grows things," Joe said.

"You mean he has a nursery?"

Joe turned away from the window and studied Charlie's inquiring face with gentle humor on his own. "I suppose you could call it a nursery. Can I stay with you for a while, Charlie? Can I live with you here inside this house?"

"What?"

"I said, yes, my father has a nursery, and then I asked if I could stay with you. Finish your eggs. They're getting cold."

Charlie did as he was told. If nothing else it bought him some time. Time to consider Joe's question. What the hell was going on here? Why would Joe think he could suddenly come waltzing, naked no less, into Charlie's life and take up residence as if he belonged here? And what the hell did this nineteen-year-old know of art, and why did it matter to Charlie so much that Joe appreciated his work, and what would his friends say if he told them he had a young man living with him who he knew less about than he knew about quantum physics, which was absolutely nothing? And how could Joe speak of souls and make Charlie change his perception of life in the time it takes to change your socks, and why was he even considering—no, why had he already decided to let the boy do exactly what he asked? And why, above all else, was Charlie so eager to have him do so? There was more than hormones at play here, but Charlie didn't have the vaguest idea what the hell it might be. All he knew was what he heard himself say.

"Yes, Joe. You can stay with me as long as you like."

"Thank you, Charlie."

"You're welcome, Joe."

"I have no money, you know."

"That's all right," Charlie said. "I do."

"You only have one bedroom. Where will I sleep?"

"With me," Charlie said. "Or on the sofa. Take your pick."

Joe downed the last drops of milk in his glass, and said, "I'll sleep with you."

"Good," Charlie said.

And that was that.

Chapter Two
...Questions and Promises....

As the summer day warmed with the rising sun and Charlie added finishing touches to his latest commission, and while the studio filled with morning light through the massive skylight he had installed when the garage was renovated, his mind made several imaginary pilgrimages to the night ahead and what it promised. But he did not linger there long. His work, as always, kept him focused on the movements of hand and brush and the colors and shapes that unfolded beneath them.

Periodically, he cast his eyes through the studio's side windows, which overlooked the lake, and saw Joe, with Mac at his side, sitting on the fender of Charlie's motorboat, pant legs rolled up, bare feet dangling in the water, staring out at the lake's far shore. He had been sitting there for hours. Charlie wondered what he was seeing, what he was thinking, and if perhaps his imagination might be taking flights to the night ahead as well. Somehow Charlie couldn't imagine it, but he sure hoped so.

Charlie wondered if the young man understood the implications of sharing a bed. On the palette of Joe's face, there was a wide-open look of such amiable innocence that Charlie could not imagine that sweet face twisted in the throes of orgasm. As much as Charlie wanted to feel Joe's body next to his, as much as he wanted to feel his hands exploring Joe, and Joe exploring him, he suspected that deep down, past the place where lust resided, was a part of him that wanted the boy to remain as he was: Innocent. Untouched. Pure.

Charlie wondered, too, if as they lay side by side beneath the sheets during the night ahead, Charlie could stay his own lust long enough to let Joe make the first move, assuming sex was his intent. Would Joe feel obligated to do so? Charlie did not want the boy to feel he owed Charlie anything. Charlie had not acquiesced to the boy's request for shelter for that reason. Why he *had* acquiesced, he wasn't quite sure, but it was not for sexual reasons. Charlie suspected he could derive a lot more from Joe's presence than Joe could ever derive from his. Joe had more to give than Charlie did. Charlie understood this instinctively. What it was, exactly, the boy could offer him, Charlie wasn't quite sure. But it was something important. That much Charlie knew.

As Charlie's brush stroked canvas, as colors melted onto linen, blended, came alive, Charlie began to understand something else. The desire he had felt for the boy when he first saw him standing naked on his doorstep had shifted into something else. The few hours he had spent with Joe, the few words they had shared between them, were more meaningful to Charlie than anything that had happened to him in a very long time. Desire was still there. Now more than ever. The boy was too beautiful for it not to be. But Joe's mere presence had given Charlie new longings, nonsexual longings, that had nothing to do with passion and everything to do with simple contentment. His presence calmed Charlie. Unflinchingly, he had accepted Joe into his life, just as Mac had. Without a moment's hesitation or misgivings, he knew Joe's presence would make him a better person. A better artist. A better everything.

The single strident note, the only twinge of unease, that came to Charlie from Joe's presence was his knowledge that his love for Joe—and that's exactly what it was, he knew that now without a doubt—would one day come back to hurt him. Joe would not be with him forever. One day he would simply leave, go off to the next place his life led him, and then Charlie would be alone again. For that was the great change Charlie knew Joe had instilled in him already. The aloneness he had cherished before was no longer something he craved. Now, that aloneness frightened him. For to be alone would mean to be without Joe. And that, Charlie knew, could destroy him.

He tried to laugh at himself for falling head over heels in love with a total stranger, and for the simple, sudden *need* that love was forcing him to confront within himself, but somehow he couldn't quite find the humor in it.

He turned again from the canvas to look out at the boy by the lake and was surprised to see Joe standing right outside the window, staring in. Joe made a sweeping gesture with his arm, drawing an arc above his head, across the sky. Smiling, he tore his eyes from Charlie's face and stared at the canvas.

Charlie turned to the canvas as well and knew immediately what Joe wanted him to do. He watched his hand reach into the empty paint can as if it belonged to someone else, for a different brush, a larger brush, soft and wide and new. Without thinking, Charlie dipped the brush in a pot of white acrylic and made a long sweeping swath across the sky above the city skyline on the canvases. Like a screaming meteor trail, it stretched from one side of the first painting in the triptych to the outer edge of the third.

That slash of glaringly white acrylic tore across the muted watercolors like an arm of light, centering the eye, drawing the paintings together, giving them texture where before there had been none. It was totally out of place, that streak of bright light, yet it was perfectly placed. Perfectly executed. It made the three paintings one.

Stunned, Charlie dropped the dripping paintbrush at his feet and stepped back, staring at what he had done. A smile crept across his face. He could feel his heart thudding away inside his chest with what might have been fear, but was more likely exhilaration, and he turned his head again to look at Joe.

The boy was once again sitting on the fender of Charlie's boat, one arm draped across Mac's broad back, staring intently out at the water.

It was as if he had never moved.

As THE sun began a slow slide to evening, Charlie and Joe, with Mac at their side, took a spin around the lake. The motorboat's powerful engine made conversation almost impossible, but that didn't bother them. Joe was clearly engrossed with the feel of wind and spray, and Charlie was content to watch the happiness on the boy's face as Joe's long hair whipped and thrashed in the wind, his lips pulled tight in laughter, exposing small white teeth as perfect as any toothpaste ad could promise. This sudden, unexpected look of jubilation on Joe's face, a face usually so calm and serene, made Charlie's own laughter bubble to the surface.

"You've never been on a boat before, have you?" Charlie screamed into the wind.

Joe took a handful of his thrashing hair and held it away from his eyes. He shook his head, his broad smile still making Charlie's heart soar, but he did not speak. Instead, he released his hair, pulled Charlie's sweater over his head, and stretched his arms wide, letting the wind pummel his body and the cool lake spray wash across his bare chest. This, Charlie knew, was how he would paint the boy. *Freedom*, he would call it. Charlie also knew, immediately, that the painting would never leave his possession. For one day, when Joe had left him, as he surely would, that painting, *Freedom*, would be all that remained of their time together: a few strokes of paint on canvas to remind Charlie what he'd once had, and lost.

This thought made Charlie's happiness crash down around his feet like a dropped basket of laundry. Slowly, he eased up on the throttle and brought the boat to a rocking stop in the center of the lake.

In that sudden secession of wind and spray and throbbing sound, Joe turned to him, still dripping, still laughing, his dark hair still tumbling across his eyes, and said, "Don't be sad, Charlie. One day we will see each other again."

Charlie felt fingers of fear pierce his chest, constrict his heart. "Are you leaving, Joe? Are you leaving already?"

"No," Joe said. "Not yet. There are things to do before I go."

With his face still glistening with lake water and his happiness still alive and bubbling inside his bottomless brown eyes, Joe laid his hand on Charlie's neck and, stepping forward, pressed a kiss to Charlie's forehead like a blessing. A benediction. Charlie closed his eyes as Joe's soft lips touched his skin, as the boy's sweet breath stirred his hair. Charlie felt Joe's essence enter into him like heat from a flame. He absorbed it eagerly, letting it feed an enormous hunger Charlie did not know he felt until that very moment. Tenderly, Joe caressed the skin below Charlie's ear with fingers surprisingly strong for all their slim elegance, and for that one brief instant, Charlie's fear vanished. Charlie felt, for the first time in his life, totally at peace.

Joe stepped back and studied the amazed look on Charlie's face. When Charlie smiled, finally, Joe smiled back.

"Now can we go in the water?" Joe meekly asked.

Before Charlie could stammer an answer, the boy was pushing his damp slacks down past his hips and stepping out of them, once again presenting himself to Charlie as naked as the first time they met. When Joe began peeling the shirt from Charlie's body, laughing at the look on Charlie's face when he did so, Charlie too stepped out of his jeans. Both naked now, hand in hand, Charlie led Joe to the fender of the boat and stepped out into the water, pulling Joe in after him.

They both gasped with the sudden shock of cold water against their skin, but Charlie's laughter died on his lips when he saw Joe sink like a rock next to him. He grabbed a fistful of Joe's thick hair and pulled him back to the surface. Only then did Charlie realize the boy couldn't swim.

He wrapped his arm around Joe's chest, holding him close, keeping his head above water, while Joe giggled and sputtered. All too conscious of Joe's naked flanks against his groin, Charlie frog-kicked back to the edge of the boat, where he placed Joe's hands on the gunwale, releasing him when he knew the boy was safely holding on.

Together, they hung there in the water, Charlie's arm still draped protectively around Joe's shoulder. Mac's grinning face appeared at the edge of the boat, giving them both friendly licks before Charlie gently pushed him away.

"I'll teach you to swim," Charlie said. "But not here. The water's too deep. Why did you step out into the water like that? You could have drowned."

Joe pushed streaming hair away from his eyes. "How could I drown with you there beside me? You protected me, Charlie, like I knew you would."

"Yeah, but my God, Joe, you sank like a brick. I might have lost you in the water."

"But you didn't."

"But I could have."

"But you didn't."

The heat of Joe's body, despite the cool water, brought warmth to Charlie's own. He cupped the back of Joe's neck with his fingers, still feeling the need to hold him above water although he was safely gripping the boat, and when Joe's leg brushing his own beneath the surface of the water began to excite him, Charlie found himself drawing away so Joe wouldn't know.

He tried to take his mind off that awkward stirring of desire by saying, "What things do you have to do, Joe?"

Charlie saw a question in Joe's eyes, as if he were perhaps wondering why Charlie had pulled away from him, but he tilted his head back against Charlie's fingers at his neck and said, "There is no right or wrong where love is concerned, Charlie. Love is simply love. A perfect, true thing. A flower. Don't be ashamed of it."

"You… you frighten me," Charlie said, almost stunned to hear his deepest feelings pouring out of him. But he could not hold them back. They needed to be said. "I don't want to push. I don't want to frighten *you*. I want you to feel safe with me, Joe. Not… beholden."

Joe laughed. "If I feel beholden to you, Charlie, then it's my choice. We have things to do together. There can be no secrets between us. No secrets and no holding back. Open yourself up to me, Charlie. Be who you are. You have more to give me than just your talent. Teach me about life, Charlie. Teach me how to live. Share it all with me, Charlie. Teach me everything you know." He laughed again. "Teach me how to swim so I don't sink like a brick."

Charlie found himself laughing too—at the boy's wistful enthusiasm, at the sweet eagerness that radiated from him like rays of sunshine piercing a rent in a clouded sky, at the hint of other lessons he seemed eager to learn, lessons of love, maybe, lessons Charlie wanted to share with Joe more than anything else in the world.

"Which would you like me to do first?" he asked jokingly, fighting yet again the urge to fold Joe in his arms.

"Feed me," Joe said. "I'm starving."

Dripping, Charlie pulled himself into the boat and pulled Joe up behind him. Still naked, he turned the ignition and, over the scream of the awakening engine, bellowed, "Consider yourself fed!"

He watched with pride and a sense of sudden possessiveness as Joe, still as naked as he, once again stood at the bow of the boat and let the wind and spray whip across his perfect young body, skin shimmering gold in the setting sun, dark hair flying loose and free, as they tore their way toward the shore and home.

Never before had Charlie's heart been so full, his sense of need so strong.

Or his fear of loss so great.

EVENING SHADOWS had settled into the corners of the cabin, and, dinner over, Charlie built a fire. He and Joe, with Mac beside them, lay on the hearthrug, staring contentedly into the flames.

Charlie had found other clothes for Joe to wear, and again he filled them better than Charlie ever had. Ever would. Joe's mane of dark hair was still damp from the shower, his face gleaming with health and happiness in the flickering firelight. It took every ounce of Charlie's willpower not to simply lie back and stare at the boy. The urge to reach out and stroke him, to feel the warmth of him, was so strong that Charlie curled his fingers into his palms and tucked them beneath his chin. Barefoot, as always, Joe slid his foot closer, touching Charlie's as if connection between the two was imperative to speech. Charlie closed his eyes for a moment, relishing the feel of that one simple touch.

A night bird trilled somewhere in the trees at the side of the house, and Joe tilted his head, listening to it over the crackling of the fire. His eyes seemed to light up with wonder at the sound of the bird's startling song. He looked over at Charlie, as if to see if Charlie heard it too, and Charlie smiled, yet again, at his innocence.

He had to speak. Slowly, he said, "So many things seem new to you, Joe. How can you know so much, and yet…?"

Joe grinned. "And yet know so little?"

Charlie grinned back. "Yes."

Joe studied Charlie's face for a long moment, his head resting comfortably on his arm, then he turned to once again stare into the flames, his grin vanishing. "What I don't know, you can teach me. You saved my life today, Charlie. I won't forget that."

Charlie remembered the way the boy had slid beneath the water, and he remembered, too, the fear that had gripped him when he did. "I want you to stay away from the lake unless I'm with you, Joe. Stay out of the water. At least until I can teach you to swim. All right?"

"Will you teach me tomorrow?"

"Yes. First thing."

Finally, Charlie could no longer refrain from reaching out, but rather than simply stroking Joe's cheek as he wanted, he pushed Joe's hair away from his eyes in a businesslike manner that probably didn't fool the boy at all. When, at his touch, Joe leaned his head into Charlie's hand, Charlie felt his heart stir, and then he let his hesitation fall away and laid his hand on the side of Joe's face and held it there, feeling Joe smile beneath his touch.

Joe pressed his lips into Charlie's palm and said, "Thank you for putting me in your painting."

"Putting you…?"

"That was me, Charlie. That streak of light. Didn't you see it?"

Charlie thought of the way that slash of white paint had torn across his canvases, thought of the way he had swept his paintbrush along the triptych without thinking, without planning, knowing that it was the right thing to do. The brush, as always, had been an extension of his body, but this time he had not led it. The brush had led him. That slash of glistening white acrylic had shot across the paintings like a meteoric ejaculation. Uncontrollable. Unstoppable. And like an explosion of hot sperm, it fertilized the painting, creating a new existence on the canvas, giving it substance, personality. Making it live. Making it a complete being. Making it whole. And Charlie did see, suddenly, Joe's presence there, Joe's life force, beaming out of that comet trail of white paint, glistening in the summer sunlight that streamed down through the studio's skylight as he worked. He thought of the motion Joe had made outside the window, his arm drawing a path over his head, across the sky, telling Charlie what to do, showing him how to breathe life into the painting he had been working on for so long. And Charlie knew now that before he swept his brush across the skyline of his triptych, there had been no life in the painting at all. It had been a dead thing. Lifeless. Resurrected at last by Joe.

Again, Charlie felt a need to know more about this young man who had come sweeping into his life like that comet, that meteor, seemingly blazing across the heavens and landing at his feet. Changing everything.

Reluctantly he pulled his hand away and tucked it under his chin once more. He let his eyes wander back to the fire, and Joe did the same. "Where is your father's nursery, Joe? Where does he work?"

A gentle smile brightened Joe's face. "My father works in many places."

"That's not an answer, Joe. Can you be a little more specific?"

"Why do these things matter to you, Charlie? Where I come from is not who I am. I am only what I am now. What you see." He turned again to study Charlie's face. "What do you see, Charlie? Are you seeing me, or are you seeing what you want to see?"

"I see both," Charlie said, smiling.

"Do I please you?"

"Yes," Charlie said. "You please me. Everything about you pleases me. Your calmness. Your… beauty. The way the firelight catches your eyes. The way your hair flows around your face. The easy way you stand as if you're rooted to the earth, as if you know exactly where you are, what you're doing in that precise place at that precise moment. And the mystery of you pleases me too. There's so much I don't understand about you, Joe."

"If I tell you everything, then the mystery will be gone. Is that what you want?"

"Yes…," Charlie said. "No."

Joe rested his head on his arm, studying Charlie's face. "If I were to tell you that you please me too, Charlie, would that be something that mattered to you?"

"Yes," Charlie said. "It would matter a great deal."

"Then you do."

At that moment, Charlie could think of a million things to say, a million feelings he wanted to express, but all he finally said was "Good."

"Why do you paint, Charlie?"

"I… don't know. It's all I've ever wanted to do."

"So even that's a mystery to you," Joe said.

"Yes. I suppose it is."

"If you analyzed that need in you too deeply, Charlie, don't you think it would cheapen it somehow? If we knew everything about everything, don't you think one day we would wake up to find we care about nothing? Don't you think maybe the first time a surgeon presses a scalpel to a human heart, that just for a fleeting moment, just for a second, he must feel a bitter disappointment to learn that love does not truly reside there, love is not something he can pluck out and hold in his hand and gaze upon? The sudden knowledge that a heart consists of nothing but throbbing muscle and seeping, pulsing blood must bring with it a horrible, sad awareness, don't you think?"

"I suppose it must," Charlie said, considering Joe's words, wondering how they could come from a boy so young, so apparently inexperienced in so many things.

"Whenever you paint, Charlie, does it ever occur to you how sad your life would be if you had the need to paint but did not have the talent to do so? Your painting is what you are, don't you think? It defines you. Without it, you would not be you."

"Without it," Charlie said, "I would be nothing."

"That's not true, Charlie. You would still be you, but it would be a different you."

Charlie had to laugh. "It would be an unhappy me."

Joe did not laugh with him. "I know. But you would still exist. Existence is not always what we make it. It comes down to what is inside us at the time we are born. You were an artist the moment you spilled out of your mother's body. When you die, Charlie, your art will die with you."

"I like to think my paintings will still be here when I'm gone. That they are my children, living on in this world after I'm no longer here."

"Maybe, Charlie. But what are children but the ashes of another life left behind? Your paintings will still be here, yes, but your art, your talent, will no longer exist. It will die with you, Charlie. If this world were to end tomorrow, think of all the talents, all the creative visions that lie unrealized in human minds that would be lost with it. It isn't only human lives that would end, but so many dreams as well. So much unrealized beauty."

Charlie tried not to grin at the seriousness on the boy's face. "*Will* the world end tomorrow, Joe?"

"No," Joe said, turning back to the flames. "Not tomorrow."

The depth of feeling in Joe's eyes, the pain that seemed to linger there after Charlie's question, made Charlie wish he had not spoken the words. He tried to lighten the mood.

"When would you like to sit for me, Joe? When will I paint you?"

Joe smiled, the sorrow in his eyes falling away in an instant. "I thought you already did."

"That wasn't you, Joe. That was… the spirit of you. I'd like to capture your face on canvas as well. Your body. All of you. I want to paint you as you were today, standing at the bow of my boat, the wind in your hair, laughing as the spray hit your face. You looked so happy out there on the lake. I want to put that happiness on canvas. To be able to look at it again anytime I choose. You were so beautiful this afternoon, Joe. I'll never forget the way you looked."

"Then why do you need to paint it? If you can pull the memory from your mind anytime you want, there's no need to put it on canvas."

"Please, Joe. Do this for me. Think of it as payment for me teaching you to swim."

"And feeding me. And clothing me. And putting a roof over my head."

"You've already paid for those things. Just having you here is payment enough." Charlie stopped himself before other words came tripping from his tongue, words it was too soon to speak, words that maybe should never be spoken to this boy who was so wise in so many things and so naïve in so many others. He would not lead Joe down any paths along which he did not want to be led. He would not force a confrontation between them, a profession of love and desire that might break the connection they'd made, sever the friendship and security he hoped Joe felt in his presence. Even in the simple kisses Joe had at various times given him, Charlie had sensed no sexual eagerness. They were kisses of friendship. Kisses of gratitude.

Kisses that could be easily misconstrued, but were, in fact, as childlike and as innocent as Joe himself. The feelings they stirred in Charlie were not necessarily stirred in Joe as well. He had shown no sign that they had. And if there was no passion, no sexual desire, stirring for him inside Joe as it stirred inside Charlie, Charlie knew he would be much happier not knowing. He was content with Joe now, and Joe was content with him too, it seemed. Passion of the body would either bring them closer together, or tear them apart completely. If it was not something Joe truly wanted, was not something he felt truly ready for, it could destroy everything. Charlie had no intention of risking so much to find out what Joe's feelings were. If passion came, it would come first from Joe. Charlie was more than willing to follow Joe to whatever destination their relationship led them. To do anything that was required of him to keep Joe at his side. His desire for the beautiful young man was great. But his love was greater. And the comfort he derived from Joe's simple presence was greater than both love *and* desire. Charlie would not jeopardize it. He would not risk the death of such a perfect, beautiful gift. It would be like destroying art. Burning canvas.

His mind was drawn away from these thoughts when Joe asked, "Where are all the people? Does no one else live here on this lake? When we were in the boat today, I saw no other people, no other houses. It's like you have this place all to yourself."

"I do. That's why I bought the property. Privacy is… important to me." *Or was*, he thought wryly. Funny how meeting one person could change your perspective entirely. In the past twenty-four hours, he had become a different person, with different priorities. What mattered to Charlie now, what mattered more than anything else, was this boy at his side. But still, there were things about Joe that bothered him. Why was he so reluctant to speak of his past? His roots? What hurts in his life had led him to the shore of this lake, to Charlie's doorstep, unclad and alone?

"Last night, Joe, when you came to my door, did you feel the earthquake? Did you see the light that came before the earthquake hit?"

Joe stared intently into the flames, lost in his own thoughts. It was as if Charlie's words had not reached him. Or he did not want them to.

"You must have seen it, Joe. It lit up everything. The cabin, the forest, the lake. It was like a sunrise at night."

"Perhaps it was a comet," Joe said, still watching the flames. "Like the one in your painting."

"You were outside. Did you see it?"

"No," Joe said. "I didn't see anything. I don't *remember* anything. Not until you opened your door and let me in."

"What do you mean, you don't remember anything? Don't you know how you got here? Where you came from?"

Joe's hair was dry now. Charlie could see faint streaks of gold amid the dark strands, catching the firelight, shimmering with the movement of Joe's head when he turned again to look at Charlie. Funny he hadn't noticed them before. They were beautiful, those lines of gold. Soft, yet intense. They radiated light. Like a halo. Again, Charlie resisted the urge to reach out and touch them, to bury his hands in those burnished locks, to feel Joe's head beneath his hands, to pull him close.

And while he thought these thoughts, he saw a hint of sorrow in Joe's eyes.

"Joe...."

"One day I'll tell you everything, Charlie. I promise. But not tonight. And probably not tomorrow. When the time is right, I'll share my secrets with you. Can you... let me do that? Will it destroy what we have between us for you to do that?"

"What *do* we have?" Charlie asked, wondering as he said it what secrets this boy of nineteen could possibly have that made him so sad.

"We have a connection, Charlie. I understand what drives you. I understand your longings."

"Do you?"

"Yes. And I understand that this is hard for you. Do as you promised, Charlie. Be my teacher. And later, when the time is right, I will be yours. I'll save you, Charlie."

"Save me? Save me from what?"

Joe reached out and pulled Charlie into his arms, stroked his hair, placed a warm hand against the back of his neck and pressed Charlie's face into the soap-scented hollow of his throat. Charlie brought his arms up to hold the boy in return. Such a flood of happiness, of contentment, washed over him that he felt a tear leak from his eye. He had to fight the urge to sob. When Joe spoke, Charlie could feel the vibration of his voice on his cheek.

"I'll save you from the misery, Charlie. I'll carry you away to a place where the misery cannot reach you. There's a great sadness coming, Charlie. But it will never touch you. I promise."

"Will I be with you, Joe?"

"Yes. You'll always be with me."

"Good," Charlie said.

And for the second night, Charlie slept peacefully in Joe's strong arms before the fire, feeling him at his side even as he dreamed dreams that he would not remember in the morning. Feeling warm breath brush his skin as the night deepened and the fire died away and darkness covered them, feeling Joe's hands occasionally move to his cheek or his chest to stroke him like a mother idly strokes a child, comforting Charlie in his sleep.

The same contented smile was on both their lips as the night wore away.

And again, when Charlie awoke in the coolness of the morning, the boy was gone.

CHAPTER THREE
...A WAY WITH ANIMALS AND ART....

COURIERS CAME for the paintings at dawn. The night before, Charlie had phoned Fosse, who, when told of the triptych's completion, had said, "About fucking time, Charlie," and had made immediate arrangements for shipping in turn. Until the art was delivered and deemed acceptable by the buyer, there would be no money coming in, and Fosse, after all, was an agent, a 15 percenter. While he dealt exclusively in art, art was not his primary motivation. Fosse didn't give a shit about art, and Charlie knew it. Hell, everyone knew it. Fosse made no pretense otherwise. But Charlie put up with him because Edgar Fosse was very good at what he did.

Fosse's impatience stemmed from the fact that the work was already three weeks overdue. The buyers were on the phone with him every day, exacerbating his ulcer, driving him nuts. Fosse had been on the phone every day with Charlie—or would have been had Charlie taken the time to answer his calls, which he didn't—trying to spur Charlie into finishing the damn canvas and hoping to maybe exacerbate *Charlie's* ulcer, which Charlie didn't have but Fosse sort of wished he did. The major motivation behind all this desperate activity was that Fosse's mistress needed breast implants, or thought she did, which Fosse's 15 percent was slotted to pay for.

The great circle of life, Fosse called it. Charlie painted, the money filtered down, everybody eventually got what they wanted, including Fosse's mistress, who was a *master* at exacerbating Fosse's ulcer if she didn't get what *she* wanted. As of this morning, Fosse had not been laid in a week. He had been cut off. Totally. Things were getting desperate.

Charlie cared little for Fosse's motivation and cared even less about his mistress's tits. The only thing concerning Charlie, as he watched the moving van pulling up the lane through the trees to his property, was where the hell Joe had gone. Wherever it was, Joe had taken Mac with him. They weren't in the cabin. They weren't in the studio. Where *were* they?

Charlie stopped his search for Joe long enough to direct the driver of the van to the studio. He stood out of the way while the driver backed the van, which was large enough for *twelve* canvases, up to the studio door, then made the driver and his assistant wait, impatiently shuffling their feet, while Charlie took a small brush and, with the same white acrylic he had used to paint the meteor trail, signed the canvas with a flourish in the lower right-hand corner of the third panel. Then he made them wait an additional ten minutes while the paint dried. The driver and his assistant, who looked like an adult version of the unfortunate banjo player in *Deliverance*, rolled their eyes and glanced pointedly at their watches until Charlie finally allowed them to wrap the paintings in moving blankets and load them onto the van.

For one desperate moment as the triptych disappeared through the van doors, Charlie didn't want to let it go. There was too much of Joe in it. He almost called the men back to tell them he had changed his mind, that the painting wasn't finished, that it was a piece of crap, *anything* to get the canvas off that damn truck and back into his studio. But the moment passed, and what the hell would he do with three twelve-by-six-foot canvases, anyway? And he needed the money, or at least *Fosse* needed the money, and Charlie knew that if he reneged on the deal now, Fosse would blow a head gasket, and Charlie needed Fosse. He didn't want to deal with buyers on his own. He needed a middleman and Fosse was it.

So, in the end, Charlie clamped his mouth shut, swallowed the ache inside himself, watched the driver and his moronic-looking assistant lock the paintings inside the van, and signed the damn transfer papers the driver held out to him afterward.

Before the two men hauled their asses back up into the cab of the moving van, Charlie heard the driver say, "Jesus Christ, would you look at that!"

Charlie followed the man's eyes.

"What the hell *is* that?" the banjo player asked.

Charlie was about to ask the same question.

Joe was standing knee deep in water at the edge of the lake, wearing a pair of Charlie's white boxer shorts, which were too big for him and looked somewhat like a toddler's full diaper from this distance, given the way they drooped off the boy's slim hips. Around Joe on the surface of the lake, the water roiled. Bubbled. Frothed. The morning sun caught the water in silver flashes of light as it encircled the boy, splashing, churning.

Charlie took a step closer before he saw the cause of the frantic motion. Fish. Hundreds of them. Flinging themselves out of the water, crashing back into it, frantically flopping around like they were snared in a net—but there was nothing holding them. Joe's arms were spread wide, and even from where he stood, Charlie could see the shuddering movement in his shoulders. He was laughing.

Beside him, Mac was laughing too, or would have been were he genetically capable of doing so. He was jumping up and down in the shallow water, his fur drenched, snapping and chomping his teeth in an attempt to catch at least one of the fish as they erupted from the lake around Joe, twisting their silvery bodies in the cool air, sending droplets of lake water sparkling around Joe like diamonds, like an aura of light, before crashing back into the maelstrom below, only to spin around beneath the surface and once again fling their bodies out into the morning air.

"Go," Charlie said to the driver.

"But what the hell is he doing? How does he get the fish to do that?" the driver asked, still staring google-eyed at Joe.

"Just go," Charlie said again. "And thanks."

"Fish for dinner," the banjo player chuckled, before pulling himself up into the cab. The driver followed and cranked up the engine, and as the van disappeared into the trees at the end of his lane, Charlie walked toward the boy in the water.

As Charlie neared him, Joe lowered his arms to his sides and turned to look at him. With the lowering of his arms, the water settled immediately into calmness, as if someone had switched off the power to a Jacuzzi. The fish that had apparently been trying to reach Joe's outstretched hands, for some unfathomable reason, swam away from him then, tiny dorsal fins slicing through the water, out toward the depths, before disappearing with a gurgle and a final flip of their strong tails, sending a last spray of diamond-laced water into the sun glare gleaming across the surface of the now-peaceful lake.

When the water was perfectly still around him, Joe gave a soft whistle, and he and Mac stepped onto the shore. There was still laughter on the boy's face, in his eyes, as he strode toward Charlie, hiking up his drooping shorts. Mac, hopping along beside him in his excitement, spotted Charlie and came barreling up the lawn to greet him, flinging water everywhere. Joe, too, greeted Charlie with a quick hug, pressing his body to his, presenting himself to Charlie like an offering. Charlie wrapped his arms around Joe, held him close, and stroked the skin of his back until he felt the first stirring of desire, then he gently pushed himself away. He was growing accustomed to controlling his lust for the boy now. Ignoring it, or pretending to. Setting it aside like an interrupted book. It seemed almost a natural response to desire, this holding back. It did not pain him like it once had. But neither did it let him go. It was always there—in his mind, in his body—every time he looked at Joe, every time their flesh touched, every time Joe whispered soothing words into his ear, or cast a smile at him from that perfect face. It was an ache that never left him, but one he could endure. And somehow, as at this very moment, Charlie found the endurance of it almost a pleasure. It was the right thing to do, Charlie knew. A *good* thing to do.

"Good morning," they said in unison.

Charlie looked over the boy's shoulders to the water, grinning. "A way with animals, huh?"

Laughter still bubbled in Joe's eyes. "You bet."

"You should have grabbed one of those fish for our breakfast," Charlie said.

Joe glanced doubtfully back at the lake, shining calmly there in the morning sun. "Don't we have other food to eat?"

"Sure. All kinds of stuff."

"Then why harm the fish? They're so playful. So friendly. Let them live. Did you see them flying, Charlie? They were like birds."

"Silver birds," Charlie said.

Joe glanced toward the studio door, still hanging open. "They took the paintings away, didn't they? You've sent another child out into the world."

"I didn't want to let it go."

"Then why did you?"

"Commitments. Promises. Money. It's how I make my living."

Joe reached over and brushed the hair from Charlie's eyes. "It makes you sad, doesn't it?"

"Not usually. But, yes. This time it made me sad."

"Did you love the painting that much?"

"No," Charlie said. "I loved the fact that you were in it."

"Maybe I'll be in your next painting too."

"I think, Joe, that you will be in everything I paint from this day forth." *You'll be in everything I do from this day forth.* But these words Charlie couldn't share with Joe. Not yet. Maybe never. Or maybe they would be the very next words he spoke. But of course they weren't.

He took Joe's hand and led him back to the water.

"Let's teach you to swim."

Like he had done on the boat, Joe reached out as they stood at the edge of the lake and pulled Charlie's shirt over his head. He stepped back and waited while Charlie slipped his trousers down past his hips and stepped out of them. Only then, when Charlie was completely naked before him, did Joe remove his shorts. Innocently. As if it were the most natural thing in the world to do.

"We'll be like fish," Joe said. "Free in the water."

Charlie laughed, flinging himself at Joe. They tumbled backward into the lake, wrestling beneath the roiling water, arms and legs entwined, giggling, spitting up great gouts of spray. When they tired of roughhousing, Charlie laid Joe out in the water, faceup, supporting Joe with his arms, teaching him to float. Joe's nakedness brushed the surface of the water. Charlie resisted the urge to lay his face across the boy's smooth stomach, resisted other urges too, and as Joe gave himself up to Charlie's teaching, trusting the strength of Charlie's arms to hold him safe, Charlie eased him farther out into the lake, still holding him, directing his body out past the place where Charlie's feet could no longer touch the bottom. Treading water, Charlie released Joe then, setting him free in the water, just like the boy had said. As free as the fish.

Floating there, untouched by any solid presence, Joe stared up at the sky with a smile of happiness and wonder spread across his face. Charlie felt Joe's freedom, and he smiled too. Gently, Charlie laid a hand to the small of Joe's back and eased him over, supporting him now with his hand against Joe's stomach. The weight of Joe's genitals brushed his arm. He could feel Joe's breath entering and leaving his body, and Charlie felt a stirring in his own genitals at the sensation of life inside the boy. And when he felt a stirring of Joe's genitals as well, or thought he did, he pulled back, easing Joe toward the shore where the water was not so deep. Joe's eyes never left his face.

Neither of them spoke. When Charlie's feet touched the muddy bottom, he released Joe, turned his back to him, and waded ashore, scooping up his clothes as he went. Without looking back, without turning to expose the excitement of his body to Joe, he headed for the house.

Silent, still floating, Joe watched him go.

LATER, THROUGH the kitchen window as Charlie stood at the sink waiting for their breakfast to cook, he saw Joe step from the lake and shake the water from his body. The growing erection Charlie was almost sure he had felt earlier, stirring beneath the water, had receded now to a flaccid beauty, nestled in its bed of damp pubic hair, swaying softly with the boy's movements, a fleshy pendulum filled with promises, the sight of which made Charlie ache with longing yet again. When his body was somewhat dry, Joe pulled on the boxer shorts he had dropped to the ground earlier and walked off toward the trees that edged the lane. He did not seem angry. He did not seem sad. He seemed only curious and determined, as if something called him there. With Mac at his heels, he disappeared among the firs.

Charlie turned to scoop eggs and bacon from the skillet onto a plate and turned off the stove before leaving the house to follow. Something in Joe's stance, in the eager way he had walked away, drew Charlie after him. The boy was a magnet, pulling Charlie along behind him like a fleck of metal. Charlie's desire no longer troubled him. Not really. He had once again managed to close that interrupted, unfinished book. Now he was simply curious, like Joe. Something important was about to happen. He could feel it in the air, sense it in a tingle of the skin at the back of his neck, like tiny jolts of electricity spurring him to action.

Still barefoot, but dressed again in the same jeans and T-shirt he had awoken in that morning, Charlie padded over the lawn, wincing as he crossed the stony lane. He trailed Joe into the shadows of the wood that bordered the cabin.

Here among the trees, where the morning sun had not yet penetrated, a blanket of mist still spread across the ground. Later, it would be dispelled by the heat of the day, but for now, it was a pleasant coolness on his naked feet. The evergreen scent of morning was one of the things Charlie most dearly loved about this place, and as he walked among the bristling pines and junipers, the air was heavy with it. The scent of pine was so intense Charlie could almost feel it on his skin like a living touch, caressing him, urging him forward, drawing him into the shadows of the wood like the scent of food leads a starving man.

Above Charlie's head and at his feet, all manner of life was stirring. Birds greeted the new day with song. Squirrels chirruped from the branches. Chipmunks, like tiny windup toys, skittered through the underbrush as he passed. Charlie thought of the way the fish had leaped around Joe at the edge of the lake and wondered now if the animals in the wood were speaking to the boy who was walking among them somewhere up ahead. Did they feel the draw of him, as the fish had done, as Charlie himself had felt since the moment he first looked at him, or was this merely their usual morning chatter? Somehow he could never remember their sound being quite so… desperate. As if they were calling Joe forward. An inexplicable tension thrummed in the air that Charlie could not explain. He was humbled to be out here among so much life, with the animals, with the morning, with Joe.

Pulling himself up a small incline, Charlie spotted Joe kneeling at the edge of the lane where it turned into the trees along its winding path to the highway. Before Joe, sprawled half on the lane and half in the tangled weeds at its verge, lay a deer. A doe. The stillness of the doe's body and the way the doe's head was twisted to the side, and the blood, too, which Charlie could now see as he stepped closer, blood that had gushed from the deer's velvet snout and was soaking into the dew-laden ground beneath her head, told Charlie the deer was dead.

The van. It must have struck the deer as it turned the corner of the lane. Impotent anger surged through Charlie to think that the driver and his fool of an assistant had simply driven on then, as if nothing had happened, leaving the deer to die in their wake.

Slowly, Charlie approached the boy and knelt at his side. Joe's eyes were closed as if in prayer as he stroked the soft hair at the deer's throat. Charlie reached out and laid his hand across the deer's muzzle, feeling the warmth of it, feeling the stillness where moments before there would have been life.

A movement in the trees caught his eye, and there, across the lane, peering through the foliage, stood a fawn, trembling, still dappled with the colors of its birth, watching them with wide, frightened eyes.

Charlie turned to Joe to tell him, but the tears on the boy's face, the trembling of his body, so like the fawn's, stopped him. With one hand at the doe's throat and the other stroking her flank, Joe lowered his head, and Charlie saw a tear fall to the ground at his knees. Slowly, as Charlie watched, a smile spread across Joe's face and he opened his eyes. At the same moment, the deer opened her liquid eyes and expelled a breath, sending a mist of blood shooting across the grass.

Charlie pulled his hand from her snout, but Joe grabbed it and placed it back, holding it there below the deer's opening eyes. The doe's head trembled beneath his touch. He could hear, suddenly, the breath leaving and entering her lungs, could sense the pulsing of her heart beneath her silken coat.

"My God, Joe…."

Again, Joe stroked the doe's velvet neck, grinning when her skin rippled beneath his fingers as awareness returned to her completely. With a gentle lurch, she raised her body, folding her delicate outstretched legs beneath her, shaking her head as if wondering what had happened to her. Still, she lay there before them, but they could sense in her now the urge to run, to raise herself completely from the ground and fly away into the trees, to her life, to her fawn.

"Go, then," Joe said, pulling his hands away. Charlie gave a final squeeze to the doe's snout, and he too pulled his hand away, sensing the fear in her at his unfamiliar touch, watching her eyes suddenly dart about, wondering what to do, which way to go.

And then in a burst of movement and a scatter of pine needles, she was simply gone, flown across the lane toward her fawn, disappearing into the trees like a ghost. Blood still sprinkled the ground where she had lain. Where she had died. Charlie stared at it, then turned to Joe.

The boy gazed back at him, his dark eyes bright, a light of happiness sparkling in their depths. They were the doe's eyes. As bottomless as a midnight sky.

"I… don't understand," Charlie said, his voice sounding out of place in the sudden silence that had fallen over the wood. "What just happened?"

But Joe wasn't listening. He had turned his head to stare into the trees where the deer, with her fawn at her heels, had flown away into the mist.

"Did you see her eyes?" Joe asked. "Weren't they beautiful?"

"Yes," Charlie said, still staring into Joe's. "They were."

"They were a mother's eyes."

"Yes," Charlie said again, tearing his eyes from Joe to gaze into the trees where the doe had gone. Then, looking back at Joe, he felt his own tears creeping to the surface, blurring his vision. He felt them slide across his lashes and hover there for a moment before falling to his cheek.

Still smiling, Joe reached over and brushed them away.

OVER BREAKFAST, Joe would not speak of the deer. He merely aimed that enigmatic smile at Charlie, ignoring his questions and smiling at the excitement and confusion in Charlie's words, in Charlie's expression. Again, Joe was chomping down his food like he hadn't eaten in a week.

Finally, after seeing a trace of anger cross Charlie's face at his refusal to speak about it, Joe laid down his fork and said, "Perhaps the doe was just stunned."

Charlie exploded. "Bullshit! She was stone-cold dead, and you know it."

Another enigmatic smile. "If you say so."

"And how did you know she was out there, Joe? I saw you leave the lake and go into the trees like you had a purpose. The doe was calling to you, wasn't she?"

"How could she be calling to me if she was stone-cold dead?"

"Hell, Joe, *I* don't know! But I know what I saw."

"And what exactly did you see?"

"I saw you lay your hands on the animal and bring her back to life. *That's* what I saw. And you can sit there with that Simple Simon grin on your face 'til Judgment Day and I'll *still* know what I saw. How did you do it, Joe?"

Joe resumed eating. "You laid your hands on her too, Charlie. Maybe *you're* the one who brought her back to life. Maybe *that's* what *I* saw."

"You're impossible!"

Joe laughed. "Are we having our first fight?"

Charlie wasn't amused. He pushed his plate away and sat back, folding his arms across his chest, just staring at the boy.

"Why are you so angry?" Joe asked.

"I don't know."

"I do. You're angry because you saw something, or *think* you saw something, that you don't understand. And I think you're angry for other reasons too. I think you're angry because of what happened in the lake."

Charlie felt a flutter of nervousness deep inside himself. A flutter of embarrassment. "You mean the fish?"

Joe leaned forward and reached his hand across the table to stroke Charlie's arm. "Give me your hand, Charlie."

Reluctantly Charlie laid his hand in Joe's. As always, he fell into the depths of those brown, bottomless eyes. The gentle expression on the boy's face drew Charlie in. Drew him into that place where he always felt happy. And torn. Yet completely at peace. This too was like a laying on of hands. It calmed Charlie. His anger ebbed, flowed away like seawater leaving the ocean shore, drawn by the moon. And as it left, emptying his heart of anguish, his love for the boy refilled it. He thought of the doe opening her eyes to a day she would never have seen again had it not been for this man, this child, sitting before him now, and he realized suddenly that he and the doe were one. His life, too, had begun the day Joe laid his hands on it by knocking at his door. Everything that happened before that moment seemed now of little consequence to Charlie. It was as if he had been merely vamping to the empty beat of his existence, waiting for the real music to begin. Joe was Charlie's music. Charlie understood that now. But still he couldn't say the words. It would destroy everything.

"I'm flesh and blood like you, Charlie. My father made me that way. As your father made you the way you are. We all have talents that maybe we don't understand, but they are there just the same. And we all have feelings too, Charlie. Longings. Maybe the greatest talent, the greatest gift, our fathers gave us was the ability to love. It's a human gift, Charlie. It's the core of everything we are. I feel your love for me in everything you do. Every movement you make. Every word you speak. And I feel your fear as well. What happened in the lake this morning frightened you. I enjoyed the feel of your hands on my body, Charlie, as you enjoyed the feel of me. We are only human, Charlie. Desire is a natural thing. But love is above it. And trust is above it all. Don't be ashamed of how you feel. Don't be ashamed of what your body tells you it wants. If, at this very moment, our bodies should come together, would it make your love for me any stronger? Or my love for you? Because I do love you, Charlie."

"You do?"

"Fate brought us together. Don't you understand that yet?"

"No," Charlie said. "I don't understand anything. I don't understand why you are here. I don't understand how you can do the things you do. I don't understand why just the sight of you brings me such peace. And such torment."

"Desire is always a torment, Charlie. A beautiful torment. Savor it. But we have things to do that transcend desires of the flesh. And we have a love for each other that should not be sullied by it. Do you think I don't want to take you in my arms right now and give in to the feelings I feel as much as you do? Do you think I'm above the need for human touch? I'm not, Charlie. I'm flesh and blood, like you. If you were a woman, Charlie, would you be feeling the torment you're feeling now? Your kind of love is not a sin, Charlie, no matter what others say. Love is love. I told you that before. Nothing as pure as love can ever be a sin. The only sin is being ashamed of who you are. Of being ashamed of what your father made you. It is not because of the way you are that I do not come to you, Charlie. Nor is it because of the way I am. Because we are exactly alike, you and I. And we will always be together."

"Will we?"

"Yes."

"Then I guess that will have to be enough," Charlie said.

Joe smiled kindly at him across the table. "For now, yes. It will have to be enough. But one day it will be different. I promise. One day I will take you in my arms, and on that day, I will open myself up to you completely. Be patient with me, Charlie. Let me come to you in my own time. Life is new to me, Charlie. I want to savor every moment of it. I want to savor our desire for each other before we take that final step, for when we do, what we have now will be lost. I don't want it to end yet. This is all so new to me, Charlie. Give me time to experience it."

Charlie felt the strength in Joe's hand as it held his own. There was a look of such intense feeling on the boy's face, in his words, that Charlie would have given him anything at that moment. What he was asking was such a small thing, really. Patience. Patience from Charlie. Patience and understanding. And the continuation of innocence for a little while longer. Charlie realized suddenly that it was what he wanted too. He ached with his need for Joe's touch, to feel him writhing beneath his hands, his lips. To taste Joe as the juice of passion poured from his young body. To feel him surge and buck beneath him, to cry out with the intensity of the lust that pulled them closer with every passing minute until it spilled out over them like a forest mist, bonding them together, cementing their love for each other.

Their love that, in reality, did not need that one final act at all. It was a perfect thing the way it was. Like Joe had said—a flower.

Charlie tore his eyes from Joe's face to stare out the window, seeking out that one perfect blossom by the fence, but what he saw was a riot of color, rippling gently in the morning breeze. He gasped. The flowers in the flower bed, long thought dead, had bloomed. All of them. Irises. Marigolds. Tiny daisies as yellow as butter. Chrysanthemums heavy on their stems. Their bowed heads glistened with dew in the morning sun. Awake now. Returned to a world Charlie thought they would never see again. As the doe had returned. As he himself had returned.

All because of this boy, Joe. Charlie closed his eyes and, smiling, savored the warmth of Joe's hand in his.

LATER THAT morning, Joe stood before him in a crystal beam of light that cascaded through the skylight of his studio like a waterfall. With arms outstretched, Joe patiently watched Charlie work with sketchpad and charcoal, transferring his likeness onto the paper in front of him.

The boy was nude, for this was how Charlie knew he must be painted. Once his sketch was completed—no doubt after having been revised a dozen times before Charlie was satisfied with it—he would begin the process of putting Joe's image on canvas. But for the moment, he was simply mapping out what it was he wanted to paint.

As always, his nakedness seemed of little concern to Joe. And in truth he had no reason to be ashamed of his nakedness, for never before had Charlie seen such perfection in human form. It went beyond sexual desire, what Charlie experienced seeing the boy so exposed before him. It was as if he were in the presence of a masterpiece. Michelangelo's *David.* *The Pieta.* Seurat's *La Grande Jatte.* The same sense of amazement, of wonder, that had overcome Charlie the day he stood in the Louvre with a bored Jason at his side, gazing on the face of da Vinci's *Mona Lisa.* And it was just such an aura of purity, like the Mona Lisa's, that flowed from Joe now. Joe's beauty held such an astonishing power, Charlie had to force himself to continue working and not simply sit there in front of his easel, gaping like a fool.

As he studied the contours of Joe's body, his fingers followed along, bringing the boy to life on paper. He seldom worked with models, but this time Charlie knew he must. It was not simply a male nude, anonymous and generic, he would be painting this time, but *Joe.* There were so many aspects of the boy he wanted to capture that he could not have done so from memory, although every line, every shape, every nuance of Joe's body and face were indelibly etched in his mind.

But it was not just the body and face Charlie wanted to capture on canvas. It was the fire behind Joe's eyes. The knowing smile. The aura of gentle sweetness that flowed from him. The innocence, and the wisdom too, and above all, the otherworldliness that, in Charlie's eyes, was the very essence of Joe's being.

Charlie sat for long minutes, staring at Joe's slim fingers, at his outstretched hands and elegant wrists, before daring to make a single mark on paper. Those hands, as much as the face, were the true heart of the boy. Those gifted hands that could, with a simple touch, heal hurts. Even banish death. For Charlie knew what he had seen that morning among the trees. Over and over in his mind, he thought of the *chuff* of expelled air, the spray of bloody mist that had exploded from the doe's snout when Joe laid his hands on her neck and somehow took back all that had happened to her. He had tried to make light of it later as they sat in the kitchen, eating their breakfast, watching the day unfold outside the window. Joe had almost laughed at the awe on Charlie's face, seeming to find humor in Charlie's amazement at what he had done. But Charlie was not fooled by the laughter in the boy's eyes.

And remembering these things, Charlie stared at Joe now with what could only be called reverence. This was no mere man-child he was about to paint. This was special. Important. Even Joe seemed to sense that. One of the first things Joe had said to him on the night they met, the night that had changed Charlie's life so completely, was that Charlie could paint him if he wished. At the time, Charlie had thought it was presumptuous, even egotistical, for Joe to say such a thing. But now he understood this was meant to be. From the first moment Joe had stepped into his life, this was where their journey had been leading them.

As he worked, Charlie thought these thoughts, and he thought of other things as well. He realized suddenly that, aside from the one tiny sip of Scotch on the morning after Joe's arrival, he hadn't had a drink since the night Joe had walked into his cabin. Had not so much as *thought* about having a drink. One of Judith's major gripes about Charlie was that he drank too much. Jason had sometimes looked askance at him too when he poured that fifth or sixth drink of an evening. And to tell the truth, Charlie sometimes looked askance at himself at those times, wondering why he needed, *craved*, the alcohol so. He had tried to laugh it off, telling himself that artists were always a little strange, always a little overly dependent on outside stimulants. And besides, if he wanted to drink himself into a stupor every night of the goddamn week, who the hell's business was it anyway?

Now, apparently, he no longer needed the liquor. Perhaps this child, this man, standing before him was all the stimulus he needed. Joe had certainly awakened love in Charlie. Love he had sometimes wondered if he was incapable of giving. To anyone. And with that love, Joe had given him other things as well. Restraint, for one. The ability to hold back. To let something remain innocent and untouched, as it was intended to be, without being pawed and analyzed and torn to shreds until there was nothing left but the *memory* of innocence.

For the first time in his life, this relationship, this… whatever it was he shared with the boy, was not driven by Charlie's own needs. It was not his dick leading him through the motions of love; it was, for the very first time, his heart. It was not his own selfish desires that steered him and urged him forward, but a sense of sharing. Of giving. And taking as well, but only what was offered. It was not his own happiness that was the center of his universe now, but Joe's. As he sat there before his easel, his fingers blackened by the charcoal, gazing at the amazing spectacle of Joe standing so patiently, so openly, nude in that unforgiving swath of sunlight, Charlie knew a certainty he had never known before—the certainty that, given a reason, any reason, he would gladly sacrifice his own life to give this boy one more minute of happiness on the earth. When this realization came to him, he dropped his hands to his lap and closed his eyes for a second, humbled, accepting the truth of it. At the same time, Charlie wondered what it was in Joe, what power he possessed, that could make Charlie feel this way.

Charlie was accustomed to this introspection. It always came to him as he worked. His hands, he sometimes thought, held all his talent, for his mind could be a million miles away from what his fingers were doing, and still the work proceeded. But never before had his idle thoughts carried such weight. Never before had they been so important to him. The places his mind took him were suddenly a pleasant wonder to Charlie. He felt better about himself than ever before. Happier. And the presence of Joe, standing so near, gave him, as always, peace. That Joe was the catalyst of Charlie's happiness was beyond dispute. "We will always be together," Joe had told him, and Charlie knew this to be true. For even if Joe left him tomorrow, there would never again be a day when he would not feel Joe beside him.

If Joe left him now, Charlie would survive. Joe had filled him with so much love for another human being that some of it had spilled over, and in the spilling, Charlie had bestowed a part of that love on himself. With Joe gone, he might be a shell of the complete man he was at this very moment, but he would go on.

Perhaps for the first time in his life, after only three days in the presence of this remarkable young man, Charlie was content, and proud, to be who he was.

Joe, and his love for Joe, had given Charlie that much, at least.

The canvas he would soon be painting was the most important work he would ever do. Without a doubt. And every brushstroke of this painting would be executed with love and purpose. There was no money involved. It would never hang for anyone but him. Not while he lived. But this portrait, this *Freedom*, would be the culmination of all his years of work and study. The culmination, too, of all he had learned in his time with Joe. So much. Trust. Compassion. Need. And above all, love. That was what Joe had brought to the world. That was what Joe had given to Charlie. The ability to love. It was a skill he never knew he lacked until Joe showed him differently. And now, with his art, Charlie would make that love eternal.

Like the world around him, this portrait would live forever.

LATER THAT day, two hundred miles north on the twenty-sixth floor of a very expensive piece of real estate up the street from Marshall Field's and a stone's throw away from Oprah's fourteen-million-dollar Chicago condo, three men stood staring at the three canvases recently delivered and propped, at the moment, against the east wall of their reception area.

Switzer, Pevin, and Jenaslovitch were not amused. Albert Switzer, in fact, was downright furious because, as founder and owner of the law firm that carried the names of all three but in reality was solely his own, he was the one who had paid for this travesty.

His latest wife, Sally, thirty years his junior, who looked like an angel but could spend money like a drunken lottery winner, had taken it upon herself to redecorate his suite of offices, and she was the one who had insisted on this triptych, or whatever the damn thing was called. She had insisted on this artist; the size, subject, and colors of these canvases; and even which goddamn wall the fucking things would hang on, when Albert would have been perfectly content with simply slapping a new coat of paint on the walls and hanging a couple of cheap posters—nicely framed of course, nothing too tacky. Jeez, he wasn't completely without taste.

Albert Switzer, the lawyer—who had heard at one time or another every anecdote, rumor, factoid, and insipid joke concerning Albert Schweitzer, the great humanitarian, philosopher, musicologist, medical missionary, Nobel laureate, savior of Africa, and a man with whom, aside from a couple of displaced letters in the spelling of his name, our Albert shared no character traits whatsoever, but who liked to think he did—had shelled out over twelve thousand bucks for this monstrosity on the strength of a blowjob. His wife always asked for things when her lips were wrapped around his pecker for some reason (she was no fool), and now Albert wondered if he was going to be forced to look at this piece of crapola every time he walked into work for the rest of his long, dreary, miserable life.

He was also wondering if he should simply refuse to pay for the artwork, which he had stupidly accepted from the courier before even looking at the paintings, for Christ's sake, and if he did, would his wife be so pissed about it that she would never again wrap those talented lips around his schlong. And why else did he marry a woman young enough to be his daughter if not for those few precious moments of marital bliss when he could spray-paint her throat with jism, making her eyes bug out like a fucking praying mantis? He might be nearing sixty, but he could still shoot with the best of them, which in the grand scheme of things was pretty much beside the point at the moment.

"Why the hell is the city on *fire*?" he asked the ceiling, though his two pseudopartners were standing right next to him. "I wanted a simple painting of Chicago, but not in the era of Mrs. O'Leary's cow. Was that so much to ask?"

Pevin, fat, pushing forty, and with an embryo of a tumor blossoming inside his head he knew nothing about that would kill him in less than a year—if nothing else killed him first—putting an end to all his worrying about life, love, and career, *especially* career, was looking nervous as usual. He always figured his name could be removed from the firm's logo as easily as it went on, which it could. Sucking up to the boss was a way of life with Pevin. He lay awake at night thinking of new and exciting ways to poke his nose up Switzer's ass farther than it already was, while in reality he should have been thinking about a brain scan and a yearly physical. Which was the last thing on his unknowingly diseased mind, unfortunately.

"Yeah," he said now. "What was the artist thinking?"

Jenaslovitch, the youngest of the three and a placater by nature, didn't like the painting any more than Albert did, but thought maybe he should try to find the good side of a bad situation.

"I don't think the city is meant to be on fire, guys. I think maybe that's supposed to be the sun reflecting off those windows."

"Looks like fire to me," Pevin said, looking to his boss for backup.

Switzer leaned closer to the canvas. "I can see faces behind the glass in that building there. See 'em? They look like—" He leaned even closer. "—they're screaming."

"Holy shit, boss! That's *our* building!"

"My God, it is! There's the diner on the corner."

"I don't like this," Albert said. "Why do artists always have to be such a pain in the ass? He's getting back at us, that's what he's doing. He's getting back at us for letting Sally all but paint the goddamn thing herself, the way she told him what colors to use and what the subject matter had to be and how big the thing had to hang, and while we're on the subject, could these things *be* any fucking bigger? With one more of these panels and a roof we could build a house, for Christ's sake, except a house would probably be cheaper!"

Jenaslovitch was eyeing the bold sweep of white paint that streaked across the top of the three panels. "Is that a jet trail? A comet? An incoming ICBM? Did the painter sneeze while he had the paintbrush in his hand? What the hell is it?"

"It's *wonderful*!" cried a voice behind them, causing all three men to jump.

They turned to see Sally standing there in a two-thousand-dollar frock it still annoyed Albert to see her in, considering what it cost and the fact that it could have come from Walmart for all the style it had, although it did show off her figure to a nice advantage. The way it draped across her perky breasts made Albert want to pluck them out like cantaloupes every time he saw her in it. Sally knew this, of course. That was why she had bought the dress in the first place.

At the moment, her peach-colored lips were forming a perfect O, just like they did when Albert's schlong was in there. Maybe Sally knew this too.

"Albert, it's lovely!"

"But the city's on fire, dammit! Why is the city on fire?"

She patted his cheek and stepped closer to the canvas, checking the signature in the corner before speaking. "Oh, Albert, don't be silly. The city's not on fire. It's Chicago at dawn. Just like I asked for. And look how the sky matches the color of the carpeting. It's perfect!"

"It's a piece of shit!"

"It's an honest-to-God Strickland, that's what it is. And the biggest one I've ever seen. You should be proud to own it. One day this painting will be worth a fortune."

"It's already worth a fortune!"

"Oh, Albert, calm down." Sally nestled up beside him, tucking her hand into the back pocket of his trousers in a familiar sort of way that made him wonder first if she was going for his wallet, and second, if he could get her into his office for a few minutes of private time with those perky cantaloupes and delectably peach-colored lips.

As her fingers did a little massaging of his left buttcheek, making Albert's schlong spring to attention beneath the flap of his suit coat, she rested her head on his shoulder, still staring at the canvas.

"Every lawyer in town is going to be green with envy, Albert. And your clients will know they are dealing with a reputable law firm when they see a Strickland on your wall."

"My clients are mostly con men, pedophiles, and murderers. They wouldn't know the difference between an honest-to-God Strickland and a snapshot of Bugs Bunny with a carrot up his ass, and would care even less."

"Oh, Albert. If nothing else, it's a tax write-off. Maybe. File it under 'renovation of business property.' One day you'll thank me for this. You'll see."

"He has us screaming," Pevin said.

"What?" Sally asked, looking at Pevin as if he were a toad that had leaped onto the dinner table and peed on her prawns. She didn't like Pevin, as she had told Albert many times. Never had.

"In the windows," Pevin said. "Look in the windows. Right there. That's our building, and he's got us screaming inside."

SALLY PULLED away from Albert and leaned closer to the mural to the spot where Pevin was pointing with his fat little finger.

"What are you talking about, Roger?"

"Right there. Don't you see it?"

This close, Sally saw only swatches of red watercolor surrounded by lines of gray. In fact, with her eyes six inches from the canvas, she couldn't tell what the hell she was looking at. You had to pull back to comprehend what the painting was supposed to be at all. And she certainly didn't see any screaming people in there, either up close or pulling back. Roger was an idiot.

"Albert, do you see screaming people in there?"

"Well… I thought I did. You know, for a minute."

Sally laughed. "Must have been sticker shock. It was probably your own reflection you saw, screaming at the price. But don't worry. In five years' time, this painting will be worth ten times what you paid for it. Maybe we'll commission one for the house."

"Oh, God…," Albert groaned.

Thirty minutes later—with a cushion under her knees for comfort and Albert's trousers bunched around his hairless, skinny ankles while she tried to keep his hands out of her hair as he leaned his white, sagging ass against his desk and prepared to once again fill her mouth with sixty-year-old sperm, which she hated but thought of as the price she had to pay for unlimited checking—Sally's mind wandered to that sparkling trail of white paint sweeping across the canvas in the outer office.

There was something about it. Something… unsettling.

It reminded her of an illustration she had seen as a child growing up in Kansas. An illustration in her mother's Bible, which always rested on the coffee table of their farmhouse in the plains east of Topeka. It was a glimpse of heaven, she seemed to remember. A glimpse of heaven as seen from the depths of hell. The drawing had frightened her as a child, and she was faintly surprised to realize that it still frightened her today.

Her mother had been a sweetly religious woman, and Sally wondered, suddenly, if she was looking down at her now from her perch in heaven.

A blush spread beneath the makeup on Sally's cheeks, more from embarrassment than exertion, and as Albert made that little sound in his throat that was her cue to prepare for incoming, she pulled her lips away and turned her head to the side, causing Albert to shoot his sperm onto the bodice of her two-thousand-dollar dress.

Poor Albert looked as if he had just been denied seating in his favorite restaurant.

"Sorry," Sally said. "Had to cough."

Albert was too winded to complain.

Sally dabbed at the mess on her bodice with a tissue she pulled from her purse and wondered where the nearest church was. Maybe she'd pop in for a few minutes, say a little prayer of thanks for everything God and Albert had given her. Maybe her mother would see her. Maybe her mother would see her in church and forget about everything else she had no doubt seen her daughter do for the past thirty years.

Sally hoped so. She had always liked her mother. Sort of.

CHAPTER FOUR
...GLIMPSES....

IT IS said that drawing the human hand is arguably the most difficult hurdle for an artist to master, and Charlie agreed with that assessment 100 percent. Charlie made eight separate sketches of Joe's hands before he was satisfied that he had captured their elegance. Their slim, incredible beauty. Their... power. The sketch he was most pleased with showed Joe's hands, fingers together, pointing upward, with palms touching in the classic prayer position. After adding a final bit of shading to the turn of the wrists with gentle strokes of his pinky, softening the lines of the charcoal, Charlie mentally stepped back and stared at it as Joe stood patiently in place, never changing his pose, not seeming tired or bored or restless, although he had been standing in the same position for over two hours, watching Charlie work. Joe still stood in what Charlie thought of as the *Freedom* pose, arms outstretched, head back, presenting his naked body to Charlie to do with as he would. Charlie wondered if Joe had any idea that Charlie had been sketching only Joe's hands for the past half hour and that the pose Joe held so perfectly was, in fact, unnecessary. But looking at him gave Charlie such peace, such *inspiration*, that he let the boy hold the pose for a while longer before guilt got the better of him and he told Joe to take a break.

Joe slowly lowered his arms and, without peeking at the sketchpad on Charlie's easel as most models would have done, stepped to the window and looked out at the lake.

As he stood there, Charlie flipped a page in his sketchpad and began following the clean lines of Joe's back, Joe's buttocks, Joe's long muscular legs, the sharp curve of his calves, the elegant ankles, transferring their likeness onto the paper in front of him. He was filled with such love for this boy standing before him, such fascination, that his fingers did not hesitate once as he worked. The charcoal stroked the paper as Charlie's hands would have stroked Joe. With reverence. Charlie could imagine the feel of Joe's skin against his fingertips. While his hands did the work, his mind was filled with that moment the night before, in front of the fire, when Joe had pulled Charlie's face into the hollow of his throat and held him there. Charlie closed his eyes for a second, remembering the boy's scent, remembering the vibration of Joe's gently timbred voice against the skin of his face. Remembering everything.

That same voice brought him back now.

"Your triptych has been delivered," Joe said.

Charlie opened his eyes and continued to sketch, working now with sweeping strokes of the charcoal, trying to make Joe's thick mane of hair fall just right across his shoulder. That done, he made a rudimentary outline of the window Joe was standing at, framing the boy's body with the frame of the window. Charlie realized suddenly that, as he had told Joe that morning, he *could* spend the rest of his working life with no other subject to draw from. His talent had never before felt so easily tapped into. His hands worked with a skill and a speed that was almost impossible. For him. For anyone. Joe brought it out in him. Joe inspired him. The only drawback was that every time the boy moved, every time he took a different stance, every time he found another backdrop, Charlie was impelled to draw that image as well. His original idea for painting Joe, his idea for *Freedom*, was all but lost in the urge to sketch Joe's every movement.

It took a while for Joe's words to soak into Charlie's consciousness.

Charlie looked up. "How do you know?" he asked.

When Joe didn't answer, Charlie tore his eyes from the sketchpad and gazed at him. Joe was still standing with his back to the room, staring out at the lake. Charlie saw a tremor in the boy's shoulders. As he had done that morning in the lake, standing knee-deep in water while the fish fairly flew around him, Joe was silently laughing.

"Joe? How do you know the triptych's been delivered?"

Instead of answering, the boy asked, "Do you believe in God, Charlie?"

Charlie considered the question, setting aside once again Joe's seemingly psychic intuitions that popped up every now and then, stunning Charlie and making him wonder where Joe acquired such insight, and wondering too if the boy could truly possess those insights at all. Somehow, Charlie never quite doubted them. After what he had seen that morning in the wood, how could he? So, like his physical desire for the boy, these questions too were set aside, stored away in that hidden place in his mind where he kept things he could neither act upon nor understand.

Charlie considered his answer carefully. "God is like the human soul, Joe. How can we know if either of them exists? It's like that surgeon you mentioned trying to pluck love from a human heart. We like to think it's there, but there really isn't any proof, is there? I'd like to think there's a God looking over us, but if he is, I have to wonder why he does some of the things he does. Why does he collapse a church on a group of praying peasants in the Andes? Why does he send a busload of school children flying off a cliff in the Rockies? Why does he bring such misery into the world, or allow it to be brought in, when he has the power to forestall it? If he is so all-powerful, Joe, why are so many people unhappy? Why do they suffer?"

"Suffering makes us stronger," Joe said, still staring through the window. He reached out one hand and laid it against the cool glass. Splaying his fingers wide, Joe cocked his head and stared through them like a child, still watching the lake. Charlie wondered what it was he saw out there, what it was about the lake that drew the boy's eyes so inexorably toward it.

"It also makes us miserable, Joe. What's the point?"

"Maybe there is no point. Maybe it's just our lot in life."

"Geez, Joe, what sort of a philosophy is that? If God created us in his own image, I'd like to think he had better things in mind than to make us live out our lives in utter misery and desperation."

"It's only through misery, Charlie, that we ever truly find God. It's only our desperation that makes us *seek* God."

Charlie had to laugh. "Sounds a little flaccid, Joe. It's a little like saying we have no use for cops unless we really need one."

Like Charlie, Joe laughed now too. He turned from the window with a wide grin on his face. "It really is, isn't it?"

Their eyes locked on to each other's.

Still chuckling, Charlie said, "Why do you ask me these questions, Joe? Does it really matter what I believe? Hell, half the time I don't even believe in myself."

"I believe in you. So does God. It doesn't matter what you believe. God wouldn't have given you the talents he gave you if he didn't believe in you. Maybe you were put here for a purpose, Charlie. Maybe God has plans for you. Did you ever think of that?"

Charlie let the charcoal move again on paper. A new sketch. Drawing the boy's smile. Something he always thought to be as difficult as human hands. But this time his fingers captured it perfectly. Sometimes they didn't. Sometimes they never could.

"If he does exist, I'd be more interested in learning why he sent *you* here, Joe. It's your talents that need explaining. Not my own."

"My powers are the same as yours, Charlie."

"Oh, please...."

Joe left the window then and stepped across the studio to pluck the stick of charcoal from Charlie's fingers and set it aside. He took Charlie's hands in his, placed one upon Charlie's chest and the other upon his own.

"Do you feel my heartbeat, Charlie?"

Charlie resisted the urge to stroke the skin beneath his hand, to simply pull Joe into his arms and hold his nakedness against him, losing himself in the boy's warmth. Once again, he felt the stirring of desire, but this time he closed his eyes and let it come.

"Yes, Joe. I feel it."

"Do you feel your own?"

"Yes."

"Make them stop, Charlie. Make our heartbeats stop. Will it to happen. Think of silence inside my chest. Inside your own. Will a stillness to settle into us. Think of that stillness as a place of utter contentment and beauty."

"Joe, I...."

"Do it, Charlie. See it in your mind and make it happen."

Charlie closed his eyes then, absorbing the heat of Joe's velvet skin against his palm, feeling the muscle and bone and *life* beneath his hand, letting Joe's words fill his mind. Seeing the stillness. Willing it to happen. Waiting for that stillness to settle around them like falling snow, pushing thoughts of desire and the texture of the boy's skin away from him. Burying his desire in the wish for silence.

For one brief moment, Charlie looked down on them both from a different place, like a spectator, trying to ignore the urge to see what they were doing as an absurdity, trying to do what Joe asked him to do, but knowing the impossibility of it. The *silliness* of the whole thing.

And then it happened.

A quiet such as Charlie had never sensed before filled his body. Filled Joe's. Total silence settled over them like a cloak. Utter silence. Utter stillness. The thudding of their hearts ceased beneath his hands. Inside their chests, he felt an empty wind blowing as if through tall canyon walls. Barren stone. Empty space.

Eyes closed, Charlie let the stillness engulf him. Suddenly he felt no need for air. His breathing stopped. The sensation of his clothes upon his body, the floor beneath his feet, and Joe's chest beneath his hand fell away from him like his desire, leaving him floating in a place of deep serenity. No sound of the world around him entered his ears. No feeling of hot summer wind against his skin. No rustle of branches or song of birds. The pungent smell of paint and charcoal, scents he so dearly loved, no longer filled the air.

He opened his eyes and saw nothing but a glowing white light that hovered around him. Joe was gone. The studio. His world. Everything. He was afloat in a sea of empty air and light and memory. In his mind he still saw what should have been there, but wasn't. It was gone. All of it.

Charlie knew then how death would feel. But there was no fear in it. No cold. No darkness. There was a pleasance to it that filled his silent body with such inner peace that he did not want to leave the place he found himself in. He was content there, far away from the hungers of mind and body. Away from doubt and sorrow and simple daily pressure. There was no tunnel of light leading him forward. But for the silence and the serenity, there was simply nothing.

Through the haze of nothingness, Joe's voice spoke to him, though he could not understand the words. He felt Joe's fingers move across his chest. Felt his own fingers where they lay upon the boy's breast. His sense of touch had returned. His sense of… life.

And through open eyes that could previously see nothing, he watched Joe's face suddenly reemerge from within that glowing light, still smiling at him as gently as before, still as beautiful as the first time Charlie had laid eyes upon it. The sweetness of that face and the love it brought reverberating through his mind and body again made Charlie gasp. And at that moment, their heartbeats resumed. His own pulse beat again inside his head. Inside his chest. The boy's heart pounded beneath his hand. Charlie drew a ragged breath of air into his lungs, not from hunger for air, but from force of habit, a bodily function Charlie had no more control over than his love for the boy.

Slowly, the hazy light dissolved around Joe's face, and Charlie found himself once again standing in his studio as the summer sunlight cascaded through the skylight, through the windows, through the open door, bringing him back to the place he thought he had left behind forever.

The place that, had it been taken from him for all time, he now knew he would not have missed at all.

His hand still rested on Joe's chest, and once again he could feel the boy's heart pumping blood beneath his touch. Feel the expansion and retreat of air flowing into Joe's lungs. He, like Charlie, again breathed life. And as if nothing at all had happened, Charlie's desire to hold the boy against him returned with such an explosion of force that he could not stop himself from pulling Joe into his arms and burrowing his face into the hollow at the base of Joe's throat, breathing in the warmth, the scent, the essence of Joe, like a drug addict desperate for a fix. Joe was Charlie's narcotic. And when Joe pressed his lips to Charlie's hair and slid his arms around Charlie to pull him close, stroke his back, comfort his hunger, Charlie gave himself up to the boy completely.

"It was your power," Joe said, whispering softly in his ear. "You made it happen. Not me. Did you see the light, Charlie? Did you see how beautiful it is?"

"Yes," Charlie said, still breathing in Joe's scent, his lips brushing the boy's throat, aching to draw him closer. To tell him how much he loved him. How much he wanted to make him happy. How glad he was to have Joe there beside him. In his arms. In his life. In his heart.

But Joe already knew. The words didn't need to be said, although it would have comforted Charlie to say them. But he let the moment pass. Again his fear of pushing Joe away led him to hold his words, and his feelings, deep inside himself where they could not drive a wedge between him and what he held now in his arms. Charlie couldn't risk losing Joe. Not now. Not ever.

"We were dead, Joe. Just for a moment, we were dead."

"No, Charlie. We're like the flowers in your garden. We never really die."

"Was it really me and not you who made it happen?"

The boy laid his hand on the back of Charlie's neck, pressing Charlie's face more firmly to his throat, as if he knew that was the place Charlie most needed to be.

"Yes, Charlie. Everything that happened, you did alone."

"I still don't understand."

"Someday you will. Someday soon."

Charlie closed his eyes, giving himself up completely to the boy's embrace. Not until desire again made him pull away did Joe let him go. For it was Joe's desire too. This time there was no mistaking it.

"Paint me," Joe said, stepping away.

"All right," Charlie answered, fighting against the tremor in his voice.

And as Joe resumed his *Freedom* pose, arms reaching out to either side, head tilted back as if he were preparing to soar to the heavens, his penis, filled with blood and longing, stood tall as well, it too seeming to reach for the sky, needing to soar, needing to fly away. Joe ignored it, unashamed, and unaffected also, apparently, by the bulge in Charlie's jeans, the tremble in his body, proclaiming his own desire as clearly as a beacon.

As Charlie picked up the charcoal again, his longing for Joe was tempered now with contentment. Contentment in knowing that Joe was drawn to him too. Charlie's desire was a brushfire burning through him, but like Joe, he strove to ignore it. He transferred his longings, his emotions, into the charcoal in his hand.

And his talent swept through him to his fingers, as strongly as his lust, as perfectly formed and realized as Joe's lust on display before him.

Their love for each other, the need they both now felt and could no longer hide, filled the air Charlie breathed like the scents of summer wafting through the open windows.

But still, Charlie knew, it was Joe's desire, not his own, that would lead the way to whatever came. At least now, knowing that Joe felt it too, Charlie could wait. And be content in doing so.

While thinking these thoughts, Charlie almost forgot the amazing thing that had happened minutes before. He understood death now, it seemed, although life and desire overshadowed the truth of it. He still did not understand Joe's purpose, or his own, but compared to his love for the boy, something as mundane as purpose didn't seem to matter very much.

He had Joe. And Joe wanted him. That was matter enough for one lifetime.

CHAPTER FIVE
...A MEMORY... A CLEANSING....

THAT AFTERNOON, with a ream of sketches scattered across the floor around him, Charlie gave in to the ache in his neck, the cramp in his fingers, and set the charcoal aside for the day. The emotion his work always brought out in him, that tense, wonderful expulsion of creativity that at the best of times focused every atom in his body onto the work at hand, had been present since he first began drawing hours and hours ago. Having Joe as a subject, having Joe beside him during these beginning steps of the creative process, having Joe to draw upon and simply look upon, had given his talent wings. He was exhilarated and exhausted. And more than pleased with the work he had done.

The physical expression of desire, which Joe had finally shown him beyond all doubt, had subsided long ago. Now Joe stood before him once again, as innocent as a child, his body no longer displaying lust or longing. His penis nestled softly, chastely, in its nest of coarse dark hair, swaying occasionally with the boy's movements, but no longer reaching out to Charlie. To anyone. Charlie wondered if Joe truly felt desire as he did. Perhaps it had not been desire at all that caused Joe to react the way he did. Perhaps it was simply the rush of vitality, of *living*, returning to his body after their heartbeats had stopped, refilling every part of him with blood and life and awareness.

Charlie's own desire had not diminished in the least. Still it pressed against the fabric of his jeans, pent up, straining to be freed. Like a teenager, Charlie longed for a few minutes alone, just a few private minutes, to stroke away the longing. That his mind would be filled with thoughts of Joe as he did so was a given. Not for years had he felt such a need for release, but he tried to push it from his mind. A sad and lonely act of masturbation would do nothing to ease his need. It would only make it worse. Without Joe's body to feed upon, he would rather let the need continue to eat at him like a beautiful cancer. If he gave in to his lust now, privately, stealthily, something more than desire, something *important*, would be diminished. If he could not share his release with Joe, he would rather not experience it at all.

While Charlie gathered up the sketches at his feet, Joe slipped into Charlie's bathrobe and began sifting through the dozens of paintings stacked against the studio walls. Mac, as always, followed the boy's every movement, as, from the corner of his eye, did Charlie. There was a power in Joe that drew the eye, centered the mind. Watching him make the simplest of gestures was enough to take one's breath away. Charlie could still find no word that better encompassed the boy than *otherworldly*. Joe appeared as alien to this world as the world sometimes appeared to him, as if he had fallen into it with no past and no experiences of it to draw from. But that simply could not be.

"What were you like as a child, Joe? Did you have the powers then that you have now?"

Joe was studying a pencil sketch of the lake, one Charlie had drawn a few years ago when he first settled on its shore.

"I like this one," Joe said. "You should work in pencil more often."

"I prefer colors," Charlie said. "And don't change the subject."

"I told you, Charlie. Before I stood at your door, I remember nothing. I don't think I ever was a boy. I came into the world as you see me now."

"Joe, you know that isn't possible. The way I see it, there's one of two possible scenarios taking place here. Either you remember your childhood and for some reason don't want to tell me about it, or you truly do remember nothing before the night of your arrival, which would mean you're suffering from amnesia. That seems a little melodramatic to me, so I'm guessing the first hypothesis is the true one. Either your youth was too painful for you to talk about, or you just plain don't want to share it with me. You told me once there could be no secrets between us. Remember? You seem to know everything about me, Joe. Some of it I've told you, and some of it you seemed to figure out on your own. But about you, I know absolutely nothing. And don't give me the heart surgeon metaphor again. I've already heard it."

Joe grinned. Charlie could sense it, although the boy had not turned to look at him. He continued to flip the canvases, gazing for long seconds at some, bypassing others perfunctorily, as if they were unworthy of Charlie's talents, which they probably were, Charlie conceded to himself. But the fact that the boy would think so irked him a bit. My God, even Picasso must have painted a few boners in his day. Not in the literal sense, of course, but with Picasso who could tell?

"What will you do with my painting, Charlie? Where will you send it? Will it be sold like the triptych, or will it stand against the wall like these, buried to anyone's eyes but your own?"

"Neither," Charlie said. "It will hang with me. Wherever I live. Above the mantle. Or over my bed. It will never leave my side."

"No," Joe said. "It has to go out in the world. People have to see it. Someplace public. Not like the triptych, decorating the office of sinners."

It was Charlie's turn to grin. "So, even without a past you seem to have discovered a dislike for lawyers. Pretty universal, that. Wait a minute, Joe. I never told you the painting was commissioned by a law firm. How did you know?"

"You must have mentioned it."

"I don't remember telling you th—"

"*Freedom* has to be given to the world, Charlie. Do you understand what I'm saying? It must be *given*. It can't be sold for money. You can donate it to a museum."

"What makes you think a museum would take my work, even if it was handed to them on a silver platter?"

"They will. You know they will. And that's what you have to do. For me, Charlie. Do it for me."

Charlie sighed. "All right. If that's what you want."

"It is."

Once again the boy had evaded questions about his past. Charlie wondered if he should go online, check out the Ten Most Wanted list. Maybe he would see Joe's picture there, sandwiched between a drug runner from Jersey and a murderer from Modesto, California who liked to slaughter transients in his spare time and bury them on his pig farm. *Not likely*, Charlie thought. There was nothing in this boy to fear. There were no crimes in his past. If he had a past at all. Joe said he didn't. But Charlie couldn't quite wrap his mind around that one. *Everyone* had a past. How else could they reach the present?

There was something else Charlie didn't quite understand. For the past few mornings, he had listened to the news on the radio (he would not allow a TV on the premises, and he was too far out in the middle of nowhere for newspaper delivery), and not once had the announcer mentioned the earthquake from a few nights ago. This wasn't California. An earthquake here, even a small one, should have sent the Midwesterners into a state of frenzy. They should have been all agog at the power of the earth to actually move beneath their feet, a power most Californians pretty much took for granted. Charlie had even checked a couple of news sites on his computer. Nothing.

Charlie estimated the jolt at somewhere between five and six on the Richter scale. That should have turned a few heads. And the fact that the nighttime sky had lit up like the Fourth of July should have turned a few heads too. But it hadn't. For the first time since burying himself here on the edge of this secluded, unnamed lake in northern Indiana, Charlie wished he had a neighbor or two to confer with about it. The fact that no one lived within twenty miles of him had always been somewhat of a comfort before. Now he began to wonder what sort of person would pull away from the world as he had. Perhaps in his own way, he was as strange as Joe. Maybe this was what brought them together. Two weirdass wackos drawn to each other like the only two Americans on a cruise ship full of Namibians.

Chuckling inwardly, Charlie gave his head a little shake, clawing his way back to reality.

"You spoke of your father, Joe. If you don't remember your past, how can you remember your father?"

"I just can."

"What about your mother? Do you remember her?"

With his finger, Joe was tracing the outline of a female nude on one of Charlie's canvases. It was Judith. She had posed for him one night, still glistening with perspiration and the residue of passion, back when passion still existed between the two, before it was replaced by anger and recriminations and the loss of everything that for a little while they had shared between them. Jason had destroyed that relationship. No, not Jason. Charlie. Judith could not bring herself to share her husband with another man. At the time, Charlie thought it rather a prudish way for her to feel, but now seeing Joe before him, he wondered what it would be like to share him with someone else, and suddenly Charlie understood Judith's feelings of abandonment and hurt. To see this boy in the arms of another, be they man or woman, would have sent Charlie into a spiraling insanity, or worse. Simply thinking about it created an ache inside him. As Judith had no doubt ached.

"She doesn't love you now, Charlie. Or at least she thinks she doesn't. You don't need to feel guilty about it anymore. She's moved past it. She has another man in her life. He's using her, but she doesn't know that yet."

"What the hell are you talking about, Joe?"

"Your wife. She's forgiven you."

Charlie stared at the painting in front of Joe. "How do you know that was my wife?"

"I can see you in her eyes. On the day she posed for this, she loved you very much."

"That didn't last long," Charlie said.

"No. Not long. But while it did last, it was a perfect thing. A flower."

"Well, I pretty well managed to wrench it from its stem and grind it into the mud."

"Yeah. You did. But it grew again. Somewhere else."

Just as my own love grew again, Charlie thought. *In you.* But these words he could not say.

"I asked about your mother, Joe. Tell me about her."

"I can see only her face," Joe said. "But it's a face from another time. Long ago. I can see her resting on a bed of straw. Strangers stand before her, offering gifts. She doesn't want to take them."

"Why not?"

"She's a simple woman. The gifts are too rich. They embarrass her. Her body still aches from my birth. She's still bleeding down below. She's afraid the bleeding will never stop. Afraid the bleeding will take her life. If it does, she won't be there to help me grow. All her thoughts are centered on me. I see her pulling me to her breast. I feed from her. After that, I remember only pain. Then nothing. The next face I remember seeing is yours, Charlie."

"But how can that be?"

Joe shrugged. "It just is."

Charlie began to wonder if amnesia *was* the only explanation. If the boy wasn't lying, what other explanation could there be? And why would Joe remember his mother lying on a bed of straw? Were his parents so poor they had no home? Not even a cot for the woman to give birth on?

"Where was this, Joe? Do you know where you were born?"

"No," Joe said. "Because it wasn't me. Not really."

"Now you've really lost me. What the hell are you talking about?"

Joe turned to him then. There was a softness in the boy's eyes that caused a flutter in Charlie's chest, like butterflies he had once seen, beating their gossamer wings against a window of the cabin, confused perhaps by the invisible barrier, as if they were trying to get inside, away from the day, away from their mundane lives, hoping to explore new territory, new dimensions. The feathery sound of their wings slapping the sun-drenched window on that long-ago morning was the same sound Charlie heard now inside himself. The vaguest flutter of noise. A gentle unease.

"What's wrong?" Charlie asked.

"Do you love me?" the boy asked.

"Y… yes. You know I do."

Joe brushed his long hair from his eyes. For the hundredth time, the look of innocence, of purity, on Joe's face, made Charlie's heart give a tiny lurch, as if it had skipped a beat or two. At that moment he would have given Joe anything. And perhaps the boy knew this.

"What do you want me to do?" Charlie asked.

Joe smiled as if pleased at the easy way Charlie spoke the words, at the resignation with which they were uttered.

"I can make you pure, Charlie."

Charlie almost laughed, but bit down on it before it could escape his lips. The assuredness on Joe's face, the childlike conviction with which he had said what he said, made Charlie pull back into himself. He would not hurt the boy by mocking him.

"Joe. Pure is something I will never be. Even *your* gifts are insufficient to *that* task."

Joe did not hold his own laugh back at all. A wide grin spread across his face as his eyes continued to bore into Charlie's, at the look of wry incomprehension in Charlie's eyes. And the doubt there too. What was he getting at? What was he about to ask Charlie to do? Could Joe see these questions in Charlie's eyes as clearly as he could see the lake outside the window?

Charlie looked through the window at the water. He stared at his boat bobbing beside the jetty, at the pine trees bordering the entire perimeter of the lake that abutted the back of his property. The lake he had once loved so much. It had always been a place of serenity for him. Until yesterday. When it tried to take this boy away from him. Charlie could still see Joe's head disappearing beneath the surface, pulled down into the depths. Could still feel the fear that ricocheted through him, and the relief he felt when the boy was once again hanging safely from the edge of the boat. Fear, relief, desire, so many emotions had bombarded Charlie at that moment that he found it almost impossible to sort them out. Until now. At this moment, for the first time, Charlie knew he would never look at the lake again in the same way. The lake had tried to steal Joe from him. It could not be forgiven for that. Charlie would never draw solace from it again.

As always, Joe seemed to understand his thoughts.

"Do not hate the water. It can kill, but it can also give life. It can cleanse you, Charlie. It can save you as you saved me."

"Save me from what?"

"Save you from yourself. And save you from the punishments that will one day be doled out."

An unreasonable anger suddenly welled up in Charlie, and when he opened his mouth, the anger spilled out of him.

"What the hell are you talking about, Joe? For once in your life, can't you say what you mean? You speak in riddles half the time. Parables. Incomprehensibilities. It's annoying, and it's really starting to piss me off."

Joe came to him then, wrapped him in his arms, stroked his hair. And with the first touch of Joe's hands upon his body, Charlie's anger fell away like the last leaf of autumn dropping from a tree, shivering and naked in the nearness of winter. Charlie closed his eyes and let Joe comfort him, untroubled by desire, untroubled by anything but the warmth of Joe's goodness seeping into him. Resting his head on Joe's shoulder, Charlie closed his eyes, feeling peace flow through him like a vapor. Feeling the anger drain away.

Again he said, but softly this time, "What do you want me to do, Joe?"

"Let me wash your hurts away, Charlie. The peace you feel now, I can give to you forever."

"Are you going to kill me?" Charlie asked in a hushed voice that barely reached his own ears. Even death, at that moment, did not frighten him. Wrapped in Joe's arms, he would have welcomed it. Wrapped in Joe's arms, he would have welcomed anything.

But Joe only laughed. "No, Charlie. I'll give you life."

"Don't I have that now?" Charlie asked.

"Not forever," Joe said. "Not yet."

"Is this another riddle?"

"No, Charlie. It's a promise."

Joe pushed Charlie gently away from him then, held him at arms' length for a moment, studying his face, then took his hand and led him through the studio door to the balmy summer evening outside. With his hand still firmly clasped in Charlie's, he led them both to the edge of the water. There, Joe let the robe slide from his shoulders and stepped naked into the lake, pulling Charlie, still fully clothed, along behind him. When they stood in water to their waists, Joe turned to Charlie and cupped his face in his gentle hands.

"Let me into your heart, Charlie," he said.

And Charlie smiled. "You already are."

"Then you are ready," Joe said, and resting one hand in the small of Charlie's back and the other on Charlie's breast, Joe laid him back in the water. Charlie closed his eyes as the water flowed across his face, giving himself up entirely to the power in Joe's hands. And for a moment, as the cool water settled over him, he opened them again to see Joe's face hovering above him, dimmed and distorted by the water. There was a smile on Joe's face as the boy looked down at him, as his hands continued to hold him firmly in place, and just as Charlie felt the dawning need for breath, for oxygen, the boy lifted him from the water.

Charlie tore himself from the boy's grasp and, stumbling, fought his way toward the shore, where he dropped to his knees. Tears streamed from his eyes, mixing with the lake water, as he had seen tears streaming from Joe's eyes a second before as he lifted Charlie to the surface. Like the gift of a comforting fire on a winter evening, warmth spread through Charlie, through his body, his legs, down the length of his arms to his paint-encrusted fingertips where they rested in the grass at the edge of the water. He did not sob. He felt no need to do so. But the tears continued to flow from his eyes as the warmth tore through him, comforting, ravaging, burning away the pain of a million forgotten sins, cleansing him like a brushfire cleans the earth of grass, each and every blade a transgression now reduced to ash.

When Joe dropped to his knees beside him and pressed a hand to the nape of Charlie's neck, Charlie turned his head to look at him, wondering what he would see, wondering if his perception of the boy would be altered by what had just transpired. But in that regard, nothing at all had changed. The boy, unclothed beside him, once again brought a rush of desire to Charlie's trembling body even as the tears still pooled in his eyes.

Joe pulled Charlie's hands from the grass, brought them to his face, and pressed them to either cheek. Charlie felt Joe's smile beneath his touch.

"Now you belong to me, Charlie."

Charlie swallowed the lump in his throat and finally forced the words from his lips. "That's all I've ever wanted," he said.

Joe opened Charlie's hand and pressed his lips into his palm. "I know," he said.

Again, Charlie had to fight to get the words out. "I feel empty, Joe. I… I can't explain it."

"You don't need to," Joe said.

"I think I know who you are now, Joe. I think I know where you came from."

Joe reached out and pushed the wet hair from Charlie's forehead. "Do you still love me?" he asked.

Charlie blinked back final tears, felt his pulsing heart calm a little inside his chest. "More than ever," he said.

Joe laid his hand across Charlie's eyes, blocking out the summer day, blocking out the sight of himself and everything else that lay before Charlie as he knelt by the edge of the water on this balmy summer evening. The darkness comforted Charlie. The warmth and pressure of Joe's hand, the nearness of his body, thrilled him. The emptiness inside him dissipated as the warmth spread. Charlie breathed in the clean summer air and smiled around his tears.

"Now we are one," Joe said through the darkness.

Chapter Six
...Miracles and Laughter....

That night, as the moon hung low over the lake and the evening sounds of crickets and night birds filled the shadows, Charlie sat at the edge of the water, a cigarette burning forgotten in his hand. The evening breeze blowing off the water, cooling his face, registered faintly through his thoughts. In the distance, that same breeze rattled the pine needles in the trees that bordered the lake, creating a sound as soft and comforting as the rustle of crisp clean sheets on a newly made bed where a traveler at long last lays his weary head.

Charlie thought of the deer and her fawn, wondering where they were now. Wondered, too, if they understood the miracle of their being together at all. At this moment the doe should have been rotting at the side of the road like battered carrion while the fawn slowly starved to death, frightened and alone, somewhere in the underbrush. Did they know that Joe had come between them and death? Did they understand the concept of an interrupted fate, or was the fawn suckling now at her mother's teat, oblivious to everything but the reassuring sound of her mother's heartbeat, the warmth of her mother's milk, comforting her, giving her life, nurturing her to an adulthood she would otherwise never have known? Would she live on to one day give birth to a fawn of her own, and would she tell her child of the miracle that happened on a long-ago day at the side of a country lane when a young human man, not much more than a child, laid his hands on her mother's neck and stole the emptiness of death from her mother's eyes even as she watched, trembling in the brambles? Or would it all be forgotten? Or worse yet, never understood at all?

If Charlie could not understand it, how in the world could they?

Charlie jumped when the cigarette, smoldered down to the filter, suddenly burned his fingers. He flipped it out over the lake and watched it spiral down to the water like a tiny meteor crashing to earth. He heard the soft sizzle of the ember extinguish when it hit the water. Saw the tiny ripples on the lake where the butt had landed, reflecting in circles of light cast down from the moon overhead.

The emptiness he had felt that afternoon, when he tore himself from Joe's arms and crawled from the lake on hands and knees to feel the grass between his fingers, and later, when he felt Joe's hands lay across his eyes to block out the sun and comfort him as he still stooped there, dripping and emotionally drained, was still with him. It seemed funny that he could be so filled with emptiness, so sated by nothing at all. Like too much helium in a balloon, maybe. Or too much darkness in an empty room. It was like his body contained nothing in that moment but vast spaces of wasteland. Fallow. Infertile. Waiting to be tilled.

It was a wonderful feeling, really. Like pages of an empty book waiting to be filled by a writer's hand. Or a blank canvas, waiting for the first brushstroke of color to bring it to life.

That was it, he told himself now. He was an empty, blank canvas. Cleaned of all marks. Restored to pristine whiteness. He could start anew with the painting of his life on clean linen, the canvas taut and ready in its frame, the mistakes of his past life gone, erased by Joe's simple ritual of lowering him beneath the water like a soiled paintbrush dipped in acetone.

There in the darkness, alone at the side of the lake, Charlie almost chuckled at that analogy. But the chuckle died before it ever reached his lips when he thought of Joe, his hand pressed to Charlie's eyes, blocking out the light, blocking out the pain, telling him that they were now one.

Charlie realized it was not only emptiness that filled him now, but love as well. His love for Joe was still there. How could it not be? And, too, that newfound love for himself, for his own life, still drifted around in the emptiness inside him—the emptiness, he knew, that came from the cleansing. Joe had erased his past like a child erases a teacher's blackboard. Erased his mistakes. Erased his… sins. Leaving nothing behind but love. Charlie's talent remained, of course. And his desires survived as well. His passion for the boy had not diminished even one iota. But Charlie knew how to handle the passion now. Knew how to control it. Knew how to push it away until it left only a gentle ache inside, not a gnawing agony.

Charlie closed his eyes and searched his memory for the sight of Joe, naked in that beam of noontime sun pouring into the studio as he posed for Charlie, arms outstretched, strong young legs rooted to the floor, spread wide, giving himself to Charlie in the only way he was ready to do so. And Charlie found the boy there, in his mind, where he knew he would be.

He remembered his sketch of Joe's praying hands. The perfect symmetry of them. He knew those hands. Had felt them on his face a dozen times. The warmth of them. Their assuredness. Their strength. The remarkable things those hands could do. Blood flowed through Joe's body as it flowed through his own. But Joe was not like him. Joe was different. Joe was special. Charlie knew that now. Perhaps he had always known it.

Still, he could not bring himself to form the words in his mind, to admit to himself, to *accept* the fact, that Joe was… not… quite… human. For humanity is flawed. Joe was not. Though he was certainly past the cusp of manhood, Joe's innocence was utterly childlike. And his purity was beyond even that of a child. He was a perfect being. Beautiful. Kind. Wise. And good.

But Joe's perfection of body and heart were merely the icing on the cake. What lay beneath was even more remarkable. Charlie had seen the boy rekindle a dead flame in the body of the doe. He had seen him, too, stop his own heart, and Charlie's, then send life once again pumping through their still bodies. Joe had given Charlie a glimpse of death, and because of that, Charlie no longer feared it. Perhaps he never had. Perhaps at one time in his life, he would have welcomed it. Why else had he drunk so much? Why else had he let his body, his desires, take him to places he never should have gone, hurting people along the way, hurting himself more than them? If not for his painting, what would Charlie have become? Where would he have ended up? Alone, certainly. Unloved. And unhappy, without a doubt.

Now he felt himself to be none of those things. Now he felt whole and complete for the first time in his life. This newfound perspective gave him no desire to change the world, or even to change his own life. He still wanted to paint. He still wanted to be himself. But he could do it better now. He could do it without causing pain to others. He would probably never be a saint, he admonished himself with a chuckle that *did* reach his lips this time, but he could be a better person than he was before.

And he had a goal now. One that he felt it within his grasp to attain. He would paint Joe. He would paint his *Freedom*. And as Joe had told him to do, he would give that painting to the world so everyone in it could look upon this boy and understand who he truly was.

The world should see Joe's face before the torments came, the torments Joe had alluded to more than once speaking to Charlie. Charlie did not understand what the torments would be, did not know if it was God who had decided to dole out punishments or the boy himself, but Charlie knew those punishments were coming. And by an incredible stroke of luck, Charlie knew he had been saved from this pending wrath by the simple fact that the boy had come to him first. Not because of any inherent goodness within himself, but because of his talent as a painter. The boy wanted to be seen by billions. And Charlie could make it happen. Charlie could show the world who this boy really was, who he himself now knew the boy to truly be.

God's child.

God's love.

And ultimately, God's punishment.

Joe was not sent here to atone for man's sins. Not this time. Charlie suspected that this time around, God had decided to take a more hands-on approach. Joe was sent here to wipe the slate clean, as he had wiped Charlie's own slate clean.

But not by baptism. Not for the rest of them. Not for the sinners. This time God was going to knock their lights out.

Charlie closed his eyes to the nighttime sky, and for the first time in many years, maybe ever, he found the words of a prayer forming in his mind.

They did not come easily, but they came. And Charlie let them flow. Like Joe, splayed and naked in the noontime sun, Charlie laid himself open to God, telling everything. His feelings for Joe. His gratitude at being given the talent to paint. His sorrow at the pain he had caused so many people over the years. His wasting of love. His sins. His mistakes. His regrets.

And as he emptied himself even further, creating almost a vacuum inside himself as he dug into the corners and dredged up every moment of unhappiness he had caused himself and the people around him, Charlie slowly realized that now the cleansing that had begun with Joe's strong arms dipping him beneath the surface of the lake was finally complete. He was like Joe now. An empty vessel, unsullied by the dregs of a past life. A vessel ready at last to be refilled with the clear, crystal wine of a new beginning.

He was reborn.

Wearied by the emotional turmoil of spilling his guts out to a God who only days before he had not believed in at all, Charlie laid himself back in the cool grass at the edge of the lake and opened his eyes. Again he heard the sounds of a simple summer night. Wind whispering through the trees. Night birds chortling off in the distance. A croaking bullfrog somewhere in the reeds at the edge of the water off to his right. The whine of a mosquito. The smell of clean earth and water and pine. Nighttime smells. Nighttime sounds.

Taking in the sky above his head, he saw the moon shining down upon his face, glistening off the water, surrounded by so many stars that it would have taken lifetimes to count them all. So vast. So perfect. So unbelievably beautiful.

And as he watched, he felt his heart leap as a streak of light swept overhead, the faintest trail of white slicing through the heavens, billions of miles away, perhaps. A comet, streaking off to some far-off destination Charlie would never see, could never comprehend, leaving behind itself nothing but, for a brief moment, the beauty of its passing.

Like Joe's comet, it was a sign of things to come. Charlie knew this with the same certainty with which he felt the earth beneath his back, the wind upon his face.

Punishments were coming. Joe had said so.

And Joe spoke for God.

A cleansing was about to begin.

LATER, WITH Mac at his heels, Joe came to sit beside him by the water. He laid his arm across Charlie's shoulder, and together they stared silently out at the lake. Wearied to the point of collapse by all the feelings that had surged through him and out of him, Charlie laid his head on Joe's shoulder and once again closed his eyes, letting Joe's strength restore some of his own. Joe pulled him close and pressed his lips to Charlie's hair.

Joe's words were barely audible over the gentle sounds of the summer night around them.

"You've spoken to the nurseryman, then," Joe said.

Charlie nodded, too spent to speak. Instead, he lifted Joe's hand and pressed it to his lips. He could feel Joe smile in the darkness beside him.

"You're a new man, Charlie. Your life is just beginning."

Charlie pushed his weariness away and turned to the boy. "But how many other lives are going to end? What's going to happen now, Joe? Have you saved me only to watch the world die around me?"

"The world will not die, Charlie. Not yet." He pointed to the shining new moon hanging overhead. "There will be many, many more of those before it does."

Charlie lifted his head from the boy's shoulder to look at him.

"Are you talking months?"

"No, Charlie. I'm talking lifetimes."

"I don't understand."

"I was not sent here to end the world, Charlie. Is that what you think?"

"Yes."

"Even the great flood did not end the world, Charlie. You know that. Good survived. This time will be no different. Only sin will perish."

"How, Joe? How will it perish? Will there be another flood?"

"Fire, Charlie. This time it will end in fire."

"You mean nuclear war?"

"No. A nuclear war *would* kill the planet. Fallout. Nuclear winter. Nothing alive would survive it. That will not be allowed to happen."

"Never?"

"No. Never."

"Can you do this by yourself, Joe?"

"My father has not entrusted everything to me alone," Joe said.

"Your father, the nurseryman?"

Joe laughed. "Yes. The nurseryman. He has many sons, Charlie. I'm only one."

"Where are they now?"

"I don't know. Doing whatever my father has told them to do, I suppose. It isn't only here that the punishments will come. Sin is everywhere, Charlie. A plague. We're going to stamp it out."

"You and your brothers?"

"Yes. Me and my brothers. My father says it's time."

"Was Jesus truly one of his sons, Joe? Like you? Like the Bible says he was?"

Joe bowed his head, and even in the dim moonlight Charlie could see a sadness pass over the boy's face.

"Yes. Jesus was the first. He was sent here to teach the world about goodness and faith, but men would not listen. They laughed at him. And ultimately, they murdered him."

"Then it was all a waste of time. A waste of life."

"No," Joe said. "There were many who listened to my first brother's words. Many lives were changed by his coming here. But not enough. Too much sin remained behind. The world is too vast a place for one man to make a difference now. This time my father sent many sons. Even so, much sin will survive. But the lessons to be learned from what is about to take place will be unmistakable to those remaining. And my father does not want to punish the good for the sins of the bad. Unlike the great flood, this time only the evil will suffer."

"But not all?"

"No. Not all. But hopefully enough."

"Why was I spared, Joe? Why did you come to me?"

"Even if I had not come to you, you would not have died with the others, Charlie. You were not evil. You were merely… astray. Like I told you on that first morning, you have a good soul, Charlie. Your purity may have been lost, but goodness still echoed inside you. It only needed a catalyst to bring it out."

"You were that catalyst."

"Yes. Me and the love you feel for me."

Charlie pulled himself to his feet and stepped to the edge of the lake, close enough for the water to lap at his toes. "My love for you wasn't just goodness, Joe. It was lust and longing and… sin, I think. I still want to hold you in my arms and make love to you. I want it so badly my body aches with the need of it. Isn't that a sin, Joe? Doesn't that make me… one of them?"

Joe came to him then and, taking his hand, led him along the shore of the lake toward the trees.

"From the moment you laid eyes on me, Charlie, I knew of your need for me. I understood your feelings. And I felt your desires in myself as well. But there was love there too. There was a great crying out in you for something to give your life meaning. I still sense it sometimes when you talk to me." Joe tugged Charlie to a stop and gently pulled his face around so their eyes were centered solely on each other. "You don't need to cry out for meaning anymore, Charlie. You have a purpose now. Your painting is your purpose, more now than it ever was before. I chose you to bring my face to the world, Charlie. Only you can do it. If things are predestined, as my father says they are, then your talent was given to you, even as you grew inside your mother's womb, for just this reason. Your painting of me will give the world a human face to center their beliefs upon. I don't know why my father chose my own face for this honor, but he did. Jesus was alone when he came here. I am not. But my brothers will remain hidden behind me. Only I will be the Savior in the eyes of your people. And you will give me to them."

"Did you come here in a meteor, Joe?"

"No. My father set me here by his hand. The light you saw on the night of my arrival was the light of my father's goodness reaching down to lay me at your feet."

"The earth trembled that night."

"Yes. My father does not touch this place often. When he does, the world feels it. Not the people, perhaps, but the earth itself knows he's here. He created it. It feels his anger. And his blessings."

"Are there many of those? Blessings?"

Joe smiled. "More than you could ever know."

"Do your brothers look like you?"

"I have never seen my brothers, but I expect they are as varied as the people living here. Why?"

"I just wondered if they were all as beautiful as you. Your beauty astounds me every time I look at you, Joe. It takes my breath away a hundred times a day."

Again Joe smiled as he cupped Charlie's cheek in the palm of his hand. "It is not my beauty you see. It's your love for me."

"No."

A shadow crossed Joe's face. "There is still doubt inside you, Charlie. I can feel it. For us to be one, you have to trust me completely. You have to believe beyond all doubt in everything I've told you."

"I do," Charlie said.

"Perhaps."

"I've watched you raise the dead, Joe. Just like Jesus. How could I ever doubt you?"

"Take my hand," Joe said.

Charlie slipped his hand in Joe's, wondering what the boy intended to do, what lessons he intended to share with him now. *Was* there doubt inside him as Joe had said? How could there be after all he had seen?

"All right," Charlie said, twining his fingers through the boy's, waiting for whatever was about to come. "Show me beyond all doubt that you are who you say you are."

"Do you love me?" the boy asked.

It was Charlie's turn to smile. If there was any fear in him for whatever was about to happen, it was lost, buried deep beneath his all-consuming love for this young man standing before him now.

"You know I do," Charlie said. "I've loved you since the night you knocked on my door."

"Then walk with me," Joe said. And pulling Charlie along behind him, the boy stepped out onto the surface of the cool water. Charlie followed, expecting to feel the water engulf his feet, his ankles, but when it did not, he looked down. The lake water shimmered beneath his feet like dark porcelain. He could feel the coldness of it on the soles of his feet. He took another step forward, and the water stayed beneath him. Wet. As cold as a fish's flesh. But unyielding. As firm as granite.

And as the moonlight poured over them and Mac watched from the shore with his head cocked in confusion, the two men walked out toward the center of the lake, hand in hand.

Far from shore, with Mac only a tiny speck on the shoreline behind them, Charlie's laughter bubbled up at the feel of the water tickling his feet, at the motion of their bodies bobbing precariously atop the sway of the gently undulating water.

"You're full of tricks," Charlie said, beaming his happiness at the boy.

"You have no idea," Joe said, smiling back, and taking a firmer grip on Charlie's hand, he lifted them both from the surface of the water, straight up into the air until the lake was nothing but a patch of glass far below their feet.

A cool wind whipped his clothes around him as Charlie gaped at the panorama laid out beneath him. He could see the cabin and the studio, the horizon circling round them, and there, a tiny speck beside the water far below his feet, stood Mac, staring up at them in the moonlight and barking his fool head off. Charlie laughed out loud at the sight, and Joe giggled, too, at the dog's excitement.

Reaching out his hand, Joe pulled a great torrent of water from the lake. Charlie gasped as it spiraled upward with a roar of sound like a thousand locomotives, a waterspout so immense it blocked out everything beneath them. The massive eddy of spinning water rose into the sky, and when it brushed the soles of their feet, it stopped climbing. Charlie felt his body settle upon it like a statue clattering into place upon its pedestal. The water still swirled beneath their feet, but it was as solid as cold marble, accepting their weight as easily as a giant lifting a child to his shoulder.

Still churning beneath his feet, the spinning funnel of water bent in the middle, and Charlie could feel the wind of it tossing his hair around his head in a whirl of air and motion. High above the center of the lake, the waterspout swooped down, bending its neck like a swan. It carried them forward, him and Joe, across the water until it reached the shore, and there it set them gently to the ground. With solid earth once again beneath his feet, Charlie watched as with a rush of sound the waterspout collapsed in upon itself. The tons of water inside it crashed back into the lake like a waterfall, a deluge. The silence that followed was deafening.

Mac shook his head in wonder to see the two of them once again standing beside him in the grass at the edge of the lake.

Charlie's heart was beating so fast he thought it too would spiral out of his body and soar off into the sky as the waterspout had done a moment before. He looked around, at the trees, at the cabin, at the once again soothing summer night, and then he turned to Joe standing beside him.

"Do it again," Charlie said.

Joe laughed. "Tell me the words I want to hear, Charlie."

Charlie pushed the boy's damp hair away from his perfect face and stared into those bottomless eyes with a look of love that flowed out of him like a wind.

"You are who you say you are," he said. "You are your father's son."

The boy gave a barely perceptible nod of his head and then stooped to pat a still confused Mac, who was standing at their feet looking from them to the water and back again as if he couldn't quite figure out what had just happened.

"I am indeed," Joe said. "And now I'm hungry. What time is dinner?"

Charlie giggled, still trembling with the excitement of all that had happened. He took the boy's hand and, on rubbery legs, led him toward the cabin.

"Come on, then," he said. "We'll fry up some chicken."

"Do we know how?" Joe asked, looking doubtful.

"Hell, no. But if you can fly, conjure up a waterspout, and walk on water, surely you can figure it out."

JOE HAD a devastated look on his face as he glumly poked a fork at the incinerated chicken carcass. His eyes were bright red and he could barely breathe through the smoke that permeated the entire cabin. Even Mac, curled up in the corner, was gasping for air and looking morose. To say that dinner had not turned out quite the way Joe expected would have been a vast understatement.

"I'm afraid this unfortunate beast died for nothing," Joe finally said, trying to restrain a cough. He turned to Charlie with such a wounded expression on his face that Charlie almost peed his pants laughing.

"You may be the son of God," Charlie sputtered, "but you can't cook for beans. Even you couldn't bring that thing back to life."

"Poor creature," Joe said, still eyeing the burnt, dismembered carcass through a stream of tears. "There must be a trick to it we don't know about."

By now, Charlie was laughing so hard he had to prop himself against the kitchen counter. "Mac will eat it," he managed to gasp, while tears streamed down his face and a rope of snot dribbled off his nose like a watch chain. "At least, I think he will."

Like a scientist gathering up the deadly residue from some failed nuclear experiment, Joe carefully scraped the charred pieces of their intended dinner onto a plate. He set it on the counter to cool before giving it to the dog.

That task completed, he turned to Charlie and asked, "Now what's for dinner?"

"Can't you beam us up a rump roast or something?"

Joe narrowed his eyes. "No."

Charlie was still laughing. "Then how about frozen waffles?"

Joe perked up. "Sounds great. Any sausages left?"

"I think so. Check the freezer."

Twenty minutes later they were dining on waffles, sausage, and the instant mashed potatoes that were supposed to go with the chicken, which Mac was now scarfing down with utter abandon. He seemed to enjoy his chicken burned obsidian black and as dry and crunchy as gravel.

"If he chokes to death," Charlie said, watching him, "you can bring him back to life."

Joe was busy eating. "Gotcha," he said around a mouthful of food.

When their hunger was appeased somewhat, the eating slowed and they eyed each other across the table. The moonlight still beamed down on the lake outside the kitchen window. The night was growing late.

"What now?" Charlie asked.

"Sleep," Joe said.

"And after that?"

"Who knows?" Joe replied cagily, a somber look in his eyes.

"That sounds ominous," Charlie said.

A silence settled over them, and in that silence, the vestiges of their previous laughter slowly died away like embers cooling on a grate. As Charlie stared at Joe's face, he saw a wisp of sadness cross the boy's eyes.

"The bad people are feeling the fear now, Charlie. It's beginning."

"You mean they know what's going to happen?"

"No, but some of them know something isn't right. They feel a weight of doom hanging over them. An unexplainable unease. Some of them are starting to turn their minds to my father for the first time in years, but it's too late. They should have reached out to him a long time ago, Charlie, before they did the things they did. Before they hurt the people they hurt. Before they angered him. Their souls are already lost, Charlie. Their lives are over. They just don't know it yet."

"When you say they will end in fire, Joe, do you mean actual fire here on earth, or did you mean the fires of… you know, hell?"

"Both."

"So hell does exist?"

"Yes. They will know of it soon enough, I think. And being there, they will feel the continual pain of their fiery mortal deaths through all eternity. I do not envy them that."

Charlie stared at his own reflection in the kitchen window. "Seems so… cruel."

Joe snaked his arm across the table and laid his hand over Charlie's. "No, Charlie. It is just. These are not merely unkind people my father is angered by. These are the true killers of good."

"Criminals?"

"Not all of them. Some are pillars of their community. The things they did that angered my father are things that might not be immediately attributed to them. But if you follow the trail of evidence, as the police are fond of saying, you will find their faces at the end of it. The commandments were not written in stone because there wasn't any papyrus handy. They were written in stone because they were meant to last. Forever. These people broke one or all of those commandments, Charlie, and they did it without a moment's hesitation, uncaring for the pain they caused to the people around them or to my father himself. Sin isn't just against fellow men. It strikes at my father too. He feels the pain of it every day of his life. He finally grew tired of the pain, I think. Now he's ready to dole out some of his own."

Charlie quoted from one of the few scriptures he thought he knew. "The Lord thy God is an angry God."

Joe smiled. "Actually, that's *jealous* God, but you've got the drift."

"When will the 'doling out' begin?"

Joe poured syrup over a fresh stack of waffles.

"Soon, Charlie. Maybe it already has."

"You mean, like… today?"

Joe forked a sausage from Charlie's plate. "As good a time as any, don't you think?"

CHAPTER SEVEN
...BEING MAN....

FOR THE first time since the boy came to Charlie, he and Joe shared the bedroom loft at the top of the stairs. One triangular wall of the loft, from floor to pointed ceiling, was constructed entirely of glass. Through it, from the head of the bed, they could see the lake stretching out below them, shimmering in the moonlight of another perfect summer night.

"It's so beautiful here," Joe said from the darkness at Charlie's side. "The lake. The sky. I wish I could see all of the other wonders my father brought to this planet when he blessed it with life. There must be miracles of beauty far beyond even this in hidden corners of the world."

Charlie could feel the weight of the boy resting on the bed beside him, could smell the clean flesh of him lying there in the shadows at his side. He was glad for the darkness that covered them. It hid many things, that darkness. Desire, for one. Charlie did not want Joe to see the ache in his eyes yet again, the ache that came from Charlie's longing to pull Joe's body next to his, to taste his skin with his tongue, to feel him tremble beneath Charlie's touch. He was not ashamed of his love for Joe—he could never be ashamed of such a taintless emotion—but the lust that came with it was more than he was willing to expose. Especially now, lying as they were unclad beneath the sheets. It felt wrong somehow, the lust that burned inside him, even though Joe had told him more than once that it was not.

Still, if a touch other than one of friendship ever entered into this bed, it would have to come first from Joe. As Charlie's eyes adjusted to the darkness, he began to see the outline of the boy lying beside him in the purple haze of moonlight that shone across the bed, across the room, and on seeing him, Charlie could suddenly feel the heat of the boy as well.

Knowing it would make his desire even more unbearable, Charlie nevertheless reached out to lay his arm across Joe's back as they stared out over the pillows at the serenity of the silent lake looming there in the night beneath them. Charlie closed his eyes for a moment at the white-hot blast of feelings the touch of Joe's skin against his own brought crashing across his senses.

Then, swallowing his desire, he opened his eyes and said, "Have you never seen the world, Joe?"

Like a child, the boy snuggled closer to him in the darkness. "Never," he said. "My father has spoken of it many times, but I never saw it with my own eyes. Only in my mind, in my imagination, has this place ever existed for me. To be here, at last, is like a dream. I wonder if it feels the same to my brothers who are here."

"What did you do before you came here, Joe? What was your life like before? Before you came to me?"

Joe let silence settle over them for a moment before speaking. In his words, when he finally spoke, were both melancholy and happiness: fond memories, yet unfulfilled yearnings never quite forgiven.

"I was only light," Joe said. "There was no physical being to me that I can remember. I was emotionless. A mind without a body. Smoke without fire. I was everything. And nothing. An eye without a tear."

He turned to gaze at Charlie beside him, and Charlie could see the glimmer of moonlight sparkling in the boy's eyes.

"Before I came to you, Charlie, I was a bloodless, silent heart. Content, but empty. I felt love only for my father. It was a kinder love than the one I feel here with you. Love on this planet is as much ordeal as pleasure. I see the pain your love for me causes you every time I gaze into your face. Even now in the darkness, I can sense your longing. But it's not a one-way street, Charlie. I feel it too. I told you once before, Charlie, that I am as much flesh and blood as you. To feel your body next to mine is a wondrous thing to me. I am no longer simply light, Charlie. I am man now. Just as you are man. My heart is no longer bloodless and silent. It beats with the rhythm of yours. Together we are like one pounding machine. I never understood the concept of desire until I came here," he quietly added. "Seeing it in you, I seemed to have found it in myself."

Charlie let his hand slide up the boy's back until he buried his fingers into Joe's thick mane of hair. "When you asked me to be your teacher, Joe, pain was not one of the lessons I would have wished you to learn. I'm sorry. I'm sorry I'm not better at hiding my own longings. Without sensing them inside me, you might never have experienced them yourself."

Joe sighed, and turned away to once again stare through the glass at the night outside the window. "You did not teach them to me, Charlie. It's this place. This world you live in. There's something about it that breeds pain and sorrow and longing. There is much happiness here too, but sorrow always lies beneath it, waiting to reach up and slap the happiness away." A wry smile played at the boy's lips. "It's like frying chicken, Charlie. There must be a trick to living here that I don't yet know."

Charlie let the soft warmth of the boy's hair caress his hand. "Maybe the trick is to appreciate the happiness when it comes," he said, "and when the sorrow overrides it, to simply wait until the happiness returns. It always does, you know. When you feel the pain inside me, Joe, you should never think that pain is all I feel. My happiness at being with you is worth every pain in the world to me. In a way, even the pain is a happiness. It means you are here beside me. The important thing is that we share. Pain. Happiness. Whatever. As long as you are here with me, I don't care what the emotions are. The fact that they are *ours*, not mine alone, is the important thing. The pain I feel because of my desire for you is nothing to the pain I felt being alone. My life did not begin until the night you knocked at my door, Joe. If you brought pain along with you, I'm more than willing to endure it if it means I can stay at your side. You promised me that I would always be with you, Joe. Do you remember that?"

"Yes. I remember."

"You love it here. I know you do. You love the calmness of the lake. The smell of the trees. You love it as much as I do. We can be happy here. We can grow old together on the shore of this lake. When your work here is finished, you can stay with me forever. I'll hide my desire from you, Joe. I swear I will. I don't want you to feel my pain another second."

"Charlie...."

"And if there are things you have to do, places you have to go, then I will come with you. Together we can—"

Joe stretched out his hand in the darkness and laid his fingers gently over Charlie's lips, silencing him.

"Just as I have no past, Charlie, I also have no future. Not here. If you grow old on this planet, it will not be with me."

Charlie gently pushed the boy's hand away from his mouth. "But you promised we would always be together."

"And we will. But not here."

"You mean by this lake?"

"I mean here in this world. My time is short. Where I go you cannot follow. Not for a while. One day we will see each other again, and when we do, we will never again be parted."

"But why do you have to leave? Where are you going?"

Joe closed his mind to Charlie's questions then. It was like the shutting of a door. The snapping of a lock. He was pushing Charlie away. Retreating to a place where Charlie was not welcome. Joe turned away from him and raised his head slightly to stare out at the nighttime sky.

"I will miss this place," Joe said.

Charlie grew almost feverish in his anguish at being pushed from Joe's mind. It was as if every moment they had shared, everything they had gone through, had been a waste of time. And worse, a lie.

"But *where* will you go?" Charlie insisted, fighting to control the tremor in his voice. Striving to quell the pounding of his injured heart.

"Back to my father," Joe said sadly. "He will call me home when my work here is finished." He turned to gaze lovingly at Charlie beside him. "You can't go with me, Charlie. I won't let you."

"But why?"

Joe gave the slightest shake to his head, as if even he could not say the words that needed to be said. Instead he closed his eyes and burrowed his face into the pillow.

"Go to sleep, Charlie. In the morning you must paint me. There isn't much time."

"Time for what?" Charlie asked, but Joe did not answer. At the moment he closed his eyes, Joe seemed to will himself to sleep.

Charlie gently extracted his hand from Joe's tangled hair and rolled over onto his back to stare blindly at the darkness above his head.

He thought of that roaring, monstrous flume of water Joe had conjured from the depths of the sleeping lake outside his back door and wondered for the first time just how much power the boy might be capable of wielding with those incredible hands of his. Was he an extension of God? Were there any limits at all to what the boy might do in the name of goodness if the mood took him? If he was truly his father's son, and Charlie could think of no reason to believe he was not, then his power, his strength, could be boundless.

If he wanted to stay here, Joe could make it happen, no matter what his father had told him to do. But if he would not, if he insisted on leaving this place as he said he must, then Charlie was determined to go with him.

If death were to take the boy, then Charlie would accompany him in death. He did not fear it. The absence of Joe was the only fear Charlie carried inside himself.

But there was anger inside him too. Anger at the father.

Anger at God.

Charlie would not give Joe up without a fight. Joe was his life now. They were connected in a way that could not be undone. Not by God. Not by anyone. Charlie would follow Joe wherever their paths led them. Nothing must be allowed to separate them now.

Nothing.

And if his anger at God, the God he had only that day discovered, should lead Charlie into hell, then even that would be preferable to a life without Joe. Maybe nothing but the endless fires of that awful place would be strong enough to burn away the pain of losing Joe, to have him no longer there to look upon or to reach out and touch when Charlie felt the need of him.

Maybe, when all was said and done, hell would be a blessing, erasing one anguish and replacing it with another.

Without Joe, Charlie could spread his arms and welcome the searing comfort of flames to extinguish the memory of him completely.

Maybe only then, with new agony to feed upon, would Charlie find peace in being alone.

DEEP IN the night, as a predawn coolness swept through the cabin but the first notes of songbirds had yet to be heard in the eaves, Joe reached out in the darkness and laid his hand across the fevered brow of the man tossing and turning beside him. He could sense the anguish in Charlie as surely as he might have sensed his own. Even in sleep, Charlie's mind was torn by desire.

With a gentle pressure of his fingertips, Joe eased Charlie from his tortured dreams and, in doing so, sent Charlie spiraling down into ever-deeper sleep, down into a sleep so heavy that nothing could penetrate it, down to a place where there were no longings, no needs, no sense of self at all.

In the soft gray light of that approaching dawn, Joe watched the lines of tension evaporate from Charlie's face, leaving him with nothing more than a peaceful calmness to mark his handsome features. The slightest of smiles twisted the corners of Charlie's mouth now, and Joe traced the lines of it with his fingertip. He felt Charlie's sleep-warm breath brush the skin of his hand. The heated scent of Charlie's sleeping body filled Joe's nostrils. Joe drew the finger that had traced the line of that vague smile along the warm skin of Charlie's neck, then down to his chest, where Joe laid his hand flat to the smooth flesh and the beating heart buried beneath.

The living heat of the man's body beneath his hand sent a shiver of desire pulsing through Joe's own, as it had on the night of his arrival when, standing by the fire, he had pressed his palm to Charlie's cheek, thanking him for the robe the man had handed him to cover his nakedness.

On that night, only seconds into the new life he found himself in, Joe had felt himself drawn to this man. There was a goodness in Charlie that Joe had sensed from the very beginning. Charlie's talent as an artist filled his body like the scent of rosebuds permeating a garden. Joe had recognized Charlie's desire for him too. Even on that first night, in their first few minutes together. It was almost as if Charlie, like Joe, had for the very first time felt the electric feel of another's flesh against his skin. And in feeling it, wanted more.

On that first night, as Charlie slept at his side, carried off to sleep purposely by Joe because Joe could not understand the feelings rushing through him and needed time to think about them, Joe had opened the robe he wore and run his hands along the length of his own body, feeling the sensation of touch, of self, for the first time. To be flesh and blood instead of light was a wondrous thing. To have Charlie's sleep-scented shoulder against the side of his face, Charlie's arms surrounding him in the darkness, was an awakening miracle to Joe.

His love for Charlie was born on that first night.

Joe did not stop to think if that love would please his father. He did not stop to think if the feelings rushing through him could be accounted a sin. He did not stop to think at all. His newly formed body did the thinking for him.

Only now, as he lay in Charlie's bed with dawn creeping into the sky outside the window by his head, did Joe let his hands truly explore the man beside him. Deep in a heavy sleep that Charlie would not awaken from until Joe himself released him from it, Joe gave rein to all his curiosities concerning this human man who he had loved from the first time he laid eyes upon him.

Sitting up, Joe brushed the sheet from Charlie's body and gazed upon his nakedness. He slid the hand resting upon Charlie's chest down across the smooth stomach, past the hips, caressing the length of Charlie's leg, feeling the brush of hair against his palm, longing to taste the skin beneath his touch. Joe's desire for the man beside him was a stone between his legs, but he ignored his own desire and closed his eyes to better absorb the velvet feel of Charlie's flesh beneath his hand.

He laid that hand now across the softness of Charlie's sleeping genitals, felt the heat and texture and *life* of what lay beneath his touch, closed his eyes yet again as he tried to bury his own desire somewhere in that sense of touch, and then he pulled his hand away.

Bending low, Joe tasted Charlie's lips with his own. Felt the stubble of Charlie's morning shadow across his chin. Inhaled the scent, for the first time, of a warm breath other than his own. When Charlie stirred beneath the gentle pressure of his lips, Joe laid his hand once more across Charlie's brow and sent him deeper into sleep.

Licking the taste of Charlie from his own lips, Joe raised himself up and sadly pulled the sheet back over Charlie's body, hiding it from the night and from himself.

He rose from the bed, ignoring the hardness of his desire, and stood at the window, gazing out across the lake. Slowly, he lowered himself to his knees and, closing his eyes, pressed his forehead against the cool glass.

"Tell me what to do, Father," he whispered in his mind. "I do not want this man to suffer. I love him too much. I cannot leave him yet. His work is not finished. But if he follows me, he will die. You know this."

Joe's only answer was the sounds of the night surrounding him. Crickets in the field. The stirring of a breeze across the cabin's roof. The lap of water at the edge of the lake. The birds were yet silent, but still the night echoed with life. Joe could hear and feel the pounding of his own heart beating a rhythm of pain inside his head. Could hear, too, the gentle sounds of slumber from the bed where Charlie slept. Charlie's breath echoed through the darkness like a calming wind. It eased Joe's pain to know Charlie was there, peacefully lost in a dreamless sleep where his troubles could not reach him.

Charlie could not understand the events that would soon unfold. He had not taken the time to learn lessons from the past. But Joe knew. He knew what awaited him. He would not let Charlie suffer with him.

This man, this artist, could have a long life ahead of him. Joe would not let his actions now shorten that life for even a moment. They would have an eternity of time together. But the life Charlie had now, the time he was allotted to live in this wondrous world as a mortal man, must not be taken from him until the last possible second of his natural life.

Either in happiness or pain, life was still life. A precious thing. A gift from the father. As wondrous as love. As perfect as a flower.

On his knees, Joe knelt there in the darkness, the cool glass still pressed against his forehead, cooling his body, softening his desire, and waited for comforting words from his father. Waited for his father to tell him what he must do. But those words did not come. Joe's mind was as empty as a carafe of spilled wine. Nothing but his own pain echoed through it. If his father heard his prayer, he had chosen not to answer.

And in that moment, Joe too felt a surge of anger blossoming inside himself at his father's silence. He remembered the words of his first brother, tearing from his dry, dying throat, as he hung suspended above the hill of stone where he was led to die. He felt the agony of his first brother's hands and feet, pierced by spikes. Felt the sharp press of splintered wood tearing at the lash marks across his first brother's bleeding back. Felt the ache in his first brother's shoulders as the weight of his body tore at his ligaments, pulling muscle from bone even as that damnable crown of thorns tore into his forehead, sending rivulets of hot blood raining down to burn his eyes, blinding him to the sight of his blessed mother kneeling in the rocks below his bleeding feet. Joe felt even now the heartbreaking sense of desolation and abandonment brought on by the failure of his father to respond to his first brother's anguished plea in the tortured moments before his death.

Joe did not speak his first brother's final words, but they echoed in his mind like the howl of a wild dog, wailing its loneliness to the world from some far off windswept hill.

"Why have you forsaken me, Father?"

When his own anguished, silent plea was left unanswered, as his brother's had been left unanswered two thousand years earlier, Joe pulled himself wearily to his feet and laid his naked body across the sheet that covered the man next to him. As if, even in the deepest sleep, love carried memories of its own, Joe felt Charlie's arm reach out and pull him close. Joe buried his face into the sleep-warm crook of Charlie's neck and closed his eyes as the man's hot scent wafted through him like a sun-laden breeze, filling him with so many emotions that he could not sort them out. Could not even try.

Joe let his mind go blank of all emotion, all memory. He let it empty itself of everything but the feel of Charlie's arms and the scent of Charlie's body. Even his returning desire no longer tortured him. It was simply there. A throbbing comfort.

When, still in sleep, Charlie turned to press his lips to the boy's forehead, Joe opened his eyes to gaze at the face before him.

At that moment, with his thoughts alone, Joe released Charlie from the well of sleep in which he had placed him, and as Charlie's eyes slowly opened to meet Joe's, so close beside him, filling Joe's vision completely as if nothing else in the world existed, Joe laid his lips once again to Charlie's mouth, truly tasting the waking man for the first time.

At the touch of Joe's lips on his, Charlie's eyes opened wide. His pulse thudded like war drums, so loud Joe could hear the sound of it on the air. Joe offered Charlie a taste of his own hunger. Then another. It was the same hunger Joe sensed in Charlie. Unquenchable. Blinding. Sexual.

"What are you doing, Joe?"

Breathless, Joe spoke with his lips still pressed to Charlie's. "What I've always wanted to do. Teach me, Charlie. Teach me to please you. Teach me to please myself."

As if weakened by desire, Charlie did not ask again, but gave himself up to Joe completely.

As Joe tore the sheet aside with a trembling hand and their naked bodies at last melded together into one, Joe voiced the other words that were tearing through his mind.

"Forgive me, Father," he said, his voice a whispered sorrow even as his flesh rejoiced.

Soon, all thoughts of his father were lost in the wonders that followed.

Chapter Eight
...A Hint of Smoke....

THE THREE panels of the triptych depicting the Chicago skyline hung now from the east wall in the reception area of Switzer, Pevin, and Jenaslovitch, Attorneys at Law, just where Sally Switzer had intended them to hang from the very beginning. Some who looked upon them saw screaming faces behind burning windows. Others saw only the painted reflection of a red sunset on panes of glass. Sally herself thought she had seen a glimpse of her own blonde hair through one of those fiery windows as she passed one of the panels on the second morning after its arrival, but when she turned back to inspect the painting more closely, she had disappeared. It was all imagination, of course. There were no people in the painting. Only glass and steel and stone and sky. And paint. Sally knew this. She was no fool. And she was no romantic either. What she thought she had seen was just a wisp of imagination. Perhaps truly fine art was *meant* to trick the eye like that. And with a price tag of twelve five, this was fine art, she told herself. Hell, what else could it be?

"It's beautiful, isn't it?" a voice said behind her.

Sally turned to Miss Jacobs, Albert's receptionist for the past twenty years, a woman so primly rigid that Sally expected to see a broomstick poking out of her ass every time she looked at her. Twice Sally had caught the woman perusing a Bible on her lunch hour, when she should have been out with the rest of the boys, downing martinis at the corner bar. Or maybe the peons didn't socialize with the men who signed their paychecks. Actually, Sally doubted if Emily Jacobs socialized at all. Ever. With anyone. If she had ever been laid, even once, Sally would have been surprised right out of her Wonderbra—if she had been wearing one at the moment, which she was not.

As always, Sally found herself being a little put out by the mere presence of the woman who sometimes gazed at her like she was the town slut instead of the wife of the firm's owner. And to tell the truth, sometimes Sally felt like the town slut when Miss Jacobs looked at her like that, like she was doing now, as if she knew exactly what sometimes took place inside the boss's office. Sally felt the urge to pull out her makeup mirror and check her lipstick again, or find a full-length mirror somewhere and check for semen stains on her bodice for the umpteenth time.

But Miss Jacobs wasn't looking at her now. She was eyeing the painting on the wall.

"Mr. Strickland had a showing of his work in a gallery on Lakeshore Drive a few months ago," Miss Jacobs was saying. "I was most impressed. He has a wonderful eye."

Somehow Sally couldn't quite grasp the concept of Miss Jacobs donning her cloth coat, pulling on her orthopedic shoes, and poking a few more bobby pins into her prissy little bun of drab graying hair before grabbing an El across town to attend an art show.

"I know," Sally lied. "That's when I got the idea of having him do this work for us." Actually, Sally had chosen Strickland because she had heard his name mentioned at a cocktail party. "I'm glad you approve," she added, with a hint of superciliousness.

Miss Jacobs didn't rise to the bait. Sally figured she knew which side her bread was buttered on.

"I only wish he would have been there," Miss Jacobs said. "At the showing, I mean. I would love to have met him. But I understand he's somewhat of a recluse. Doesn't like parading himself around in public." Here Miss Jacobs *did* give Sally a little sidelong glance, and Sally was more than aware of the disapproval in it. Sally wondered, not for the first time, if this old broad had the hots for Albert. Or maybe she simply didn't like younger and prettier women. In the old bat's shoes, Sally supposed she wouldn't have liked herself either. Women were intensely jealous creatures, every single one of them, right down to the bone. As long as she was the one being envied, Sally didn't mind that fact at all.

"Strange thing about your painting, though," Miss Jacobs said in a conversational tone, one woman to another. "Certain people seem to see things in it that aren't there. Almost like an optical illusion. Do *you* see people in it, in the windows, Mrs. Switzer?"

"No," Sally said, not liking the way Miss Jacobs had said "certain" people, like maybe they were morons or something. She didn't like the way the woman said "*Mrs.* Switzer" either, but there wasn't much she could do about that. And she certainly wasn't going to admit she was almost certain she *had* caught a glimpse of her own image in the painting only minutes before. "I see only a lovely skyline. Chicago is such a pretty city. Especially at dawn."

Miss Jacobs gave her that funny glance again, as if she knew for a fact Sally hadn't seen a sunrise for more than a decade. Hard to appreciate a sunrise when you slept past noon every day.

Sally turned away from that disapproving glance, ignoring it like a queen might ignore a servant's unwanted gesture of familiarity, and pointed to the streak of white across the top of the painting. "What do you suppose this is, Miss Jacobs? A comet?"

If Sally meant to catch the woman off guard, it didn't work. Miss Jacobs answered her question without so much as a beat of hesitation. "It's God's hand, Mrs. Switzer, sweeping across the sky. What else could it be?"

Sally stepped back and eyed the painting again. *Good lord, the old bat's right. That is what it is. Or might be.*

At the sound of the door opening behind them, Sally saw Miss Jacobs go even more rigid than she already was. A look of such intense dislike crossed the woman's face for a second, before it was quickly buried behind a cool veneer of businesslike greeting, that Sally turned to see what manner of beast had entered the room.

The man striding into the office like he owned the place was a knockout. Sally took in the thousand-dollar suit, the slim physique, the stunningly chiseled black face, and found herself resisting the urge to pat her hair like a schoolgirl waiting for a prom date. The man stood well over six feet and radiated sex appeal like waves of heat rolling off a desert highway. She knew this man. She couldn't remember his name at the moment, but she had seen his photograph in the paper a dozen times since Albert gained him an acquittal for the vicious murder of his wife, a white woman as stunningly beautiful as the man himself. He played football, or basketball maybe, Sally couldn't remember which. What she *could* remember was that the evidence was overwhelming in the prosecutor's case against him, and still Albert, and a jury practically handpicked by Albert himself, a fact Albert still chuckled over occasionally, had found the man innocent of all charges against him. Celebrities were easy to defend, Albert had told her once. And here was living proof standing before her now. That the woman's real murderer had never been found—and the fact that no one was looking for him—did not cross Sally's mind even once. Nor, apparently, had it crossed the jurors'.

The man cast an appreciative eye at Sally, nodded, and said to Miss Jacobs in a rich baritone voice that made Sally's toes curl, "Is Albert in?"

"He's expecting you," Miss Jacobs said, tersely but efficiently. "Go right in."

Before stepping around the desk and heading for Albert's office, the man cast one more appreciative glance in Sally's direction, taking in her voluptuous figure like a man inhaling the scent of a lime, and Sally knew in that instant the man had indeed murdered his wife. She could see it in his eyes. Rather than shocking Sally, the realization made her toes curl again, and she wondered if she was actually getting wet down there or was it simply hot in here, and she wondered, too, what it would be like to bed a black man. This one in particular. She gazed at his strong hands, neatly manicured and as perfectly chiseled as his face, and wondered how it would feel to have those hands caressing her body, delving into her most intimate places.

She opened her mouth to speak, to say good morning, *something*, but the man's eyes had drifted away from her already, focusing on the panels behind her. A look of such surprise crossed his face that Sally too turned to gaze at the paintings.

There, in a window high above the watercolored street, she saw herself again. Her face was twisted in fear, a silent scream erupting from her mouth. Standing behind her at the window, his hands at her throat, was the man standing before her now. In the shock of what she saw, Sally dropped her purse, which practically exploded when it hit the floor, scattering stuff around her feet.

The man's eyes did not waver from the painting. He did not offer to help Sally pick up her belongings. He merely glanced at her one more time, glanced back at the painting, then spun on his heel and walked away. After he disappeared into Albert's office, Sally turned to the triptych again, but she and the man behind her in the window were gone.

"You look like you've seen a ghost," Miss Jacobs said, moving around her desk and stooping to help Sally gather up the contents of her purse. "It's the painting, isn't it?"

"No," Sally said, bending to help the woman. "It was… that man. I think he *did* kill his wife." No sense trying to tell the woman what she thought she had seen in the painting. She couldn't even explain it to herself.

Miss Jacobs continued to scoop things into Sally's purse after giving her an incredulous look.

"Of course he killed her," she said. "Everyone knows that."

"But… but Albert got him off."

Miss Jacobs heaved herself slowly to her feet and helped Sally up as well. "That's what we do here, Mrs. Switzer. We free the sinners."

Sally thought of those big black hands surrounding her throat in the window in the painting. She thought of the scream she had seen on her own lips. And she thought of the leering smile she had seen on the face of the man behind her as he… what? Choked the life from her body?

Sally remembered the Bible she had seen Miss Jacobs reading on those days when she should have been out to lunch with the other girls, or the guys, or *someone*. The Bible that undoubtedly rested inside her desk at this very minute. A Bible just like Sally's mother's.

"Then why do you stay?" Sally asked. "Why do you continue to work here?"

Miss Jacobs smiled at her like she might have smiled at a child who had asked an inane question. "Because we also free the innocent. It doesn't happen often, but it happens. That's reason enough to stay, don't you think?"

"I suppose it is," Sally said, her eyes once again drifting back to the paintings, afraid of what she would see there but unable to stop her eyes from going back to them all the same.

"There's a church on the corner of Adams and Fifth, just a few blocks from here," Miss Jacobs said kindly.

Sally tore her eyes from the painting and back to the older woman's face. "Thank you," she said.

It wasn't until later, as she clutched her purse to her chest and strolled among the crowds on the sidewalk outside, her mind an eddy of confused thoughts, that she realized she had never asked Miss Jacobs for directions to the nearest church.

How had the woman known?

THE CHURCH Miss Jacobs directed Sally to was Greek Orthodox, beautiful and ornate. Sally had never been inside a Greek Orthodox church in her life, had not been inside *any* church for as long as she could remember. After climbing the long bank of steps, she stood outside the door for a moment, torn between walking on and walking in. She looked around at the mobs of people going this way and that on the crowded sidewalk below her, wondering where they were all headed, but not really caring.

They were always there, those throngs of people. Like the buildings were always there. And the traffic. She had never seen humanity behind those nameless faces before, had never looked for it even once, and she did not see it now. They were simply a part of the landscape of Chicago. And they apparently did not see humanity in her face either, for no one looked in her direction, and Sally was glad of that. She felt completely out of place, standing like a fool on the steps of this big gaudy church. Sometimes it was a good thing to be anonymous, unknown, and she was glad to be shielded by that anonymity now. It comforted her somehow.

She glanced at the sky above her head and almost dropped her purse again. There, streaming across the sky, just as in the painting in Albert's office, was a stream of white slicing across the heavens. The hand of God, Miss Jacobs had said. Sally glanced again at the nameless, faceless strangers on the sidewalk, all intent on getting from one place to another, not looking around, not doing anything but simply walking. Jostling. Checking watches. Patting wallets to be sure they were still there. Cattle moving toward the slaughterhouse, marching toward death, but mindlessly, oblivious to the fact. No one stared at the sky. No one even bothered looking up. Their eyes were centered on their own feet. Going nowhere. Everywhere.

The masses of moving people ignored Sally as they ignored everyone else around them. Except for one man. He stood at the corner in rags; one of the thousands of homeless that survived in the city, by the look of him. He was a young man, thin to the point of emaciation, with long, greasy hair protruding wildly from beneath a filthy ball cap. The cuffs of his too-long trousers were frayed from being trod upon. Like most of the homeless, he carried no belongings. He simply stood there empty-handed, staring up the steps of the church, at Sally, as she stood there looking down at him.

When their eyes met, he gave her a gentle smile and the faintest nod of his head. Then his eyes rolled over her and took in the sky above their heads, at the crisp summer skyline and higher, toward the stream of white vapor tearing across the sky from one horizon to the other.

He sees it, Sally said to herself. *I'm not crazy. That man sees it too.*

When she looked back at him, the homeless young man reached into his pants and pulled his penis free. The gentle smile he had given her a moment before had transformed itself into a wicked leer. He stroked himself and watched her like a tabby cat might watch a mouse. Sally felt a trickle of cold sweat slide down her rib cage.

People on the sidewalk strode past the young man, ignoring him completely, almost as if they didn't see him at all. His penis was erect now in his hand as he continued to stroke it, continued to stare into Sally's eyes as she stood on the steps of the church wondering why no one stopped him, why no one called for a policeman, why no one so much as glanced in the young man's direction. As always, there wasn't a cop in sight when you needed one.

The homeless man took a step toward her, and in that split second of time, Sally lost all fear of the church in the fear she felt for the man. She ran through the open doorway, out of the sunlight, away from the street, away from that comet trail of white tearing across the sky. But most importantly, she ran from the man with his unwashed, throbbing penis in his hand and the look in his leering eyes that told her he knew what kind of woman she really was.

Standing in the shadows of the vestibule, Sally felt herself trembling with fear. She thought of Albert spraying his sperm across her dress and felt such a rush of shame that she pushed the thought away as quickly as she could.

Stepping through the ornately carved archway leading into the chapel, she saw two old women sitting in prayer in one of the pews. Side by side, they bowed their heads, their gray hair covered in tattered lace. Sally realized that in this church, perhaps, women were required to cover their hair, so she pulled a scarf from her purse and laid it across her head.

On quivering legs, she moved to the last pew and all but fell into it, thankful to have gotten this far without collapsing to the floor.

But for herself and the two old women, the chapel was empty. Silent and cool. Sunlight filtered through stained-glass windows on either side, casting colored shadows over everything. Watercolor shadows. Like in the mural in Albert's office. Now, like before, when she had seen herself and the black man in the painting, she felt herself to be inside a canvas. She could picture herself trapped behind layers of watercolor, looking out at Miss Jacobs sitting at her desk. Sally was trying to get out, trying to claw her way free of the walls of paint confining her. She could feel the weight of that heavy streak of white acrylic hanging over her head like an executioner's ax. Sally imagined herself screaming at Miss Jacobs to grab the letter opener on her desk and slice through the canvas so she could escape, but her voice was silenced by the layers of color in front of her. No one could hear her screaming. Her pleadings echoed inside her own head, but they could not carry past the narrow prison in which she found herself. In her imagination, Sally felt a presence behind her and spun to see the black man, with the homeless man beside him, both converging on her now. Both exposing themselves to her, both stroking themselves and leering at her breasts, at her body, at her fear. She felt a tear slide down her cheek, and she squeezed her eyes shut to block out the vision. From a distance, sitting in the pew like the two old women, head bowed, eyes closed, Sally looked as if she were praying, but there was no prayer in her mind. Only fear. She knew she *should* be praying, but she wasn't exactly sure what she should be praying for. Wasn't even sure why she had come here, really. Wasn't sure if God would listen to her if she did pray.

A hand came out of nowhere and laid itself across her shoulder, causing Sally to jump and cry out. The two old women turned in the silent church to look at her as Sally turned to look at the old priest who was standing beside her now in his long black robe, looming over her like a shadow.

"You don't belong here," the priest said.

"But I've come to pray," Sally stammered.

"No," the priest said. There was no kindness in his voice. Only contempt. "Please leave."

Sally looked over at the two women, who were now leering like the man in her vision. They were laughing at her. Their teeth were black and jagged. Their eyes blood red. And when she looked again at the priest's face, she saw that he was laughing at her too as he took her arm and roughly pulled her to her feet. Only then did she see the lines of blood seeping from the corners of his eyes. Bloody tears coursed down the stubble on his cheek and dripped onto his cassock. Sally gaped at those spattering tears, but the priest ignored them. He seemed to find amusement in the horror on her face.

When he spoke again, his voice was an unholy gurgle of sound, as if the blood flowing from his eyes had filled his throat and lungs as well. "God is coming for you, Sally. You cannot be here when he does. It puts the rest of us at risk, you see." He was still laughing as he spoke, and the pressure he applied to her arm made her wince as he propelled her toward the door.

"But there's a man out there…." she tried to say.

"Go," the priest said again, pushing her forward.

At the vestibule, he gave her a shove, and she flew through the doorway, landing on her knees on the tiled floor. She felt her nylons tear, felt the skin of her knees give way in a blast of pain that made her gasp. Looking back at the priest from the floor through swimming tears of both pain and fear, she watched him gaze down at her through those awful bleeding eyes. Before he disappeared, before the door closed in front of him with a bang, she heard him say, "The fires of hell are waiting for you, Sally. You can't escape them here. You can't escape them anywhere. You are destined to burn. The man outside will show you the way."

With that, he slammed the chapel door. She heard it latch and thought she heard the turning of a key.

God had locked her out.

Groaning, Sally pulled herself to her feet. A rivulet of blood was oozing down her shin, and pulling a tissue from her purse, she dabbed it away with shaking hands. She let the bloody tissue fall to her feet and tried to arrange her dress. She was sobbing now, both from anger and from the pain of her torn knees. Fucking priest. Why she ever thought she could find comfort in this place was beyond her now. Why had she come here? What was she so afraid of? She tried to analyze her fear. Was it because of what she thought she had seen inside the painting? Is that what had spooked her?

Then she remembered the comet trail of white that was not only in the painting, but was also in the summer sky outside this church, or had been a few minutes ago. Had it been her imagination? Or did it really exist?

Pulling herself together as best she could, she stepped through the outer doors and back into the summer sunshine outside. She had almost forgotten about the homeless man exposing himself on the street corner. Her concentration was centered on the sky above her head. The clear, unblemished summer sky. As blue as a robin's egg now. Untouched by cloud or anything else.

The comet trail was gone.

But the man on the street corner was still there. He was no longer exposing himself to her, but he was moving toward her now in a shuffling lope, as if he had been waiting for her to reemerge. He was climbing the steps of the old church, heading straight for her, his arms reaching out to her as if greeting an old friend, but there was nothing friendly in his eyes. They were filled with hatred. And madness.

No longer caring how she looked, no longer feeling the pain in her torn knees, Sally flew down the opposite side of the long flight of steps, away from the man, away from the church, back to the only sanctuary she could think of at the moment. Albert's building.

If those inhuman faces on the street saw the fear in the eyes of this woman running among them, they showed no signs of it. They did not look at her at all. It was as if she didn't exist.

Two blocks away, she could run no more. Gasping, she leaned against a building and waited for the young man to reach her, to take her neck in his dirty hands, and do with her whatever it was he intended to do. She was too weak to fight him. Whatever happened would happen, and there was nothing she could do about it.

When nothing did happen, when people began to look at her again, standing there with her bloody legs and disheveled hair, she conquered her fear long enough to look behind her.

"The man outside will show you the way," the priest had said, threatening, the memory of his bleeding eyes yet again chilling her heart.

But the homeless man was gone.

CHAPTER NINE
...TWO MURDERERS....

SALLY WEPT in a cubicle of the ladies bathroom down the hall from the reception area where the newly acquired Strickland now hung. It was the first time she had ever been inside this bathroom. On any other day of her life, she would have used Albert's private bath connected to his office behind the desk where Miss Jacobs sat five days a week, ten hours a day. Sally was, after all, the wife of the firm's owner. All perks honoring him honored her as well. She saw to that. But the main reason, perhaps, that she did not use her husband's private bathroom was because he was at this very moment sequestered in his office with the black man. The murderer. Sally remembered all too well the look on that handsomely chiseled face as he stood behind her in the window of the painting, his strong dark hands digging at her throat. And she remembered, too, the horror on her own face as she stared out of the canvas at her own reflection. She could not face that man right now. Perhaps she would never be able to face him.

She wasn't exactly sure why she was crying. Fear, certainly. Fear of Albert's client. Fear of the homeless young stranger on the street who had taunted her with his engorged penis. And anger, too, at the way the priest had treated her. She figured now that the blood she had seen pouring from the old priest's eyes was strictly a figment of her imagination, brought on by stress and confusion. She could still see the way it dripped onto his robes. Could still *hear* it dripping onto his robes. She remembered, too, the blood-red eyes of the old women sitting in the pew in front of her. Like Russian peasant women, sitting in some turn of the century synagogue buried to hell and gone in some seedy village perched atop the frozen soil of the Siberian steppes, a million miles from anywhere anybody would ever want to be. What the hell they were doing in the middle of Chicago on this Tuesday afternoon was anybody's guess. Maybe they were on their lunch hour from central casting. Maybe they were doing a remake of *Fiddler on the Roof* in one of the theaters in the downtown area. This thought was so ridiculous, Sally actually laughed at herself until she peeled her torn panty hose off, and the pain of the nylon pulling at the scabs on her knees killed her chuckle deader than a

Christmas goose. It also started the blood flowing again. She peeled off a yard of toilet paper and dabbed at her knees, her shins, wincing as the rough paper dug at her wounds.

She considered locating some office flunky and sending him out to buy her a new pair of panty hose, then decided against it. Her legs were good. And even dark hose wouldn't cover her cut knees, so why bother? She supposed she would be wearing slacks for the next few days. Nothing less appealing than a woman with scabby knees, no matter how shapely her legs were.

She peeled off another yard of toilet paper and blew her nose. Her tears were winding down now, but her anger hadn't decreased to any measurable extent. She was still mad as hell. Perhaps she would wait for Albert to finish his meeting and then convince him to take her home. He was the boss. He could leave any time he wished so long as he didn't have a case to prep or a client to kowtow to or another murderer to set loose upon the world.

Guilty or innocent, Albert once told her, every defendant had a right to a spirited defense. What Albert didn't mention was the fact that the spirited defense was multiplied exponentially by the ability of the defendant to *pay* for it. Albert did run a business, after all. It would make no sense at all for the firm to drain its resources on behalf of a client who didn't have two nickels to rub together, whether that client was guilty or innocent. That it might be the right thing to do was beside the point. Business, after all, was business.

With hands that still trembled, Sally pulled a cigarette from her purse and lit it as she continued to dab at her wounded knees, staunching the seeping blood.

The cigarette calmed her. After a while, the tremble faded from her hands. She stared at the blood-soaked tissue paper and thought of a day long ago. A day that she tried never to think of. The day of her mother's death. She wasn't sure why she was remembering that day now. She had spent the better part of her life trying to forget about it. But there it was, inside her mind, before her eyes, as she sat high above the earth in this bathroom cubicle, twenty-six floors up, on this strange, strange day, as if all the ensuing years had meant nothing at all. Not once in all those years had that day haunted Sally's nighttime dreams. It always came to her like this. On bold feet in broad daylight.

As ever, worms of guilt accompanied the memory. And as it always did, the guilt angered her, eating at her just as persistently as the cancer that had once eaten at her mother's withered, reeking body.

She remembered her mother's foul breath. The breath of sickness. And she remembered the stench of the bedclothes. No matter how often Sally laundered them, the smell of the dying woman lying atop them never went away, as if the corruption in the woman's body had seeped into the very fibers of the fabric.

It was Sally's first summer out of high school. She was eighteen. And beautiful. She had looked forward to this summer for as long as she could remember. It was time for her life to begin. Time for her to leave Kansas behind and find her place in the world. Her youth and beauty were the only tickets she would need, but before those tickets could be punched, before she could step aboard a plane and soar away to whatever future awaited her, her mother had fallen ill.

The cancer moved quickly through her mother's body, but not quickly enough for Sally. She did not see her mother's suffering as she lay there in her reeking bed day after day, rotting away like an injured animal at the side of a road. Sally saw only her own suffering. It did not once occur to her that her mother might have plans of her own for what she would do with her life after her daughter left. Sally saw only the interruption of her own plans.

On the day that Sally remembered now—as she dabbed at her bloody knees inside this bathroom cubicle far above the bustling streets of downtown Chicago, a thousand miles away from where her memory was centered—she saw again her mother reaching out to her, trying to speak, maybe trying to tell her daughter how sorry she was for putting this burden on the young girl's shoulders. And on that day, Sally was more than wearied by the whole thing. She found herself unable to hide her resentment from the dying woman reaching out to her.

Sally pulled her hand away from the cold tentacles of her mother's grasp, and she saw the hurt in her mother's eyes as she did so, but her heart was not touched by it. All Sally wanted was her freedom. All she wanted was to never again smell the stench of sickness, never again carry fouled bedclothes to the washer on the back porch, never again wipe the feces from her mother's reeking legs, never again look at that horrible place in her mother's body where, eighteen years earlier, she had squeezed herself out into the world. Even her mother's shame angered her.

And on that day, Sally decided to end her own suffering. That what she was about to do would end her mother's suffering as well did not truly enter her mind until years later, when she would claim her mother's suffering as motive for her actions.

It was a simple thing, really, to end a human life. She had seen it done in countless movies. Read about it in countless books. The thought of it had been in her mind for weeks before the day she finally set about doing it.

The straight razor had lain in the medicine cabinet for years. It was the only possession of Sally's father's that remained in the house after he left years earlier to find his own beginning with a woman he once worked with, a woman as different from her mother as night from day. He too, like Sally, had tired of the constant Bible reading, the constant prayers for guidance, the constant sweetness of the woman lying as good as dead on the bed in the other room. Sally did not blame her father for leaving. She understood his actions completely.

Her father had had to find his own way in the world, as Sally had to do now.

With steady hands, Sally had taken the straight razor from the medicine cabinet, opened it with careful fingers to gaze upon the gleaming blade, and carried it into her mother's bedroom.

When her mother saw what she was carrying, she did not protest, but simply closed her eyes. Sally could see her mother's lips moving in silent prayer as Sally drew the edge of the razor across the woman's bony wrist. Saw her mother almost cry out in pain as Sally opened the veins on the other wrist as well. And as the hot blood gushed out across those damnable reeking sheets, Sally placed the straight razor in her mother's hand, the hand the woman had tried to reach out to her daughter with moments before.

Sally turned her back to the woman then and walked from the room, latching the bedroom door securely behind her. She went to the living room, switched on the TV, and lost herself in the faces on the screen until she was sure her mother's life had ended.

Only then did she phone for an ambulance.

As the paramedics carried her mother's body away, Sally received their words of condolence with cool acceptance, feeling no guilt and no grief. Only immeasurable relief.

During the closing of her mother's estate, if one could call it that, Sally came away with little more than a thousand dollars, and that was mostly from the sale of her mother's furniture. Not once did anyone suggest that her mother's death was perpetrated by any hand other than her mother's own. And not once in the ensuing years did Sally think of the actions she took that day as cold-blooded murder. Her mother was suffering, and she had ended it. That her own suffering had also ended was merely a fortunate by-product of the actions she took that day. Sort of a bonus. Time was a great healer of wounds (all but her mother's), and Sally had convinced herself that what she did on that long-ago day was a mercy killing. Nothing more. Nothing less. The act of a loving, caring daughter who could not bear to see her dear mother suffer another day, another week, another month. She had ended the suffering in the only way she knew how. And set herself free in the process.

A few years later, she met Albert, here in this very city where her wanderings had taken her. Using her beauty as a net, she had captured him, and the rest was history, folks. She did not tell Albert of the hundreds of men she had bedded. She did not tell him how she had taken a straight razor and ended her mother's life. And she did not tell him that it was the money, not the man, which drew her to him, this successful defense lawyer with all the morals of a goat, and a body and a libido to match. This man who seemed as old as Methuselah to her, but who she quickly learned was as randy as a twenty-year-old. The first time she took his erection into her mouth and coaxed the sperm from his pale body, she knew he was hers. A thousand times since, she had swallowed her disgust (as well as his sperm), given her body to him in other ways too, in every way, all for the privilege of living the life she had always dreamed of.

Her mother's death had made it all happen, and not once did she regret her actions on that day when her mother's blood seeped onto the bedclothes of her reeking bed after Sally opened the veins on those pitiful, withered wrists. She would do it again in a heartbeat, she knew. Perhaps one day, one day *soon*, she would even do the same for Albert. With his money, her freedom would be complete. And she did so hunger for younger flesh to bed.

Like the black man.

They did, after all, have a few things in common, she and the killer sitting in Albert's office at this very minute. And if he frightened her, what did that really matter? Fear was exciting in a way.

With her panty hose removed, she was naked beneath the billowy-skirted sundress she wore, another creation that had set Albert back a goodly number of dollars. She laid her fingers across the damp heat of her vulva and closed her eyes, thinking of the black man's hands encircling her throat, feeling the heat of his body against her back, his cock burrowing into that moist, hot well of pleasure she had opened up to him. She imagined him filling her like no man had done before.

As her body bucked beneath the touch of her hand, as the nub of her clitoris cried out at the brush of her fingernail, she felt his hands tighten around her throat. Just as they did in the painting.

And as she felt the white-hot rush of orgasm pouring over her fingertips, she imagined the young homeless man, stinking and naked in front of her, pushing his foul cock between her lips as the black man pounded her from behind.

She almost laughed.

God, if only Albert could see her now.

ALBERT, AT that moment, was staring at the check in his hand. The check was written very neatly, in very precise handwriting, and signed by the grinning sports hero slash cold-blooded murderer sitting across the desk from him. There were a lot of zeroes in the check, and it did not occur even once to Albert that the damn thing would bounce like a kangaroo on its first journey through the bowels of Chase Manhattan Bank, if it ever made it that far, which it wouldn't. His deposit was about to be interrupted by future events, but of course Albert didn't know that either.

Willis Jefferson, star receiver for the Indianapolis Colts—currently on permanent hiatus after his arrest two years earlier for the murder of his wife and only recently exonerated on national TV, thanks to the efforts of the man sitting in front of him—had learned that his contract with the Colts had not been renewed due to a public outcry by angry citizens because of the outcome of his trial. It seemed most of America was convinced of his guilt even if the jury was not. In the end, Willis's fickle fucking fans had turned against him.

This bothered Willis, but not to any great extent. He had enough money to live comfortably for the rest of his life, so long as he didn't pay this goddamn lawyer the outrageous fee he had charged for the privilege of making Willis the most hated man in the country.

Willis Jefferson owned a good deal of property in both Chicago and Indianapolis, or had until quite recently. He had not squandered his money like so many other players in the NFL, many of whom were as strong as oxen and as fleet as deer when it came to pounding opponents into the AstroTurf or sprinting across a football field, but didn't have the God-given brains to write their names on a piece of paper without misspelling it two times out of three. Willis had agreed to liquidate much of his property and hand over most of the proceeds in return for Albert's promise of acquittal on all charges. It seemed like a good idea at the time, standing as he was in an eight-by-twelve holding cell, facing either a lifetime behind bars or death by lethal injection. Hell, he would have promised Albert Switzer *anything*, and had.

The fact that he was actually guilty of carving the bitch up like a Thanksgiving turkey did not seem to really factor into the equation. He had pushed his guilt from his mind two minutes after the act was carried out. She had it coming. There was no doubt about that. He had given her everything, and she'd repaid him by sleeping around like a common whore, instead of the wife of one of the most respected names in American sports.

He wasn't respected anymore, of course, and he would simply have to learn to live with that, but he'd be damned if he was going to live with it at the poverty level.

Upon the ignominious return of his rubber check from the bank, Willis had no doubt that the old fart in front of him would drag his ass to civil court in an attempt to recoup his losses, but Willis wasn't worried about that either. At this very moment, in his condo on Lakeshore Drive, already sold but not yet vacated, was an envelope containing a first-class ticket on American Airlines. ETD: 8:05 this evening. Destination: Bern, Switzerland. And on the shore of Lake Geneva there was a nice little chalet Willis had recently purchased, sight unseen except for photographs, where he would live out his days in luxury. And in a numbered Swiss bank account in Zurich were the proceeds from the sale of his real estate holdings, which he had been quietly liquidating since the day of his arrest, per Albert's instructions. But Albert Switzer wasn't as smart as he thought he was. He had not followed the money trail after the sale of Willis's property. If he had, he would have known the money was already safely sheltered from his greedy little hands.

No, Willis was no fool. He conceded it might have been a lapse of judgment that had led him to repeatedly poke a paring knife into the luscious young body of his whoring wife, but hell, everyone had lapses of judgment from time to time. The trick was not to let it bring you down.

Willis would miss the accolades afforded a sports star, but he would have missed his freedom more. And his money. He chuckled inwardly to think that Albert Switzer would soon be missing his money too. Albert would just have to learn to be satisfied with the six-digit retainer Willis had paid the man at the beginning of the trial. If he could have thought of a way to get *that* back, Willis would not have hesitated doing so, but that money was gone and, he had to admit, well spent.

So Willis sat here now, watching the dollar signs flash and sparkle in old Switzer's piggish eyes, and thought about the Swiss misses he would soon be banging daily in his little chalet on Lake Geneva, while this goddamn *lawyer* fussed and fumed and ranted and raved a half a world away at the dawning realization that he had been outwitted by a *nigger*. Just as Albert himself had outwitted the judicial system. Tit for tat, Willis figured.

And while Willis Jefferson thought his private thoughts on one side of the desk, Albert Switzer was contemplating a few private thoughts of his own on the other.

Saving Willis Jefferson's black ass had been the case of a lifetime. He was taking some heat from the press for his role in manipulating the courts, but hell, that's what the practice of law was all about. That and the garnering of large amounts of money, such as the sum he now held in his hand.

Albert had foreseen the backlash that would come his way from the acquittal of this client. He had also foreseen that he could throw the press's and the public's outrage back in their faces with a couple of pro bono cases he was working at the moment. One a murder case, and the other a priest brought up on child molestation charges. Both with the potential of being fairly high profile, and both with defendants that, if not *certainly*, at least *possibly*, were actually innocent of the charges brought against them.

Guilt was not a major concern for Albert—unless, of course, the evidence was so blatantly stacked against his client that no jury in the world would ever believe their innocence. He had wrested both clients from the hands of the public defender's office in the eventuality that damage control would be needed for the sake of his firm, and damage control was *exactly* what was needed at the moment. Sometimes Albert's foresight astounded even him.

To be honest, Albert had a few misgivings about the innocence of the priest. If he had to, he would throw the man to the wolves. He hated pedophiles as much as the next man, especially when they were incapable of paying for a decent defense. Well, he would have to see how that trial unfolded. Albert wouldn't take another public relations hit over it, that much was certain. Two hits in a row could damage the firm irreparably.

Not that he truly had to worry about that either. With the amount of money written on the check in his hand, he could retire tomorrow, even if he weren't already as rich as God. Perhaps he would show this check to Sally before he lost it to the hands of the banking establishment. Large amounts of money always got her juices flowing, in more ways than one.

Even as he sat here with this murdering bastard in front of him, he remembered the feel of Sally's lips on his meat. God, the woman was incredible. Tonight, perhaps, he would stick his tongue up her ass and wear her like a hat. She liked it when he did that. Albert liked it too. Liked it a lot.

Willis Jefferson's deeply timbred voice tore Albert away from these pleasant thoughts.

"I've hired a private investigator to find Natalie's real killer. The police are obviously not up to the task."

Albert almost laughed. Who the hell did this guy think he was fooling? Every third grader in the world knew he had chopped his wife up like ham salad.

"That's good, Willis. The public should know we are sparing no expense in hunting the bastard down. You've been through enough. It's time the real killer is brought to justice."

Albert figured if a murdering bastard like Jefferson could lie this convincingly, then he could do the same.

"I'd like the names of the jurors, Albert. I'd like to compensate them for their sacrifices in putting their lives on hold for my sake during the course of that interminable trial."

This was another lie. Jesus, this guy must think Albert was an idiot. "Can't do it, Willis. Not allowed. You'll have to be satisfied with the fact that they know they did the right thing and leave it at that. It's the American way."

Two of the jurors had already been paid off handsomely in the guise of book deals they were smart enough to make with a New York publishing house. The others got their fifteen minutes of fame. They would have to be content with that. It was more than they deserved, probably. There certainly wasn't a Mensa member among the lot of them. If there had been, the trial would have come to a decidedly different conclusion.

"Well, if you say so," Willis droned. He glanced at the check now lying on the desk between them. "We're square then?"

"More than square, sir. Now you can get on with your life. Sorry about the Colts. I heard they canned your… let you go."

Willis grinned. "Yeah, well, fuck 'em."

"Fuck 'em, indeed," Albert said, standing and reaching his hand across the desk.

Willis stood, too, understanding that the interview was over. "Thank you for everything," he said in his most obsequious manner as he shook Albert's hand.

"You bet."

That formality completed, Willis buttoned his suit coat primly across his broad chest and glanced one final time at the worthless check lying on the desk.

"Don't take any wooden nickels," he said.

Albert smiled, wishing the bastard would leave already.

"And you be good," he couldn't help saying.

Both men laughed.

Chapter Ten
...A Gathering Darkness....

The scent of Joe's body pulled Charlie awake from a dreamless sleep, but when he opened his eyes, the boy was gone. The sun had risen long ago, and he lay alone in his big brass bed, uncovered, his body caressed by a morning breeze rolling off the lake. But the air was not filled with the smells of summer. It was filled with the smell of Joe's skin. Joe's breath. The scent of Joe's hair. On his lips, Charlie could taste Joe's passion that, in his dream, had filled his mouth like sweet nectar. In his mind, he recalled Joe tasting him too, as Charlie writhed beneath him, impaled inside those warm, persistent lips. Remembered Joe's hands foraging across his body, seeking out the most intimate places, finding wonder in them, tasting them as he went along, letting love lead his hands, his lips, his every movement. Never before had Charlie felt such delicate passion in another's touch. Shy, but unhesitant. Tender, yet eager. Starved, but ever gentle.

Charlie pressed his hands to his face, inhaling the aroma of their lovemaking as if it truly existed, as if it had not been just a dream. Still, he felt Joe's hands upon his skin. Saw himself opening up to the boy as the boy opened himself up to Charlie, holding nothing back at last, offering themselves to each other with no restraints, no rules, no fear.

Charlie closed his eyes and tried to will himself back inside the dream. If he let it go, it would evaporate like the dew, burned away by the awakening of another day. He would lose it forever.

But soon, even as Charlie tried to hold on to it, he felt the dream pull away from him, going back to that place in his mind where it had been born, burrowing itself into the depths of Charlie's brain. Into the shadows. Into the past. A past that never really was.

Unable to grasp it, unable to keep it with him, Charlie watched it go. In moments, the memory of his dream had wrapped itself in an envelope of darkness deep inside him, in a place where Charlie could not reach.

When Charlie opened his eyes again, it was simply gone. The scent of Joe's body and the feel of Joe's lips had lost themselves in the morning light. All memory of their lovemaking vanished from Charlie's mind like morning mist burned away by a rising sun.

Sitting up, Charlie swung his legs off the edge of the bed and rubbed the sleep from his eyes. Gazing through the glass wall at the head of the bed, he looked out upon the lake.

The sun was high in the sky. It was not yet noon, but noon was approaching. He had slept the morning away, and with the memory of what he thought to be a dream no longer with him, he wondered why.

Pulling on jeans and a T-shirt, he set off in search of Joe, thinking how odd it was that in all the days he had known the boy, not once had he awoken to find Joe with him.

The cabin was empty. Joe had not eaten, for there was no smell of cooking on the air. Mac, too, was gone, trailing along at the heels of the boy, no doubt. They were inseparable now. Had been since the night of Joe's arrival.

Charlie stepped out the back door, breathing in the scent of the flowers blooming by the fence and the pines surrounding the cabin. The sky above his head was cloudless. A perfect blue. He wondered idly if he could bring that blue to canvas, or was it beyond his powers to duplicate? Perhaps only nature could draw that color from a palette. Perhaps only nature should be allowed to try.

He whistled for Mac and heard a whimper of sound coming from somewhere behind the studio, down by the lake where the shore was hidden from his eyes.

Barefoot, he set off across the cool grass, and at the softness of it beneath his feet, he looked down. What had once been dead and brown was now as green as a field of young wheat. Charlie blinked, staring at it. There had been no rain for weeks. He had thought the lawn as dead as the flower bed, but now they were both alive and flourishing. Only Joe could have accomplished that. Only Joe would have thought it necessary to do so.

Charlie smiled at that thought and once again set off to where he had heard the sound of Mac whimpering by the water.

When he rounded the corner of the studio and looked out to the edge of the lake, he saw Joe lying facedown in the mud at the water's edge. Naked. Splattered with muck. The dog sat beside him, and as Charlie watched, a howl of misery and anguish erupted from Mac's throat as he wailed his pain at the sky above his head.

Charlie ran to Joe and threw himself down beside him. Pulling the boy's face from the mud, Charlie gently turned him over, cradling him in his arms.

Joe's eyes were open, but he turned away from Charlie's face and stared out at the water. Tears streamed from his eyes, and his body convulsed with sobs.

"What is it?" Charlie asked, his fear a living beast clawing at his breast. "What's wrong?"

Joe turned his spattered face to him then, and as Charlie wiped the mud from the boy's cheek, Joe said, "Last night was just a dream."

"I know," Charlie answered, his own tears climbing to the surface now, seeing Joe's. Feeling Joe's pain. Not understanding it, but not caring that he didn't. The fact that the boy was suffering was enough to tear Charlie apart. That Joe's words made no sense was beside the point.

"Let's get you inside," Charlie said. "Let's clean you up."

He awkwardly scooped Joe into his arms and carried him to the cabin.

As they entered the kitchen door, Joe looked into his eyes and said, "I don't want to go back to my father, Charlie. I want to stay here with you."

"Hush," Charlie said, even as his heart sang to hear Joe say the words. Laying Joe gently on the sofa in the living room, he dragged the afghan from the back of it and covered the boy's nakedness.

Only then did Joe close his eyes and sleep, his hand clasped tightly in Charlie's as if afraid to let him go.

Charlie sat on the floor beside him until the sun began to drop toward the trees along the lake.

Not once in all that time did the boy release his grip on Charlie's hand.

As evening shadows gathered around them with the approach of another night, Charlie heard the boy weeping softly in his sleep, uttering words that Charlie could not hear. Charlie leaned closer and pressed his ear to Joe's lips.

Joe's words were barely audible. Charlie had to hold his breath to hear them.

"Forgive me, father," the boy was saying as, even in sleep, a tear crept from beneath his closed eyelid to dampen his lash. "I was weak."

And in that moment, Charlie's dream returned to him. Or was it a dream? Once again, Charlie tasted Joe's passion. He heard Joe cry out as the semen poured from his body for the very first time. He felt Joe's hands on his own flesh. Clutching. Kneading. Remembered his own orgasm screaming out of him. Charlie remembered all of it. And Charlie suddenly knew, as he knelt there now at the edge of the sofa in the gathering gloom of evening with Joe's hand squeezing his and Joe's fevered breath on his cheek, that it had not been a dream at all. The boy had come to him in the night, and Charlie had eagerly accepted everything Joe offered him, just as Joe accepted everything Charlie had eagerly offered him. Without hesitation. All in a blur of exquisite hunger.

The thought of it tortured Joe now, and Charlie knew that what they had done should be torturing him too. So like Joe, Charlie closed his eyes and, laying his head upon Joe's chest, prayed to his newfound God for his own forgiveness.

But Charlie knew, even as he spoke them silently in his mind, that every word of his plea for forgiveness was a lie. If Joe should open his eyes at that very second and offer his body to Charlie again, Charlie would accept it.

And he would do so eagerly, without a moment of hesitation. His hunger for Joe, even now with the words of his false prayer still banging around inside his head, was no less consuming than it had been the night before.

Charlie let the words of his false prayer stutter away to silence. He replaced it in his mind with the scent of Joe's skin against his face, the beat of Joe's heart pounding in his ear, the feel of Joe's fingers still tightly gripping his. It was as if Joe was afraid to let go, afraid he would sail off into the sky like the mist he once was, losing himself to Charlie forever.

The father had given Joe life.

Somehow, Charlie must see that the boy was allowed to live it.

With him.

He would not let the father take Joe now. The sins of the world meant nothing to Charlie. Only this boy meant anything to him at all.

Joe was his perfect flower. Selfishly, Charlie would keep Joe with him. He had to. And even if their bodies never came together in a passionate embrace again, Charlie would still have the memory of the one time they did. And he would cherish it. Always.

God be damned.

As CHARLIE fitfully dozed, his head still resting on Joe's chest, his legs folded uncomfortably, cramped and aching beneath him, Joe opened his eyes and saw him there.

He brushed his fingers through Charlie's hair and knew, in that instant, that Charlie remembered everything.

Again, Joe closed his eyes to the memory of what he and this man had done. No, what Joe alone had done. He closed his mind, too, to the knowledge that in another moment of weakness, it could happen again. The act of bringing their bodies together had opened up a whole new world to Joe, but he knew it was not a world the father would ever allow him to experience again. He had not been sent to this place to find love. That had happened on its own. He knew that when he and Charlie opened themselves up to each other as mortal men, something of himself had been found, but more had been lost.

There were things he was sent here to do, and with that one shared taste of each other's bodies, Joe knew Charlie would never again look at him in the same way he had before. The memory of it must be erased from Charlie's thoughts, or it would threaten everything.

So, with an ache in his heart, Joe once again laid his hand over Charlie's brow, and with nothing more than a wisp of thought, erased the memory of last night's lovemaking from Charlie's mind. But not before pressing his lips to Charlie's sleeping eyes, one after the other, and inhaling the scent of the man one last time.

Erasing that perfect memory from his own mind would be more difficult. And erasing his love for Charlie would be impossible. Joe would not even try. That much he would keep for himself, safely buried in the shadows, deep in the bottommost wells of his heart, away from the light, away from Charlie, away from himself. But most importantly, away from his father.

In places of the world far away from this beautiful Indiana lake, Joe gradually felt the cleansing begin. Not his own, but the world's. Screaming began to echo in the recesses of his mind, growing slowly louder. It was the wailing cry of unheard prayers, not unlike his own prayers, which Joe had muttered before as he lay weeping in the mud at the edge of the lake. They were being screamed to the heavens, those desperate prayers, in a hundred different tongues, in a million unknown voices, and they were falling on the same deaf ears as Joe's plea for forgiveness had fallen earlier. As his father had turned his back on Joe, he had now turned his back on the world. The screams grew more terrified, more frantic, and Joe felt human flesh begin to sear. He heard the sizzle of melting fat, the snap of heat-twisted bones, the shriek of tortured, flame-filled lungs. He smelled the reek of burning skin, smoldering hair, boiling blood. Feeling those flames, those burnings, on his own flesh, Joe gasped at the pain of it.

AT JOE'S sharp intake of breath, Charlie stirred and opened his eyes.

"It has finally begun," Joe said as a tear rinsed a clean trail through the dried mud smeared across his cheek. "Close your eyes, Charlie. Close your eyes until it's over. Don't look at me." Joe began to weep. Confused, Charlie did as he was asked, turning his eyes from the boy's face, burying it once again into the velvet softness of Joe's heaving chest.

When the sobs grew deeper, more tortured, Charlie took Joe into his arms and held him close, waiting for the pain to end.

But for the weeping, Joe lay like a dead man in Charlie's arms, neither resisting nor accepting Charlie's comfort.

He simply wept.

Soon, Charlie wept with him.

And darkness fell.

CHAPTER ELEVEN
...A GREAT BURNING....

In Aurora, Illinois, not a hundred miles from where Charlie held Joe's trembling body, weak and weeping in his arms, a man in a late-model blue Chevy opened the passenger door and released a young girl, a child no older than the car itself, and left her standing at the side of the road. The child's clothes were ripped, and she was bleeding from where the man had inserted his fingers into her torn vagina. Her face was oddly devoid of expression, and her eyes had the vacant, lifeless look of those in an ineptly painted portrait. This was because the child's pain did not reach her mind. It was waylaid before it ever got there, lost somewhere in the dark place where fear had taken her hours before.

A sharp stone from the man's spinning rear wheel lifted from the gravel road as he took off. It sailed through the air as if perfectly thrown, like a bullet well aimed, to tear the skin of the young girl's cheek below one of those dead, lifeless eyes. That hurt, too, was lost before it ever reached the pain center of her clouded brain. She did not so much as blink when the stone sliced into her smooth, cherubic skin, then clattered to her feet, its momentum spent.

The child did not see the car disappear around a corner of the rutted gravel path, and she did not hear the sound of the automobile exploding as it struck a particularly deep rut in the road, smashing the gas tank against the chassis, creating a spark when metal struck metal that ignited the leaking fuel and engulfed the Chevy in flames.

Little Bridgett, for that was her name, although she would not remember it for many months to come, did not hear the shriek of terror from the man whose fingers had torn into her, ever deeper, ever more insistently, as he masturbated, leering at her misery minutes earlier. She did not feel the flames reach through the car windows now with hot grabbing hands and sear the skin from the man's face as neatly as a housewife peels the skin from a peach.

She did not hear the Chevy strike the concrete railroad abutment as it lazily wended its fiery path away from the road, unsteered by the screaming man inside. And she did not see the large sliver of metal from the dashboard nail the man to his seat as the car came to a metal-screeching halt, securing him in place as surely as a moth by an entomologist's pin.

Lung pierced, but otherwise unharmed by the crash, and still lucid but for the pain of the flames upon his skin, the man flailed like a puppet at the end of its strings, held in place by that cruel spike of metal, while the fire, unhindered now by movement or wind, surged through the vehicle like a starving beast, seeking naught but flesh to feed upon.

And like a beast, the flames fed slowly.

The man felt every wisp of the fire that dug at him with hot claws. Felt it enter his screaming mouth, blistering and blackening his tongue. Felt it forage upward across his face to explode his already blinded eyes. Felt it enter into the very depths of him, just as his cruel fingers had sounded the depths of the small girl he had taken from the schoolyard earlier—digging, tearing, searing.

And when his heart burst from terror and pain and heat, stilling his body as it turned to ash in the gutted car, the man's pain continued on like an endless road.

It did not waver. It did not abate. It did not stop.

Ever.

FOLLOWING THE path of the setting sun on this day that none would forget until time buried it in the waste of ten thousand others, a woman in Arkansas looked down upon the bodies of her three children, all dead now, all as motionless as dolls. They were still drenched in the water of their final bath. The echoes of their screams had at long last faded into the walls of the house they called home. Those screams had torn from their young throats as their mother's cold, unrelenting hands held their small heads, one after the other, beneath the soapy bathwater she had drawn for them moments before. She had placed in it the bubble bath the children loved so much, thinking that might somehow ease the pain they would soon endure, and when it did not, the mother wept. Still, her hands did not release the children from the fate she had decreed for them.

When their thrashing bodies lay still beneath her hands, she had lifted them from the water, one after the other, and laid them on her bed.

"Are they dead?" the man said from the other room.

"Yes," the mother said softly, covering the children's open, accusing eyes with a quilt. Their tiny hands seemed so still as they lay at their sides. She had never seen those busy little hands so still.

The drugs in the mother's body took the edge from the pain she felt at seeing her children's little hands so calm, so unmoving. She felt, as always, when in the throes of the drug, nothing but hunger for the body of the man in the other room. Six, small, unmoving hands were not enough to shake her from the drug's grasp, nor would a hundred small unmoving hands have done so.

"Set the fire," the man who was not the children's father said. "We have to go."

His drug was wearing off. His body, larger than the woman's, absorbed it more quickly than hers. While the woman hungered for him, he hungered only for the drug.

He looked down at the blood-spattered face of the man who *was* the children's father, making sure the gun was gripped securely by the dead hand it lay in.

Four hundred thousand dollars, he thought to himself. Insurance money. One hundred thousand for each of the children cooling in the other room. Another hundred thousand for the corpse at his feet. Enough money to ease the drug hunger for a long time to come.

That hunger was breeding panic in his mind now, gnawing at his brain like the chittering teeth of a hundred thousand rats, all chomping away inside his head.

"Set the fucking fire!" he screamed at the walls. "Set the fucking fire *now*!"

The woman tucked the last of her children's faces beneath the quilt and turned to a gasoline can standing in the corner. The can was large. Five gallons. She had barely been able to lift it when she dragged it into the house earlier. Now she did not even bother trying. She simply unscrewed the cap and tipped it over, watching the amber liquid spill out onto the carpet as the fumes of it seeped into her head and made her dizzy until she buried her nose in the sleeve of her blouse.

Pulling a kitchen match from her pocket, she thought of the man's cock inside her, thought of his strong arms around her face, his large body hovering over hers, repeatedly burying himself inside her as she worked her fingers into his anus, urging him deeper. As she struck the match against the sole of her shoe and tossed it at the soaking patch of carpet in the corner, she remembered his climax tearing out of him and into her, felt both their bodies convulse at the intensity of that one split second of time when his drug-riddled sperm poured out of his beautiful cock and sought refuge in her eager womb, where it would lie until she washed it away, part of him becoming part of her.

Like an exploding star, a nova, the gasoline ignited, driving her back toward the door, away from the heat, away from the flames.

She felt the man's strong hand grip her arm then, pulling her toward the front door. She glanced one last time at the man with the bullet hole in his forehead, lying beside the TV in the living room. He had been a good husband, but this man was better. And with drugs, this man was perfect.

As smoke began to fill the house, the man beside her fumbled with the doorknob, turning it this way and that, doing everything but opening the door. She nudged him aside, and as she did, she felt the doorknob beneath her fingertips freeze to immobility, as if someone had welded it in place.

"It's locked," she said, not yet feeling her own panic. "It's locked from the outside."

Flames had erupted suddenly through the bedroom door where the children lay, no longer cooling but cooking now, on the big double bed where the woman had placed them. She thought she smelled the stench of burning hair, but perhaps it was just the mattress.

She led the man through the kitchen to the back door. That doorknob, too, was immobile. It did not do so much as jiggle in her strong grasp.

"Break a window," she said, still calm, almost, ignoring the panic of the man beside her. "We have to get out of here before anyone sees the flames."

"I know that, you stupid bitch!" the man bellowed, and lifting one of the dinette chairs from the floor, he crashed it into the window that overlooked the garden in back. The chair bounced off the glass as if the window were made of rubber. In his surprise, the man dropped the chair and, stepping forward, crashed his fist into the glass.

Nothing happened. Not only did the glass not shatter, it repelled his stroke with one of its own, sending his arm back into his shoulder as if shot from a shotgun. The pain of it made him cry out, and he cursed the woman yet again.

Flames were creeping across the living room now, eating away at the carpet, the drapes, the paint on the walls. The stench of it tore at their throats. Their eyes streamed tears.

Panic finally reached the woman when a finger of flame crept around the kitchen door, licking at the cupboard, cutting off their retreat.

She could not see the man beside her now. The smoke was too dense. And at the first touch of heat on her skin from the nearing fire, she cried out for him, but he did not answer. Not until his fist came flying out of the smoke and crashed into the side of her face did she know where he was.

"Get us out of here!" he screamed.

The woman dropped to her knees at his feet, stunned by the blow of his massive fist. When she reached out to him to pull herself to her feet, his fist came crashing down upon her again.

"You bitch!" he screamed. "You stupid fucking bitch!"

And when the first tongue of flame reached his back and lingered playfully there for a moment before burrowing into his skin, he cried out yet again. This time to God.

Blinded by the blows and the smoke and her panic, the woman cowered at his feet, listening to the man's screams, and listening then to her own.

Soon, the flames lapped at them both like surf pounding rocks.

And like the surf, the pounding was endless.

Where the children went, the woman did not go. That was not her fate. Nor was it the man's.

As the flames licked hungrily at her skin and his, she saw again her children's struggling faces beneath the soapy water as they fought to breathe. She saw again the light of awareness dim in their terrified eyes and felt their bodies grow still as their lives left them.

But even their deaths, she knew, were preferable to the one she now endured. And as the flames sucked the last breath of air from her lungs and cracked the skin of her face like sun-hardened mud in the river delta where she was raised, she lost all thought of the man beside her.

Her mind was filled with nothing but her own pain and the innocent faces of her drowning children, clawing at her unyielding arms, crying out in muffled screams from beneath the soapy water.

The children's own pain would be quickly forgotten, lost in the comforting arms of the robed man who welcomed them with gentle hands to their new home for all eons to come. But the mother's pain would never end. Within the hungry flames that gnawed her flesh, those little faces would always be there. Staring back at her. Accusing. Unforgiving.

It would always be so. The faces of her children would torture her heart, even as her burning skin sloughed from blackened bone. Even as her screams echoed in her own ears.

The guilt of what she had done would never leave her. To the end of days, she would wail in grief and suffering. Alone and lost. A well of misery, writhing in flame. Tortured by memory and pain.

And even then, still wracked with a never-ending hunger for the drug that had killed them all.

THE SUFFERING traveled west, behind the sun, ahead of the rising moon, a rolling wave of flame, and in that flame, tears of the punished turned to vapor, dimming the ever-moving horizon.

Following that mist of tears came the screams. They raged across the countryside, through the cities, over the treetops, like an avalanche of fetid snow, every granule a tortured soul, every echo of anguished sound a weeping voice, begging forgiveness, pleading for the pain to stop.

But forgiveness did not come, nor did release from pain.

Those who begged for death did not know until it came that it gave but a glimpse of comfort before that cruel, never-ending pain truly settled in, burrowing beneath the skin, filling the mouth, expanding the lungs with fouled air, clawing at the body until it buried its gnawing head into the viscera, into the bone, into the very soul. And once it came, the pain did not leave. It was simply there. Forever.

Smoke filled the earthly skies from countless fires, each and every one a cleansing. In those fires, evil writhed and crisped and turned to ash. Tortured shapes of men and women were reduced to smoking cinders as their sins and their bodies burned away.

A momentum built. The fires increased in number. They moved now in every direction, not just west, blossoming out to every point of the compass, petals on a burning flower, consuming sin with tongues of flame that burst from the earth like spouts of fire. The flames consumed only the worst of mankind, picking and choosing as they swept along, sailing over the bowed heads of the devout, the good, the young, and crashing down upon the wicked before they knew it was there.

In New Orleans, a serial killer, a man with the blood of a dozen prostitutes on his hands, burst into spontaneous flame as he stood at a bus stop. In his pain and panic, blinded by fire, he ran screaming through crowds of people who did not feel the heat of his burning body as he passed among them. He ran until his body crumbled to ash on the sidewalk and was swept away in the breeze of passing cars.

In Atlanta, huddled in a doorway, a drug dealer lit a crack pipe for a client, and before the drug could reach their lungs, both were consumed by a rain of flames that showered down upon them.

And less than a block away, in a tenement hotel room with ragged curtains hanging in the yellow windows, a woman whose children had not been fed for three days because the food stamps had been traded for cigarettes and beer, looked out upon the burning doorway across the street, before she too erupted into flames as she stood at the window. The woman screamed and crumpled to the floor while her hungry children watched from the bedroom doorway. The heat of the flames devouring her body did not so much as singe the frayed and filthy curtains.

In Mexico City, a rental van containing almost half a ton of explosives, soon to be parked outside the American consulate and detonated in retribution for the thousands of Mexican field workers who were denied work across the border due to new immigration laws, exploded on a lonely street before ever reaching its destination, taking with it fourteen members of the terrorist cell who had planned the operation.

And in Washington, DC, the Republican senator who had instigated the legislation concerning immigrant field workers, and by doing so assured continued poverty and hunger for innocent thousands, stepped inside his limousine at the very moment the car was consumed by flame. The driver, a young Mexican national who, only the night before, had been threatened with deportation by the senator, a man old enough to be his grandfather, if the young man did not concede to the drunken senator's demand for sexual favors—which he finally did, in fear, weeping in shame as the old man pawed and slavered hungrily at his body—and who had closed the limousine door for the senator only seconds before the fire erupted, escaped unharmed.

In Montreal, a young transient who had stolen a motorized wheelchair from an old woman on the street after knocking her senseless to the ground, was consumed in flame as he pushed the chair along a desolate unlit street toward the fence who would pay him enough money for it to buy drugs for a week.

In London, a man and woman who kept their young son locked in a shed behind the house because they were ashamed of the boy's retardation and cleft palate, were drenched in burning liquid when the propane tank burst beside the house as they sat next to it in lawn chairs, sipping wine, enjoying the evening, and quietly plotting the child's murder. Their screams could be heard three blocks away.

In Sao Paolo, a young man, not yet sixteen but big for his age, a child of the ghetto who breathed in fear like oxygen and expelled hate like carbon dioxide, turned away from the weeping, naked body of the young woman he had just pulled from the street and raped in the shadows of a burned-out storefront. Before he could press a knife to the woman's throat, silencing her cries and insuring his own safety from retribution, he watched in amazement as the ground at his feet breathed forth a flame that climbed the length of his body and engulfed him completely in a pillar of fire before the knife could fall from his hand.

In Kobe, Japan, a middle-aged man, a teacher, sat at his desk in front of a class of uniformed schoolchildren. His eyes fell upon the young boy he had abused only that morning. A punishment, he had told the boy, for passing notes in class. He watched without pity as tears of shame still flowed down the boy's cheeks as he wept silently at his little desk. The teacher reached beneath his own desk and calmly stroked his erection, remembering the feel of the boy's smooth body beneath his hands, the small penis, so perfectly formed, so incredibly tasty, slipping between his lips. He felt the first glorious twinge of a coming climax shudder through his body, even as the children, all but the weeping child, sat with their little noses pressed to their little books. Alone among his classmates, the boy looked up in time to see the man erupt in flames like the ignited head of a match. The fire reduced his abuser to ashes before so much as a scream could be heard. Amid the looks of shock and horror on the other faces in his class, the boy smiled.

In Nimule, South Sudan, just below the burning wastes of the Sudanese desert, a man, a chief, stood before a village of Muslim peasants. There were only women and children in the village at this time of day, since the men were in the fields. The chief watched a line of machete-armed warriors emerge from the jungle behind him. The warriors were there to avenge the loss of the man's son, taken from him by the simple sin of falling in love with a woman of the Muslim faith, a young woman from this very village, who had lured his son, through her womanly wiles, to an eternity of damnation in the fires of hell. As the chief raised his arm as a signal to release his warriors and send them hacking and slicing a bloody swath through the village of heathens, a grassfire erupted at his feet. It was swept along by a sudden hot wind from the desert to the north. The flames quickly engulfed them all, warriors and chief alike. In seconds, before the village women even knew they were there, the chief and his warriors were incinerated to a fine black powder. As soon as the hot desert wind carried their drifting ashes away across the fields, the flames went out like the snuffing of a thousand candles. No livestock were harmed, no fields were burned, nor a single villager lost. Only the chief and his warriors had died. They awoke in a place, their bodies burned, their voices shrieking in pain, where the heat of the Sudanese desert would have seemed a cool oasis indeed. They would never leave that place of fire. They would never know coolness again. And the chief's son would never join his father there, for love is not a sin.

In Perth, a man sold guns from the back of a green van. He was always moving, always one street ahead of the law that sought him. The guns he sold had caused more pain than he could ever have imagined. In robberies. In cripplings. In murders. But the man did not think about such things. He was simply trying to make a living. That was all. What people did with his merchandise was their business, not his. And as he parked beneath the shade of a eucalyptus tree at the end of this most profitable day, he counted his money with dirty hands and looked only vaguely surprised when the ammunition that surrounded him, sweltering there in that windowless van, exploded in the Australian heat and tore his burning body to shreds before he could blink his greedy eyes. His death brought him no pain. It came too fast. The pain came later. And it came to stay.

A young man in the Castro District of San Francisco, gay since birth due to a pairing of proteins in one of his forty-six chromosomes, and infected with the AIDS virus for the past three years due to a glitch in his sense of caution, spread his naked legs and unfolded his naked arms. Smiling, he offered himself to the hands and lips of a dozen naked men arranged on their knees in a circle around him. The young man was lying atop a massive, massive bed in the pitch-black orgy room of the Vulcan Bathhouse, just up the street from his tiny studio apartment, which was not much bigger than the bed itself. Already, in his three years of infection, he had knowingly deposited his diseased sperm into more than a thousand orifices, many of which, more than half, in fact, had accepted the infection as eagerly as the orifices accepted the sperm. Those half a thousand young men, all in the prime of life, would eventually die, some sooner, some later, depending on the care they took with their bodies once the infection was diagnosed. Each of those deaths would be accompanied by suffering and shame. AIDS did not offer an easy demise. The young man splayed wide across the bed knew this, but he did not care. He had set a mission for himself, a mission born of anger and vengeance, to share his coming death with as many others as he could manage before his body, his beauty, disintegrated around him. But at this moment, his mission was forgotten in that blissful forest of unseen hands and probing tongues that foraged across his body in the darkness of this sweat-and-sperm-scented room, stroking, tasting, causing his body to tremble, causing his breath to catch, causing his voice to ring out in pleasure, even as he stroked and tasted and killed the men around him.

From the total darkness, a warm mouth in an unseen face pressed itself to his lips. Another warm mouth encircled his testicles. And yet another warm mouth fell around his engorged penis. It was at that moment that the young man felt another warmth building deep inside his chest, where no tangible warmth should ever reside. In moments, the warmth turned to heat, the heat turned to fire, and as the young man opened his eyes wide and screamed, causing the naked bodies around him to pull back as if scalded by that horrific sound, bright orange flames erupted from the young man's chest. In seconds, the young man's body was consumed in a flame that created no heat at all, except to him. It reduced his lovely infected flesh to red embers, then to coal, and then to ash.

A dozen naked men ran screaming from the room, erections lost in panic, and behind them nothing was left in the darkness of the Vulcan Bathhouse orgy room but the finest sifting of a dark, reeking sand, which lay sprinkled atop the crumpled, unburned sheet.

In Paris, a middle-aged woman in a rusted Citroën sedan gasped as the wheels of her old car passed over the screaming body of a child who had wandered into her path. She had not seen the child step into her path because the alcohol she had consumed had blurred her vision. She saw the small body only now, in her rearview mirror, as she pushed her foot to the accelerator and sped away into the crush of cars at the intersection ahead. She turned the corner, wheels screeching on asphalt, forcing another motorist up onto the sidewalk, and as she began to think perhaps no one had seen her, perhaps no one had copied her license number onto a slip of paper, the car's tires, all four of them, burst beneath her, sending the Citroën into a spin that took it straight into the wall of a brick warehouse, black with age and smog. As the old car struck the stone wall, it burst into a bright orange fireball that lit up the woman inside like a roman candle. Pedestrians, unable to reach her through the flames, watched as she screamed and flailed and died before their eyes. At the closing of her burnt eyes and the silencing of her wailing mouth, the flames went out with a *whuff*. Later perusal of records by the Paris police would show that the woman had six prior violations for driving under the influence, and her license had been revoked more than four years earlier. "It won't happen again," one policeman said, pushing his hand beneath his cap and scratching his scalp.

The child survived.

In Stonehaven Maximum Security Prison in the frozen foothills of an Alaskan mountainside, a flash fire swept through a cellblock housing more than one hundred eighty of the world's most violent offenders. The men were locked in their cages when the flames swept over them, flames fed by nothing in the concrete cellblock but the wrath of God. The inmates were later found huddled in the corners of their cells, their bodies burned clean of sin, their tattoos no longer offending, their minds no longer plotting new evil or contemplating old.

One inmate, the man in cell 245, an African American welder from Spokane, Washington, sentenced to life for the brutal slaying of a woman he once dated and supposedly became obsessed with, survived the fire without a blister. He was later proven innocent when the actual killer confessed to not only the young woman's murder, but six others, just before bursting into spontaneous flame in a precinct house in Salem, Oregon. The inmate was released two months after the fire and returned to Spokane to take up a new line of work. He could no longer stand the smell of the arc welder's smoke, he told his new wife. It reminded him too much of hell.

In Puerto Nuevo, Colombia, fifty bone-jarring miles north of the Tomo River and hundreds of miles farther from the populous western half of the country that bordered the Pacific Ocean, the leaders of three drug cartels met in the massive and ornate hacienda of Pedro de Castilla, a man who, like the other two, had reaped millions from his exportation of cocaine to a thousand cities around the world. The purpose of the meeting was to once again raise the price of their cocaine, bringing it up, finally, to almost that of heroin, the other drug of choice for millions of the world's mindless. This would serve to enrich their cartels, and if the addict on the street suffered from the cost increase, he would simply have to steal more stuff to pay for it, the drug lords laughingly told themselves.

More than forty men, mostly bodyguards and sentries, surrounded the hacienda as the wives and children of the three cartel leaders gossiped and ate on the terrace above the central courtyard.

One man had yet to arrive. Luis Santiamo was scheduled to fly into the small airstrip at any moment, bringing with him his four Alsatian hounds, and leaving his six children, his wife, and his string of mistresses back in Cali.

When the men heard the sound of helicopter rotors blatting in the skies to the southwest, they knew he would soon be landing. They quickly moved to the all-terrain vehicle waiting for them on the circling drive outside the hacienda to drive them, drinks in hand, to the airstrip to see Santiamo's new toy, the Huey helicopter he had purchased from the American government. Americans could always be relied on to grab a peso when the opportunity presented itself.

As they neared the airstrip, the Huey swooped down on them like a soaring condor, then playfully sailed away. The other cartel leaders stepped from the SUV at the edge of the freshly mown field, packed firm by peasant feet to accommodate landing aircraft. Looking up, they sipped their drinks and laughed at the antics of Luis's pilot.

Their laughter died in their throats and their drinks tumbled from their hands when the Huey made one more pass, and this time, they saw that the rotors had slowed. The Huey, directly above them, fell from the sky like a homing bomb, and when it struck the ground not more than twenty feet from where they stood, the flames shot out of it even while the burning, fuel-drenched rotors blatted one last time before sweeping across the ground, mowing the men from the earth like a peasant's scythe chopping coca plants. Santiamo and his hounds died on impact, the other cartel leaders were torn to bits by the flying rotors, and the helicopter fuel ignited the surrounding jungle, creating an inferno that swept up the hillside, consuming everything in its path.

As the flames subsided, hours later, only the hacienda stood, untouched, amid a hillside of burnt stubble. The forty sentries burned in the blaze. The wives and children, and even the mistresses, remained unscathed. The amount of cocaine available on the streets of cities around the world was cut in half for months to come.

And the leaders of the four cartels, along with their henchmen, all responsible for more human suffering than even the gun seller in Perth, than even a thousand gun sellers across the world, felt the flames gnaw at their flesh from that day forth.

AND THE burning continued.

Drug dealers. Meth cookers. Cocaine and heroin distributors. Poachers of endangered animals and tormentors of the nonendangered. Purveyors of prostitution. Child pornographers. Sweatshop proprietors. Thieves. Murderers. Rapists. Abusers of the young. Abusers of the old. And those who were not criminals in the eyes of the law, but in the eyes of God were deemed unworthy to escape the holocaust. CEOs of institutions who, either through the products they sold or the overpricing of necessities, created hardship and suffering for millions. Utility conglomerates. Energy suppliers. Pharmaceutical companies. Housing and rental monopolies. Tobacco and alcohol manufacturers.

And through every burning, always nearby, stood a young man off in the shadows, or looking down from a window or standing at a street corner. A young man with the purity of Joe. A young man with no past. A brother, directing the flames.

In a matter of hours, across the globe, from the smallest village to the largest city, the flames sought out evil, reducing it to ash, moving on, burning again, until the very sun and moon, depending upon which time zone one stood in, were hidden from the eye by the veil of smoke, the stench of burning flesh that hovered over everything like a miasma of righted wrongs.

A pedophile in Vatican City. Another in Tucson. Another in Belgrade.

A murderer in Kentucky. Two in Peru. A dozen more in New York City.

Scores of terrorist cells in Tokyo, Madrid, Lima, Helsinki, Bonn, London, Berlin.

Slumlords in the Bronx, Mexico City, Rome, Hong Kong.

Torturers of political prisoners in China, North Korea, Algeria, Iran, Iraq, Libya.

Cruel dictators in African, Asian, and South American states.

Serial killers in Australia, New Zealand, the Americas, and Europe.

The list did not stop. Screaming echoed everywhere.

And as the cleansing began to wane, as the light of a million fires, large and small, began to dim, in Chicago, two hundred miles north from where one young man alone wept at the world's suffering as he lay in the arms of the man he loved but could not have, Sally Switzer stepped from the cubicle in the public restroom on the twenty-sixth floor of the high-rise office building where her husband worked, and reentered the offices of Switzer, Pevin, and Janaslovitch for the very last time.

EMILY JACOBS was gone. An unreasoning fear had driven her from the office only moments earlier when she looked out the windows of the reception room, so high from the streets below, and saw the sunlit summer day turn to a brown haze before her eyes. It was as if the earth, the very earth, was burning beneath her. She had plucked her beloved Bible from the desk drawer where it always lay and, leaving her purse behind (she wouldn't think of it until hours later), fled the building just as a man on the street not twenty feet away from her burst into flame as he waited for the traffic light to change. The man, well-dressed, his hair neatly styled, but with a heart as black as midnight, invisible to all but God, had turned his horrified eyes to her as the flames swept up his torso. Emily turned and ran before she could hear the scream escape his blistering lips.

The street was a war zone. A car burned on the sidewalk, a charred and bleeding arm hanging from the shattered window. Up ahead, a building burned. At her feet, she saw the outline of a human body, pitifully sketched in ash.

Lost in panic now, Emily Jacobs squeezed these terrible images from her mind as she cowered at the base of the building beside her. She pressed the Bible to her eyes to block out the horrifying sights that seemed to bombard her from every angle.

Closing her eyes in prayer, she waited for the fire to find her too.

It never did.

SALLY STARED at the empty desk, wondering what had happened to the old bat who usually sat there, but she was relieved to find her gone. She was not in the mood to explain her appearance to Miss Jacobs, or to anyone else for that matter. Did not know how to *begin* to explain it, in fact.

Averting her eyes from the newly acquired artwork on the wall, afraid for the first time of what she might see there, Sally opened the door to her husband's office just as Albert and the black man were shaking hands across the desk. The office was brightly lit by overhead lights, but the blinds were drawn, blocking out the smoke-filled skies outside the windows, as the windows themselves blocked out the screaming from the street below.

Albert registered the briefest expression of surprise at the way she looked, a small inquiring gesture of a raised eyebrow as his eyes traveled over her bleeding legs and rumpled dress, and as he opened his mouth to speak, to ask what had happened to her, cries were heard through the door she had at that moment closed behind her.

Willis Jefferson tilted his head to the sound, and said, "What the fuck is that?"

Sally turned and reopened the door behind her, and as she did, she was met with a wall of flame that singed the hair from around her face before she could register what she was seeing. She cried out and raised her arms to block the heat from her already blistering cheeks, and as Willis Jefferson and Albert Switzer bellowed in shock behind her, Sally's white dress absorbed the flames and blossomed into an inferno around her.

Blinded by panic and pain, Sally fled from the doorway. She carried the fire with her, igniting the room, igniting the men behind her. Her blackened, hairless head was a mask of horror now, her voice a banshee's wail that dwindled into the distance as, with unseeing eyes, Sally crashed her ruined body through the plate-glass window and sailed out over the street of burning bodies below. Her flaming white dress billowed around her as she fell.

Like a comet.

PART 2
EMBERS

Chapter Twelve
...Tears and Rain....

By the time the burnings ended and the last flickers of a million scattered infernos had dwindled down to ash, an ash now drifting away on a cleansing wind that suddenly swept across the planet, Joe was sick with grief and hunger. He had not eaten all day. Nor had Charlie. Twice the boy stumbled outside the cabin to vomit bile onto the green new grass beneath his feet. Charlie followed him there each time, holding Joe's trembling head and stroking his brow as he retched his empty misery onto the ground. Charlie comforted Joe as best he could, not understanding the torments that led him to such anguish. As he stood there with Joe in the coolness of evening, Charlie stared uncomprehendingly at the copper skies above his head. He was amazed by the colors, confused by the distant screams he imagined he heard on the freshening breeze that slowly swept the burnished colors from the sky. In the air, Charlie could smell the burnings. Could smell the charred flesh. The stench of it, even after the skies had cleared, remained in his mind for days afterward.

Charlie did not know that the world had changed around him as he dozed with his head on Joe's chest, his senses blunted by Joe's sweet scent. He knew something momentous had happened. He could see it in the pain living behind Joe's eyes, could see it in the eerie streaks of umber burned across the sky, but he did not know what it was. That the earth could have been swept clean of evil in the space of a few short hours was beyond Charlie's comprehension, and the fact that Joe had felt the pain of each and every burning death did not enter Charlie's thoughts.

In Joe's mind, however, the pain was a caged, pacing beast that would not rest. He had wept so long and so hard at the suffering he sensed around him, even as Charlie nestled his sleeping face against the beating of his heart, that tears could no longer reach his eyes. The well from which they came had been emptied long ago.

Joe could feel his father reaching out to him now, but as his father had done to him only hours before, Joe turned his back and would not listen. He pushed all thoughts of his father as far away as he could, down into the farthest recesses of his tortured mind, into the deepest shadows he could delve, leaving them there, ignored, unacknowledged. He did not want to see his father's face in his mind's eye. He did not want to hear his father's words ringing in his ear, echoing inside his head. He let all memory of his father drift away and disappear into the darkness inside himself as the ashes of death were drifting and disappearing from the face of the earth in the wake of his father's cleansing wind.

Instead, Joe let his fingers trace the warmth of Charlie's brow. Let the wind of Charlie's breath cool his fevered chest. He tried to ignore the sickness he felt, the disgust, the sheer sorrow at the loss of life, at the agonies that had been unleashed. But the pain inside him was as unrelenting as his father's burnings. He could no more escape it than the wicked had escaped their destinies on this day of days when good survived and evil perished. That the final agonies of a million burning souls should come to rest in him was not something he had been prepared for. And even more surprising was the pity he felt each time he thought of the suffering those people endured, the suffering they still endured, the suffering they would never cease to endure until the final sunset had fallen on this earth at the end of all time.

That they deserved their fate was beyond dispute, but that truth only made Joe's suffering more incomprehensible to him.

The reek of human ash was such an abomination to his senses that he stumbled outside one last time before night completely fell around them on that first day. Reaching his arms to the copper sky, even as Charlie watched in wonder, Joe drew forth a bank of rolling cloud that swept across the lake, blocking the unholy colors from his eyes, and from those black thunderheads, he pulled down a torrent of cold rain to sweep the last vestiges of the stench from his nostrils.

Hand in hand, Charlie and Joe stood beneath the downpour of clean, fresh rain and felt the horror wash away. Drenched and shivering from the icy deluge, Joe turned then to Charlie and forced a weak smile to his lips.

"It's over," he said. "It's finally over. Forgive us, Charlie."

And as Joe spoke the name of the man who loved him, and who Joe loved in return, his eyes rolled up into his head and he collapsed to the ground at Charlie's feet.

JOE LAY in a fever for three days and nights as Charlie watched over him, nursing him, forcing soup into the boy whenever he could, washing his brow with a cool, damp cloth when the fever raged too high. He held Joe's hands firmly in his own when the boy struck out at invisible demons that came to pester his fevered dreams. It was not only the fever that seemed to rage inside the boy, but anger as well. He cried out his father's name many times, always in fury, always in words Charlie had never before heard the boy utter. Many times Charlie sat stunned, listening to the curses that poured from the boy's sweet lips, curses that, until that moment, Charlie would never have suspected the boy knew.

When the anger took him, Charlie closed his own eyes and prayed for the father to forgive the words erupting from Joe's mouth. It was the illness speaking those words, he tried to explain in his prayers, not the boy. But as he prayed, even as Charlie beseeched the father to forgive his son for the angry words he spoke in his delirium, Charlie knew somehow that his prayers were not being heard. And soon, before the first day of illness passed, Charlie stopped praying. He erased all thoughts of the father from his mind and concentrated his energies on making the boy well again.

Charlie carried the boy to the bed in the loft upstairs on the second day, caring for him there. He sat for hours at Joe's side, stroking his hands, whispering calming words in his ears, trying to bring a smile back to that perfect face. At those times when Joe's sleep seemed to be without tortured dreams, Charlie did other things. He prepared food he thought Joe might eat, although but for a bit of soup, Joe never did. He gently washed Joe's body, erasing the final vestiges of mud from the edge of the lake where Charlie had found Joe earlier, with Mac at his side howling his misery into the sky. He tried to sketch Joe sleeping in his bed, but at the first stroke of pencil on paper, Charlie set both pencil and paper aside and never tried again.

Mac never left Joe's side during his illness. The dog lay at the foot of the bed, his chin resting on the boy's leg, occasionally opening his liquid eyes to gaze up at Joe's face, as if reassuring himself that Joe was still there. When words of anger poured from Joe, Mac whimpered but did not move. Once, when a gentle word arose out of Joe's delirium, Mac gave his tail a little wag, as if sensing Joe had finally returned to him, and when the word trailed away and silence again ensued, Mac raised his head as if waiting for another.

On the third day, Charlie went to his computer, booted it up, and foraged through the news sites to see if the momentous events he suspected had taken place were mentioned there. What he found was beyond anything he could have imagined. Fires had erupted the world over, it seemed. And all in the space of a few hours. The fact that many people had died was clearly stated, but no mention was made of the type of people they were. Governments on every continent seemed to be blaming other governments for the outrage. Accusations flew back and forth like lightning, but in all the denunciation, no one seemed to think to blame God.

In the online chat rooms, the story was different. Average citizens seemed to understand what had taken place even if their governments did not. God had finally returned, many said. Charlie could imagine them bowing their heads in prayer, thankful for being spared as they typed their words onto keyboards to send them out into cyberspace to be read and commented on by millions of other grateful souls.

But the words printed across his computer screen meant nothing to Charlie. Time and again, he raised his head to listen, to gaze at Joe, to see if the boy was awake, to see if his fever had broken. All he wanted was Joe's return. He did not care that the world had changed around them.

Charlie began to understand Joe's torment. And in his understanding, his anger turned once again to the father. Why did he let Joe suffer like this? Why did he let Joe take the burden of the father's acts, the father's guilt, onto his own shoulders? It had not been Joe's doing that so many people had perished in flame. It had not been Joe who had pointed his finger and sent flames shooting across the world, blackening skin and turning bones to dust. It had not been Joe who had turned his back to the screams and let them pierce the air, unheard and unpitied.

Weary, Charlie switched off his computer and let the silence of the cabin, the whisper of the trees beside the lake, comfort him as they always had.

He moved again to Joe's side, took the cloth from a pan of cool water on the stand beside the bed, and, for the hundredth time, pressed it to Joe's forehead, hoping to ease the fever, hoping to calm the boy's tortured dreams. And as he did so, for the first time in three days, he watched Joe open his eyes. The boy's eyes, no longer wild with pain, gazed calmly into his own. Joe reached up to touch Charlie's cheek, and pushing the uncombed hair from Charlie's face, he smiled.

And with that one simple smile, Joe unleashed Charlie's tears. Charlie dropped his head to Joe's shoulder and wept into it like a child.

And like a father, Joe stroked Charlie's back and cooed soothing words into his ear until the weeping stopped.

CHARLIE LED Joe, trembling with weakness, down the stairs to the kitchen, where he settled him at the table and, all but scurrying in his happiness and relief, laid enough food in front of Joe to feed a dozen. Joe ate but without the gusto with which he had always eaten before. Thirst seemed to trouble him more than hunger, and Charlie refilled his glass with milk many times before the boy motioned he had had enough.

There were dark circles beneath Joe's eyes now. He was thinner. His hands were as beautiful as ever, but there was a tremor in them when he raised the glass to his lips. The illness had taken a toll on him. Charlie noticed too that Joe looked at him now with a knowing in his eyes Charlie did not understand. He could not see what the boy was seeing. He did not know that the boy was remembering their time together as they lay in the moonlight, on that night Joe had erased from Charlie's mind, while a flood of passion consumed them both. He did not feel again the release of that passion as Joe did, or recall the taste of that passion on his lips, in his throat. He did not remember the heat of their bodies, the twining of their limbs, or the crying out at that final moment when their love exploded from their bodies like hot, searing lava.

But Joe did. Joe remembered every second of their lovemaking. And it no longer troubled him. He had finally, at some point during his days of sickness, while his mind was lost on other roads, accepted the love he felt for Charlie. What he would do with this knowledge, Joe wasn't yet sure. It was not fear of his father's anger that troubled him now. Joe no longer cared what his father thought of his feelings for Charlie. It was his own fate that troubled Joe. And it was not for himself that he was troubled, but for Charlie. The wave of suffering was not yet over, and Joe did not want Charlie to be swept away inside it.

At that moment, as he sat there with Charlie's honest, open eyes upon him, Joe realized he would have to leave. When his portrait was completed, Joe would simply have to walk away and face his fate alone.

Someday Charlie would understand.

Joe did not know that Charlie already understood. He did not know Charlie had already committed himself to Joe's fate, no matter where it led. He did not know Charlie would prefer to meet a thousand deaths with Joe rather than live his life alone.

Joe could not understand these things, for Joe, with all his talk of love, was too new on this earth to understand love's full power. His naïve wisdom could not reach that far, could not quite grasp the reality of what love really meant.

But soon it would.

FOR MORE than a week, Charlie cared for the boy, trying to bring a glimmer of his previous health back to Joe's weakened body. He stood with Joe beneath the warm spray of the shower and bathed his body. He knelt before the boy and bathed his feet when Joe spoke of a burning in the soles that never seemed to leave him, as if in his imagination he was treading on the smoldering remnants of the dead. He washed the boy's long hair time and again, for Joe said he could smell the smoke of charred flesh in it. Charlie lay for hours on end, simply holding Joe close to him, comforting him as best he could, stroking his cheeks, his back, petting his hair, letting the warmth of his own body bring warmth to Joe's, for always, the boy seemed taken by a chill that he could not escape. His thin limbs trembled with it. His teeth chattered behind his lips. It was nothing to be concerned about, Charlie whispered into Joe's ear as Joe's frail body shivered in his arms. He was simply weak from his sickness, and soon it would pass. But in his own mind, Charlie wondered if Joe would ever completely recover. His hurts seemed to go too deep.

Charlie thought of driving the boy to a hospital he knew of in a nearby town, but at the first mention of it, Joe said he would not go. He made a brave face then, for Charlie's benefit, and told him he was feeling much better. He even tried to rise and walk outside, as if thinking fresh air would help him heal, but halfway to the door, he swayed on his feet, and Charlie rushed to his side to catch him before he fell.

As the sun rose on the seventh day after Joe's awakening from his fever, Charlie opened his eyes from sleep and saw Joe sitting on the doorstep of the cabin, with Mac at his side, staring out at the lake. He sat straighter, it seemed to Charlie, and he was stroking Mac's head, something he had not done for many days. In the dog's happiness, Mac's tail was thumping a tattoo on the doorstep.

On hearing movement behind him, Joe turned and, seeing Charlie, beamed a smile at him. It was a smile Charlie had thought he might never see again. When Joe spoke, his voice was strong.

"Come sit with us, Charlie."

Charlie did, studying Joe's face as he lowered himself down beside him. Joe's color had returned, most of it, although there was still a tinge of paleness in his cheeks. But his eyes were clear. The haunted look that comes with sickness and pain was gone. Joe had obviously bathed himself that morning, for his hair was still damp and smelled of Charlie's shampoo. Joe was wearing Charlie's bathrobe again, the same one Charlie had handed to the boy on that first night when Joe came to him.

Charlie reached out to take Joe's hand, bringing it to his lips, pressing a kiss into Joe's palm. Smiling, Joe cupped Charlie's chin in his long elegant fingers and gave it a little shake.

"Thank you, Charlie," he said.

Joe's hand felt warm against Charlie's skin, not cold as it had been for days past when chills had wracked his body and heat had seemed something the boy would never again acquire. It was the warmth of healthy human flesh, not the fire of the fever, which came before the chills; not a blaze of misery beneath the skin, but the simple heat of life. Charlie relished the feel of it.

"Have you eaten?" Charlie asked.

"No. I was waiting for you."

"Are you hungry?"

Joe thought about that for a moment, then smiled. "I'm starving."

Charlie smiled back. "I guess that's a good sign."

"Good as gold," Joe said. Joe's eyes left Charlie's face to gaze up into the morning sky. "Look, Charlie. The sky is clear again. The burning is just a memory now."

And there it was, that incredible blue Charlie had seen only once before, the blue he had wondered if he could ever duplicate on canvas. The sky was filled with it. From horizon to horizon. It shone overhead without a blemish of cloud, without a tinge of copper. The air smelled as fresh as a spray of daisies sitting on a sideboard. The sun was rising across the lake, and as he watched, Charlie saw a fish fling itself out of the water as if it too wished to gaze upon the crystal beauty of that cerulean sky without the boundaries of a watery prison getting in the way. Charlie could hear the distant splash when the fish fell back to the lake. And as if that small splash had awoken his senses, he suddenly heard songbirds singing their morning song in the fir trees that edged the water, heard the hum of bees plucking nectar from the blooming flowers by the fence, heard the soft rustle of wind through pine needles, the lap of water as it touched the shore. The air was alive with morning sounds and smells. Charlie closed his eyes for a moment and let himself be buried in the music.

Joe's voice brought him back. "After we eat, Charlie, we have work to do."

Charlie nodded. "I know." He glanced at the studio, felt the pull of it as he always did. He had not touched a brush to canvas for days on end, and he hungered for it now. It was time for him to set aside his love for the boy and do the job he had promised to do. It was time to put this incredible young man's image on canvas and present him to the world as Joe requested.

It was time for *Freedom* to be born.

Charlie's fingers itched to begin.

CHAPTER THIRTEEN
...IN THE EYES OF A WOMAN....

ON THE seventh day after the onset of Joe's illness, and before the sun had reached its zenith in that flawless sapphire sky, Joe stood once again before Charlie, nude, arms outstretched, his face lifted high in *Freedom*'s pose, and watched Charlie work. Standing as he was, so nakedly exposed in the harsh rays of the summer sun, which once again streamed through the studio's glass roof like a waterfall of light, Charlie could see the changes etched in the boy from his days of sickness.

Always trim, now the boy looked frail. His ribs peeked out through the skin of his chest. His arms, once so elegant and strong, seemed to have withered slightly, as if the muscle beneath had simply wasted away. Joe's face, which before had always shown a zest for life, a curiosity, an astonishment at the sights of this new and exciting world he saw around him, now displayed a look of tired patience. His eyes, still beautiful, still dark and bottomless, no longer beamed with wonder. They were simply there, looking out at Charlie as if seeing but not seeing, and in their depths Charlie could still find vestiges of the pain that, if not for Charlie's care, might have brought Joe to the very brink of death. For with all the miracles waiting to burst forth from the boy's wondrous hands, the power to heal himself was apparently not among them.

Still, with all the changes wrought in Joe by his days of suffering, Charlie had never seen such beauty. The golden skin. The strong, waving hair. The tall, sleek stance that seemed now to be a torture for Joe to maintain. If there were dark circles still beneath his eyes, there was also the glimmer of a smile always ready to burst forth, lighting the room when it did, like a klieg light aimed at Charlie alone. If he still suffered, as Charlie suspected he did, fraught with guilt at the suffering the world had endured, Joe was still determined to keep all signs of that torment from Charlie. The goodness, the kindness, inherent in the boy since he first set foot on this planet, since he first stood naked at Charlie's doorstep, had not been lessened even one iota in all the days of his illness. Despite it all, Joe was still Joe. And Charlie loved him more than ever.

As Joe stood before Charlie, sometimes a tremor of weakness passed through his body, but when Charlie begged him to sit, the boy would shake his head no and, with a look of concentration piercing his eyes, once again straighten his shoulders, reach out his arms, and regain the pose Charlie needed. Reluctantly, Charlie would continue his work.

The canvas Charlie had chosen for the painting was a large one. Three feet by five. In the back of his mind, he always remembered the sense of disappointment that struck him when he first laid eyes on da Vinci's *Mona Lisa*. That marvelous portrait had seemed so small, so unfinished, somehow, hanging alone beneath its plexiglass dome. He remembered people crowding up to it to better see the artistry of Da Vinci's brush strokes, the unsullied perfection of a work of art brought so unerringly to the world.

People would one day visit *Freedom* too. They would come to lay their eyes on the child of God who had come to this world to set things right, and Charlie did not want to see them crowding forward, jostling, straining to see his rendering of this perfect being standing before him now. The momentous importance of the subject matter demanded size, demanded clarity of image that only a large canvas could provide. Charlie wanted people to see every nuance of this man-child as Charlie himself saw them. He wanted people to feel they had come face-to-face with a living presence. Chaos, Charlie's stock in trade, would not be brought to this canvas. He envisioned simplicity of perfection for this, his greatest work. He wanted nothing less than to bring the boy to canvas, exactly as he was in life. He wanted the world to see the pain in Joe's eyes, but he wanted the world to see the wonder there too, the childlike innocence that had captured Charlie's heart the first moment he looked upon the boy. He wanted the world to feel the power of those perfect hands reaching out to either side as if gathering the world to him. He wanted the world to know there was goodness in life, and this goodness emanated solely from this one perfect boy standing before them on the canvas.

As always, when the passion of Charlie's work tore him completely away from the world he stood in, when the skill in his hands made the brush a living entity he neither guided nor controlled, but followed, his thoughts sometimes wandered to places he had never been, or to places he most dearly wished to see again. And now, while his hands did the work, his mind played. As Joe's image slowly unfolded on the canvas as if the boy were stepping through a curtain of mist, Charlie thought of the feel of the boy's skin beneath his fingertips. Remembered the beauty of the boy on the day of the deer, when he stepped from the lake and shook the water from his naked body. Remembered the laughter in Joe's eyes when he looked down from that vast pedestal of swirling water he had drawn from the lake and saw Mac barking in confusion at the edge of the water far below. Remembered the innocence on the boy's face as he slept beside Charlie in front of the fire. Remembered his sweet breath upon Charlie's hair. Remembered the warmth of Joe's fingers idly caressing the skin beneath Charlie's ear as he told him of his father. Remembered, too, the brush of Joe's genitals against his arm as he hung suspended in the water, guided by Charlie's strong hands. Buoyant and beautiful.

Charlie remembered other things too. The fear that gripped his heart when Joe sank beneath the surface of the lake on the day they stepped from the boat. The tear that fell from the boy's eye as he stroked the lifeless body of the doe. The pain of watching Joe suffer through the endless fever, and later, the weakness on Joe's face, the emptiness in his eyes, as he fought against the chill that seemed to have settled into his very bones. Charlie remembered, too, the horror of finding Joe, lost in delirium, lying in the mud beside the water and the weight of the boy's weeping body as he carried him to the cabin.

If Charlie's mind had retained the memory of their night of passion, he would undoubtedly have gone there first. Gone there and stayed. But he did not know. Joe had stolen the memory from him.

So now, as Charlie worked, as Charlie's mind traveled to those places that meant the most to him, or most frightened him, it was Joe whose mind traveled to that place, to that one perfect hour of time when their bodies had come together at last.

As he tried to ignore the weakness in his body, as he tried to maintain the pose Charlie needed from him, Joe's mind settled inside the warmth of that memory and never left it. As Charlie concentrated on the canvas before him, Joe recalled every moment of that night. Tearing the sheet from Charlie's body. The first taste of Charlie's skin against his lips. The first touch of Charlie's hands, Charlie's mouth, caressing Joe's manhood, exploring, tasting, reveling. Never before, until that night, had Joe known earthly passion. Never before had his newly formed body been taken to that place where the flesh of another had led him to feed and to be fed upon. Never before had he known the ecstasy of his juices flowing over hungry lips. Felt the stroke of a hand upon his leg, upon his chest, while his body bucked and trembled as his passion gushed forth. And never before had Joe tasted the passion of another. He could not have known until that night that the sweet taste of it would always be with him. Each time he looked into the face of this person he loved so much, he would hunger for that taste again. And again. Love on this planet seemed to be an endless circle, always returning to that one perfect moment when the flesh opens up, all inhibitions fall away, and the lust of each body spews forth to anoint the other.

And now, even weak from illness, Joe felt the rising of his passion again, felt the stirring of his penis as it awoke beneath him, felt a tremble in his body that did not come from weakness alone. To bury it, to hide it from both Charlie and himself, Joe cast his mind toward those thoughts that truly haunted him—those thoughts that perhaps he had been trying to keep from himself all along—laying their horror like a blanket across the only true beauty he had ever known.

Again, he felt the searing of flesh. Heard the screams of anguish. Felt the desolation of unanswered prayers from the lips of dying men and women. They were gone from the earth now, those men, those women, but their suffering continued, even more greatly now, perhaps, because they knew they no longer had the release of death to free them from it. The tortures they felt at this moment would be the same tortures they would know a hundred years from now. A thousand. It would never stop. Pain would be all they would ever know from that day forth, from the day their earthly bodies had turned to ash and the pain had settled around them like a gnawing womb, trapping them inside, tearing at them through all eternity. An unending, writhing torture.

As Joe thought these thoughts, a renewed weariness settled into him. Again, the taste of bile rose in his throat. He sensed a tremor in his outstretched arms and strove to control it before Charlie noticed. The ache he remembered from his illness seemed to once again take hold of his body and he closed his eyes for a moment, willing it to cease. Behind his eyelids, he saw his father's face, his father's hands, reaching out to him. Touching him. Smiling that gentle smile Joe remembered so well. With the sight of him there, Joe let his anger at his father fall away from him as easily as if it had never been, and drawing strength from the image behind his eyelids, Joe felt the bile drop, the aching lessen, the tremors stop. He opened his eyes and saw Charlie before him, working at the easel, a furrow of concentration between his eyes, and seeing him there, Joe smiled. His mind returned to love. It was a far better place for it to be during these long hours of forced stillness. And while he held Charlie's pose, while he watched Charlie work, he waited for the completion of the painting that would also herald the completion of Joe himself. For once the portrait was finished, his own life would begin to end. Joe knew this and accepted it.

His death was approaching now. He could sense it. He could feel it drawing nearer as surely as he felt the rays of sunlight warming his weakened body, as surely as he felt his love for Charlie grow with every passing second, as surely as he longed to taste Charlie's skin beneath his lips one more time, to feel himself drawn into Charlie's embrace, and there to bury the knowledge of his fate, losing it in the feel and scent and taste of Charlie's strong arms surrounding him, vainly trying to protect him from something he could never be protected from.

He had discovered so many emotions in his short time here. Love. Pity. Sorrow. Happiness. And now he discovered another. Loneliness. It came from the memory of Charlie's body and his becoming one, hungrily devouring the essence of each other as they let their senses, their needs, their passion, override all else. But it was not the act that brought Joe such loneliness now. It was the fact that he was the only one who carried the memory of it inside himself. For from Charlie, the memory of their moments together had been winnowed out, like chaff from wheat. Joe had torn the memory of their lovemaking from Charlie's mind as surely as his father had torn evil from the world. But had he not, Joe's relationship with Charlie would have been irrevocably changed, and his own sense of determination lost. For to see that passion in Charlie's eyes again at the memory of their time in each other's arms would have made it that much harder for Joe to leave. Would also have made his leaving that much more painful for Charlie.

And leave he must. This mortal body, which Joe had learned to cherish so deeply because of the happiness it had once given Charlie, would die around him. That had always been his fate, and it could not be changed now by such a simple thing as love.

Joe's death would leave Charlie alone, and Charlie did not need memories of passion to make the parting more painful. Charlie had many more years of life to live before they would see each other again. Joe did not want those years to be a torment. He wanted Charlie's time on earth to be happy. Fulfilled. He would find other loves. Maybe many. But he would not compare those loves to a boy he once knew, to a boy he once adored more than any other, for on that road Charlie would find no happiness.

Death would part them as surely as rain would again fall to water the earth, as surely as all recollection of the cleansing would be buried in the vacant tombs of time, as surely as evil would one day rise again. Joe saw his own final breath approaching with the same clarity with which he saw Charlie standing before him now.

He saw it in the eyes of a woman.

She would soon come. And coming, would bring his death with her. This knowledge brought him no fear. His own death mattered little to him. Joe was born for such a death. It had always been his destiny.

But regret was another matter. Regret that he did not have more time to spend with the man before him filled Joe's every thought, every moment, like a bitter wine poured to the very brim of a cup.

But the woman was needed. Without her, he would pour that cup of regret to the ground, never tasting it, never knowing its pain. Joe would forsake all that his father had brought him here to attain, for on his own, he knew, he did not have the strength to bring about his own death, nor the strength to leave Charlie behind.

The world demanded such things from those they worshiped. If the people of this world were ever to see Joe as his father's son, they would have to kill him first. As they had two thousand years ago.

And the woman would be the implement from which death came. It had always been so. Eve's legacy still lived in his father's eyes. All that was good, and all that was evil, was centered in woman. She gave life as easily as she doled out death. She brought happiness to man while she tortured his very soul.

The goodness of woman would once again be twisted to evil by the very nature the father had instilled in her at the beginning of time. She was a rose, a perfect being, but as in every rose, there are thorns, waiting to prick the flesh of those who come too close.

And now, as then, those thorns would once again draw blood. The woman would not understand the consequences of her actions, just as the thorn did not understand its power, but still the damage would be done.

And this time, the damage was needed.

The woman would make it happen.

Joe forgave her even now, before he laid his eyes upon her living face. He prayed that one day Charlie would forgive her, too, for it was the woman closest to Charlie who would bring it all about.

The woman in the painting.

The woman who had once loved this man in the same way Joe loved him now.

Judith.

Joe's Judas Iscariot.

AS THE day progressed and evening neared, Joe's mind became ever more filled with thoughts of his own death, wondering how it would come about, wondering if he would know such pain as his first brother had known. His body, still weak from sickness, ached now with the effort of holding the pose Charlie asked from him, but that pain was as nothing compared to what his first brother had been forced to endure.

Perhaps it was the pose he held that brought such thoughts to Joe, for the pose of *Freedom* was also the pose of crucifixion. Ever in his mind's eye, Joe saw the heavy wooden cross his first brother had carried through the streets of Jerusalem and then been borne upon into the sky. Was it made of cedar, that cross? His father, in his sorrow, had never said. Had other bodies died upon it? Did it reek with the blood of others spilled on those very beams? Did the stench of that blood fill his first brother's nostrils as he hung there in the reek of his own? Were they truly evil people, those who had died on that cross before him? Were their punishments deserved? Or did they, like his first brother, die a faultless death, lost in the bureaucracy and hypocrisy of unholy men? An amusement for the masses more than anything else. An exercise in power.

Joe looked now at his hands reaching out to either side of him and imagined them pierced by nails, imagined his feet, crossed one upon the other, pierced as well, nailed to the wood from which he hung. He imagined the weight of his head pulling at the tendons in his neck. Imagined, too, the mocking sign placed above the crown of thorns that pierced his forehead. INRI. King of the Jews. He saw the smiles on the faces of the Roman soldiers beneath him as they stood on the hillside watching him die, impatient but enjoying the spectacle. He felt the life ebbing away from the two misguided souls hanging beside him, their miseries as profound as his own. He tried to find the strength to reach out to them and ease their suffering, but his body was too weak. He could no more release them from their pain than he could relinquish his own.

Joe saw himself as Jesus, concentrating his mind away from his own pain and onto the view afforded him by the hill and by the height of the cross from which he hung. Skull Hill, the peasants called it in the city. A fitting name. He could see the rooftops of Jerusalem spread out before him, the walls of the city surrounding them. As Jesus, he thought of his childhood in Nazareth. A happy time. His mother's gentle hands and the strength of his father's, the carpenter, also gentle. Their simple meals together. He remembered the freedom they had given him to roam the hillsides around the city. The freedom to find his own path. And when the time came, the freedom to leave, to wander the roads of his own destiny. The roads that led him… here, nailed to this wood, his body dying around him.

His parents were with him now. Kneeling at his feet. They had traveled far to find him, to be beside him at the end. His mother was reaching up to him, but he was too far away. Mary was there too. Mary Magdalene, the woman who perhaps loved him more than any other. Her head was bent in prayer. He could see the tears sparkling on her cheeks as she clutched his father's strong hand.

And as the eyes in his memory closed in death, beseeching the great father one last time for comfort that would not come, Joe opened his own and saw Charlie standing before him.

The woman who would bring his own death was close now. Very close. She had come a long way to find him, although she did not know it yet. That was her destiny, just as death was Joe's. He did not blame her for bringing death with her. She was a pawn, guided by the hand of his father, and without her, Joe's own destiny would never be fulfilled.

On her, he could smell the perfume of betrayal. It wafted through the screaming rays of sunlight that flooded over his naked flesh with a velvet heat. That inevitable betrayal, like a living touch, brought a shiver of fear to his hot skin, but a shiver of expectancy too. Much suffering had already occurred; now only his own remained. It was his duty to accept it. And he would. Bravely, he hoped. As his first brother had done.

Joe felt heat on his palms, and before he could react to it, before he could turn his head to see what had caused it, Charlie's brush clattered to the floor. He saw Charlie's face, twisted in horror.

"My God, Joe! You're bleeding!"

Joe turned then to his hands and saw the blood dripping from the wounds in his palms. Looking down at a wash of heat on his feet, he saw blood there as well. He felt no pain, only the gentle flowing of warm blood across his skin.

He closed his hands, and when he opened them again, the blood was gone.

A look of confusion crossed Charlie's face. "Good lord, I thought…."

"It was nothing," Joe said. "Just echoes from the past."

Charlie's eyes were as wide as saucers, staring still at Joe's hands. He saw a drop of blood on the floor at the boy's feet and knew then he had not imagined what he had just seen.

"I'm sorry," Charlie said. "You're tired. I should never have kept you standing so long. We'll stop for today. You need to rest. You need to eat."

"No," Joe said. "There's another hour of sunlight left. I'll be all right."

With a ripple of thought that flowed as easily as liquid from his body, Joe, unmoving, willed the brush from the floor and sailed it back to Charlie, positioning it perfectly between his thumb and forefinger, just as it had been before it fell.

Charlie looked at Joe, glanced down at the brush in his hand, then back to Joe. "Thanks, kid," he said, worry still etched on his face, but a trace of humor too.

Joe had not altered his pose even once. "You're welcome, Charlie."

Once again, Charlie dipped the bristles of his brush into the smears of color on the palette in his left hand, stopping only when he heard Joe say, "Your wife is here."

Charlie looked up then, away from the palette, away from the easel. "*Who* did you say is here?"

"Me," said a familiar voice at the open door behind him.

Charlie turned, almost dropping the brush again.

"And that would be *ex*-wife," Judith said, tearing her eyes away from Charlie's startled face long enough to appraise the naked young man standing in the center of the room.

"Some things never change," she said with a wry shake of her head, then bent to pet Mac, who had come to greet her.

Still, Joe did not alter his pose. He stood there, naked and unashamed, staring at the woman until Charlie came and draped him in his robe. Only then did Joe move his aching legs to the window and gaze out upon the lake, turning his back to the people behind him. Turning his back, not with anger but with kindness, on the woman who carried his death with her through the door. As his first brother had carried the cross, the implement of his own demise, this woman carried Joe's, though she did not know it yet.

He listened to the two's words of greeting, heard the surprise, and a trace of discomfort, in Charlie's voice as he spoke welcoming words to the woman who had once shared his life, his bed.

And at that moment, Joe learned another emotion.

Jealousy. Jealousy at the time these two had spent together, wrapped in each other's arms, exploring each other's body, speaking soft words in each other's ears. Time to learn all there was to know about the other person. Time he and Charlie would never have.

But he forced the jealousy from his mind and pushed all thoughts of these two away from him, concentrating instead on the stillness of the lake outside the window, and in that stillness, Joe found peace.

Just as he always had.

Chapter Fourteen
...THE BIRTH OF BETRAYAL....

ON THE day of the cleansing, Judith had looked up from her laptop and watched in horror as the man who shared her life now, the man who had buried the pain inside her at the loss of Charlie, the man who had taught her to love all over again, burst into flames as he stood at the window looking out on the streets of Dallas. She remembered every writhing moment of his death. His screams. The tortured expression on his face. His hand, sheared of skin by the flames, reaching out to her for help, a help she could not give, before he crumbled to ash on the living room floor of the condominium they had leased together only a month before.

As she leaped from behind her desk, dragging the laptop with her and sending it crashing to the floor, she stood screaming out her anguish, her confusion, her disbelief. And as her eyes traveled through the window that Tom had only moments before been gazing through, she saw the smoke of other burnings, countless burnings, filling the sky outside.

That Tom had gambled away her life savings, every penny she had acquired in the divorce from Charlie, she did not yet know. That Tom had other sins in his past as well, sins that had brought the flames of this day to him as assuredly as the sun rises in the east, she could not have begun to imagine. She thought he had loved her. She did not know that already he had planned his escape from her. She would find the airline ticket in his valise the following day. And on that day, too, she would learn that her money was gone. Her grief at the loss of Tom would turn to hatred in a heartbeat, and in that hatred she would lose all interest in the whys and wherefores of the burnings, for that knowledge could not return to her all that had been taken. That her own life had been spared from the flames did not once occur to her. She saw only her loss.

Now when she remembered Tom's strong body, the body she had made love to mere hours before, engulfed in fire, she did so without pity. He had suffered the misery he had earned.

Four days later, still stunned by everything that had befallen her, she packed up her clothes and those few belongings that meant the most to her and left Dallas, driving north, seeking cooler air, for the heat of this Dallas summer reminded her of the burnings. She might have stayed in the city had she the money for another month's rent, but she didn't. She had little more than two hundred dollars to her name, only what she found in her purse.

At first, as the miles began to unwind beneath the wheels of her car, she had no thoughts of what her destination would be. She thought merely to escape the memories. And the heat. But as time passed, as cities and towns fled by her windows, she gradually came to realize where she had been heading all along. Back to Charlie. He would help her, she knew. He would have to. For all his faults, Charlie was as different from Tom as two people could be. He had never intentionally hurt her as Tom had. Had never stolen anything from her but her trust, and even that had not been taken through malice. Charlie battled his own demons. She had been merely an innocent victim of a war he continually fought, and continually lost. Battle after battle. Although she no longer loved Charlie—there had been too many recriminations, too much betrayal for that—she did still respect him. Respected his art. Respected his passion for his work. Even respected him for his never giving in to the demons that pursued him. It was not his fault her body had not been enough for him. If he craved men as well, that was something inborn. She had left *him*, after all, or so she remembered it. He had not left her. The fact that she was unwilling to share him was her weakness, not his. She had never quite forgiven him for not at least *offering* to change, but perhaps he knew it was not within his power to do so, and by offering an impossible change, he would have only prolonged her torment at his infidelities.

There were other friends than Charlie she might have gone to for help, but with anyone but Charlie, the shame would have been too great. Her pride was her downfall. It always had been. As Charlie had his infidelities, she had her all-consuming pride. With Charlie she could swallow that pride. God knows she had done so time and time again during the years of their marriage.

But as Judith stood now in the doorway of Charlie's studio, the studio she had helped him design, she felt yet again that familiar rush of anger she had come to know so well during the time they were together. It was the same feeling Joe felt as he stood with his back to her at the window, although Judith would not have thought to call it what Joe did. She did not see it for what it truly was. To her, it was merely an indescribable ache. Had she been a stronger woman, she might have laughed at herself for feeling it. She had not known, as she drove up the familiar winding lane to the cabin, that the pain of losing Charlie was still raw inside her, could not have imagined she had hidden it even from herself for the three years they had been apart. But seeing the beautiful young man standing naked in the studio, seeing the look the young man had given Charlie when she stepped through the door, and seeing the look Charlie had given the boy in return, brought that sense of loss bubbling up inside her. And for the first time since the days of their marriage, or during the years since it ended, she found the courage to call that feeling what it really was. Jealousy. She did not see mere lust in Charlie's eyes when he looked on the boy posing so unashamedly before him. No. Charlie looked at this boy in the same way he had once looked at her. When their eyes met, Charlie's and the boy's, when their thoughts joined, a spark like electricity flew across the room. That spark was love.

The boy had looked at her then as if he knew why she was here. And in her shame at that realization, her resentment of the boy was born. It was him, or others like him, after all, who had destroyed her marriage to Charlie.

That Joe had seen in her his own death, she could not have known, and perhaps it would not have troubled her if she had. But it planted a seed in her, a seed of hatred that would one day bring about everything Joe had known was coming all along. He had not intentionally planted that seed, but as he stood with his back to the room staring out at the lake, he could feel it growing behind him inside the woman. It took him, he knew, one step closer to the end that was ordained for him. He felt no pity for himself, only sorrow that it would one day hurt the woman standing at the door. The woman Charlie had once loved.

Judith tore her eyes from the boy, and from Charlie too, and they came to rest upon the canvas Charlie was working on. It was immediately apparent that Charlie's talent had matured since she saw him last. Although as yet unfinished, far from it in fact, the painting drew her eye like a leaf is drawn, unfurling, to the warmth of the sun. She saw the beauty of the boy standing at the window so perfectly captured on canvas that it all but took her breath away. The lines and texture of his skin were almost photographic in their perfection. Charlie's blending of colors brought such life to the boy's image that Judith almost expected the boy to move across the linen. Those elegant outstretched arms reaching to either edge of the canvas seemed to pull her into their embrace. She could almost feel those arms folding themselves around her, drawing her into the safe harbor they offered. But it was the eyes on the canvas that held her. She could see such compassion in the way Charlie had brought them to life with nothing but brush and paint that, had they been living eyes, they could not have touched her more deeply. Her resentment of the boy was almost lost in the beauty of those eyes. She had to force herself to turn away from the kindness she saw in them, and when she did, she let her own eyes settle once again on Charlie's face.

"You've grown," she said.

"Taller? Fatter? Cuter? Uglier? Let's be a little more specific, shall we?"

She let a weary smile settle across her tired face. "No, Charlie. Your work."

Charlie did not glance at the canvas. He merely continued to stare at the woman who was once his wife. She looked exhausted. Had she driven here from Dallas, the last place he knew she was living? She must have. Her clothes were rumpled, her hair windblown, but still she was as pretty as the last time he'd seen her. He did not look at her now through eyes of love, as he once had, but through the eyes of an artist. He saw colors and shapes, not emotion. The high cheekbones. The titian hair. The flawless skin that spoke of Irish ancestry, and the courageous, stubborn tilt of her head that spoke of Irish pride. She was a small woman, but the certainty of her own worth that carried her through life did not lend itself to an impression of smallness. Her green eyes had always fascinated him, and they did so now, but he no longer saw love for himself in them. They were not cold, exactly, those eyes, merely disconnected. In the time they had been apart, a distancing had grown in them. A distancing from the past, a change in priorities. He knew immediately that Joe had been right when he told Charlie she no longer loved him. If not for his love for Joe, Charlie thought that the distance he saw now in Judith's lovely green eyes might have crushed him, for he had once loved her as much as she had loved him. He wondered if she could see the same change in his own eyes. If she did, she kept it well hidden behind that cloak of self-assurance that always protected her.

Her eyes traveled from him to Joe.

"Since when do you work with models?" she asked in a voice as businesslike and disconnected as her eyes.

The dislike he saw on her face as she stared at Joe surprised him. And angered him.

"I seem to remember you posing for me once," he said.

Her eyes once again centered on him. The hint of a smile, a remembrance, twisted the corners of her mouth.

"I had almost forgotten," she said, the edge of petulance disappearing from her voice. But it returned quickly enough when she turned once again to the boy standing with his back to her at the window. "Afterward," she said, "we made love right there on the floor. Remember? By the time we were finished, there was as much paint on me as there was on the canvas. Tell me, Charlie, do you still make love as ferociously as you once did?"

Her words were aimed at Joe, Charlie knew, not at himself. He decided to ignore them, but his face grew stern.

"What do you want, Judith? Why are you here?"

This was not how she had seen their reunion progressing. She could not have known all the anger and resentment that had once torn them apart would so easily resurface. *Did* she still love Charlie? Why else would she be acting like this? She decided to backpedal. She was here, after all, because she wanted something from Charlie. Antagonizing him wouldn't help her get it.

She ran a hand across her face, pushing a lock of hair from in front of her eyes. "I'm sorry, Charlie. I'm worn out. I've been driving nonstop for two days. I need a bath. I need a drink. And I need to stretch my legs." She cast an embarrassed look at Joe, but still Charlie saw resentment in her glance. "Can we take a walk along the lake? I need to talk to you." *In private*, she didn't add, or need to. Charlie caught her drift.

Charlie set his palette and brush aside and wiped his hands on his trouser legs.

Before he could step away from the easel and the unfinished canvas, he saw her turn again to Joe. Once again, her words were meant to wound. Charlie had almost forgotten what a bitch she could be if she really set her mind to it. Oddly enough, at the beginning, that was one of her traits that most appealed to him.

"Isn't that the robe I bought you for one of the few anniversaries we shared together?"

"I don't remember," Charlie said, his voice flat.

"I do," she volleyed back. "I bought it at Macy's."

Joe turned from the window then and gazed upon her with the same eyes that had gazed at her from the canvas. There was such kindness in those eyes that Judith felt a twinge of embarrassment at the way she'd been acting. If her words had hurt the boy, he did not show it. He merely smiled at her, then at Charlie, and shrugging out of the robe as if he no longer cared for the feel of it, as if he no longer felt the need to hide his nakedness from anyone, least of all her, he let it fall to his feet and stepped naked across the room.

At the door, he turned long enough to say, "I'll let you two have some privacy." To Judith alone, he said, "You must be hungry after your long drive. While you talk, I'll start dinner. Come inside whenever you're ready."

With that, he stepped out into the sunlight and padded on bare feet across the lush lawn with Mac at his heels, like an unclad Adam with not so much as a fig leaf to hide his secrets, strolling through the garden of Eden without a care in the world.

"He's beautiful," Judith whispered in spite of herself. She almost smiled at the way the boy had dropped the robe to the floor. She understood that act completely. With that one simple gesture, he had told her in no uncertain terms that he needed nothing from her. Nothing at all. It was a gesture she herself might have made under the same circumstances.

Charlie watched Joe and Mac disappear into the cabin and close the door behind them.

"I know," Charlie said quietly, his voice as soft as the rustle of pine needles in a morning breeze. "He's his father's son."

CHARLIE SAT with Judith at the edge of the jetty and watched the sun slowly dip its blinding eye behind the trees that bordered the lake. As the shadow of the forest settled over them, the air grew cooler and the smell of pine grew stronger.

Judith had removed her shoes and stockings and was wearily paddling her feet in the water. Charlie lifted one of her shoes from the ground beside him and held it in his hands, feeling the warm contours of it, the heat of her body still alive inside the leather, as she spoke. He knew why she was here now. She had told him everything.

"He took it all, Charlie. Every dime."

"I'm sorry."

"I didn't know who else to turn to."

"I know. I understand."

When she looked at him, her eyes were dry.

"Can you help me? I don't know why you should, but can you? I don't need much, Charlie. Just enough to get me back on my feet."

Charlie remembered the blurred image of Joe's face hovering over him on the day he held his body beneath the water, on the day he cleansed Charlie's sins from him as cleanly as a million fires had cleansed the world. He thought perhaps that Tom's burning had been a cleansing for Judith as well. It certainly cleansed her of her money, at any rate. She wasn't used to being broke. He could see the fear of it in her eyes when she looked at him. And he could see the shame there too. It must have been hard for her, coming here like this, swallowing that stubborn Irish pride. And then finding him with Joe. That must have *really* sent her into paroxysms of ecstasy.

"You know I will," he said. "I'll give you whatever you need."

Only then did he see tears rise in her eyes. Tears of relief. "Thank you, Charlie. I'll pay you back."

A silence settled over them until she asked, "What happened, Charlie? What does it all mean? I listened to a dozen talk radio stations as I drove out here. There are as many opinions about it as there were fires. What do you think really happened? Why did so many people die? Was it God, like they say? Do you believe that?"

"Yes," Charlie said. "I believe it."

She cocked her head as she gazed at him. "I thought you were an atheist, or an agnostic, or something."

"I was," Charlie said simply. "Now I'm not."

"Why? What changed your mind?"

Charlie gazed back at the cabin. He could smell cooking on the air. It smelled like hamburgers and onions frying. Thank God it wasn't chicken. He realized suddenly how hungry he was.

"Joe," he said. "Joe changed my mind."

"Your model? What the hell does he have to do with it?"

Charlie smiled at her. "He has everything to do with it."

"You're in love with him," she said. There was a sadness, a flat finality in her voice when she said it that surprised even her. "That boy in there isn't just another conquest, is he? This has all the makings of a full-blown affair of the heart. Am I right? Don't lie to me, Mr. Charles Allen Strickland. I'll know if you do."

Charlie smiled at her, at the memories her words dredged up. "I always knew I was in trouble when you used my full name."

"Don't change the subject. You're in love, aren't you? You're in love with that kid."

"He's not a kid. He's a man."

"Barely."

Charlie looked up into the darkening sky. A few stars had awoken, Sirius the brightest of them. It hung there over his head like a glimpse of heaven. He wondered if Joe's father was there at this very moment, looking down on him through that pinpoint of light, waiting to hear the words he would speak next. Or did he already know?

"Yes. I love him. But it's more than that."

"What do you mean?"

"It isn't just my art that's grown, Judith. My heart has grown too."

"God, Charlie. You sound like a dime novel."

He ignored her comment. "After you've spent some time with him, you'll understand."

"Understand what?"

An animation lit Charlie's eyes for the first time since Judith had looked into them this day. He dropped her shoe to the ground and gently gripped her shoulders, twisting her to him. His eyes were bright and eager as he stared into her face. There was an unreadable smile on his lips she had never seen before. A smile with wisdom behind it. The wisdom of angels, she thought, wondering even as she did why the words had come to her like that. Jealousy once again reared up and kicked her in the gut.

"Judith…."

"What the hell are you talking about, Charlie? He's a model, for Christ's sake."

"No."

Judith's anger surged up before she knew it was coming. "How does it work, Charlie? Do you fuck him, or does he fuck you? Or is it one of those one size fits all things? I hope you're using protection, Charlie. You take some kid in out of the blue and start banging away between poses, and the next thing you know you're popping pills for the rest of your life and waiting for the AIDS virus to rip you to shreds, and for what? Fresh meat? And why the hell is he in there right now cooking dinner? Does he live here? If you two are married, I sure as hell didn't get an invitation to the wedding."

"Stop it."

"I saw only your car in the driveway. Where's his? Or isn't he old enough to drive?"

"He doesn't need to drive. He can fly."

"Right."

"He can do anything he wants."

"Well, he certainly seems to be doing it with you. You don't really think he loves you back, do you?"

"I know he does. He loves you, too, Judith. He loves everyone."

"Well, that's magnanimous of him. And what did you mean when you said he had everything to do with the burnings? I suppose that since he can fly, he's the one who flew around setting the fires?"

Charlie grinned, amused suddenly by Judith's anger. "No. His father did that."

"Can his father fly through the air, too?"

"His father *is* the air."

"*Jesus*, Charlie!"

Charlie's grin turned into a full-blown laugh. "Yeah. Something like that."

Judith took a deep breath, trying to bury her anger, or at least hide it. "Charlie, I think this kid is taking you for a ride."

"Oh, yes, he's certainly done that."

"How did you meet him? Where did he come from?"

"You said it yourself. He came from the blue."

"The blue."

"Yep."

She pointed skyward. "Like *that* blue?"

"None other."

Judith's eyes flashed. "It must be every faggot's dream, having a handsome young cocksucker fall out of the sky like that."

Charlie slapped her then. Hard. Her eyes flew open with the shock of it. Before she could speak, before she could do anything, he laid a gentle hand to her reddening cheek and said, "I'm sorry. I shouldn't have done that."

At the touch of his hand, her tears began to flow. "You've never hit me before, Charlie."

"I know. I...." Gently, he wiped the tears from her face. He cupped her face now in both his hands and captured her eyes in his own. "You can't talk about him like that, Judith. You don't understand who he is."

She pushed his hands away, trying to control the sobs that were about to burst from her throat. She couldn't let him see her cry. She never had and she never would. She blinked away her tears, her head still buzzing from the slap.

She forced a calmness to her voice that was as far from how she really felt as night was from day.

"So what are you trying to tell me, Charlie? Just spit it out. Who is he exactly, this young man of yours?"

The gentlest smile she had ever seen on a human face now transformed Charlie's features into something as clean and pure as rain. His crystal eyes reflected light from the rising moon, and in their depths, she saw a love that was unlike any he had ever directed at her. Her heart ached at the sight of it.

"He's the son of God," Charlie said, his voice little more than a whisper.

He turned away from her then, and gazed out across the water. His hand found hers and pulled it to his lips. She felt his tears fall to her hand and slide across her fingertips.

They were so warm, those tears. As warm as the ones falling from her own eyes, she suddenly realized.

"You can't honestly believe that," she said.

Charlie released her hand then and she lowered it to her lap, still feeling the heat of his tears upon her skin. He turned to her and gave her a little shrug, the smallest movement of shoulders and head, that brought a flood of memories washing through her, memories of their first days together, memories of the moment she first realized she had fallen in love with him. It seemed so long ago, but in the course of a lifetime, it really wasn't.

She knew then that, as easily as her love for Tom had slipped away from her, her love for this man, this artist, had survived inside her, buried in an all-too-shallow grave beneath the anger and the hurts and the jealousies of a troubled marriage.

His love for her, however, was gone forever. She could see it in his eyes. Now he loved only the boy inside the cabin. She could feel him ache for the boy even as he sat beside her on the dock.

Could his love for the boy be so strong that it had stolen his reason?

"Charlie. Listen to yourself. Listen to the words you're saying."

"I'm only saying what is true."

Her eyes flashed in anger. "Bullshit. You're only saying what the boy wants you to believe."

Again, Charlie smiled. "I know. Because it's true. There are no lies in Joe. He doesn't know how."

We'll see about that. Judith collected her shoes and pulled her feet from the water. The skin of her cheek still burned from Charlie's slap, but she ignored it, wiping her tears away with the palm of her hand.

"I need a drink, Charlie. Maybe your new boyfriend will turn some water into wine for me."

She said it with malice, but Charlie did not hear it that way.

He merely pulled himself to his feet and said, "Maybe he will."

Shaking her head, Judith followed him to the cabin.

CHAPTER FIFTEEN
...A HOT BATH AND
A GLASS OF WINE....

As THEY ate, sitting at the kitchen table, Judith kept her thoughts to herself. Her back still ached from the long drive, and she was all too aware she needed a bath. Needed to lie down. Needed some time to think things through. That she would come back here to find Charlie all but mesmerized into insanity by the boy sitting across from her, the boy who occasionally reached out to push Charlie's hair from his face, or touch Charlie's hand as they spoke, was something she never could have imagined until she saw it with her own eyes. Charlie had never been the stablest of human beings, but what artist was? Once upon a time, his eccentricities had amused her—the ones that did not involve sex with other men, at any rate. But this was no mere eccentricity. This was full-blown delusion. And it frightened her.

She noticed that the damn kid had even mesmerized the dog. Mac was sitting beside Joe's chair right now, his chin resting on Joe's leg, occasionally gazing up into Joe's face as if his own happiness depended solely on the happiness on the face above him.

Still, with all the resentment blossoming inside her at the way this kid had wormed his way into Charlie's life and Charlie's mind, she could not take her own eyes away from Joe's face. He was certainly gorgeous, even though he looked as tired as she felt. He looked, in fact, as if he might have been recently ill.

Didn't he own any clothes of his own? Right now he was wearing a pair of Charlie's baggy shorts and a T-shirt she had once bought for Charlie after an Aerosmith concert. She chose not to mention the fact, however, afraid the boy would simply pull the T-shirt over his head and toss it to the floor like he had the robe. She had already seen more of Joe's body than she ever cared to. Had seen it all, in fact. And even now, the thought of that young body in Charlie's arms as he and Charlie lay naked on the bed upstairs, imagining the nights of passion the two must have shared, like the ones she and Charlie once shared, gnawed at her mind and made her strike out in the only way she knew how. With words.

"No offense, Joe," she said, forcing a tease to her voice that she certainly didn't feel, "but you aren't much of a cook."

It surprised her when Joe and Charlie both laughed. Mac thumped his tail on the floor at the sound of it.

"It's a talent I've yet to acquire," Joe said, his face suddenly beaming with happiness.

"No kidding," Charlie agreed.

Judith watched the two and wondered what the joke was. "Well, maybe you have other talents that I don't know about."

Joe shrugged. "Maybe I do." He reached across the table and touched her hand. "Would you like something else? We have frozen waffles. They're pretty good."

Charlie laughed again, even as Judith pulled her hand away from the boy's touch, ignoring the kindness of the gesture. Ignoring the warmth of it. She saw a flash of insight gleam in Joe's eyes at the feel of her skin on his, and she wondered what it meant. But even that thought did not distract her from her anger.

"No. This is fine." Her words were clipped. Terse. All pretense of friendly teasing gone in the space of two seconds.

She took another sip of wine, the wine Joe had poured for her unmagically from a bottle. Charlie, she noticed, was drinking milk.

To him, she said, "Are you on the wagon?"

Charlie answered around a mouthful of food. "I seem to have lost the urge for alcohol."

"Never thought I'd hear you say that," Judith said, honestly amazed.

Charlie gave a sheepish nod. "Me neither."

Joe was staring at her face intently now, as if he wanted to say something.

"What's wrong?" she asked, her annoyance more than apparent, although she hadn't intended it to be. It sort of got away from her. "Why are you staring at me like that?"

Joe gave her a timid smile that angered her ever further. "You shouldn't be drinking," he said.

Charlie looked over at Joe, then at Judith.

"Why do you say that?" she asked, forcing a smile to her face, ignoring Charlie, focusing all her attention on the boy. As if to show her independence, she lifted the glass of wine to her lips and took another sip.

Joe again made a move to reach out and touch her hand, perhaps to even take her glass away, then thought better of it. He laid his hands in his lap and said, "Your body has accepted his seed."

Her eyes flashed. "What the hell are you talking about?"

"You're pregnant."

Judith remembered Tom's sperm shooting into her only hours before he went up in flames like a torched Christmas tree, the bastard. Remembered his apologizing for it. Remembered, too, the way she had laughed it off, telling him not to worry. After four years of marriage with Charlie, and no small number of affairs before and after, she had never been pregnant yet. At thirty-two, in fact, she was beginning to wonder if she might not be barren, not that it mattered. A child was the last thing she wanted. Then as now.

She plastered a patient smile on her face that was about as sincere as Tom's apology. It felt all right, so she left it there. "I know Charlie thinks you have some special insights into this world that the rest of us don't have, but this time, Joe, I'm afraid you're barking up the wrong tree. In fact, you're talking out of your ass. Why the hell would you think I'm pregnant? I had my period three weeks ago and it was just as goddamn messy and miserable as it always is. But maybe you don't know much about women's bodies. Being queer, you probably don't know anything about them at all, so I'd appreciate it if you'd keep your opinions and your stupid extrasensory predictions to yourself."

Joe grinned as if he found her anger amusing. "It's a boy. Or will be. Right now it's little more than a mass of gelatin. Wouldn't you rather have a glass of milk?"

Charlie rested his hand on Joe's shoulder. "Are you sure?"

Seeing that look of unquestioning, insipid belief on Charlie's face was too much for Judith. She flung her napkin over her plate and pushed herself to her feet.

"If it isn't too much of an imposition," she said, looking directly at neither one of them, "I think I'll go clean up. I'd like to wash the bullshit off before it soaks in."

She grabbed her glass and, as an afterthought, the wine bottle, and stalked from the room.

When she was gone, Joe turned to Charlie and said, "I was wrong. She still loves you." He was still grinning.

Charlie grinned back. "Oh yeah. About as much as she loves you. I could feel the love just pouring out of her. Is she really pregnant?"

"Yes."

"Well, I guess she'll figure it out in a week or so when it's time for another period."

"How does that work, exactly?" Joe asked, like a basic math student asking his professor about the intricacies of higher geometry.

"You mean you don't know?"

"Well, not exactly."

"I'll explain it to you later."

"What's a queer?"

"What?"

"She said, being queer, I wouldn't understand about a woman's body."

"Never mind, Joe. It's not important."

Charlie took another bite of his overdone hamburger and thought, once again, of Joe's innocence when it came to the ways of this new world he found himself living in. The boy seemed to teeter constantly between ancient wisdom and guileless inexperience. At one moment he could be as naïve as a six-year-old, yet in the next moment be capable of such wonders that Charlie could barely understand the scope of all he was seeing.

Joe turned to Charlie and once again Charlie saw that incomprehensible *knowing* in Joe's eyes he had noticed only hours before. Charlie wondered at the meaning of it. He could not have imagined that the satin heat of Charlie's trembling body clinging to his in those first moments after their passion had burst forth claimed Joe's mind. Again, Joe saw the moonlight flooding across their damp bodies as their heartbeats slowed, as the taste of each other's climax still lingered sweetly on hungry lips. Joe knew it was a moment they could never experience again. He longed to free Charlie's mind to the memory, to let Charlie, too, remember that incredible hour they had shared, wondrously exploring each other, slaking their thirst for each other, but he knew he could not. The memory of that night would have to live in Joe's thoughts alone. It could be no other way.

"Joe," Charlie said. "Judith has never wanted children. Can't you… take it away from her?"

"No," Joe said. "The child already has a destiny of his own. He's alive even now, Charlie. He's in that field of white mist I once showed you. But soon he'll be here. To stop his journey now would be an unforgivable sin. My father has plans for him."

"What plans?"

"He will carry the truth about me into the next generation, Charlie."

"Judith's child?"

"Yes."

"But he doesn't know you."

"He will."

"How?"

"You will tell him."

"Joe. Judith doesn't believe you are who you are."

"Before it's over, she will."

Charlie thought about that. He laid his hand on Joe's arm, felt the heat beneath his palm, against his fingertips. Longed to feel even more of him. Tried to bury the ache of that longing beneath a blanket of words.

"She may try to abort the child herself, Joe. It's legal, you know. If she decides to do it, there's nothing we can do to stop her."

Joe smiled. "When she understands about me, she will understand about the child."

"But the child came from evil. His father was one of the burned. Doesn't that make a difference?"

"No, Charlie. Evil does not beget evil. Only goodness does that. And what evil could reside in the heart of a fetus? It's a creation of love. Nothing else. My father will not let evil touch the boy. His work is too important. You will not let evil touch the boy either."

"Me?"

"Just as you taught me, you will teach him. You will keep him safe from the world until he's ready. He will understand his fate, even if you do not. Take him safely into manhood, that's all you have to do. Judith will help you. She is a good woman, Charlie. She will be a good wife for you again. And she will need your help too. More than the boy, perhaps."

Charlie almost laughed. "I seriously doubt if she would consent to be my wife again, Joe. Even if I wanted her to be. And I don't. I want to be with you."

"While I am here, you will be."

"When you leave, Joe, I'm going with you."

Joe covered his sorrow with a grin. "We'll see. Now go to her. Talk to her. Show her that you still love her. Because I know you do."

"I love you more," Charlie said.

Joe stood and, bending over, pressed his lips to Charlie's forehead.

"I know," he said simply, and with Mac at his heels, he walked into the darkness outside the cabin, heading for the lake.

Charlie watched until the shadows swallowed them up.

CHARLIE TAPPED at the bathroom door. Without waiting for a response, since he figured the chances of her tossing out a welcome mat were pretty thin, he stepped on in as if he owned the place, which of course he did.

Judith was lying in the tub with bubbles up to her chin. The glass of wine next to the bottle, now half-empty he noticed, sat on the floor beside her. She arched her eyebrows when he walked through the door but said nothing. She studied him as he lowered the lid of the commode and sat down facing her.

"This is cozy," she finally said. "Where's Houdini?"

Charlie ignored the sarcasm and said, "He's out by the lake. He seems to draw inspiration from the water."

"Oh, good. Maybe he'll be inspired to learn how to cook."

The eyes hovering above the bubbles were still furious, Charlie saw. "Talk to her," Joe had said. Yeah, right. Would she listen? Seriously doubtful.

"So what's so special about the lake?" she asked, her words still laced with sarcasm. "Is it like a big crystal ball? Is that where he sees… whatever the hell you think it is he sees?"

"It calms him," Charlie said.

"Has he walked on it yet?"

"Yes."

Judith methodically squeezed the bathwater from her hair. "I see. I walked on it once myself. Of course, it was frozen solid at the time. I don't suppose it was frozen solid when Joe walked on it?"

Charlie's eyes crinkled with silent laughter. "No, dear."

"You're my ex. You have no right to call me 'dear.' So what did he do after he walked on water? Did he feed the masses with a couple of bluegills and a catfish?"

"There were no masses to feed, or I suppose he would have. I'm going to thoroughly enjoy your apology when he shows you who he truly is."

"When do you think that will be, Charlie? You know how I hate suspense."

"I don't know. Whenever he thinks the time is right, I imagine."

He watched her reach for the wine glass with a soapy hand. When she saw a flicker of concern cross Charlie's eyes, she stopped all pretense of banter. "Oh, for Christ's sake, Charlie! Don't you think I'd know if I was pregnant?"

"Maybe not. It's still early."

"You honestly believe this, don't you?"

"Yes."

"And he even knows the sex of the fetus."

"That's right. He said it's a boy."

"Amazing."

"Yes, he is."

Her eyes narrowed. "Stop talking about him like he's God. You sound like a fool."

"I never said he was God."

"Oh, that's right. He's only the *son* of God."

"Yep."

"What's it like having sex with the son of God? Does he know when you're about to come, even before you do?"

"We've never had sex."

"Oh, please. Judging by the way he looks at you, I think there's very little you haven't done together."

"That's true. But sex isn't one of them."

"Let me get this straight. Not only have you given up booze, but you've given up sex as well. Is that right? So now you're… what? An apostle?"

Charlie thought about that for a moment. *Was* he an apostle? Is that how history would think of him? Or was he nothing more than what he knew himself to be?

"I'm the painter," he said, putting it into words. "I'm the one he came to first because I can give his likeness to the world."

Judith's voice was flat. "His likeness."

"They'll want to know who they are worshiping."

"Worshiping."

"If you don't stop echoing my words, I'm going to hold your head underwater until you drown. Have another drink."

"He's taught you empathy, I see. Fine apostle you are."

"You're being stubborn and pigheaded. How else am I supposed to act?"

"I can't believe you expect me to buy this ridiculous story and maybe even bend down and kiss the little bastard's feet. He's a con man,

Charlie. It's the only explanation. Maybe he knows hypnosis. Maybe he hypnotized you into thinking you saw all these miracles you say you saw. Or maybe you're so madly in love with the fucker that you'll believe anything he says."

Charlie's mouth became a colorless, narrow line slashed across his face. "Don't talk about him like that."

"I'll talk about him any way I choose. Feeling the urge to hit me again, Charlie?"

"What about your friend, Judith? What about the baby's father? Joe told me even before the burnings he was using you."

"How could he know anything of the kind?"

"Who knows how he knows what he knows?"

"I've always admired your grammar."

"He wants me to help you raise the child."

Judith slapped the bathwater, and suds hit the wall. "There is no child!"

"When is your next period?"

"None of your business."

"He wants us to remarry."

"Hell, no."

"He thinks you still love me."

"He's crazier than you are."

"He thinks I still love you too."

"Queers don't like women. It's a biological fact."

"Have another drink."

"I think I will."

But she didn't. She studied Charlie's face instead.

"I know you love him, Charlie. It couldn't be any plainer if you painted it across your forehead in Day-Glo green. But you have to understand how… *silly* this whole thing is. A lot of people have gone a little wacky since the fires. Maybe that's what it is. Sort of a mass hysteria. People are as hot on religion now as they once were on Hula-Hoops. It's kind of a national pastime. Maybe you simply got caught up in that."

"You're wrong."

"Did Joe know the fires were coming?"

"Yes. He told me punishments were about to be doled out."

"So God was truly pissed this time."

"It would seem so."

"Why didn't Joe try to stop it? If he's another Jesus, why didn't he take the sins of the masses onto his own shoulders and give the poor sinners a break?"

"I guess God figured it didn't work so well the last time, so why flog a dead horse. This time he took a more hands-on approach."

"He certainly did."

Charlie looked at her. "So you believe now that it was God who set the burnings."

Judith shrugged, causing the bubbles to ripple atop the water. "I can't think of another explanation for it."

Charlie reached out and touched her hand as it rested on the edge of the tub. Her fingers, he noticed, were beginning to prune. "So don't you think that if God went to all the trouble to incinerate a few million sinners, he would also send a messenger to speak to the people who were spared? To let them know what happened? And why? He must know how stupid people are. They would otherwise probably have blamed the burnings on a new strain of flu or something."

Judith giggled. "The Asian Brimstone flu. You don't get it from chickens anymore. Or pigs. You get it by being a wicked asshole."

"Answer my question."

"Even if God did send a messenger," Judith said, "what the hell do you think the chances are that he would come to *you*? A bisexual artist with all the morals of a goat. Frankly, Charlie, I'm a little surprised that you weren't among the burnees."

"Thanks."

"Sorry. Didn't mean that."

A silence settled over them that wasn't entirely uncomfortable. She seemed to remember an evening exactly like this once upon a time, with Charlie sitting on the lid of the commode and her soaking in the tub in front of him as they talked about… what? Love? There was passion between them once. They had been happy together. For a while.

"*Do* you still love me, Charlie?"

Charlie's hand still rested on hers. "I… don't know."

"Do you love Joe?"

"Yes."

"Do you love him as a lover, or do you love him as a god?"

"Both."

She gently pulled her hand away from his. "I won't share you again, Charlie. I can't do that."

"I know."

"And I can't live in a loveless marriage."

"Do you think that's what we had?"

"I suppose not."

"He baptized me, you know."

"What?"

"In the lake. He held me beneath the water, and when I came up, I was a different person. I can't describe it to you. But I'm not the same person now as I was when we were together. I'll never be that person again. He's shown me things that I never knew existed. If you'll just open yourself up to him, he'll show them to you too."

"You sound like one of those pomaded televangelists. I hate you like this."

"I wish I could make you understand what is happening here. I wish I could make you believe the truth of who Joe is."

"The son of God."

"Yes."

"Maybe only Joe can do that. Have him show me a miracle, Charlie. Have him walk across the lake for me. Then we'll talk. Then maybe I'll believe what you believe."

"Will you?"

"Probably not."

"Why? Does it seem like such an impossibility to you?"

"Yes, Charlie. It does. I think you need help, Charlie. I think you need to get away from this person. If you could just sit back and listen to yourself, you'd know how insane this all is."

"He wants me to help you raise the child," Charlie said again, wearily this time, as if he knew it was a lost cause even as he uttered the words.

"There is no child," she said. "But if there was, I'd take care of it myself."

"But you don't work. How will you support a child? You can't even support yourself. You live off what you took from the divorce."

"What I *took*?"

"You know what I mean."

Her eyes were flashing again, and Charlie's eyes were beginning to flash right back at them. "I said I'd take care of it, Charlie. I didn't say I'd raise it."

"You're talking about abortion."

"Brilliant, Holmes. Now you see the light."

"He won't let you do that."

"Who? Joe? What business is it of his what I do with my own body?"

"It's not your body I'm talking about. It's the body of the child." Charlie heard his voice rising in anger and tried to control it. "There are things the child will do with his life that mustn't be stopped. It's important that he grow up to do them."

"Oh God, Charlie. Don't tell me we're talking about another apostle here. How many apostles does this guy need? Why doesn't he just go on national TV, do a few miracles for the press, a few holier-than-thou photo ops, and be done with it?"

"You will not abort the child."

"I'll do whatever I want."

"Then you'll do it on your own without any financial help from me."

"Fine."

She lifted the glass of wine to her lips.

"And stop drinking!" Charlie yelled.

"Fuck you, Charlie."

She took a long pull of wine from the glass and her eyes opened wide. She held the glass away from her and looked at it. "What the…?"

Charlie lifted the wine bottle and sniffed it, then tipped it up to take a sip. It was water. Pure, crystal water. Joe had apparently taken the matter of Judith's drinking into his own hands.

Charlie laughed until the tears squirted from his eyes.

CHAPTER SIXTEEN
...AT THE EDGE OF THE LAKE....

WHILE JUDITH furiously blew her short hair dry, all the while resisting the urge to fling the blow-dryer through the bathroom window, Charlie stood at the back door and watched Joe's silhouette as the boy stared out at the water. The lake shimmered with moonlight. Mac sat patiently beside Joe in the darkness. Later, perhaps, when his present canvas was finished, Charlie might pluck this image from his memory and put it to paper. It would be best done in charcoal. Simple linear strokes forming shadow and light. The colorless, leaden calm of night and silence. A pensive sketch. The son of God gazing out upon a newly cleansed world.

Or just a boy and his dog.

Charlie chuckled at that thought.

He could hear Judith slamming things around in the bathroom. She had never been one for sulky silences. If she was mad, you damn well knew it, and Charlie knew it now. He drew some comfort in knowing she could not abort the child without money, but he also knew if abortion was something she really wanted, she would find a way to do it. He supposed it would rest on Joe's shoulders to see that she didn't, for Charlie himself would be powerless to stop it. It wasn't even his child. And it was true that, as Judith said, a woman could do with her own body what she wanted. In the eyes of the law, at least.

Perhaps when she understood who Joe truly was, she would reconsider. What choice would she have? Certainly, the chardonnay turning to water must have given her something to think about. Good old Joe. That was a good one.

Charlie could hear Joe at the moment, humming softly to himself as he stood by the lake. It was a hymn Charlie remembered from his own childhood, his mother's favorite. "In The Garden." His mother was gone now. His father too. Because of his mother's love for the hymn, it was one he had chosen for their joint funeral after the car crash took their lives several years earlier. Charlie wondered if Joe knew about that. He probably did, Charlie decided. There was very little the boy seemed *not* to know, aside from such mundane things as how to fry chicken or the correlation between a woman's menstrual cycle and pregnancy or the demeaning and insulting definition of the word "queer." Yet even in his innocence, Joe could still pull rain from the sky and a waterspout from the lake and save a sinning artist from the miseries of a burning eternity, changing the contents of his heart with nothing more than a flick of his fingertip. Joe could not only raise the dead, but the living as well. Raise them high above what they actually were. If the boy could do this for him, he could also do it for Judith.

But even that thought troubled Charlie. In proving himself to Judith, Joe would be sharing himself with her. It would be the first step, perhaps, in his sharing of himself with the world. And with every instance of sharing, Joe would be pulling farther away from Charlie's side.

As Charlie continued to watch the boy standing in the moonlight, Judith stood in front of the bathroom mirror and stared at her reflection. How *had* the wine turned to water like that? Could Charlie be telling the truth? She could still see the anger on her own face in the mirror, but she was beginning to see doubt there too. Charlie was many things, but a fool wasn't one of them. He had certainly changed. Judith could see that as clearly as she saw her own growing confusion in the fogged-up mirror. If God had taken the trouble to burn sin from the world, he *would* send a messenger to explain it to the masses. But why would the messenger come here, to this out of the way place in the middle of nowhere? And why, of all the people in the world, would he come to Charlie? If Joe wanted his image presented to the masses, why didn't he just go online and beam his likeness out into cyberspace? Or make an appointment at Sears and sit for a couple of 5 x 9s and a few billion wallet-sizes?

Wrapped in a towel, Judith climbed the stairs to the loft and found something to wear from her suitcase, which Charlie had put on the bed. Feeling no need to impress anyone, she donned faded jeans and a Ship 'n Shore blouse that she had worn for a decade. It was the most comfortable thing she owned. As she rummaged deeper into the bag looking for her sandals, a glint of dark metal caught her eye, and she pulled the revolver from the tube sock she had wrapped it in back in Dallas. She stared at the gun for long seconds while a dozen thoughts went stampeding through her mind. Thoughts of Tom, of course, for it was his gun she now held in her hand. She had thought it might come in handy for a single woman driving across country, but now she wondered if it might not serve another purpose. Maybe she could scare some sense into Charlie with it, or better yet, maybe she could scare some sense into Joe. Perhaps even drive him away. It would be for Charlie's own good if she did. Maybe Charlie would even thank her for it one day. Or maybe he would never forgive her. Either way, she thought it was worth the risk. A bit of shock therapy seemed to be exactly what was needed here.

Judith was no atheist, as Charlie once was. Nor was she agnostic. She had always believed in a higher power, a belief embedded in her through years of Sunday services and Bible schools when she was a child growing up in a small town in Ohio not more than three hundred miles from where she now stood. Her parents were devout Methodists. They had instilled in her an acceptance of God, and although her own life had perhaps swayed her from the path a few times, she still did not doubt God's existence.

She did doubt, however, that Joe was his messenger. His son. She had seen the way Joe looked at Charlie. She knew desire when she saw it, and she had seen it there in Joe's eyes. Charlie might *say* the two of them had never had sex, but Judith knew better. The idea that the son of God might come down to earth in the body of a homosexual—a *faggot*, for Christ's sake—was not a hypothesis Judith ever remembered hearing in Bible school. She was pretty sure her mother would have keeled over in a dead faint just to imagine such a thing.

No, the boy had simply used Charlie's love for him, twisting it into an impossible scenario Charlie was too smitten to see through, and it was up to Judith to knock some sense into his head. What the boy really wanted from Charlie, Judith didn't know. And frankly, she didn't care. She just wanted Charlie freed from his clutches, one way or another. She wasn't about to shoot the kid, but she thought a little of that primal fear that came from looking down the barrel of a revolver might serve to clear the air considerably. And maybe even send the kid packing.

Deeper in her mind, down past the place where she thought of helping Charlie by scaring the boy away, she also thought of getting Charlie back. She did still love him, of course. She supposed she had always known that, although she had never let herself admit it. But seeing him again had changed her perspective. And seeing him with Joe, seeing what Joe had done to Charlie, seeing how Joe had made such a fool of Charlie, making him believe the son of God had come to him and him alone, infuriated her. She knew without a doubt that while Joe was still in the picture, she would never get Charlie back. The kid would have to go.

One way or another. She would not share Charlie again. With anyone. And certainly not with a con artist.

After tucking the revolver in the waistband at the back of her jeans and covering it with the tail of her blouse, hoping all the while she wouldn't blow her own ass off, she slammed the suitcase shut and headed back downstairs.

Not once did she think her actions were being directed by Joe himself. Not believing in the boy, that realization was beyond her. As Joe, smiling in the darkness by the water's edge, knew it would be.

AFTER LISTENING to Judith climb the stairs to the bedroom, Charlie stepped outside and joined Joe by the lake. As he drew near, Mac turned to look at him at the same moment Joe stopped softly humming Charlie's mother's favorite hymn.

Charlie placed a hand on Joe's back, and together they stared out at the water. Joe cocked his head at the sound of an owl hooting somewhere off in the trees, then said, "She has to be made to understand, Charlie. It's the only way the child will survive."

Charlie sighed. "I tried talking to her, but she's got her Irish dander up. There's no way to get through to her when she's like that. Trust me. I know. Hell, she doesn't even believe a child exists."

"She needs a miracle," Joe said. "That's all. One simple miracle."

Charlie smiled. "Yeah, turning the wine into water didn't quite do it. Nice touch, though."

Joe smiled too. "Would like to have seen the look on her face."

Charlie chuckled again at the memory. "That *was* worth the price of admission. But I think you'll need to be a little less subtle. How about another waterspout? Or a leisurely stroll across the lake?"

"The matter's already been taken care of. Judith will create the miracle herself." *And that will set other wheels in motion.* But Charlie did not need to know of those. If he even suspected what was about to happen, Charlie would do everything in his power to stop it, and that could not be allowed.

Joe spoke quietly in the darkness, his words meant for Charlie's ears alone. "I cannot heal myself. You know that, don't you?"

Charlie thought of the days of illness when fever and chills tore at the boy's body. It had not occurred to him even once to wonder why Joe did not lay his hands upon himself, turn his incredible powers inward, and make the pain, the sickness, go away.

"Y-yes. I guess I know that. But what are you telling me?"

"I'm telling you to do what your heart tells you to do, Charlie." He reached out and laid a warm hand to Charlie's cheek. "Just as you've always done."

Charlie leaned into the warmth of Joe's palm and brought his own hand up, laying it over the boy's. "I will do whatever you want me to do."

"No," Joe said. "You must do what *you* want to do. If you believe in me, Charlie, if you trust me, no harm will be done."

"What sort of harm?" Charlie asked, fingers of worry beginning to claw at his stomach.

Once again, Joe pressed his lips to Charlie's forehead. The boy's breath was as sweet as spring rain on Charlie's face. "Just love me, Charlie," he said, "and I will protect you as you've always protected me."

"You know I love you."

"Then don't worry."

Charlie sighed. "All right."

At the sound of the cabin door opening and closing, they both turned to watch Judith approach them through the moonlight.

Joe saw his own death approaching as clearly as he saw the new moon hanging over his head.

But not tonight, Father.

Tonight, Joe knew, death was reserved for another.

THE GUN pushed against the small of her back like a pound of scrap iron, as cold and hard as a chunk of ice. It weighed her down like the drag of an anchor holds a ship in the tide. She seemed barely able to move. Guns had always frightened her, and here she was packing one like some undercover movie cop, only the one she carried wasn't a plastic prop, but the real thing. Loaded and ready to go, or so she assumed, since she wasn't completely sure how to check and see. But she couldn't imagine Tom leaving an unloaded gun lying around. What would be the point? Besides, for what she intended to do that night, it didn't matter if the gun was loaded or not. She had no plans to shoot anyone. Before she could think what it was she really *did* intend to do, she was already standing in front of Charlie and the boy, and for a moment, she had the sensation that she was not directing her own movements. Like that undercover movie cop, she seemed to be taking directions from somewhere off set. And that was a good thing. Without it, she might not find the courage to do what she felt needed to be done. In the darkness, she could not see the compassion, the sympathy, on Joe's face. Before the night was finished, Joe knew, this woman's life would be changed forever. He pitied her the pain she would soon suffer, but it could not be avoided.

He patiently waited and watched as his own fate began to unfold. Seeing it as from a distance, as if it were not choreographed by his own hand. Choreographed, indeed, in three precise acts. Murder. Resurrection. Expulsion. And those three precise acts would be performed by each of the three players standing now at the edge of the lake. Judith, Joe, and Charlie.

And then, performed before a cast of thousands, the most important act of all. Betrayal. The reason for it all. Only after tonight's events could that final act occur. It would happen here, by this very lake, and it would happen soon. Not tonight, but soon. Joe's time as a living man would then be over, his purpose fulfilled. For even as Joe directed these players, the father directed him. And as the father chose death for the first son, he had also chosen death for the second.

This woman would make it happen.

And it would destroy her.

I'm sorry, Joe thought, watching her. *Please forgive me.*

THERE WAS a tremor in Judith's voice when she spoke, but there was determination in it too.

"I want you to leave, Joe. Tonight. Right this minute. Pack your bags, if you have any, and get the hell out of here."

It was Charlie who answered her. "Judith, what do you think you're doing?"

"I'm saving you, Charlie. In the only way I know how."

"Don't be stupid." His anger was rising. Even Mac could sense it, tensing at his feet. "You're the guest here, not Joe. What makes you think you can waltz into my home and start barking orders at every…?"

"There's no other way," Judith said, and before she knew she had done it, she pulled the gun from behind her and aimed it at the boy.

In the darkness, Charlie did not see the look of sadness cross Joe's face as the boy stood silently beside him, as if patiently waiting for the drama to unfold. Charlie saw only the gun in Judith's hand.

"What are you going to do?" Charlie asked, forcing himself to remain calm even while his heart did a somersault. "Shoot him? What the hell's wrong with you? And since when do you own a gun?"

Judith ignored him, staring only at Joe. "Go now," she said. "Go back to wherever it is you came from, Joe. You aren't wanted here."

Joe's answer was barely audible. "No," he said quietly. "I can't do that. Not yet."

Charlie took a step toward her. "Judith, you don't understand." Then he turned to Joe, desperately seeking out the boy's eyes in the shadows. "Show her who you are, Joe. Make her believe like you made me believe."

Softly, to Charlie, Joe said, "She will believe before the night is over. Don't be afraid."

"My God!" Judith fumed, her hand now trembling as much from anger as from the weight of the gun. "Would you listen to you two? Charlie, the kid's got you mesmerized into thinking he's something he isn't."

"No," Charlie said, "he is who he is."

"A con artist."

"The son of God, Judith. This boy is the son of God. Damn it, Joe! Show her!"

Joe calmly pushed his hair from his eyes. "No."

"Because he can't!" Judith raved. "Because he's a fraud!"

"Because I don't wish to," Joe said, once again staring sadly through the darkness at the woman.

The fear inside Charlie was no longer something he could hide. Things were getting out of hand. "Give me the gun, Judith. Just give me the gun, and we'll talk."

"No," she answered. "There's been enough talk."

And in the darkness, Charlie heard the ratchet of the gun as she pulled the hammer back. The sound of it surprised Judith as much as Charlie. Only the boy seemed unaffected by the sound.

"Go now," she said again to Joe, her resolve strengthened by that unholy sound of metal on metal ratcheting through the darkness. The weight of the gun in her hand seemed to be the center of her being now. It no longer frightened her. It gave her strength. She knew now that she could do what she had really not intended to do at all. She could kill this boy. She *wanted* to kill this boy. She smiled as the realization hit her.

This is the right thing to do.

"Judith, no!"

Charlie flung himself between the two just as Judith, blinded by hatred and by other forces she knew nothing about, calmly pulled the trigger.

CHAPTER SEVENTEEN
...SOWING THE FINAL SEED....

THE MUZZLE flash strobed their faces in an explosion of light, creating a momentary tableau in crisp black and white there in the darkness beside the moonlit lake. Could Charlie have stepped back and witnessed that fleeting chiaroscuro of madness with his artist's unbiased eye, he would have been sorely tempted to put it to canvas.

In that mind-numbing scream of light and sound, Judith stood with her arm outstretched, the gun in her hand spitting fire, illuminating the cool fury in her eyes. There was a determined, yet clinical, tilt to her head, as if she knew she had every right in the world to do what she was doing.

Mac lay at her feet, cowering flat to the ground beneath the weight of that unearthly explosion of noise, his eyes wide and fearful.

Joe stood calmly in the strobe, handsome and serene, observing the woman dispassionately, watching events unfold he alone had set in motion. The moon-sparkled water of the lake shimmered like a quilt of diamonds behind him. A gust of evening air playfully lifted the hair from his forehead at the precise moment the light of the gunshot exploded over him.

And Charlie, the only one with fear on his face—fear for Joe, not himself—stretched his mouth wide in a silent, anguished scream as the bullet meant for Joe tore into his own body. He looked down in surprise as a blood-red flower, as beautiful as any in his garden, blossomed from his chest. The bullet burrowed deep inside Charlie's flesh, seeking a home for itself as it left a trail of bleeding destruction in its wake. It silenced Charlie's heart before his spattering blood could fall to earth. His life was gone before the echoing concussion of the gunshot had died around them, plunging them all back to a silent darkness.

In those returning shadows, Judith heard the sound of Charlie's body crumpling to the ground. The realization of what she had done suddenly flooded through her. The gun fell from her hand, and a wail of horror erupted from her throat as she flung herself over Charlie's silent body. She felt the heat of his blood surging over her hands in the darkness. And she felt the heat of damnation too, as it closed down around her. Weeping, she waited for flames to engulf her, as they had engulfed Tom, but the flames did not come. The burnings were over. Other anguish awaited her. She could feel it in the silence of Charlie's body beneath her. Could smell it in the cool air, no longer a pleasure, but chilling now, biting, wafting off the lake.

Gentle hands pulled Judith to her feet, and in the moonlight, through her tears, she saw Joe's face before her, the untroubled smile on his lips the last thing she expected to see. She opened her mouth to speak, but there was nothing she could say. Her shame silenced her as completely as death had silenced Charlie.

"Do not fear," Joe said. "Let me help him."

Scooping Charlie's limp body into his arms, Joe carried the only human he had ever loved, the only human he had ever harmed, through the door of the cabin and laid him gently on the kitchen floor.

Judith watched in stunned silence as the boy bent over Charlie's still body. He tore the blood-soaked shirt aside to lay his hand upon the horrible wound in Charlie's chest, which still oozed blood even in death. She watched in trembling silence as the boy bowed his head to kiss the wound, to lay his young hand, bloodied now, on Charlie's forehead. As a tear fell from his eye and dropped to Charlie's flesh, the wound closed, the oozing blood stopped seeping, the flower that had opened in Charlie's chest pulled its petals together and disappeared completely. But for a smear of blood, the chest she had so many times kissed in passion became as flawless and beautiful as Judith always remembered it being.

When Charlie took a ragged breath and slowly opened his eyes, Judith collapsed to her knees and sobbed as if the weight of the world had just been lifted from her shoulders. She reached out a trembling hand to touch Charlie's cheek, and feeling the warmth of life beneath her palm, the flutter of his eyelashes across her fingertips, she laid her head on Joe's bended knees and clutched Joe to her. She buried her face into the warmth of Joe's strong legs, understanding his power, now, and knowing at last who the boy truly was, believing it all, just like Charlie had said she would.

"Joe," she whispered, "forgive me."

And Joe rested his bloody hand softly atop her head. "You are forgiven," he said.

She raised her face, still streaming with tears, to look at him, but as their eyes connected, she heard Charlie's voice. She gazed down at him, already seeking the words in her mind to ask for his forgiveness as well, but the anger in his eyes silenced her before the words could be found. A look of such hatred burned in his gaze that Judith recoiled from the heat of it. Never before had human eyes looked at her with such loathing. Her shame returned in an overwhelming rush that made her gasp.

"Oh, God, Charlie, I'm so s—"

"Get out," Charlie said, his voice torn by both emotion and by the trauma his body had just endured. And by the hatred, too, that billowed out of him like an icy tide. "Get out of my house."

"Please, Charlie," Judith pleaded, dropping her head to Charlie's chest, not caring about the blood there, not caring about *anything* but the need to stem the tide of self-loathing that Charlie's words had burned into her. "I didn't mean to...."

Charlie roughly pushed her away, and she gasped again as those hands, which had so many times carried her to a place of passion, now rejected her completely.

Charlie raised himself to one elbow, feeling the weakness of blood loss but no pain as he stared back coldly at the shattered look Judith gave him. He felt no pity in his heart for the woman before him. The tears on her face meant nothing to him. Her pleadings were a mindless noise that merely angered him further.

His words spat out of him with the same force, and with the same intent to inflict damage, as the bullet had spat from the gun. And his words tore into the woman's heart as fiercely as the bullet had pierced his own.

"You tried to kill him, you fucking *cunt*! You fucking *Judas*! You should have burned with the rest of them!"

"No, I...."

"All the others were choirboys compared to you! They only murdered each other! But *you*! You tried to murder the only decent thing that's left in this world! He came here for you, you know! He came here to protect you! He came here to make the world a better place and all you can think to do is put a gun in his face and pull the trigger! A thousand hells would be too good for you!"

"No, I...."

Charlie's face grew as red as the blood drying upon his chest. Spittle, like venom, flew from his pale lips. "Get out! Now!"

"Charlie, please...." In horror, Judith felt Charlie's hands grip her shoulders and push her away from him. Away from Joe. Losing her balance, she fell to the floor, her tears almost blinding her. The hatred from Charlie's face she saw swimming in her vision began to seep into her from her own mind. What had she done? This wasn't her. This couldn't be her. How could she have done what she did?

She reached out to Charlie with a trembling hand, but he slapped it away. Seeing the cold hatred still burning in his furious eyes, she collapsed to the floor and buried her face in her arms. She wailed out her grief for what she had done, tried to hide her guilt even from herself as she closed her eyes to the room, to the night, to Charlie's fury. She felt the cold floor against her face, the hot tears streaming down her cheeks. She fought to breathe through her rasping sobs, but tried most of all to forget the sound of that horrible gunshot stabbing the night. To take it back. To push it all away from her as if it never happened. But the memory of it would not go. And in that instant, she knew it never would. She would carry this night with her for the rest of her life. Charlie would never forgive her.

Just as she would never forgive herself.

She felt a gentle touch at the back of her neck. A brush of fingertips. A soft caress of compassion. Opening her eyes, she turned, hoping to see Charlie there, but it was Joe's face that hovered over her. It was Joe's hand that offered her solace. She saw no hatred on the boy's face as he looked down at her. Only pity.

She wiped the tears from her eyes and gazed up at the boy, understanding once again who he truly was, and understanding yet again what she had almost done to him.

At the feel of the boy's hand sliding gently across her cheek, she closed her eyes and felt his forgiveness enter into her. But the words he softly spoke were not the words she expected to hear.

Cringing still from the look of hatred on Charlie's face, Judith dropped her eyes and listened to the words the boy whispered in her ear.

"Leave us," Joe said, one warm hand resting at the nape of her neck, the other still caressing her cheek. "Fulfill your purpose."

Feeling the glare of Charlie's burning eyes upon her, she took a great shuddering breath and asked in a fearful voice, "What is my purpose, Joe? What is it… you want me to do?"

The boy lifted her hands, still covered in Charlie's blood, to his face and, kissing each of her palms, smeared the blood onto himself. She tried to pull her hands away, but his grip was strong. She could not escape his hold. When she gazed up into his face again, his eyes were cold. As cold, as full of hate, as Charlie's.

Frightened now, she tried to pull away, but Joe would not release her. He was hurting her. Purposely. Her hands were aching in his grasp.

"You know what you have to do," the boy quietly said.

Again, she tried to pull her bloodied hands away from his. Anger began to rise in her with the pain of his fingers pressing into her flesh, at the look of loathing on his face where she had only a moment ago seen forgiveness.

"Soon," Joe said, "this will be *my* blood on your hands. That's what you really want, isn't it?"

"Yes!" she spat, still trying to free her hands from that awful pressure. Her fingers were turning white under Charlie's blood. Soon she would hear the crack of bone as her fingers gave way beneath Joe's twisting, unrelenting grip. Her hatred for the boy flooded through her again, as it had the first time she saw him standing naked in the studio. She didn't care at the moment who he was. She only knew she wanted him dead.

He leaned closer. So close his lips brushed her ear. Feeling his breath upon her skin, she heard him say, softly so that Charlie would not hear, "Betray me and I will die. Only then will Charlie be yours." He laid his hand to her stomach, and she knew in that instant that there was a life there, growing inside her, just as the boy had said. "If anything happens to the child, you will burn forever. Now go."

Joe released her then, pulling his hands from her body as if the mere touch of her caused him pain.

Laying her bloody, aching hands to the floor, she crawled away from him, away from Charlie, far enough to be out of their reach, and then pulling herself to her feet, she fled the room, the cabin, still sobbing—as much from anger in that moment as remorse. She wore her rediscovered hatred for the boy like a shroud as she flung herself out into the night. And with her went the gelatinous mass that was her unborn child growing inside her.

At the sound of her car's tires on the gravel lane receding into the distance, Joe dropped his head to Charlie's chest, exhausted, spent. His show of taunting hatred for the woman, although a farce, had drained him. The pain he had caused her, the remorse she had offered him but that he had seemingly turned his back to, made him feel small and cruel. Tears began to pool in Joe's eyes at the memory of the woman's face, crushed beyond all hope of salvation, when he had spoken his cold words to her. They were words she needed to hear to make her do what was expected of her. But they were words, perhaps, that she would never truly understand.

Charlie wrapped his arms around Joe and pulled him to him, and at the feel of Charlie's living body beneath him, Joe wept.

"What did you say to her?" Charlie finally asked.

But Joe did not answer. He merely pressed his lips to the warmth of Charlie's chest, tasting the cooling blood and feeling the renewed heartbeat beneath. He let his tears fall unashamedly once again upon the flesh of this man he loved so deeply. The man he would soon leave behind. But his tears were for the woman, not for Charlie. Not for himself.

Forgive her, Father, Joe whispered in silent prayer, closing his eyes to the memory of Judith's pain.

And to himself, he said, *There. It is done.*

Raising his head to gaze upon Charlie's face, he wiped the tears from his eyes and said, "We have work to do, Charlie. We must finish the painting tonight. Before the sun rises."

And to himself, he said, in words that only he could hear, *Before death finds me.*

Taking Charlie's hand, he led him out into the darkness, and for the last time they entered the studio together. There, at the basin against the wall, Joe washed the blood from their bodies, and when they were clean and their bloodied clothes thrown into a corner and forgotten, Joe stood once again before Charlie, unclothed and unashamed, and reached his arms out to either side in *Freedom*'s pose. Charlie, clad now only in the bathrobe the boy had draped across his shoulders, took a brush in his hand and faced the unfinished canvas.

As Charlie entered that special place where his painting always took him, Joe closed his eyes and willed all memory of what had transpired this night from Charlie's mind. Just as the memory of their night of passion no longer lived in Charlie, now Charlie's death at the hands of the woman he once loved did not live within him either. Until the day of his true death, Charlie would carry with him no memory of what had happened on this night at the edge of the lake.

Only Judith, miles away now, would carry that burden within her.

And she always would.

CHAPTER EIGHTEEN
…BLOOD MONEY….

WEEPING, ALMOST blinded by tears, Judith manhandled the lurching car along the bumpy, winding path that led from the cabin to the highway. Her heart was a dull ache, a thudding misery, pounding away inside her. It did not beat, it throbbed. A screaming wound. Judith's every thought, every emotion, was blunted by shame and humiliation.

At a turn in the rutted lane, her headlights illuminated a doe and her fawn standing just off the road among the trees. They looked up, startled, as the headlights swept over them. At any other time, Judith would have slowed the car to better appreciate the beauty of those two sylvan creatures standing in the moonlight, but not tonight. She could not know that they were there, alive on this summer night, only because of Joe, and had she known she would not have cared.

She had already seen the boy's ability to resurrect life. Another example of it would have meant nothing to her.

What mattered most to Judith at this moment was the stench of blood on her hands and clothes. She rolled the windows down to let the night air sweep through the car and carry it away, but still she could feel the blood drying on her skin. She fumbled in the darkness of the back floorboard for something to wipe it away. She found a cloth—in the dark she couldn't tell what it was—and she stopped the car at the edge of the lane and poured water from a bottle of stale Evian that rested in the cup holder beside her onto the cloth, which she now saw was a blouse, and washed the blood away as best she could.

When she was finished, she threw the blouse out the window and drove on. She could feel the eyes of the doe and her fawn watching from the trees as her taillights disappeared in the distance. And she could feel other eyes upon her as well. Joe's eyes, perhaps. Could he see her now? Was he following her on the wind, hovering above her, just out of sight, watching every move she made? Were his eyes still accusing, still burning with hatred, like Charlie's had been, or were they now filled with compassion, as they had been for a little while after the shooting? She had seen forgiveness there in those bottomless brown eyes, hadn't she? If only for a moment? Where had it gone? Why had his look turned to loathing so suddenly? She had felt Joe's forgiveness enter into her, she knew she had, only to be replaced by a cool and calculated hatred moments later.

Again, the echo of the gunshot blasted through her mind. The sound of Charlie's body striking the ground, dead before he ever reached it, reverberated through her like a boom of thunder. She recoiled at the memory, felt her tears rain down yet again as she gripped the wheel and blindly drove on through the night, not knowing what her destination would be, only knowing she must escape. Escape from the echoes. Escape from her guilt. Escape from Joe.

Charlie had saved the boy. He had offered up his own life to do so, as if he knew his death would be taken back. He had thrown his body between Joe and the gun without a moment of hesitation. Did he have such faith in the boy's powers that he would forfeit his own life to protect Joe's, in the unwavering certainty that Joe would allow no lasting harm to come to him? Did he honestly believe that as long as the boy stood there beside him, even death could not touch him?

And it was true, wasn't it? No harm had come to him. She recalled the way the bloody hole in Charlie's chest had simply closed before her eyes with a gathering together of flesh when Joe's tears fell upon it. Joe had returned Charlie's life to him as easily as a magician produces a rabbit from his hat. But this was no illusion, no Hollywood special effect. There was nothing false or deceptive in what she had seen. It had been simply…

… a miracle.

What was it Charlie had called her? Judas? Is that what the boy meant when he taunted her, when he all but *commanded* her to betray him? Did he *want* her to tell the world about him, to give him up for thirty pieces of silver, or whatever the hell it was? Did he want to make Judith hated for all eternity, to make her name synonymous with betrayal for all the ages to come? Was that the role she was destined to play in Joe's little drama?

Did he want to die, just as Jesus had died, and was that the only way his destiny could be fulfilled? Was that what this was all about? Was she to be the implement of his death, and with death, his martyrdom? But what would be the point of martyrdom now? The world was already burned clean of evil, wasn't it?

Or was it? She was still here, wasn't she? Her actions tonight had been the purest form of evil. Maybe Charlie was right when he said she was worse than all the others. If she could have done it, she would have killed the boy tonight. Only Charlie had prevented it from happening. Where had her hatred for Joe come from? It couldn't be merely jealousy that made her do what she did. She wanted Charlie back, yes. She knew that now. But would she kill for him? Did she act on her own, or had her actions been prompted by Joe himself?

The boy *was* God's messenger, God's son, she believed that now without a doubt. But why would God send the boy to the shore of that secluded lake? What message could Joe deliver to the world from there?

Judith recalled Charlie's painting of the boy. *Freedom*, he called it. The beauty of that portrait, even unfinished, had struck a chord inside her when she first looked at it. The eyes in the canvas had gazed out at her as if she were the only person they were meant to see. It would be the same for anyone who saw it. Those eyes. So sweet. So beautiful. So forgiving. They would explain it all. The burnings. The deaths. The destruction of sin. Everything. And they would offer hope. Hope for the future. Just as Charlie had said it would, the painting would give the world a face to worship. Not just an abstract idea, but a living face. On the canvas, Joe's outstretched arms had seemed to enfold her, protect her, as they would for anyone who gazed upon them. Charlie was right when he said his talent as a painter was the reason Joe came to him. She could see the truth of that now. Charlie could make Joe a living entity to the masses. He could make him real.

But to be real, to be worshiped, Joe would have to be brought to the attention of the world. And only the sin of betrayal would accomplish that. It was a sin, it would seem, which she alone had been chosen to perform. Would she burn in hell for it, or was she merely a pawn? Would Joe forgive her if she gave him up to the world, dragging him into the limelight like a lamb to the slaughter? Would God forgive her? Or would they both turn their back on her as Charlie had done?

And what of the child? Joe had told her she would burn in hell if any harm came to the child growing inside her, and she believed him. Above all else, if for no other reason than to save herself from eternal fire, she must protect the child. Why Joe was so adamant in protecting the child she did not know or care. She cared only that her own survival depended on it.

But how could she care for a child? She had counted her money before she reached the cabin that night, and she had only twelve dollars to her name. It was all that remained of the two hundred dollars Tom had left her with. She could live for a while on her credit cards, she supposed, but how long could that charade last? Where would she find work? What was she trained to do? Would she be destined to live a life of poverty and drudgery to keep food on the table, or would Charlie take her back as Joe said he would? Was Charlie as much a pawn in all this as she was? Had Joe orchestrated everything that was happening here?

Thirty pieces of silver….

She was on the highway now. It was so late at night there was very little traffic. The solitude gave her time to think. A plan began to form in her mind. There was one way to get money without having to humble herself and beg it from Charlie, who would probably turn her down anyway. He had, after all, driven her from his house in shame. Spat her out of his life like sputum from a diseased lung. He was with Joe now. Perhaps they were laughing at her, remembering the way she had slunk away, remembering the way she had gaped so stupidly when Joe healed Charlie's wound, the wound she herself had inflicted.

Joe wanted death. That much she understood. A glitter of hatred burned in her eyes as she stared out blindly at the empty miles of highway unfolding beneath her. Yes, she thought. Why not? If it's death the boy wants, then why shouldn't she be the one to give it to him? She would play her role as the boy directed. And with him dead, Charlie would take her back, if for no other reason than to protect the child.

The child she already hated as much as she hated Joe.

As she drove on through the night, burning up the miles, getting as far away from the cabin as she could, away from Charlie, away from Joe, she saw around her the evidence of the fires that had swept across the world only a week before. Blackened husks of automobiles dotted the highway. In her headlights, behind a patch of well-kept lawn bordered by heat-seared roses, she saw the spire of a charred brick chimney poking up from the ashes where a house once stood. Who had died inside that house? Inside those cars? What were their crimes? Were they any greater than her own?

Up ahead she saw the lights of a service station. She steered the car off the highway and parked it beside a dusty phone booth standing at the edge of the lot like a lone sentinel. Rummaging for coins in her change purse, she thought…

… thirty pieces of silver.

She would, she knew, betray the boy for far less than that if she had to. But why should she? There could be profit in this if she played her cards right. Profit and revenge.

Judith would give Joe what he wanted.

And she would enjoy doing it.

Coins in hand, she dug through the flotsam in her purse until she found her little black book of phone numbers. There, as she knew she would, she found the number she sought.

Stepping from the car, she entered the phone booth and closed the door behind her, triggering the light overhead. As she pushed her coins through the slot with a hand still tinged with blood, one word kept screaming inside her head.

Judas…. Judas…. Judas….

EVER SINCE the day of the burnings, Edgar Fosse's mistress had been driving him crazy, dragging him to church every day of the goddamn week, insisting suddenly on a wedding ring to take the stinging miasma of sin, or what she *perceived* as sin, from their relationship, and making him feel like a card-carrying *husband*, for Christ's sake, even before the ceremony had taken place. He *would* marry her, he supposed. What choice did he have? He had four thousand bucks invested in the woman, after all. Invested in her tits, at least. Two thousand each, if you wanted to break it down. And he had to admit, they were something glorious to behold. Or just hold.

He had paid for them, not from his commission from Strickland's latest painting as he had planned, but out of his own pocket, it turned out, since the man who should have paid for Strickland's last masterpiece, not to mention Molly's tits, or at least one of them, via Edgar's commission, had gone up in smoke with the rest of the world's assholes. Along with the painting.

But Edgar figured he maybe shouldn't get too worked up about that. In the long run, he was probably lucky he wasn't a little pile of ashes right now himself. He had never been the most amiable of men, he grudgingly admitted, but he supposed that wasn't enough, really, to attract the wrath of God, if that's what the burnings really were, and he could think of no legitimate reason to think they were not. That's what Molly said, anyway. And she said it with such conviction, standing there with her shiny new tits poking piously up to the heavens, that Edgar was beginning to believe her.

He had only that evening learned about the fire that had destroyed his check and Charlie's triptych of the Chicago skyline, the skyline he could see right now through his bathroom window. In the morning he would phone Charlie and tell him, assuming of course that C. A. Strickland himself, artiste extraordinaire and royal pain in the ass, wasn't also a little pile of ashes right now, drifting in the wind and settling into the crevices of a lush, fragrant Indiana countryside like the stinky residue of some cheapass cigar. He wondered what Charlie was working on at the moment, or if he was working at all. If not, then it would be up to Edgar to get the bastard painting again. Maybe something spiritual this time. Shoot for what the market demands, that was Edgar's motto, and the world, like Molly, was suddenly so enamored of religion and all things holy that something along those lines would be sure to fetch a commanding price—of which Edgar Fosse, agent extraordinaire, would reap 15 percent. Art? Patooie! Religion? Who gave a shit? Money's what mattered. It might be a brave new world they were all living in since the fires, but some things never changed, and money happened to be one of them.

The hour was late. He could hear Molly snoring softly beside him in their four-acre California King. She never used to snore. Maybe the weight of her new tits was compressing her lungs like a bellows, squeezing the air right out of her. He could see them now in the moonlight, like two hills poking out of the prairies. God, they were magnificent! Well worth the price. And to think he had almost talked her out of them. Well, live and learn.

He snaked his hand across the wide expanse of sheet to sneak another feel, hoping she wouldn't wake up, hoping for a little quality time with one of those magnificent mounds of flesh and whatever the hell the doc had packed them with, pudding maybe, without having to explain why he was waking her up in the middle of the night, yet again—which she should be able to figure out on her own by now but probably wouldn't—when the phone rang.

He dropped his dick and picked up the receiver, leaving his other hand where it was. On Molly.

His side of the conversation didn't amount to much as he lay there fondling Molly's new left tit and barely listening to the voice on the line. But soon, even Molly's bulging breast was forgotten as revelations poured out of the phone that made Edgar see dollar signs lazily floating across the bed like sheep just waiting to be counted.

"Judith, you're nuts," he finally muttered.

He listened some more.

"You actually *shot* the bastard? Good for you. I've wanted to do that for years."

Finally, with the phone still pressed to his ear, Edgar crept from the bed and slipped into the bathroom with it, closing the door silently behind him. Squatting on the john, he gave his full attention now to what the woman on the phone was telling him. His hard-on had petered out long ago. All of a sudden, he had other things on his mind. Profitable things. Maybe he could even recoup the losses the flaming fucking lawyer had left him with. Dollar signs hung over his head like ripe fruit as he emptied his bladder into the toilet bowl. While he pissed, he soaked up every word Judith was telling him.

"And you saw this with your own eyes?" he asked, staring blindly at the damn swans on the shower curtain Molly had picked out. The woman liked swans. Go figure.

Suddenly Edgar's face darkened, and his eyes grew leery. It was his haggling face. "How much money are you talking about?"

His eyes narrowed even further. "Judith, Judith, Judith. You must be joking." But to himself, he said, *Hell, we can do better than that.*

If what Judith was telling him was true, this would be the scoop of the century. Hell, the millennium. Make that *two* millennia. Jesus! (No pun intended.) This could make him even richer than he already was. The wire services would pay a fortune for the information this woman was giving him. Of course, if Judith was as flaky as Molly, he would just laugh off what she was telling him. But she wasn't. He had always suspected, in fact, that Judith was a lot like himself. She might not be able to hold on to a dollar for more than five fucking minutes, but she certainly knew the value of one. Why else would she have put up with her fruity husband for as long as she had? And why had she so cleverly raked him over the coals during the divorce, taking more for herself than she left Charlie and apparently not feeling a moment's qualm about it?

No, Judith certainly knew the value of money, and by all appearances, she sounded pretty desperate for a little of it right now. Still, Edgar wasn't sure she fully understood how deep this gold mine of information could go, and Edgar wasn't above raking *her* over the coals to get his hands on a goodly portion of it.

Of course, there were *religious* aspects to what she was telling him that had to be taken into consideration. If Judith was Judas, as Charlie had told her, then what the hell did that make himself? Pontius Fucking Pilate? King Herod? Would old Edgar the agent go up in flames like all the rest of the world's assholes if he even *considered* doing what he had already pretty well convinced himself he was about to do? Maybe not. If what Judith said was true, this was what the kid wanted. Edgar didn't quite see why fingering the kid to the media would result in his death, but Judith seemed convinced of the fact. Hell, the kid had practically told her as much. Edgar wasn't exactly up on biblical lore. In fact, as far as he could remember, the only time he had ever so much as *touched* a Bible was when one fell on his foot one day in a downtown bookstore by the 12th Street El station when he was groping around for something else. It was one of those big fat illustrated suckers too. Must have weighed ten pounds.

Edgar shook his head and got back on track.

He had connections. He could think of four or five people off the top of his head who would pay good, good money for this story. Reporters, mostly. But why waste his time on them? The tabloids could always be counted on to cough up sizable wads of money for a story they thought the knuckle-dragging public would be intrigued by. But this wasn't just another two-headed Elvis sighting. This was important stuff. Much better to go for the big kahuna. CNN, maybe. Of course, if Judith's scoop of the century turned out to be some diabolical hoax, then his credibility would be shot forever. But he believed her. She was sniveling on the other end of the line right now, blathering on about the kid's tears healing the hole she had punched in her ex-husband's chest with a revolver, for Christ's sake. Lord, she must have been really pissed to do something like that.

Well, hell hath no fury… yada yada yada.

According to Judith, Charlie had already finished, or was still working on, a portrait of the boy, this Messiah of his. Gads. Just thinking about it gave Edgar goose bumps. That painting would be worth a fortune. The poster rights alone would make them all rich beyond their wildest dreams. Every religious fanatic in the world would want a copy of that kid's likeness hanging over the mantle, and since the fires, there were more religious fanatics roaming around than you could shake a stick at. Of course, Judith had also told him the boy had made Charlie promise the painting would not be sold for money. It would be simply *given* to the world.

Over my big fuzzy ass, Edgar told himself. He had been steering Charlie's career for more than a decade now, and he wasn't about to let the fool make a monetary fuckup of such mind-boggling scope as that. Hell, Charlie wouldn't have to paint so much as his fruity toenails ever again. They could all retire in the lap of luxury. Him, Judith, Charlie, Molly, and Molly's new tits. Even the kid could retire, if Messiahs did that sort of thing.

But the first thing Edgar had to do was get his hands on that portrait.

He was, at this moment, maybe a two-hour drive from where Judith stood at the edge of an Indiana highway. Three hours, tops, to Charlie's lake. He could be there before morning. Sneak in, grab the painting, and run like a fucking rabbit.

No, he couldn't do that. Charlie might be annoying as hell, like all artists were, but he had always been square with Edgar. If he was intent on giving the portrait to the world for nothing, then Edgar would have to accept that. It wouldn't affect the poster rights, really. They would still have that. They would also still have whatever chunk of loose change he could extract from whoever Edgar chose to bless with this remarkable information. And that chunk, he was convinced, could be considerable.

He dragged his attention back to the woman still yammering on the phone. Good old Judith. Blah blah blah. He didn't know what the hell she was blathering on about now. Didn't much care. There was a coldness in her voice, though, that was beginning to give him the fantods. A woman scorned, indeed. This broad wanted revenge. And Edgar had a sneaking suspicion that she would be willing to bring the world crashing down around them all to get it.

But still. The money....

WITH MOLLY still sawing logs like a lumberjack in the bedroom, Edgar cranked up the computer in his den and took a spin through cyberspace, seeking out the most profitable news agency with which to share this blockbuster information that had suddenly fallen into his lap. He put out feelers, by way of e-mails, to CNN, the *New York Times*, the *Sun*, the *San Francisco Chronicle*, the *Chicago Trib*, and as an afterthought, to the *Christian Science Monitor*. He might even have notified the Pope since the Catholic Church was known to have more money than God, but he couldn't find an e-mail address for the old geezer.

As he pecked out his message with two fingers, typing not being his greatest talent, Edgar continually expected the chair he was sitting in to go up in red-hot flames, roasting his sorry ass like a tom turkey, but after a while, when it didn't, he began to relax.

He reread the message he had so painstakingly typed up. *The greatest story ever told is about to hit the airwaves. The Messiah is here and I know where He is. For a price, I might be willing to share that information with a properly motivated second party. Interested?*

With his e-mails sent, he set about pouring a drink for himself, something to sip on while he whiled away the time, but before he could put ice in the glass, before he could even figure out what it was he wanted to drink, his computer notified him that he had incoming mail.

Jeez Louise. That didn't take long.

THREE THOUSAND miles away, in the labyrinthine offices of the *San Francisco Chronicle*, a young copyboy by the name of Chester Winfield, or Winnie as he was known to most of his gay friends, which in truth were the only sort of friends he had since he was as gay as a goose himself, saw the e-mail coming in. He immediately felt his heart doing a Greg Louganis triple gainer inside his skinny but well-tanned chest. This could be the break he was looking for. One good story under his belt could get him out of the copy room and into the reporters' nest upstairs, the holiest of holies, a place he had longed to be for as many years as he could remember. And if what he was reading on the computer monitor wasn't some sort of feeble hoax, this story could take him there.

Winnie had called in sick that morning because he hadn't been in the mood, as usual, to drag his ass out of bed at the crack of dawn. So here he was now in the middle of the night—not for the first time—in the all but empty offices of the newspaper, catching up on the work he should have done during the day.

Without giving himself too much time to think about what the powers that be would do to him for sticking his nose where it didn't really belong, he plopped himself down at the computer terminal and typed in the user name at the bottom of the incoming message. Then, under the heading of the *San Francisco Chronicle*, he sent his own instant message right back. *Tell me more.*

Two seconds later he had a response. *Can you deal?*

Yes, I can deal, Winnie lied with his fingertips, after which he nervously ran a hand through his spiky hair—which was platinum blond at the moment and apt to stay that way for a while since his hair stylist had gone up in smoke the week before in the orgy room of the Vulcan Bathhouse, giving a whole new meaning to the term "flaming faggot."

A responding IM popped onto the screen. *For one million dollars I will give you the exact location where the Messiah may be found. This is not a joke. Still interested?*

Winnie was more than aware that in the past week there had been a groundswell of public interest in the possibility of a Second Coming. Rumors abounded. The newspaper had received more than three hundred "Letters to the Editor" speaking of the new Messiah in the past three days alone. Where would he arise? What would he do when he got here? Religious frenzy was at an all-time high since the burnings, and Winnie had been caught up in the rumors as much as everyone else. Now, here in front of him via AOL, seemed to be a person with actual knowledge of it.

A bead of sweat rolled down Winnie's nose and plopped onto the keyboard, but he ignored it. This was no time to chicken out. His future could be at stake here.

He typed *On verification of the information to our satisfaction, one million dollars will be wired to you at your chosen location.* Which was pretty funny, really, since Winnie had $227.35 in his checking account at the moment. He hit Send.

A moment later a new message popped up. *This correspondence is being recorded to disk, making our agreement a solid contract, viable in a court of law. Do you understand that?*

Winnie was sweating like a field hand now. He looked around the massive maze of offices, and the only human in sight was a Filipino janitor in khaki emptying wastebaskets into a rolling dolly three desks down.

The janitor didn't look like he gave a shit about much of anything, least of all what the nelly copyboy was doing, so Winnie typed *Understood and accepted.* Then, as if he actually knew what he was doing, Winnie added the caveat *Assuming, of course, that this information is proven correct and presented to us alone. If the story gets out from any other source before we have a chance to break it in the* Chronicle, *then all agreements here will be considered null and void. Is that understood?*

A pregnant pause ensued, if that's what it's called in cyberspace, and then the message came up. *Understood. Give me your name.*

This was a question Winnie hadn't expected. After only a moment of hesitation, he typed in *J. William Peterson III, Editor in Chief, San Francisco Chronicle*, wondering as he did so if he had just crossed the line from computer sneakery to full-blown wire fraud.

New words then scrawled across the screen that made his heart do a little Gilbert and Sullivan patter song. *The big boss, huh? You're working late.*

Winnie tried for humor to cover his unease. *All great men do. LOL. Forward the information, please.*

The responding IM read *No time for chitchat, huh? That's the way to do business. Okay, here goes....*

And as the words unscrolled before him, Winnie jotted the information down on a slip of paper, typed in a perfunctory *Thank you*, deleted the e-mails, and signed off before his informant could ask any more questions.

Staring now at the blank monitor, Winnie wondered what to do with the story. Was it a joke? Hopefully not. If he acted on it, would it make him famous, or would he spend the rest of his life in some high-security prison bending over a cot and being plowed by every inmate with a boner? As much as he enjoyed sex, that thought didn't really appeal to him much. Those people only showered twice a week.

But the Messiah! Holy cow! This was Pulitzer Prize-winning stuff. No two ways about it. Those snobby reporters up on six would be pulling their intestines out and spitting toenails and body hair to think that some lowly copyboy had scooped their story right out from under them. He was going to enjoy this.

Winnie gathered up his backpack from the locker assigned to him on the second floor and, once outside, splurged on a cab to get himself home. This was no time to fool around waiting for a bus. Once he reached his apartment in the Castro District thirty-six dollars later, he logged on to his PC and proceeded to make the biggest mistake of his life.

Phoning his buddy Jerry, once a lover but now a friend, he told him the whole story and begged him for the money to catch a flight to O'Hare where he could rent a car with what little credit was still available on his credit card, and haul his ass down to that unnamed lake in Indiana where his informant told him the Messiah could be found. There he would write the story that would make him famous. Maybe get the Messiah to perform a few miracles for him, which he could film on his home movie camera and in the process make himself the reporter of the century. As famous, maybe, as the Messiah himself.

The weakest part of Winnie's plan, a plan that was simply brimming with weaknesses, and one he didn't even once consider, was his friend Jerry's penchant for spending the major part of his life online, telling everyone he knew, and everyone he didn't, everything he thought might be of interest to anyone and everyone who would listen.

Twenty minutes later, with his bags packed and his cheap movie camera slung across his shoulder, Winnie hailed another cab, this time to Jerry's apartment to pick up eight-hundred dollars in cash (Jerry did a little dealing and always seemed to have a generous supply of cash on hand). With a quick kiss for luck from his ex-lover, Winnie headed in the same cab to the airport where he would snag the first plane to Chicago with an empty seat, and by the time he had that seat four hours later and was taxiing down the runway on the biggest adventure of his life, the story of the Messiah holing up on the shore of an unnamed lake in northern Indiana, with corresponding directions on exactly how to get there, had, thanks to good old Jerry, inundated cyberspace.

On the World Wide Web, the story of the handsome young Messiah who had fallen to earth to erase the world's wrongs took on mythical proportions in a matter of hours. Hundreds of men and women in the Chicago area alone clicked off their computers, locked their doors behind them, and set out in search of this mysterious unnamed lake where the blessed boy could be found. Like Muslims seeking Mecca, they set out from their homes with little more than the clothes on their backs, carrying with them their sick, their blind, their afflicted, and for many, nothing more than their curiosity. Seeking cures. Seeking forgiveness. Seeking salvation. Seeking excitement.

At this merest rumor of a Second Coming, the world was spurred to action before another dawn crept over the horizon. From as far away as Asia, people began to move. In Europe and South America, airports were swamped with calls for reservations on the first flight out. In the States, the highways filled with automobiles, all heading toward the center of the country where their Savior was waiting. People who, until the burnings, had never prayed a day in their lives now sought God's guidance in finding the boy who waited for them somewhere out there in the wilderness.

News crews from a dozen news agencies pored over maps, seeking this mysterious lake. Even if the story of the Messiah coming to earth turned out to be nothing but rumor, the story of the thousands who sought him, migrating now along the nation's highways, would be a newsworthy event in and of itself.

Unbeknownst to Chester Winfield, a lowly copyboy at the *San Francisco Chronicle*, sitting now in an aisle seat of Flight 292 on Southwest Airlines, destination Chicago, sipping a three-dollar plastic glass of lousy chardonnay and wondering how he would handle his newfound fame once the story broke, the world was traveling right along behind him.

What had once been a secret was a secret no more. Winnie's scoop had been scooped right out from under him.

AND ON the edge of a deserted nighttime highway in northern Indiana, Judith, aching with weariness, sprawled out uncomfortably in the backseat of her car and tried to sleep. As she lay there twisting and turning, she wondered how she would get the money Edgar had promised her. She wondered, too, when the heat of this summer night would turn to a devouring flame and reduce her to screaming ashes.

Like Tom.

Like the rest of the world's sinners.

Or did God have an even more torturous fate prepared for her?

Finally, too tired to care anymore, she dozed, her tears turning to dust upon her cheeks. And in the place where her uneasy sleep had taken her, she saw Judas in flaming robes reaching out to her through a wall of fire.

Welcoming her home.

Chapter NINETEEN
...FREEDOM BORN....

STILL WEAK from his illness, Joe fought to maintain the pose Charlie expected of him. He tried to ignore his pain by watching the sun crest the eastern shore of the lake outside the studio window. It rose so slowly, that sun. And in its light, the world slowly awoke. There was so much beauty to be found in this world. So many things of wonder he had not expected to find here. His father had centered all his power into making this place a garden of delights, but evil had still managed to creep in. Time and time again. Even after his father's burnings only days before, the evil was already rising yet again, like the sun. Perhaps evil, like that burning globe of fire creeping now over the horizon, was an unstoppable force that simply could not be contained. Perhaps it was even necessary, for without a choice to be made between good and evil, how could the people of this world ever truly choose goodness?

Joe turned his eyes from the brightening dawn outside the window and rested them once again on Charlie. He was standing at his easel, his brow furrowed in concentration, with a hint of a smile dimpling his cheek. Charlie looked happy and more than a little surprised by the wonders unfolding beneath the touch of his glistening brush. If he was wearied by his work, he did not show it. Charlie was doing what he loved to do. Joe smiled to see him so content.

The robe Joe had draped across Charlie hours before had now slipped from one shoulder unnoticed, exposing a hint of the wonders hidden beneath, the wonders Joe had tasted once but would never taste again. The boy, standing naked before this man he loved so much, wished, not for the first time, that he could be truly mortal. To be able to openly savor the body and mind of this man, and to let the man savor him, as they shared a real life together. A life bound by nothing but the love they felt for each other. Their kind of love, Joe knew, was not a sin in the eyes of his father. It never had been. Love was simply love. Nothing more. It was one of the wonders with which his father had blessed this world at the very beginning of time. That he should find that love in the short time he was destined to be here was, to Joe, nothing short of a miracle.

To his father, Joe supposed, it merely complicated matters. He had not sent his son to this place to find love. It had simply happened. Yet Joe did not regret it for a moment. It gave him a better understanding of the people living here than he would otherwise have had. It gave him a better understanding of their pain.

For it was the same pain Joe felt now. The pain of need. The pain of longing. And in the end, the pain of leaving.

Joe could feel himself being pulled away from Charlie already. Events were happening in the world right now, events that Joe himself had set in motion, events Charlie knew nothing about that would tear Joe forever from Charlie's side. In this world, at least. They would see each other again one day, just as Joe had promised Charlie they would, but when they did, nothing would remain of the love they shared now except… the essence of love. Their bodies would be gone. Their flesh merely a memory. The taste and feel of each other's bodies would be as unattainable, as unreachable, as the sun now rising above their heads. It would shine in their thoughts, but they would never again know the joy of flesh upon flesh. Their love would be ephemeral. A light. Like the sun's. But even the sun was a pale and flickering thing compared to the light of real human love. All sense of touch and taste and desire would die with the death of Joe's body. And that death was approaching already. But still their love would survive.

Joe's greatest work would soon be before him, just as Charlie's greatest work was before him now. With it would come Joe's greatest sorrow. The loss of his earthly life and the loss of this man standing before him. And not even the memory of the hour they had spent in each other's arms would survive the parting, for Joe had taken it from Charlie as surely as death would take Charlie from him.

For that was how it had to be. For Charlie. Without the memory of passion, their time together would seem little more than a dream to Charlie. An interlude. Charlie's life would continue on, untorn by the regret of losing what had once been, until the day they found each other again. Among the light. And in that light, Joe would be joyously, and sadly, waiting. Joyous for what was regained, and saddened by what was irretrievably lost.

As Joe watched him now, with every muscle in his body aching from weakness, he saw Charlie step away from the canvas and drop his hands to his sides. The brush fell from Charlie's hand and splattered crimson at his feet. He slowly tore his eyes from the painting and directed them at Joe.

"It's finished," Charlie said, his face suddenly solemn, his words so filled with sorrow they seemed to be wrenched from his throat with pliers. Joe could see no joy on Charlie's face for what he had accomplished.

And in truth, for Charlie, there was none. Bringing Joe to canvas had been the most sensual experience of his life. Every brushstroke was a finger on the boy's skin. Every blending of colors, a taste of the boy's body beneath him. To finish it now was like the pulling away of passion. The cooling of ardor. Two lovers leaving each other's arms to face the world once again, alone. It filled Charlie with a sadness that tore at his heart with ravaging teeth.

Joe slowly lowered his aching arms, and with the rays of the morning sun beaming through the skylight over his head, he moved toward the canvas for the first time to see what it was Charlie had created. Joe knew, as he did so, that the completion of this work would take him one step closer to his own death.

On weak legs, Joe walked into Charlie's arms and pressed his lips to Charlie's forehead. Joe sensed turmoil there in Charlie's mind, but still he smiled to feel Charlie's arms automatically enfold him. Charlie caressed the taut muscles of Joe's back, easing the ache that filled Joe's body, even as the feel of the boy's satin skin beneath his hands eased the ache in Charlie's heart. For long seconds, in the silence of the studio, with the world awakening around them, Joe allowed himself to relish the feel of Charlie's strong arms holding him close. It wasn't until the first stirrings of desire in both their bodies threatened to steal the gentle moment away, turning it to something else, something he could not have, that Joe pulled away from Charlie's embrace and gazed upon the painting.

On the canvas, his young body, this body his father had given him to dwell in for such a short while, floated in a blaze of silver light. Hovering faintly behind him in the background he could see, as through a mist, the vaguest outline of his first brother's true cross, following the contours of his outstretched arms. Far beneath his parted feet, the earth receded into the distance as his fleshly self rose through the clouds to a darkening sky, where stars pierced the gloom like welcoming faces, calling him home. A streak of red, the crimson that had splattered at Charlie's feet, and obviously the last touch of color Charlie had added to the canvas, followed his soaring body like a contrail of blood. The blood of mankind, but his blood, too, telling of the suffering he would soon endure. The suffering his father had ordained for him. But it spoke of more than suffering, that blood. It spoke, at least to Joe, of his loss of humanness, the loss of everything he had grown to know and accept about himself in the short time he had spent in this world, in this skin. As his earthly body on the canvas rose toward the heavens, returning him to the world of light from which he came, his life's blood poured out of him, reducing this perfect body, this well of miracles and awakenings, to… nothing. An empty husk. A shell of memory.

For the first time, Joe saw himself as Charlie saw him. The man's love for him was apparent in every brushstroke. The beauty of the body the father had given him was recreated down to the finest detail. Joe's arms in the canvas, so young, so perfectly formed, seemed to reach out with a promise of comfort, begging for a chance to ease the miseries of life, to bury it in the warmth of his embrace. Joe felt his living eyes moisten, just as the eyes in the canvas, moistened by undried paint, stared back at him. Like the windows in Charlie's triptych, Joe saw life behind the eyes on this canvas. His own life. He saw, mirrored there, every thought he had ever known, every emotion he had ever felt, every wonder he had ever witnessed. He saw his love for the man who had painted him, and he saw his own sadness in the knowledge that it was a love he could not keep. He saw, too, the world, gazing as he did into those very eyes and finding peace. Finding solace. Finding a reason to live another day in the belief of something finer than earthly realities. Great good would come to those who took those eyes into their hearts, and Joe knew his trust in Charlie's talents had been well placed. He had done exactly what Joe had asked him to do.

He had brought Joe's face to the world. Joe would remain here even after his own death, just as the father intended.

"Sign it," Joe said, reaching out to Charlie and taking his hand in his own. "Sign it so the world will know who you are."

"No," Charlie said. "This painting is yours alone. I will not bring myself into it."

Joe sighed. "As you wish." Hoping to ease the anguish he could still feel in the man beside him, Joe let a smile creep across his face. Hoping for some levity to lighten the sadness that engulfed them both.

"Where's the water?" Joe asked. "I thought you were going to paint me in the boat? Standing at the bow. That isn't water I'm looking at. It's clouds."

"I wanted you free. That's flight."

Joe took a step back, still studying the painting. "That's not flight. It's ascendance. A resurrection."

"It is?"

"I'm afraid so."

"Well, good. That's even better, isn't it?"

"Well, yeah, except I'd have to be dead to resurrect."

"Oh."

Charlie looked into Joe's eyes and saw laughter there, burrowing its way upward through the sadness. He reached out to brush Joe's hair from his face, and as he did so, he forced a smile to his own face.

"Everybody's a critic," he said.

Joe gave a theatrical moan. "Ain't it the truth. Sign the painting, Charlie. If you don't, I'll sign it for you." Sadness touched the boy's eyes as he stared into Charlie's. "Sign it in red, Charlie. Sign it in the color of the blood you pulled from my body."

Charlie glanced down at the brush, still smeared with crimson, that lay at his feet. Slowly he picked it up, dipped the bristles into the puddle of crimson paint on his palette, and put his signature on the bottom of the canvas.

When he gazed back at Joe, there were tears in the boy's eyes, all traces of humor gone.

"You're leaving soon," Charlie said.

"Yes."

"And you're not taking me with you, are you?"

"No, Charlie. Where I'm going you cannot follow."

Again, Charlie reached out to bury his hand in Joe's hair. "I didn't want to paint you like this, Joe. It just happened."

"I know."

"It's as if I had no control over where the brush was taking me. I *did* want to paint you on the bow of the boat, as the way you looked that day on the water. You were so happy then. As innocent as a child. And you laughed like a kid when the spray hit you. Remember?"

"Yes, I remember. You saved my life that day."

"And you saved mine," Charlie said, remembering Joe's hands dipping him beneath the water at the lake's edge. Baptizing him. Cleansing him of sin. And suddenly, there were other memories of Joe in Charlie's mind too. Memories just out of reach. Memories of touch. Of taste. Memories of Joe's young body, trembling, writhing, arching in release. Or had that been a dream?

Joe tore his eyes from Charlie's face and gazed once again upon the canvas. "You painted what my father told you to paint, Charlie. This is the image of me the world needs to see."

"They'll never know you as I do," Charlie said, his voice but a wretched whisper with the emotions raging through him. "They'll never know the sweetness of you. And they'll never know your sorrow either. I can feel it in you right now, Joe. You don't want to leave. You want to stay here with me. Don't you? Please tell me what I need to hear."

Joe sighed. So weary. "Yes. I want to stay with you. But what I want is irrelevant. It's what my father wants that matters, Charlie. He sent me here for a purpose, and soon that purpose will be fulfilled, as your purpose has now been fulfilled. As my father gave me to you for a little while, you have given me to the world forever. Yes, Charlie, I want to stay with you. I want it more than anything else. But it cannot happen. When the time comes for me to leave, Charlie, and that time is soon, I'll need your strength to help me go. Do you understand what I'm saying?"

"No. And I don't want to understand."

Joe smiled. "You have more strength in you than you realize. You will do this for me, Charlie. I know you will. I cannot leave this place without your blessing. Without your understanding. Give me that much, Charlie. With all the power my father put in my hands, I cannot let myself be torn from this world if I know I'm leaving you unhappy behind me. When the time comes, please prove your love for me by letting me go."

Charlie dropped his head to Joe's shoulder, feeling the velvet heat of the boy's skin against his face, inhaling the scent of him and feeling his love for the boy surge through him like a flame. "Take me with you, Joe. Even if it means my death, take me with you."

Joe cupped his hands to Charlie's face, pressing his lips to Charlie's hair. "I'm leaving the child in your care. Judith will return to you, and she'll bring the child with her. You must care for them both, Charlie. Whatever the world throws at them, I need you to shelter them from it. Especially the woman. Her life will not be easy, Charlie."

"Why? Why will it not be easy?" In his mind, Charlie remembered Judith as the woman he once married. Nothing more. He had no recollection of the bullet that tore out of the gun in her hand, piercing his chest, his heart. He had no recollection of his own resurrection at the hands of the boy he held in his arms. Still, Joe might be asking much of him, but he had given back so much more. Charlie knew he could never refuse the boy anything, even if he didn't understand the reasoning behind the things he was being asked to do.

"Perhaps she will tell you one day what she's done," Joe said. "When she does, you must forgive her."

"Forgive her for what?"

For betraying me. For stealing me from you. Just as I forced her to do.

"For doing what she had to do, Charlie. The choices she made were not her own. You must always remember that."

"All… all right. But I still don't understand."

"I know you don't. But one day the truth will come to you, and you'll see it all as clearly as I see it now. The child will bring you happiness, Charlie. You must live your life for him now. Teach him the things you taught me. Teach him goodness. He has great work before him. He will need your guidance to lead him to it. Tell him of me. Tell him everything you remember. Let him know me as you do. This is your true purpose, Charlie. This is what I ask of you. What my father asks of you."

Charlie could sense the fierce need in Joe's words even as he sensed the boy's sadness at leaving. He understood for the first time that Joe had no more control over what was happening around him than Charlie did. Joe had accepted his fate, no matter the pain it brought him. The least Charlie could do was match that strength. What Charlie was giving up, the boy was giving up as well. Joe's life had been so short. Only a matter of days. What would it be like to find the beauty of life and so quickly have it taken away? Charlie could not imagine it. He did not want to.

"I will make the child my own son, Joe. I promise. I will teach him everything I taught you and everything you taught me. He will learn to love you as much as I do. Every time I look at him, I'll see you. Every time he speaks a word, I'll hear your voice. I… I'll let you go, Joe. When the time comes, I'll let you go. But when it's my time to die, promise me you'll be there waiting for me. Give me that much to live for. I have to see you again. I can't let you go forever."

"I'll be there," Joe said, smiling a gentle smile as he pressed his lips to Charlie's, tasting the man yet again, longing for more, but burying the longing somewhere in the darkness of his mind where it could not trouble him. The pain that had torn at him for so long was suddenly lifted with the words Charlie had just spoken. Now, Joe knew he would have the strength to do what he was destined to do. He would give up this life, this man. He would fulfill his father's task, and he would do so with a lighter heart. For it was true. When this man before him shed his earthly skin, when the last breath of his life was spent, when the light descended on him to carry his weary, aged body away, it would be Joe's face that Charlie saw first. It would be Joe's arms that welcomed Charlie home.

But that was then. This was now. First, Joe had his own welcoming to consider.

They were coming for him. So many. He could feel them eagerly reaching out to him, seeking his presence. Their thoughts drifted to him like pollen on the wind. Where was he, they asked themselves? Where was their Savior?

Joe released Charlie with a final kiss, and still unclothed, still as pure and innocent as Charlie had made him on canvas, a creature as beautiful on the outside as he was within, Joe stepped through the studio door, naked and unashamed. With his skin glowing gold in the light of the rising sun and the streaks of blond in his dark hair glimmering like a halo atop his head, he gazed up at the clear morning sky and let the light of it engulf him.

Raising his arms, Joe willed a pillar of darkness to boil from his fingertips. It swirled like a billowing smoke out into the air, a smoke not of burning but of hope, a smoke that rose up into that flawless dawning sky and hovered there, high above the treetops, shadowing the lake, shadowing the cabin, shadowing Charlie as he stood in wonder, once again watching the boy's power unfold before him. The great stanchion of shadow swirled and eddied and rose into the windless air like a beacon. Visible for miles, Joe knew, it would lead them to him. The seekers. Like the star that led the Magi on their quest so many ages ago, this cloud would bring the pilgrims to his feet, and once there, Joe would show them who he truly was. Just as the great star of old had led the three wise men to the birth of the first son, this towering cloud of darkness would guide the people of earth to the death of the second.

For only then could the prophecy of his life, and his purpose, be fulfilled.

Joe closed his eyes in silent prayer, thanking the father, but more importantly, thanking Charlie, for the newfound peace he felt stirring to life inside him like an awakening heartbeat, pumping the courage to do what he had always known he would have to do through every fiber of his body. The dread he had felt since the moment of his creation left him at last. His fear of death subsided. He was ready now for whatever lay ahead.

Untroubled, he would die in Charlie's arms. Joe knew this. He could see the moment of it as clearly in his mind as he saw this beacon of shadow with his living eye. How he would die, he did not yet know. He knew only that Charlie would be there to hold and comfort him as the life left his body and his heart stilled, as the pain and torment of his own death receded behind, to be lost in time, lost in memory. As Joe always knew he would, Charlie would see him through the misery that awaited him. Even death held no fear for Joe now that he knew he would face it in Charlie's arms, with Charlie's heartbeat pulsing against his own, and now, at last, with Charlie's permission to say good-bye.

Compared to the power of love, his own powers were nothing. Even death could not daunt the strength of the love he felt for Charlie. And Charlie's love for him was strong enough to let Joe go. What could be stronger than that?

This earth truly was an amazing place.

Turning to Charlie, whose startled face still looked up in amazement and confusion at that swirling black cloud the boy had conjured up to fill the sky above their heads, Joe grinned.

Pushing aside his weariness, as he had pushed aside his fear of death, the fear that no longer tormented him, Joe said, "Let's eat. I'm starving."

Bending to give Mac a good morning pat on the head, he took Charlie's arm and led him to the cabin as if it were just another day.

At the doorway, the boy stopped for a moment, listening to the sounds of the crystal summer morning awakening around him. He listened, too, for other sounds: sounds of his fate drawing ever nearer, sounds of a great pilgrimage, coming for him. Coming for their Messiah.

Would he be all they expected him to be?

Joe wondered.

Chapter TWENTY
...AND A CHILD LEADS THE WAY....

WHILE CHARLIE slept the sleep of the weary in the bedroom loft on the second floor of the cabin, the room now cooled from the heat of the noontime sun by the massive black cloud Joe had draped above them like a caul, Joe stood at the edge of the lake and let the water lap at his feet. Mac lay in the grass beside him, his head on his paws, watching Joe, wondering perhaps what miracles the boy would next perform, for even to Mac, this human was something special. In his simple mind, there were many things Mac did not understand, but kindness he could always sense as clearly as the smell of meat on the wind, and the scent of kindness rolled from this human in waves. He had kept himself near the boy ever since the day of Joe's arrival. To Mac, it was simply the place he wanted to be. He could see the young human looking down at him now and smiling. Mac thumped his tail on the ground and smiled back.

Joe watched the dog for a moment, then turned his eyes back to the lake. The water lay gray and still. He could see the reflection of the vast dark cloud hovering overhead in the mirrored surface of the water. Past the edges of the cloud, stretching to all horizons, the sky was as blue as the eyes of a newborn child. Only Joe's conjured cloud marred the beauty of it.

Joe was dressed now in a pair of Charlie's walking shorts. They were too big for him and he had cinched one of Charlie's belts around his slim waist to keep them comfortably snug atop the swell of his butt. His legs beneath the shorts were slim and strong, already turning brown in the days he had spent in the summer sun that continually beat down upon this beautiful lake. Joe's chest, with just the finest sprinkling of dark hair creeping over it, was also tanned. He had lost weight during his illness, but his beauty had not been marred by it. Only his eyes showed the effects of his sickness. Dark smudges still lay beneath them, although the eyes, as brown and bottomless as ever, were as clear as the summer air around him.

Those eyes stared out at the water now, patiently expectant, waiting for whatever would come. He glanced back once at the upstairs window of the cabin, hoping to see Charlie standing behind the glass and looking down at him, but Charlie was not there. He was still sleeping. Their remaining hours were so short. Joe wished Charlie would awaken and come down to the edge of the water to wait with him. He felt so alone. He needed Charlie's strength beside him. He needed to relish Charlie's presence a little while longer. While he still could.

A gentle breeze rolled off the water and tousled his long hair, pushing it across his face, tickling his skin. In the touch of that breeze, Joe felt his father's hand reaching down to comfort his loneliness. He closed his eyes as the wind swept over him, and in its coolness he found a new burst of strength. The strength to face what lay ahead.

A sudden thought etched its way into Joe's mind. Where would his bones lie? Upon his death, would this earthly shell of flesh he wore so proudly be carried back to the father, or would it remain here? Would his resurrection be of spirit alone, or would his physical body follow with him?

He raised his hands to his face and gazed at the perfection of them. So intricate, those hands. The workings of the human body were truly a miracle of miracles. His father had planned them well. But soon, he supposed, he would no longer need the miracle of the flesh surrounding him. In the end, what became of it would not matter. Still, it would be nice to think he could leave it here on the shore of this lake he loved so much, let it be absorbed by the earth, leaving a trace of himself in the soil Charlie would tread across every remaining day of his earthly life. Even that small comfort would ease his parting. Joe closed his eyes to ask the father to allow him this one indulgence, this one blessed favor, but his words of prayer were torn from his thoughts before he could form them in his mind.

In the distance, a thrumming noise pierced his awareness. Looking over toward the trees that bordered the water to the north, he saw the highest branches of those trees whipping about in a wind that was not the gentle wind he had felt earlier, but something stronger. Something fiercer. The thrumming sound increased in pitch, and with a roar of sound that sent Mac leaping to his feet beside him, Joe watched a helicopter, its rotors blatting, raise its snout above the treetops like some gigantic stinging insect. It hovered for a second as if unsure of the direction it should take, then headed straight for him, nose down, engines screaming. In its wake, the tall pines whipped and thrashed as it passed overhead. Joe could hear the trees tearing themselves to pieces as the machine howled over them, all noise and blasting wind, like a reaper tearing through a field of corn.

The shining helicopter, with NEWS 8 painted in blue letters along its flank, hovered over him, and Joe could feel the wind of it whipping his hair, the screaming roar of the engines all but rendering him senseless. Mac, his hackles standing straight up, growled and barked and railed, daring the machine to come any closer, and as if his threats had truly made a difference, the helicopter swooped out over the lake and disappeared in the direction from which it came, once again tearing the trees apart in the blast of its wake.

There's nowhere to land. They can't set down.

He stooped to calm Mac, who was still wailing in outrage at the empty horizon where the screaming machine had disappeared, and slowly, under the calming hand of the boy he loved so deeply, the dog's hackles fell and he gave himself up to the gentle touch of the human's soothing fingers in his coat.

Together, the boy and dog stared out at the silent horizon.

They'll soon be back. It's finally beginning.

At the sound of a door opening and closing behind him, Joe turned to see Charlie, staring as he and Mac were at the horizon to the north. His eyes were puffy from sleep, his hair a tangle of damp curls atop his head.

Joe smiled at the way he looked and said, "They're here."

Charlie nodded. His voice husky from sleep, he said, "They've found you, then." His words carried a timbre of sorrow, the fear of what was soon to come written clearly across his face.

"Yes," Joe said, brushing the hair from his eyes. "They've found me."

WINNIE FELT as if he had spent the last eight hours of his life being beaten over the head with an ugly stick. His ass was sore. His clothes were wrinkled. His breath stank. And his spiky blond hair, of which he was inordinately proud, had lost most of its spike hours ago, thanks to the cheap molding crème he had stupidly bought the week before in an attempt to save a few bucks. Well, his days of scrimping would soon be over. When this story broke, he would be rich. Or at least well on his way to being rich. How much cash *did* they award Pulitzer Prize winners?

The flight to Chicago had been interminable. The man sitting next to him in the cramped seating space of the Southwest airliner had smelled like a goat who had just been dipped in a vat of cheap cologne and stale cigar butts. And to make matters worse, the old fart had been hitting on him the whole trip, rubbing his fat thigh against Winnie's and continually trying to strike up a conversation, which Winnie had finally put a stop to by desperately feigning sleep.

At O'Hare, Winnie went to three rental car booths before he found an available automobile. It seemed that everybody and his dog had chosen this night to travel. The Volkswagen Golf he finally managed to procure after standing in an Avis line for forty minutes looked as if it had been driven in a demolition derby and lost, and must have been recently occupied by the same old fart as the one he had sat next to on the plane, because it too reeked of cheap cologne and stale cigars. It also rode like a log wagon. But at least it ran.

It took Winnie forever to navigate the confusing cloverleafs and switchbacks and on-ramps and off-ramps that finally led him away from the massive airport to an Interstate heading south. Once on it, he found himself in a long line of cars seemingly headed to the same destination he was. But surely that couldn't be.

Breathing a sigh of relief at finally leaving Chicago behind, Winnie switched on the car's radio (surprisingly it worked) and only then did he realize the story he had thought belonged to him alone, the story of the Messiah, the greatest story ever told—for the past two thousand years at any rate—had been pulled right out from under him like a rug.

Every station he turned to spoke of nothing but the great hajj now taking place in America's heartland where, it was rumored, the Messiah had finally come. Most of the newscasters were not brave enough to actually give credence to the story; they merely reported on the mass pilgrimage taking place. The chickenshits, Winnie thought, twisting the knob to another station where he was forced to listen to another chickenshit announcer giving the same slippery song and dance around the real story taking place here. Perhaps with a little bit of luck, he, Chester Winfield, lowly copyboy for the *San Francisco Chronicle*, could still break the story of the millennium.

If he could only get there in time.

THE BLARE of a car horn wrenched Judith from the deep sleep she had finally managed to lose herself in, thanks to the tranquilizer she had found in the bottom of her purse the night before. She raised her aching head from the backseat to look through the car's rear window, and on the highway before her she saw a string of automobiles that stretched from one end of the horizon to the other. They were all headed south. The direction from which she had just come.

Bleary-eyed, her skull throbbing, she checked her watch, realizing with a start that she had been asleep for almost ten hours. My God, that pill must have knocked her out good and proper. Every muscle in her body ached and she had to pee something fierce.

But these cars…. Where were all these people going? And then she knew. They were going to him. Edgar Fosse must have spilled the beans to anyone and everyone. She hoped he had made some money in the process. Money he had promised to her.

Not caring who saw her, Judith crawled from the backseat, and under protection of the two open side doors, she squatted down and unleashed a stream of urine onto the dusty roadside. When she was finished, she cleaned herself with a handful of Kleenex, straightened her clothes, and climbed behind the wheel.

Lighting a cigarette, she cranked up the engine and pulled a U-turn, heading out into traffic, squeezing her car into the line before her, heading once again… south.

Someone in this line of automobiles would be dealing out death to the boy. Joe had told her as much back at the lake. Although she regretted what she had done, her regret did not stem from the obvious reasons. She did not regret letting the world know where Joe could be found. Hell, the kid wanted to die. Someone had to rat him out. No, Judith's regret stemmed from the fact that she had not returned to the lake as soon as she spoke to Edgar.

For if death, as she suspected, truly was on its way to finding this boy, this Messiah of Charlie's, then she wanted to be there to witness it. He had destroyed her life. She would be hated forever when her part in all this was made public. Charlie hated her already. Surely she should be afforded the opportunity to see the boy struck down. After all, she was already doomed to the fires of hell. What difference could one small taste of revenge make now?

Joe had all but forced her to turn him over to the masses. She could see that now. She didn't know exactly how he had done it, but he had.

As she drove, ignoring the angry horn blasts of the cars she had squeezed in front of, she cringed once again at the memory of the gunshot that had torn Charlie's life from him in the blinking of an eye. And she remembered Joe's tears healing Charlie, giving his life back to him, erasing death as easily and as neatly as erasing chalk marks on a blackboard.

She wondered. If Joe could so easily erase death, could he not also erase her sin of betrayal? But no. She would rather burn in hell than ask forgiveness from the boy who had brought her down to this miserable place she now found herself in.

He deserved to suffer. Almost as much as she did.

In that moment, as she gripped the wheel and fought back the tears of hatred threatening to well from her eyes at the mere thought of what the boy had done to her, Judith felt a sudden stabbing pain in her abdomen, and before she could react, before she could do anything at all, she vomited a mass of bile onto her lap.

Morning sickness, she told herself, stunned by the sudden, undeniable truth of it. She wiped her mouth with the sleeve of her blouse and continued to drive as if nothing had happened, ignoring the stench that now filled the car, letting the meager contents of her stomach dry on her clothes as if she didn't care that it was there.

She thought of the fetus growing inside her. With the realization that the boy had been right about that as well, she let the tears finally flow. Pregnant and penniless and soon to be hated by the world, what else could happen to her?

Perhaps, just perhaps, she could find the courage to kill Joe herself. She was doomed anyway. What difference would murder make now?

She followed along among the snaking trail of automobiles and gave in to her hatred completely. Hatred for the boy. Hatred for the child inside her. And hatred for herself most of all.

Seeing a level field at the side of the highway, she yanked the wheel to the right and left the asphalt, gunning the car up to seventy-five as she passed the other cars creeping along, raising a cloud of dust behind her, ignoring the furious horns and yells and obscene gestures that were directed at her.

And in the madness of her desperation, Judith began to laugh. For a caravan of automobiles heading toward the savior of the world, the drivers and passengers of those automobiles were a testy lot. Downright unchristian, in fact.

She shot a finger back at them, still braying with laughter, her eyes bright with ever-growing madness, and at the end of the field, where level ground ran out, she wormed her way back into line and waited for the next opportunity to pull out ahead.

She had to get there fast. Back to the lake. Back to the boy. She looked at the gun that rested on the seat beside her. The gun that had shot Charlie. There were five bullets left in the gun. She had figured out how to check it during the time she had waited for sleep to overtake her the night before.

Maybe she had known even then that this was her destiny, to kill the young man who called himself the son of God. She was right in thinking someone in this unending line of cars would soon be doling out punishment to the boy. It was herself. Perhaps she had known it all along.

Judith wondered if he was capable of healing his own body as readily as he had healed Charlie's. Somehow she doubted it. Why else would Charlie have been so desperate to protect him?

She watched the miles roll away beneath her as she followed the string of automobiles through the Indiana countryside with the hot summer sun shining brightly overhead. As the horizon crept ever nearer, she laid the gun in her lap, letting the weight of it comfort her.

Like the weight of a child in a mother's lap.

This time, perhaps, she could finish what she had tried to do the night before. If she was going to burn, she might as well burn for a reason.

Car horns again began to blare around her, but this time they were not directed at her. Something was happening.

In the car ahead, she saw an arm protruding through the passenger window, a finger pointing skyward. She heard the voices of women, and some men too, crying out. Joyous.

Looking to the south, far away, just above the horizon, she saw what looked to be a black shadow rising high up into the sky. It was a thundercloud. Massive. As she stared at it, she saw a flash of lightning glimmer in its core, and faintly, over the sound of the automobiles surrounding her and the voices crying out in wonder, she heard the rumble of thunder.

It's a beacon, she thought. As clear as a road sign.

The boy was drawing her to him, begging for a death only she could deliver.

More laughter escaped her lips as the madness grew stronger inside her mind. Once again she swerved away from the line of traffic, pressed the accelerator to the floor, and tore ahead of the other cars, her eyes fixed firmly on that massive thundercloud looming in the distance.

And as she drove, she stroked the cool, hard metal of the revolver in her lap, longing to hear it speak again. Longing to hear it roar.

THE FIRST face to appear from among the trees was the face of a child, as Joe had known it would be. Like a curious faun stepping for the first time out of the wilderness, the young girl stood at the edge of the lake where the trees met the water and simply stared at him from across the wide expanse of green lawn. Her long blonde hair was pulled back with a red bow at the back of her head. She looked to be no more than six, her skin as pale and unblemished as porcelain. She wore a soft pink dress gathered together at the waist with a red sash. It too was tied in a bow behind her. On her feet she wore shining black slippers, dusty now from her trek through the trees. There was a scratch on her leg where a limb had lashed out at her, and as she stared at Joe from a distance with shining eyes, she reached down to touch the scratch as if it still pained her.

Joe's eyes narrowed and when he opened them wide again, the scratch was gone from the child's leg. She looked down at it for a moment in wonder, then looked back at Joe, smiling.

The child's voice when she spoke was like the tinkle of tiny bells ringing happily across the air.

"Are you Jesus?" she asked, taking one tentative step forward.

"No, child. My name is Joe. Just Joe."

"Joe," she said, as if testing the taste of it on her lips. Hearing a sound in the trees behind her, she turned, then quickly faced Joe once again.

"My daddy needs your help," the child said. "He's come a long way."

Joe smiled. "Then bring him to me," he said.

And happily, like the child she was, she spun and ran off into the trees. A moment later she reappeared, this time leading a man as pale as her by the hand, a man no older than Charlie. The man's paleness, Joe knew, did not come from a child's purity but from illness. Even from a distance he could feel the vast tumor growing inside the man's flesh as if it grew within his own.

Striding across the lawn, Joe went to help the man, who seemed to be all but spent by his long trek through the trees. Reaching him, Joe took the cane from the man's hand and lowered him to the grass.

"I'm sorry," the man said, as if embarrassed by his affliction. "I… I can't breathe. Give me a minute."

"You don't need a minute," Joe said, smiling as he laid his hand upon the man's chest.

And as that great massive thundercloud hovered above them, casting cool shadows across the lawn, and as the child kept a firm grip on her father's pale hand as if to give him strength, all the while looking up at Joe's face with a trust that knew no doubt, no hesitation, a trust that only a child's face can impart, Joe pulled the tumor from the man's body with nothing more than a wisp of thought.

A breath of clean summer air entered the man's lungs for the first time in over a year, and when the shock of it registered on the man's face, his tears began to flow like rain upon his face, a face no longer pale, but ruddy now with the glow of returning health.

He reached his hand out to the young man who knelt before him, the young man who was not much more than a boy, and after a moment of hesitation, rested it upon Joe's cheek. The man fathomed the depths of those bottomless eyes that gazed upon him, and found kindness there. In his mind, a mind no longer wracked with pain, he thought, *He is truly the one.*

"My daughter said it was you. I… I didn't believe her."

Joe grinned. "Do you believe her now?"

The man released Joe from his touch and, still weeping, pulled his daughter into his arms. Burying his face in her long blonde hair, the man looked over her to Joe, his eyes still sparkling with tears.

"Yes," he said with his daughter's small arms holding him close. "I believe."

"Good," Joe whispered.

"Others are coming," the man said, once again pulling a deep breath of clean air into his lungs as if still amazed that he could do so. "Too many others, maybe. I will help you if I can."

"Thank you," Joe said, rising to his feet and staring off into the trees. He laid his hand atop the child's head and, smiling sadly, looked back down at the man's face staring up at him.

"Are you well?" Joe asked.

The man swallowed a sob. "Yes, I am well."

"And what is your name?"

"My name is Peter."

"Then, Peter, take your child and go. Soon it will not be safe for her here. Take her home and live your lives as best you can. Remember this day."

"I will never forget it."

Joe tousled the man's hair and pulled him to his feet.

"Then go," Joe said, turning his back to the man with the blonde-headed child wrapped securely in his arms. "Go and be happy."

And as Joe walked away, back toward the cabin, the man lifted his child from the ground and settled her safely in the crook of his arm, feeling his strength returning even as he did so. His cane lay in the grass behind him, forgotten, as he carried the child back into the trees. At the edge of the forest, he looked back, but the boy who was almost a man was already gone.

Before the trees swallowed them up, he drew the child's face toward him and said, "I didn't ask his name."

His daughter kissed her father sweetly on the lips, and said, "His name is Joe, Daddy. Just Joe."

And her laughter, again like tiny crystal bells, rang out among the trees. At the sound of it, the man's tears again began to flow, and holding his daughter tightly to him, shielding her face from the stinging branches, he carried her into the shadows of the wood.

CHAPTER TWENTY-ONE
...SAYING GOOD-BYE....

CHARLIE FOUND Joe in the bedroom loft staring at his reflection in the dresser mirror. Approaching, he laid his hand on Joe's shoulder, and for the first time, gazing into the mirror as well, he saw them as they looked together standing side by side. As it always did when Charlie looked upon the boy, Joe's beauty caused Charlie's heart to falter. He was filled with so many sudden longings that it was impossible to sort them out. But above the longings, above the pain of wanting, he felt his love for the boy shine over all. And as Joe's eyes sought him out in the mirror, and as a gentle smile turned the corners of the boy's lips upward, Charlie felt Joe's love for him beaming right back at him.

"You saved him, Joe," Charlie said.

Joe's smile grew wider, but there was sadness in it too. "Yes. The child should not grow up alone."

"Where was her mother?" Charlie asked.

"She is burning."

"Oh."

Still staring at their reflection in the mirror, Charlie reached down and clasped Joe's hand in his. "He said there are others coming to see you. But you know that, don't you?"

"Yes, I know that. They'll be here soon."

Charlie stared at the battered shorts the boy was wearing. "Joe, you cannot be dressed like this when they come."

"Why should they care what I'm wearing? They come for me, not for my clothes."

"Why *do* they come, Joe? What do they want?"

"They want a reason to believe. They want their sorrows taken away. They want their dying bodies to be healed. They want as much from me as I am capable of giving. And while my strength holds out, I will give it to them. It is my father's wish."

"What about *your* wishes, Joe? What about *your* sorrows?"

"They do not matter."

Charlie clasped the boy's hand even tighter. "They matter to me."

Watching himself in the mirror, Joe pulled Charlie's hand to his face and pressed it to his lips. "I know." *Our time together is growing short, but we need not fear the parting yet. Neither of us should fear it yet.*

"You're not ready for this, Joe. You're still weak. I can see it in your eyes. You need sleep."

"There will be plenty of time for sleep later," Joe said. *Eons upon eons.*

He turned away from the mirror then, and pulling Charlie into his arms, he said, "This will be a day of wonders. Remember it, Charlie. One day, when the memory of it has settled deep inside you, paint it. Paint it just as it was. Paint it so that those who could not be here will know what it was like. I cannot reach out to everyone in this world. They are too many. It will be up to you to show me to the ones who could not find their way here. Make them believe in the miracles I perform today. Make them feel they were standing with me here on the shore of this lake. Make them see me as I truly am, Charlie. Make them feel my hands upon their bodies. Make them see my eyes settle upon them as if I stand before them in life."

"I… I'll try."

"You will try and you will succeed. You have a great talent inside you, Charlie. That's why you were chosen."

"I want to stay beside you, Joe. Whatever happens today, I want to be there with you."

Joe smiled. "Good. It will help me to see your face now and then. But whatever happens, do not interfere. Stand behind me and let me draw strength from your presence, but remember what I say to you now. No matter what happens, do not interfere."

"I'm not sure I understand…."

Joe cocked his head as if listening to a distant music. "They are coming, Charlie. Do you hear them?"

Charlie turned toward the open window. He held his breath and listened. And heard. A susurrus of sound, like gentle gusts of wind rattling leaves. Hushed voices. The soft tread of many feet. A billowy cloud of sound that slowly grew and gradually filled the summer air around the cabin like the first quiet patter of raindrops before a deluge.

Joe tightened his hand over Charlie's for an instant, then released him. Brushing the hair from his forehead, Joe walked toward the stairs. He stopped for just a moment to lay a reassuring hand on Mac's head as the dog trailed along beside him, tense and wide-eyed. His touch instantly silenced the nervous whimper emanating from the animal's throat.

"Follow me, Charlie," Joe said, looking back.

And Charlie followed.

CHAPTER TWENTY-TWO
...A HEALING SHADOW....

AT THE cabin door, Charlie looked out into that false twilight Joe's hovering thundercloud had immersed them in. Feeling the coolness of the shadowed air upon his face, he stared in amazement at the vast sea of faces awaiting them. There were so many! A shiver of fear slid up Charlie's spine, registering itself in his eyes with an almost audible click. He watched Joe, standing before him. The boy straightened his body as if pulling strength from some hidden well of courage and then stepped through the doorway. Charlie reached out to place his hand on Joe's shoulder, needing the boy's touch to buoy his own strength, but Joe had already stepped too far ahead. Charlie dropped his arm to his side, uncomforted. Taking a deep breath, Charlie stepped through the doorway alone.

That susurrus of sound that had pulled him and Joe from the cabin now dissolved to an unearthly silence so profound it seemed to echo in the earth beneath their feet. Voices stilled and all movement stopped as that great mass of expectant faces fell upon the boy for the first time. In every pair of gaping eyes, Charlie saw the humbled look of the devout shining like a fine madness. *The son of God*, those silent, probing eyes seemed to say. *I'm gazing upon the son of God.*

How did they know? Charlie wondered. His own understanding of who Joe truly was had come so slowly. How could this mass of strangers see Joe's true heart with little more than a glance?

As if on cue, Charlie heard a massive rustle of clothing as the crowd slowly lowered themselves to their knees before Joe, and only then did Charlie see the light that had formed across Joe's brow, encircling his crown of hair like a halo. It shone above him, around him, like a glimmer of fireflies on a summer evening. It illuminated the boy's face in the gloaming light, drawing every eye to Joe alone. Charlie, who had seen many miracles in the time he had spent with Joe and who thought nothing further could ever surprise him, gasped at the beauty of it.

When the silence was at its peak, when even the birds in the pines surrounding the cabin had stilled their singing as if they, too, were caught up in the drama unfolding beneath them—and perhaps they were—Joe lifted his naked arms, reaching them wide to either side, and looked out upon the crowd.

"My father welcomes you," he said, his voice a strong resonance that rippled through the air like waves upon water. At the sound of his voice, many bowed, while others simply stared. The silence was so absolute that Charlie could hear his own pulse pounding inside his head, could hear the blood sluicing through his veins like a whisper of throbbing wind in the distance. Standing behind Joe, Charlie longed again to reach out and touch him, his need for the feel of the boy never greater than at that moment, but he knew he could not. Joe was no longer his. Joe belonged to the people before him now, and Charlie knew beyond all doubt that their need for him was as great as his own. Or greater.

Charlie tore his eyes from the nimbus of golden light that encompassed Joe. He had never seen that light radiating from Joe before this moment, but somehow he knew it had always been there. He studied the faces in the crowd. Young and old had come. Children and the aged. But on every face, the same wonder was clearly written. It was not doubt that had brought them here, but belief. They had not traveled so many miles on a whim. It was faith alone that had drawn them across those untold miles to this unnamed lake in the middle of nowhere. It was the certainty of what they would find here that had given them the strength to come so far. Many were ill. Charlie could see it in their eyes, in their weakened, trembling bodies. Their journeys must have been a misery to them. But still they had come. Not for themselves. Not really. But for Joe. For this boy who stood before them now.

A flash of light drew Charlie's eyes to the edge of the crowd, and there, where the trees began, he saw news cameras blinking at him, at Joe, their lenses reflecting the pale sunlight like tiny strobes. And behind the newsmen, with their cameras pointed like guns, more people were emerging from the trees, squeezing into the small glade where Charlie's cabin stood. Already the open ground around the cabin was blanketed in bodies, all kneeling, their hands clasped beneath their chins as they gazed upon the boy they had traveled so far to find. The faces of those emerging from the trees looked out upon the carpet of kneeling bodies before them, then looked up to the steps of the cabin where the boy stood, engulfed in his glowing halo of light, his arms reaching out in welcome, and they too fell to their knees in wonder. At Joe's feet, from the steps of the cabin to the edge of the lake, a sea of faces rose up like heads of wheat, eyes shimmering, lips whispering silent prayers. All staring at Joe. At this boy. This Messiah.

Not one among them doubted who the boy was, although he had as yet proclaimed himself to be no one. If the perfect glimmering halo that hovered over him did not convince them, then the look of kindness and love that radiated from his brown, bottomless eyes did. Love seemed to flow from Joe's eyes like a cascade of light tumbling through a prism, settling onto each of them alone, as if the boy's gaze saw no other face before him but theirs.

A temblor of thunder boomed from the cloud above their heads and, raising his face, Joe silenced it with a look. A hushed murmur of wonder, a shuddering gasp, followed this display of power. Once again a deep silence fell over the crowd that still knelt, mesmerized, before the boy.

An old woman, too weak and stiff to kneel, sat in the grass beside the bottom step leading up to the porch. She reached out her palsied hand, a hand that had known more toil over the years than many of the men's around her, and laid it gently across Joe's bare foot. Her fingers were as cool as stones in a stream. Joe looked down at the feel of them on his skin and smiled.

"Rise, Mother," he said. "Do not sit before me in pain. Your body is healed."

And the woman, with tears filling her eyes, raised her old head to the sky and, pushing helpful hands away, rose to her feet to stand alone among the throng of kneeling bodies around her. She gazed about with the incredulous look of someone suddenly released from long-borne pain. She stared down at the body that had tormented her for so long as if amazed to see it standing beneath her unaided. Bending forward, she cupped Joe's foot in her aged hands and laid her papery lips to it as she once, in her youth, might have kissed a lover.

With gentle hands, Joe lifted her gray head from his flesh and gazed upon her face. "Go now," he said, "until my father has need of you."

The old woman opened her mouth to speak, but her voice was lost in the deluge of emotions sweeping through her. All she could do was nod, her shimmering eyes taking in the boy in front of her as if she were memorizing every line of him. Only then did she again look down at her own body, wondering, perhaps, where the pain had gone. Then, with an incredulous smile creasing her weathered face, she knelt with the others, dropping to her knees without so much as a glimmer of pain to dim her weeping eyes. She groped for the hand of the old man kneeling beside her, and as if knowing she could not, the old man spoke the words that his wife of so many years was incapable of speaking.

"Thank you," he said, staring up at the boy, his gravelly voice barely audible in the hush. "And bless you, son."

"Bless *you*, Father," the boy said, and turning away faced the crowd. Once again his arms reached out to either side. Once again Joe's voice rang out in the still air, stronger now than Charlie had ever heard it. His words flew out of him like eagles, sure and certain in their flight.

"The souls of each of you will find heaven one day. All those who escaped the burning will find heaven if they stay on the true path. Do not grieve for those you lost in the fires. They are beyond your help, just as they are beyond my father's help. Forget them, for they have most certainly, in their agonies, forgotten you."

A murmur of sound arose around him. Whispered voices speaking whispered prayers. All eyes were locked upon the boy as he spoke of their salvation from flame, and not one among them doubted the words they heard.

Joe saw their belief and smiled.

"I come from my father, not mortal woman. I was not sent here to teach, but to show, to renew. Those acts that you call miracles can help you know that all I say is true. There is nothing I can add to what my first brother has already told you. His words were spoken once. You do not need to hear them again. I am a renewal of those words. Nothing more."

Joe stepped into the crowd, arms wide. The light encircling his brow was a beacon, drawing every eye, every thought, every hope. A great gasp of wonder and expectation erupted from those kneeling before him. As he walked among them, as his strong young arms encompassed them, the ill and crippled and dying all rose to their feet as his shadow passed over them. Like plants bursting from the earth on trembling stalks, they stood, their miseries forgotten, their wounds healed. Joe did not touch. He did not look down. His eyes were open but directed upward to the sky as he wended a path through the crowd. And as the boy walked, the world around him seemed to waken. A fresh wind rose and the smell of pine and summer honeysuckle filled the air. Birds again chirped in the trees, as if their voices had been returned to them. Bees hummed in the blossoms. Their music sang through the sweet scented air like a hymn.

A young man no older than Joe, his body wasted to a painful thinness from AIDS, his clothes hanging on his bones like flags, with black lesions peppering his face and arms, reached out to touch Joe's leg as he passed. At the feel of Joe's skin, the lesions sloughed away, falling to the earth like ash.

"Sin no more," Joe said and walked on.

A child, his scalp shining and bare, his face the thinnest veneer of flesh, like crepe stretched over naked bone, felt the cancer leave his blood as Joe passed in front of him. He felt his heartbeat strengthen for the first time in memory. Giggling a childish laugh, he looked at his parents kneeling beside him and wondered why they wept.

As Joe brushed against her in the crowd, a woman, pale with sadness, her eyes opaque in the blindness she had known from birth, watched in wonder as the day emerged before her through the long darkness in which she had always lived. Through tears that blurred true vision for the very first time, she stood and stared at the trees bordering the glade, trees that before this day she had only glimpsed through scent and feel and imagination. She had never known until that moment how beautiful the actual sight of them would be.

The buzz of expectant voices rose as those people Joe had yet to heal reached out their arms to him, drawing him closer, and as he passed them, as his powers settled into their ailing bodies, their gasps of amazement, their murmurs of "Thank you, Lord," joined those in his wake.

All hands reached out to Joe, but the boy touched no one. Behind him, Charlie followed. His own tears flowed as freely as the crowd's. Many, when Charlie passed, stretched out their hands to touch him as well. He smiled down at them, but could not bring himself to speak. A sudden welling of emotion had closed his throat. Even if he had known what to say, he could not have spoken the words.

The miracles unfolding before him as he trailed along behind the boy through the mass of adorers had left Charlie numb. So much true suffering was being erased here that he could not help but wonder why he himself had ever felt sorrow. Ever felt pain. Compared to the people kneeling before Joe, the ones the boy had yet to reach, to heal, Charlie knew now that his own complaints had been nothing more than a shadowed image of pain. A delusion. A self-centered facade. Shame welled up in him to think that he once thought he too had suffered.

Joe still walked slowly through the crowd, arms wide, easing the miseries of all who fell in his shadow. Nearing the edge of the lake, he turned at the sound of voices in the trees. Desperate voices. Some at the brink of anger. There were people there who could not reach the glade for all the kneeling souls blocking their path. They had traveled the long miles of the highway only to be stopped now when they were so near to where they desperately wanted to be.

Joe felt their longing for him, and reaching out his hand, he knelt to touch the cool water of the lake where it lapped against the shore. As his fingers brushed its surface, and as those nearest to him watched in wonder, their heartbeats quickening, the water beneath the boy's touch turned to ice. Quickly, the ice spread outward from the shore. It could be heard like the crumple of heavy tinfoil, cracking and snapping as the frozen path of water expanded. It moved ever forward, ever outward, changing the lapping water to an expanse of mirrored ice that shone in the shadowed light like crystal. And as that sweeping blanket of ice spread slowly across the lake, reaching finally to the farthest shore, it turned the water to crystal stone before their very eyes. The summer air turned cool around them, bringing memories to many of long-forgotten childhood winters. Some smiled at the memory. Others were too stunned to smile. And still others, lost in the magic of what they had just seen, bowed their heads to pray, humbled in the knowledge that of all the souls residing on this planet, they were among the few who were here at the edge of this beautiful lake to witness these miracles.

Seeing the boy step out onto the wide expanse of frozen water, those closest to him followed, and in this way room was made in the glade surrounding Charlie's cabin for those who had yet to lay eyes upon the boy. They came from the trees as if in a daze, their eyes wide at the sights before them. The dark cloud hovering high above. The frozen lake glistening beneath their feet. The young man striding across it with the glimmering halo about his head, arms stretched wide, a gentle smile upon his face. The mob of people, no longer kneeling, followed along in the footsteps of the boy as he led them out toward the center of the lake where there was room for all to see him clearly.

Newsmen—those who were not caught up in the wonders unfolding, and they were few—jockeyed forward among the crowd. They tried desperately to get it all on film. Many doubted that the world would believe what their cameras were recording, what they themselves had just seen with their very own eyes. They had witnessed countless horrors over the years as they trailed along with their cameras and notepads from one breaking story to another. Good news didn't sell, their editors had always told them. This time, they suspected, their editors would be proven wrong.

Charlie stepped out onto the frozen lake, far behind Joe now, separated from him by the worshiping crowds that followed behind the boy. The frozen water beneath Charlie's feet was as smooth and hard as rippled glass. And just as clear. He could see down through it to the very bottom of the lake, where underwater plants and fish no longer swayed and swam in the moving water but were frozen to stillness, as if captured in time. The ice was cool beneath his feet but not cold, the surface just rough enough to give good footing.

Where Mac had gone, Charlie didn't know. He looked around for him and finally spotted the dog standing beside the young boy who Joe had healed of cancer, the boy who still wondered why his parents wept and laughed all at the same time. And as the child rested his small sleek head on Mac's broad back, small arms hugging the dog and perhaps wishing for one of his own, Charlie watched the boy stare out at the lake, where Joe had stopped now to turn and face that sea of worshiping faces. Joe sought Charlie out in the crowd, as if reassuring himself Charlie was safe. Then, returning his gaze to the others around him, Joe's voice once again rang out, as clear as the crystal lake beneath his feet.

"My time with you is short. You must all carry the memory of this day with you wherever your lives lead you. Speak of it to any who listen. Tell them what you have seen before you, for there will be many who doubt the truth of it. I cannot present myself to every soul residing in this world, for faith must still play a part in my father's teachings. Because of the things you have seen, your own faith is strong now. It beats inside you like a living heart. You must carry that heartbeat to others. Make them see my miracles as you have seen them. Make them believe as you believe. Each of you is an apostle to me now. You have all heard or read my first brother's words. You know of the message he brought to this place. This garden. Do not let yourselves believe that because I am here, the snake of evil is gone. For he will never leave this Eden of yours. He still lies waiting, coiled about the branches of the tree you pass beneath. He will still tempt you. He will still reach down his head and lead you with his lying tongue to that place where the fires have already taken so many. Do not listen to his words. Do not follow where he tries to lead.

For mine is the only light you shall follow. Mine, like my brother's, are the only words that speak truth."

Charlie watched as Joe took a deep breath, as if wearied by his speech or by the strength he had spent in his healing walk among the savaged bodies of those who worshiped before him. His healing powers came with a price, Charlie knew. Joe's body was, after all, only human. What lay beneath might be eternal and blessed, but the shell around it was flesh and blood. Charlie remembered the boy lying on his bed, weak from the illness that tore through him, and wondered yet again why it was that with all his power, with all his goodness, Joe could not heal himself.

With a start, Charlie realized that Joe was staring now directly at him as his words once again echoed over the ice.

"Many of you are still in pain," Joe said, his arms once again reaching out to encompass those before him. "I have not healed as many of you as I would like. As the day recedes behind us, I will remedy that. You have all traveled far to be here. And you have traveled far with nothing more than hope to guide you. I will not let that hope die for nothing. Each of you, before you leave this place, will be as sound of body as you are of faith. You will need your strength to carry my brother's words to others. I will not let you carry those words in pain."

The flickering light of a sad compassion lit Joe's eyes as he gazed at the kneeling crowd.

"Do not kneel," he said. "Sit. Be comfortable. I see the flame of belief in your eyes; you do not need to demonstrate it by torturing your bodies. Let me walk among you, and as my shadow passes over you, your sorrows will be lifted, your afflictions erased. When darkness falls, when my work here is done, you will all leave this place. You will return to your homes and there you will find peace. You will carry the memory of me with you, just as I will always carry the memory of you with me. Never forget who you are. Never forget what my father has given you. Share it. Give it to others. And one day, on the day of your last heartbeat, my father will thank you."

He smiled kindly on those faces closest to him, and said, "Rest now. Sleep if you wish. For even in sleep, I will find you and heal your suffering."

Here Joe's eyes sought out Charlie once again, and a playful, devilish smile twisted his lips. "The one who loves me most will bring you food before you journey home. We cannot let you leave this place with the agony of hunger gnawing at your newly healed bodies. Right, Charlie?"

And Charlie, finally soaking in what the boy had said, felt his jaw drop. He stared at Joe and blinked. *Say what? There must be two thousand people here!*

Joe blinked back at him in a parody of innocence, laughter in his eyes at the horrified look on Charlie's face.

"Waffles will do just fine," Joe said, still orating for all to hear, "and maybe some of those nice sausages." And with that parting shot over Charlie's bow, he turned to walk among those who had yet to feel his shadow. Charlie could see a tremor of real laughter now rippling across the boy's bare shoulders as he reached out his arms to widen that healing shadow while he once again strode among the adoring upturned faces surrounding him.

Avoiding the eyes staring at him as if he, too, was suddenly an entity worthy of worship, Charlie looked down at his own two hands, and thought, *What the fuck do I do now?* He knew for a fact there were exactly four waffles and six sausages, count them, four and six, languishing in his freezer compartment at this very moment. Barring another miracle, he had a sneaking suspicion—call it a hunch, if you will—that it wouldn't be quite enough.

Oh, well. That's what he got for falling in love with the son of God.

Next time he'd shoot for a 7-Eleven clerk and keep things simple.

Chapter Twenty-Three
…Destinies Met….

Chester Winfield, or Winnie as he was affectionately known to his friends, a few of which he wished he had around him now, stepped out from the trees, breathless and drenched in sweat. That big black cloud that hovered so weirdly over this stretch of Midwestern countryside might block out the heat of the sun, but under the pine trees, the air had been as muggy and dead as the air in the orgy room at the Vulcan Bathhouse on a Saturday night, when writhing bodies managed to create enough heat and friction to fry an egg on the sheets. Or a hairdresser, he thought, bemoaning once again the fiery loss of his own.

Winnie, never much for worship, saw worship in every eye around him. He was among an eager, jostling crowd of hundreds, maybe thousands, who were trudging along the highway on foot now, seeking this Messiah who Winnie had learned about from his mysterious e-mail. Where the others had learned about him, Winnie didn't know, but they had come from God knows where and converged en masse, a biblical swarm of locusts, on this vast tract of Indiana farmland, with its towering pines and flat fields of young green corn and soybeans, all plodding determinedly forward in straight, unveering rows at either side of the highway.

He had parked his rattletrap rental car miles back at the place where traffic no longer moved, thanks to the convergence of more cars than the road could handle. More cars, in fact, than Winnie had ever seen before in his life. It was never a question of *finding* the Messiah, if that's who this person truly was, but a matter of *reaching* him. Finding was easy. All Winnie had to do was follow the mob. They seemed to know where they were going even if he did not. His dream of being the first to present himself to this mythical messenger from God had died a miserable death hours ago, along about the time he realized all these cars weren't just trying to get away from O'Hare, but were seeking the same thing he was.

Stepping out of the mugginess of the trees, he raised his head to savor the cool air that hit him like the soothing breeze from a damn good air conditioner on a sultry summer day. Seeing the dark thunderhead still hovering overhead, Winnie wondered again at the strangeness of it. He shifted the strap of the movie camera, which was digging a trench in his shoulder, and wished for a nice icy root beer to drown his thirst. He breathed in the cool air yet again before he began to wonder why exactly the air *was* so blessedly cool here on this side of the trees when it was hotter than hell on the other.

Then, looking down for the first time, he saw the thousands of people all kneeling in the glade, their hands clasped piously beneath their chins as they gazed out across a flat expanse of ground to a person who appeared to be not much more than a boy walking among them in the distance. And a good-looking boy at that.

Winnie studied the distant figure of the young man for a moment, appreciating the beauty of his long limbs and lean naked torso poking out from that god-awful pair of shorts the kid was wearing, before his mind took in what he was actually seeing. Wait a minute. Was that a frozen lake the kid was walking across? In the middle of summer? On a day that was hot enough to melt the rouge off a drag queen's cheeks? Was that why the air was so cool? Out beyond this side of the frozen lake where the crowd had formed, he could see the cloud above his head mirrored in the empty ice as clearly as if it had been painted there.

Watching the boy, whose arms were spread out wide as he seemingly strolled aimlessly through the kneeling crowd, Winnie saw an undulation of movement rising up behind the boy. What were those people doing?

And then he knew.

This was a healing. Something he had read about but never believed. But this wasn't *just* a healing. It was a *mass* healing. Winnie stared in amazement when a woman in a wheelchair rose to her feet as the boy passed before her and, pushing the chair away, stood maybe for the first time on her own two legs and looked down at those legs now as if wondering why they had never worked before. Winnie could hear her wail of joy from a quarter mile away.

And the woman was not alone in her wails of joy. The air was filled with them. As people rose to their feet in the wake of the boy, suddenly finding their bodies whole once again, their cries and prayers of gratitude echoed across the air like a drumbeat. Somewhere in the crowd, a tenor voice began to sing. Pure and clear. Then others joined in. Winnie was reminded of the young Nazi standing in the beer garden in *Cabaret.* But this sweet tenor voice singing in the distance sang words of love, not hate. The song he heard now was one Winnie remembered from his childhood, when every Sunday morning his mother would drag him kicking and screaming to the Baptist church around the corner from where they lived.

"Mine eyes have seen the glory of the coming of the Lord...."

Soon the meadow before him was filled with a thousand voices, all singing from their hearts as if the fate of the world depended on it. In spite of himself, Winnie felt his throat close around a wad of emotion that, had he not experienced it firsthand, he would not have thought himself capable of feeling.

He spat up a wry chuckle and muttered, "Get a grip, Chester."

At that moment, someone stumbled into him from behind, almost knocking him to the ground. He turned, ready to snap the head off of the person who had plowed into him, then remembered where he was and opted for a bit of Christian charity instead.

"Are you all right?" he started to ask, but the words never reached his lips. He found himself staring at a young woman who looked about as worn out as Winnie felt. Like his, her clothes were wrinkled beyond redemption, and her short auburn hair had stuck to her perspiring face in damp tendrils. She looked as if she had recently vomited on herself. Winnie could smell the acrid stench of it from three feet away. Upon colliding with Winnie, the woman had stumbled to her knees, looking for all the world like another adoring worshiper, but when she raised her eyes to glare at him, he saw such hopelessness and such... *hatred*, there in those beautiful but weary eyes, that he all but winced to find them aimed in his direction.

"I'm sorry," he instinctively said, stunned by the desperate fury in the woman's haunted eyes. He reached out his hand to help her to her feet. She slapped his hand away and picked up the purse she had dropped, clutching it to her chest. As she did, Winnie saw the dull glint of gunmetal. For a split second, the butt of a revolver poked out of the open purse before the woman hastily pushed it out of sight.

He watched as she appeared to make a concerted effort to pull herself together. Her eyes fell on Winnie's face once more, this time with a little less animosity, and then she gazed around the meadow as Winnie had done a moment before. He could see her eyes fall upon the boy in the distance, and he could see the moment of enlightenment hit her when she realized what was happening in this glade with the strangely frozen lake and the weird black cloud and the thousands of kneeling travelers all staring in adulation at a kid who looked like he should be sitting in a high school biology class somewhere studying his cell constructions rather than standing in the middle of Indiana like a modern-day Jesus healing the maimed.

The singing had grown to a fevered pitch. It rang through the air like old-time revival music. Stirring. Hypnotic. Even Winnie was not immune to its power.

But the young woman apparently was. "Must be choir practice," she said. "Sounds a little flat."

Winnie didn't know what to say, so he said, "Uh...."

"Well put," the woman snapped, and clutching her purse even closer to her chest, she stepped out into the crowd, her eyes never straying from the boy in the distance.

Winnie watched her go.

Then he remembered the gun in her purse and, stepping carefully through the kneeling bodies around him, followed along in the young woman's wake. His heart did a lively Bojangles tap dance, flailing away beneath his ribs in a weirdly syncopated rhythm he had never heard before and didn't much care for, and all the while he wondered why the woman needed a gun and what the hell he was getting himself into by trailing along behind her.

Smelled like a story, though, Winnie thought. Smelled like a *good* story.

JOE WALKED among the worshipers, many of whom were sitting now rather than kneeling, as he had asked them to do. Beneath his passing shadow, lives were being changed, agonies and sorrows erased. And yet more than once as he stepped through the crowd, he felt that his shadow was now not enough to heal all the misery beneath him. For those few suffering souls, the ones most deeply afflicted, Joe stopped and laid a hand upon their heads to complete what his shadow could not fully accomplish.

Every eye that looked upon him burned with hope. Every face that gazed into his shone with the light of true worship. Before Joe lay a stagnant sea of need, and in his wake rose up a cresting, roiling surge of freedom. Freedom from pain. Freedom from anguish. Freedom from bodies that brought torment, not pleasure, to those souls held captive in their damaged fleshly prisons.

Hands reached out to him from every side, brushing his legs, touching his feet, and at every touch, at every movement of his shadow, Joe felt a little more of his power drain away. There was so much misery here, so much suffering to be cured, that already he was wearied by it. His powers were growing weaker, and even the love he felt surging back at him from those weeping, grateful faces was not enough to replenish it. Too much strength from this body his father had loaned him had been taken from him already by the illness brought about by the burnings and by his shame at allowing his love for Charlie to take him to that place where he should never have gone. Now, even as he performed miracles of healing with the power his father had given him to wield, his thoughts returned time and again to the feel of Charlie's naked body pressed to his, the taste of Charlie's passion flowing across his lips, the arch of his own back as his answering passion flowed from him to be eagerly accepted by the man he had come to love more than any other.

Once again, he turned to seek Charlie out in the crowd. He spotted him far behind him now, standing at the edge of the frozen lake. Mac was with him. As Joe watched, they turned toward the cabin, weaving carefully through the crowd. There was a tension in Charlie's shoulders that brought a smile to Joe's lips. He was wondering, Joe knew, how in the world he was supposed to feed a couple of thousand people with a handful of waffles and sausage.

O ye of little faith. Joe chuckled inwardly, then resolutely turned back to the adoring faces of the healed and yet-to-be healed who milled around him.

The smile on Joe's lips slowly faded as he once again felt his strength drain away at the sight of so many still to be helped. Was he strong enough to finish the work before him? Perhaps his own faith wasn't as strong as it should be. Surely his father would not let him fail now. So much had already been accomplished.

Closing his eyes to pray for strength, he once again let his shadow and his hands correct the wrongs that nature had done to so many here. The songs of faith echoing through the glade from so many ebullient voices helped. Music always did. Joe felt, in its power, the strength to take one more step, to heal one more ailing body, and with that one, he moved on to the next, and the next after that.

Hours passed. Slowly, oh so slowly, the long day faded to twilight.

Not once in that time, not once during all those many hours, did the crowd of worshipers cease their singing. Not once did Joe's feet stop moving. Not once did his strength or his powers forsake him. Joe could feel his father's hand leading him now, urging him forward. Guiding him toward the end.

And in his growing weariness, a weariness so deep that it was almost a death unto itself, the boy with the power of the father at his fingertips accepted the inevitable.

For in that great rush of love pouring into him from the crowd at his feet, he felt one small ray of anger aimed in his direction. One small ray of hatred, of cold malice, burning into his flesh like a fiery dagger.

She was here. Somewhere in the crowd. Like him, she had returned to finish the task the father had set for her. Joe could feel her eyes upon him even now. In the heat of those unseen eyes, he felt the piercing of his heart and the looming loss of everything he loved so deeply. His newfound life. The sky. The lake. The song of birds. The scent of dew on grass. The supple movement of his fingers. The ever-present pulsing of blood through his young body, the body whose limits he had only begun to explore. The tender, needing touch of loving hands upon his skin, and the feel of that one other's flesh beneath his own exploring fingertips.

Charlie. Always Charlie. All roads of thought led back to him. Again, the lure and power of human love, human desire, astonished the boy. It was an inescapable force, that love. Inescapable and all-consuming.

But the fate decreed for him was inescapable too. Joe knew that. He had always known it.

Sensing his own death reaching out to him in that moment from somewhere in this crowd of worshipers, he looked skyward with saddened eyes.

"Father," he spoke softly, "is it to be so soon? Can I not have but one more day?"

And in the silence that followed, he learned the answer to what he already knew.

CHARLIE STARED into his pantry like a thirsty man peering desperately into an empty well. He hadn't shopped since Joe arrived. He looked down at the few waffles and sausages he held in his hand and realized they wouldn't be enough even for Joe and him. If there was any humor in this situation, he was having a real hard time finding it. Joe had laid the responsibility for the feeding of this mob at Charlie's feet in such a cavalier manner that it made the blood rise to the back of Charlie's neck to think about it. Good lord, what was he supposed to do? Was this meant to be one of those leap-of-faith things where you plod along and hope for the best? Seemed good old Joe had a nasty little vicious streak buried somewhere beneath that veneer of pious omniscience he walked around in so beautifully. The little shit.

And finally, seeing the absolute hopelessness of what he had been all but commanded to do, Charlie laughed. Helplessly. Mac looked up at him and wagged his tail at the sound. Or maybe he was hoping for one of those sausages to fall from his master's hand and hit the floor so he could scoop it up and shorten the rations ever farther. Who could tell?

Still giggling like a schoolgirl at the impossible situation he found himself in, Charlie tossed the frozen waffles in the microwave and set the timer. Then he dropped the sausages in a skillet and adjusted the flame beneath them. He dragged out a plate from the cupboard, covered it very neatly with a single paper towel, and waited for the inevitable moment of truth.

"I'm calling your bluff, Joe," he muttered to himself. "Let's see you spiritualize your way out of this one."

Somehow, deep down, Charlie knew the boy would do exactly that. Hell, after all Charlie had seen in the last few days, one more miracle wouldn't surprise him much. Eggos and Jimmy Dean sausage patties didn't sound as impressive as loaves and fishes, but maybe history would clean it up, he thought wryly. Mac looked up at him with a sappy grin, as if he could read his thoughts, and looking down, Charlie grinned right back.

No longer worried, no longer ticked off, Charlie stared out the kitchen window and watched Joe in the distance. The singing of the crowd was so heartfelt now that it brought a threat of tears to Charlie's eyes. In the throng of worshipers now sitting or kneeling around the boy, acres and acres of tear-streaked faces all staring intently at the wonders Joe was performing, Charlie saw two people, a woman and a man, wending a path between the bodies, heading straight for Joe.

Something in the tilt of the woman's head, the shape of her body, the familiar color of her auburn hair, caused Charlie's breath to stop. He leaned closer to the window, peering out over the heads of the kneeling mob.

It was Judith. Who the man was behind her, Charlie didn't know, but that was certainly Judith walking with purposeful strides toward the boy. She was clutching something to her chest like a woman in the city passing through a throng of people and afraid of having her purse snatched away by some lowlife in the crowd.

What was she doing? Charlie could feel a threat in the way she moved. He did not know of the gun. He had no memory of it taking his life the night before. He knew only that something was not right. She had been here yesterday, hadn't she? When had she left? Why had he not seen her this morning? Why had he not wondered at her absence?

Charlie jumped at the sound of the microwave beeping off. He scooped the waffles onto the plate with a fork, quickly checked the sausages spattering and popping in the skillet, and when he looked back through the kitchen window at the mass of people once again, Judith and the unknown man were gone. Only Joe stood upright on that weirdly frozen lake and on the green, green grass of Charlie's once-dead lawn. Both the lake and the lawn were invisible now, buried beneath the throng of worshipers sitting and kneeling in the twilight of this waning summer day so unlike any other summer day Charlie had ever known.

Charlie's eyes bored into Joe walking there in the distance, arms outstretched. His lithe young body was obviously wearied now by all he had done, but still the halo of light burned warmly around him. It drew every eye to the promises Joe selflessly offered. And like the roiling wake of a ship's passage, the swell and rise of healed bodies rose up behind Joe to sing his praises as he passed, then settled back once again to humbly kneel upon the ice, as if accepting the fact that this boy, this Messiah, should be the only one to stand among them.

Somewhere in that sea of faces, Judith had hidden herself. Judith and the unknown man. They too, like Charlie, must be watching Joe. Perhaps they, too, were waiting for his shadow to fall across them, waiting for his hand to reach out and free them from their miseries.

Or perhaps, Charlie thought, they carried with them a misery not meant to be healed. A misery not for themselves, but... for another. A misery for Joe.

A nagging scrap of memory wormed its way upward through Charlie's mind. Judith. A gun. A piercing boom of noise, then silence. Joe. In the studio. Peeling bloody clothes from Charlie's body, then wrapping him lovingly in a robe.

Charlie, still standing at the kitchen window, looked down at himself. He played his fingers across his chest as if remembering a long-forgotten wound. Again he searched the crowd for Judith's auburn hair. A fear, a dread like none he had ever felt, began to settle into his thoughts.

He stared at Joe as he stood far out on the frozen lake, enveloped in his halo of light, that light Charlie knew he would one day paint.

Joe was in danger, he suddenly realized, and somehow in the tilt of the boy's head, in the angle of Joe's strong young shoulders, Charlie knew Joe could feel that danger approaching him at this very moment, drawing ever nearer, looming closer with every passing second like a long-written fate. A fate beyond any power on earth to escape.

Words suddenly screamed in Charlie's mind—words he did not want to hear, did not want to comprehend. But they came nevertheless, tearing into him like a bullet.

Today is the day. This is Joe's Calvary. This is his crucifixion!

Charlie thought of *Freedom*. The boy's perfect body, so lovingly rendered, rising into the sky on wings of glistening acrylic light. An ascension, Joe had said, looking for the first time on the painting that had sailed so easily from Charlie's hand to canvas. A resurrection. But before he could be resurrected, Joe had jokingly told him, he would have to be dead.

Only martyrs live forever, Charlie thought. Only martyrs are ever truly worshiped. Like the first brother. Like Jesus. The one they nailed to a cross.

Charlie saw it all so clearly now. And looking out at the boy in the twilight, a hot tear burned a path down his cheek.

"No!" he railed, as anger surged through him at the feel of that hot tear burning into his skin. "Not now! Not today! It's too soon!"

And Charlie flung himself through the cabin door and ran out into the waning light, but he knew even then that it was too late.

For already, out of that sea of kneeling bodies, Charlie saw Judith's auburn hair rising up from the crowd. In her hand he saw a gleam of metal.

Screaming, he ran toward her, fighting the crowd. But his movements were so slow. His voice so dimmed. He was mired as if in a dream, where the body is stunted with fear, where the monster approaches but you cannot run.

He reached out his hand, then stumbled. The ground rushed up at him. As it rose to meet him, he heard Joe's voice speaking softly to him from the dream.

"Let it be, Charlie. Let it be."

Weeping and helpless, Charlie fell, a slow, drawn-out motion that seemed to take forever. Before he hit the earth, every moment he had shared with the boy passed through his mind.

Every moment but one.

JUDITH FORCED her way through the crowd until she stood within twenty feet of Joe. Then she lowered herself to the ice, wondering at the odd feel of it. Pleasantly cool but not cold. Joe had done this, she knew. He needed more room for his worshipers to gather around him, more room for these pathetic fools to grovel at his feet like a pack of slavering dogs, begging a crumb of kindness from their master.

She glanced at the faces around her. What would they do if they knew her reason for being here? Would they rise up like animals and tear her to shreds in a frenzy of righteousness? Would they reduce her body to tattered shreds of flesh and a few splinters of glistening bone? Would her blood slowly freeze into the surface of the lake, streams of red on silver ice, like the colors in one of Charlie's chaotic paintings?

Angrily, she tore her mind from these thoughts and gazed upon Joe. Did he know she was near? Did he feel his death approaching? She wondered. Even as she walked through the crowd, he did not turn to look at her. Did he know that their destinies were tied together like two lengths of string twisted into one unalterable knot? Did he care that she suffered so in the knowledge of what she was about to do, or was she merely a cog in the machine that chugged and thrummed and led them each toward their inescapable fates?

Where her hatred for the boy came from, she did not know or care. But like the fetus of her unwanted child, it grew stronger inside her with every passing second.

Judith watched Joe now as he laid his hand upon the brow of a young woman whose body had turned on her, leaving her twisted, like a tree bent into agonizing shapes by an unending wind on the edge of some stony, stormy cliff. At the mere touch of Joe's fingers on her tortured flesh, the woman's limbs straightened beneath her. Tears of wonder flowed from her eyes. She reached out to Joe with a hand that only moments before she could not move, and Judith saw the boy smile down at her before walking on.

Judith found herself weeping as the bondage of pain and helplessness left the woman's body, but inside she railed at the injustice of it. Why should *she* suffer so when this stranger before her no longer did? Why should she alone among this crowd of fools be the only one left to writhe in torment?

She felt the weight of the gun in her purse, remembered the feel of it in her hand. It was calling to her now. Begging for the caress of her touch to bring it to life. It had but a single purpose, that gun. It was forged for no other reason but one. Yet without a human hand to guide it, it was a worthless chunk of metal. Cold and lifeless. But when it spoke, its voice could be heard above all others. *Let me speak*, it whispered to her now. *I can ease your pain even if this boy before you will not.*

Let me speak.

And slowly, Judith let her hand slide into the purse. The gun slipped into her grasp as easily as Cinderella's foot gliding into the slipper of glass. A perfect fit. As the cold metal warmed beneath her touch, Judith raised herself to her feet. Never before had she felt such exquisite resolve.

Or such thundering sorrow.

Through a blur of hot tears, she stared at Joe as he calmly turned to her at last. His angelic face was still lit by that golden aura of light that seemed to radiate from his flesh. His arms were still splayed out wide, encompassing all around him, his hands cupped upward as if grasping invisible orbs. He smiled kindly at her, even as the gun in her hand rose to the level of his heart.

And at the moment when his smile first touched her, at the moment when she first looked fully upon the sweetness of his face, the boy swam away from her, and he became in her eyes the man from her nightmare. Judas. The betrayer. The golden light that lit the boy from head to toe became a shroud of flaming robes.

Judith's eyes darkened. Her finger found the trigger of the gun that felt so at home now in her trembling hand, and as the gun opened its mouth to speak at last, a body struck her from behind. Judith cried out as the gun itself cried out. Then it cried out again. The air filled suddenly with screams as the crowd rose up around her, drowning the echo of the second shot in a wail of fear and panic.

As desperate hands pushed her down, Judith heard the gun skitter away across the ice.

WINNIE SAT in wonder as he watched the boy enveloped in golden light perform miracle after miracle. He realized that until this moment, he had never truly believed in the story of this mysterious Messiah. He had merely hoped it was true, not for the world, but for himself. For what he could reap from it. Now, all thoughts of Pulitzers and journalistic glories were swept away in the rush of emotion that bombarded his senses as he watched the boy walk among the crowd, his shadow and his hands curing each and every ill that passed within his sphere.

Winnie was so caught up in the moment, in the simple breathtaking beauty of it all, that the movie camera hung forgotten on his shoulder. Even the woman with the gun was almost forgotten. Almost.

Remembering, Winnie turned back to her now. He watched her as she sat among the crowd less than ten feet away. She was staring intently at the boy. Even from where he sat, he could see a tear wend its way along the woman's cheek. That look of venom that had so startled him earlier still burned in her eyes like a vicious ember, and seeing it, Winnie reluctantly tore his attention from the boy to study her more closely.

He could see her body tensing, like a cat preparing to pounce, and when she stood, Winnie stood with her, his heart pounding in his chest. He saw the boy turn to face her then, as if he knew she had always been there, as if he knew exactly what her purpose was. When the woman reached her hand into her purse to pull out the gun, Winnie screamed out a warning.

Tripping and stumbling across the kneeling bodies in front of him, Winnie flung himself at the woman at the precise moment the gun exploded in her hand. A second gunshot boomed around him as he drove her to the ice.

Screams erupted from the crowd. Winnie had only a moment to lift his head to see if either gunshot had found the boy's flesh. In that brief second of time, he saw the boy standing uninjured, his arms still reaching out as if in supplication, before an avalanche of bodies swept over him in panic and fear, fleeing from the sound of gunfire, driving the boy to the ground as Winnie had driven the woman to the ground. Even now she lay screaming in anger beneath him.

As the boy disappeared beneath the stampeding crowd, bodies swept over Winnie as well. Trampling feet scored his flesh. He felt a rib snap as a boot struck him from the side. Another smashed his hand, and before he could cry out in pain, before he could see his own blood begin to flow across the ice, a foot struck his forehead and drove all awareness from his mind.

Moments after the blackness of unconsciousness took him, another foot, driven by panic, came crashing down to snap his spine like a matchstick, and Winnie opened his eyes to a misty light that seemed to gather him into its warmth like a mother's arms.

Lost in the beauty of that welcoming light, Winnie did not recognize his own death for what it was, and if he had, it would not have troubled him.

SHIELDED BY the body of the man above her, Judith felt the crowd swarming over her, screaming out their panic at the sound of her gunshots, but not one foot touched her. She could feel the man whose body protected her being jarred and pummeled by a thousand rampaging feet. She saw his hand splintered into the ice beneath a bootheel only inches from her face, and she felt his body grow still above her when the final, irreparable damage was done to his flesh.

She did not know if Joe was alive or dead. But more importantly, she did not remember now why it was she had done what she did. What motivations had driven her to such a desperate act? And what did those motivations say of her? Was she truly as evil as her actions made her out to be? She had not always been so, had she? If God knew such evil lay dormant inside her, why hadn't she been taken in the fires? Why had that evil been allowed to fester and spread until it filled her like the stuffing in the battered Raggedy Ann doll she had played with as a child?

Judith closed her eyes and waited for her own death, hoping all the while that it would come quickly. But life had apparently not finished with her torment, for death did not come at all. The stampede of bodies slowed, and the panicked crowd gradually ceased their rampage. An odd stillness descended around her. As the knowledge of her own survival began to settle into her mind, Judith screamed in silent outrage at the unfairness of it.

When the blood of the battered man lying atop her seeped down across her face, and the man's silent weight, in a stillness that could only come from death, settled over her like a spent lover, Judith opened her eyes. The first sound she heard was the beating of her own heart pumping out the detested rhythm of her own unwanted life. Then she heard the eerie, awakening rustle of the stunned crowd as they began to move around her. Hushed voices murmured through the summer twilight. Soon they would come for her, these people. Soon they would know what she had done.

Where was the gun? Judith longed to hold it in her hand once more. To feel its weight. Its power.

To press it to her temple and hear it speak one last time, just to her.

A LEADEN silence descended across the frozen lake. Charlie opened his eyes to the empty sound of it. Wiping a sodden warmth from his face, he looked down to see a smear of blood on his fingertips. He raised his head to look around and saw the crowd, standing now, no longer running. They looked numbed and confused by the panic that had taken them. In every face, Charlie saw a stunned uncertainty. What had happened? In silence, they stared out at the frozen lake, and as they stared, their silence was slowly replaced by the sound of hushed whispers. Soon those whispers became a rising wail of grief that tore at Charlie's heart like a knife.

Struggling to his feet, Charlie stumbled out across the ice, searching for Joe in the crowd. Where was he? Why was he not standing where he stood before, encircled by that lustrous golden aura that had followed him through all the long hours of the day? That light had grown ever paler as the day wore on, as Joe's strength waned more and more with every healing he performed. Charlie had seen Joe gradually weaken. Why had he not tried to stop him? Why had he let Joe wear himself out dispensing mercies that none here truly deserved? Charlie did not care that Joe had eased these people's miseries; he cared only for the boy. And now he could not see him, and his own panic began to set in.

"Joe!" he cried out, pushing aside those in his path who stood around like cattle, lost in their own confusion, not knowing where to go, what to do. A growing dread settled into Charlie as he moved deeper through the milling crowd. Here, far from the shore, he saw still bodies on the ice. Ravaged bodies. Bodies torn and bruised by the feet of those who moments before had joined their voices in songs of praise. But then the singing had turned to screams. At the sound of gunshots in the crowd, the singers were driven to the ice. Trampled. Maimed.

On more than one face, Charlie saw the vacant stare of death. Many were children, those whose small bodies were less able to shield themselves from the rampage that had swooped down upon them.

Why was Joe not casting his shadow over these small, bloodied faces, erasing death, erasing wounds, bestowing life as he had done so many times before? Where had he gone? Why was he not here?

And then Charlie saw him, far out across the ice, lying in a crumpled stillness that brought a sob of fear to Charlie's lips. Filled with dread and blinded by his own tears, Charlie ran to him, shoving aside those who stood in his way, screaming out his anguish at every face that stared so stupidly at him, pushing away every hand that reached out to him for help, as if theirs was the only misery that mattered.

Only steps away from Joe, Charlie stopped, his heartbeat pulsing in his ears, his hands clenched tightly at his sides. Trembling, he stared down at the bloodied mass that lay before him.

Joe's body had been torn and trampled, savaged by the countless feet that had passed over him like a roaring avalanche of jagged stones. His arms, still stretched out to either side as if gathering the world to his embrace even now, were twisted and broken. A bright sliver of bone protruded from one and a horrible gash of shredded flesh marred the beauty of the other. His legs, once so strong, like slender trees rooted to the earth, were now flayed beyond recognition of human flesh at all. Joe's face was swollen and distorted to a tortured caricature of itself. His hair awash with blood, Charlie saw the faintest glimmer of yellow light still shine across the battered brow, winking like the final flicker of a dying candle.

"No...," Charlie whispered.

Dropping to his knees beside Joe, he laid a trembling hand upon the torn cheek, and at his touch, Joe's eyes slowly opened. The brown, bottomless well of those eyes, once so wise, so caring, so startling to look upon, were now filled with pain. But there was love there too, Charlie saw, as the boy's gaze finally settled upon his face.

"Charlie," Joe said, his breathless voice as twisted and torn as his body. "My poor Charlie."

Charlie fought back the tears that threatened to silence him, and forcing a smile to his lips, he bent to press his smile to the boy's bloodied brow. Joe's savaged arm came up to brush Charlie's cheek before it fell again weakly to the ice. He closed his eyes for a moment, as if willing the pain to leave him, but when it did not, he opened them to gaze once again on Charlie's face.

"I should have trusted you, Charlie," Joe said, his voice so frail that Charlie had to press his ear to Joe's lips to hear it. "I should have trusted myself. I should not have held myself from you. All I did in the end was exchange love for regret. I'm sorry."

Again, Charlie forced a smile to his lips. "If there is regret, Joe, then it is all in you. Not me. I don't regret one moment of the time I've had with you."

"Even this one?" Joe asked, trying to force a grin to lips that could hardly move.

Charlie grinned for him, all the while feeling his heart plummet inside him, like a cold stone sinking to the depths of the sea. "Maybe this moment I could live without."

"When I'm gone...," Joe began.

Charlie stopped him. "You're not going anywhere. I won't let you."

Joe sighed. A bubble of blood burst upon his lips. He ignored it as he ignored Charlie's words. "When I'm gone, remember the child. Remember the mother."

Anger suddenly swelled in Charlie at the memory of Judith approaching Joe. The gun in her hand. The shots that created the panic that led to Joe lying before him now, bloodied and wracked with the pain of a shattered, twisted body.

"She did this to you, Joe. Don't ask me to help her. Ask me anything, but don't ask me that."

"But that's exactly what I'm asking of you, Charlie. If you won't do it for the child, then do it for me. Please."

Charlie watched as a tear formed at the corner of Joe's eye and glistened there for a moment before falling like a drop of dew from a dying petal.

"All right, Joe. Whatever you want."

"She was forced to do what she did, Charlie. Never forget that. And never let *her* forget it. Perhaps it will ease her pain. Her suffering will be the greatest of anyone's. Help her through it, Charlie. Help her survive."

"And what about me, Joe? Without you, how do I survive?"

Joe's eyes turned away from him and stared up at that dark, hovering cloud. It boomed softly now above their heads with a renewed rumble of distant thunder. As Charlie watched Joe, he saw the mirrored image of that looming cloud of shadow reflected in Joe's pain-riddled eyes. Then he felt the first cool patter of raindrops on his face.

Joe sighed. "The father is weeping for her, Charlie."

"No," Charlie answered. "It's just the rain."

Again, Joe rested his eyes on Charlie's face. "I've taken memories from you, Charlie."

"Memories?"

"Yes. Memories of what I thought you didn't need to remember. Some bad. Some good. When I die, they will be restored to you. I cannot leave you thinking you never knew me. I came to you, Charlie. You don't remember, but I came to you. In the night. I… I don't remember now which night it was. I came to you just as I've always known you wanted me to. But I didn't do it for you, Charlie. I did it for myself. I wanted you. I still want you. Every thought that enters my head has you in it."

Charlie opened his mouth to speak, but the words would not come. He brushed hot tears from his eyes and pushed a strand of bloody hair away from the boy's face with shaky fingers.

Finally, Charlie found his voice, a thing so shattered by grief and loss that he did not recognize it as his own.

"You lied to me, Joe. You said we would always be together."

Joe, too, delved inward through the pain to find his voice. What was left of it was little more than an agonized whisper. "I did not lie. One day we will be together."

"In death?"

"Not as you know it."

"In life, then?"

"Not as you know it."

"Ah, Christ, Joe! What's left?"

Joe gave Charlie a weak smile as another bubble of blood burst upon his lips. "You'll see."

The light that had feebly glowed across Joe's brow was gone now. And the light in his tortured eyes was dimming as well. Pain was taking him away. Or perhaps it was Death himself coming for the boy. Charlie screamed inwardly at the helplessness he felt, but he buried his panic, his desperation, deep inside himself, where the boy would not see it. Joe had suffered enough. He did not need the sight of Charlie's pain compounding his own.

"Did we make love, Joe?" he finally asked. "On the night you came to me, did we…."

"Yes." Joe said. "We made love."

Charlie's breath was a rope that threatened to strangle his words. He had to force them from his mouth, buried in a sob. "Was it a sin?"

At long last, Joe was able to force a true smile to his lips. "No, Charlie. Love is never a sin. Love is…."

A whimper of anguish tore from the boy, and Charlie clutched Joe's hand to help ease him through it.

"Don't leave me, Joe. Stay with me."

Joe's fingers tightened around his own, and as the light dimmed further in the boy's eyes, he said, "… a flower."

Charlie smiled, tasting tears. "I know."

"Live a good man's life, Charlie. Remember me. Remember it all."

And as the light flickered out, as the boy's eyelids slowly closed upon this earth for the final time, Charlie felt again the boy's flesh against his own, heard the words of wonder they had breathed in the darkness on the night their bodies finally met in passion. Tasted again every moment of the time they spent in each other's arms. Each second flooded back to him, and when it did, he gasped at the beauty of it.

Feeling Joe's hand relax to stillness in his grasp, Charlie laid his head upon the boy's silent chest.

"I remember, Joe. I remember."

Then he closed his eyes, as Joe's were closed, and his grief truly began. But even in that grief, even as the sound of his own weeping began to fill his ears, he thought of the painting resting on the easel in the studio at the edge of the lake. He saw once again Joe's earthly body, on canvas, rising to the sky on a shimmering beam of wondrous light.

When the raindrops stopped, Charlie lifted his head from Joe's chest, and gazed upward to the sky. He watched in amazement as the great thundercloud opened wide. A golden ray of evening sunshine pierced its darkness, streaming downward like a finger of light and mist until it lit the boy's face where he lay upon the ice.

And as Charlie watched in wonder, Joe's wounds simply faded away. Joe's spilled blood dissolved into wisps of smoke upon his flesh, to be whisked away on a freshening breeze that suddenly swept across the ice. Joe opened his eyes, eyes clear now and free of pain, as brown and bottomless as the first time Charlie had looked into them. Sadly, Joe smiled at Charlie's tears. He reached out a hand, a hand no longer maimed and bloodied, but beautiful and strong and warm, and with a gentle brush of his fingertips, he wiped the tears from Charlie's cheek.

"Don't grieve, Charlie. Rejoice. What we shared between us will not die with my body. It lives on. In me. In you. In memory. Savor it and carry it with you always, for that's what I will do. I love you, Charlie. I'll always love you."

Joe tore his gaze from Charlie's stricken face to look around him at the injured and dead. Softly, he said, "Release them, Father. Make them whole."

On the ice around him, the lifeless bodies of men and women and the silent corpses of trampled children awoke from death to find their wounds were healed, their lives restored. Charlie watched as they, each in turn, opened their eyes to that golden beam of light stabbing down from the heavens.

Only when he knew that all were healed, that all were whole, did Joe turn his eyes back to the man kneeling over him.

"Remember me, Charlie," he said.

And Charlie nodded, causing a tear to spill from his eye. "Always, Joe. Always."

At that moment, just as Charlie had painted him, Joe began to pull away. Slowly he rose into the air on that golden shaft of light, cradled softly as in a mother's gentle arms. The light carried Joe high into the sky until he was lost to view, leaving Charlie kneeling on the ice, alone. Weeping tears of both joy and sorrow, Charlie reached out once to his one perfect flower, but Joe was no longer there. The world seemed suddenly a very empty place.

Around Charlie, the wailing of a sorrow other than his own began, as every face followed Joe's ascension into the sepia-clouded sky, as

Joe's body grew smaller and smaller until even the light that carried him was lost in the distance.

Countless tears from countless upturned faces, like rain, floated down upon the ice.

But for the weeping, the glade fell silent.

CHAPTER TWENTY-FOUR
...AND AN END.

FOR ALMOST four years, Charlie watched from the privacy of his secluded lake as the world gradually settled back into its remembered patterns of good and evil. The Day of Burning, as it came to be called, had winnowed out much of Earth's cause for sorrow, but like hidden cancer cells that, untouched by treatment, soon reconstitute themselves into a life-threatening illness once again, so too did those few untouched cells of evil that escaped the fires eventually blossom and thrive. Once again they returned to infest the earth with all the tortures for mankind that for a little while the world had been freed of. Crime. War. Famine. Hatred. They all returned.

And the Day of Burning, Charlie feared, was all but forgotten.

The two thousand apostles Joe had appointed on the day of his ascension still labored at the task of bringing the Second Son's message to the world. The torment they carried with them through every moment of their lives at their unintended participation in the new Messiah's death gave fervor to their preachings. It was, Charlie knew, a desperate attempt to right the wrong of what they had done, to mitigate their own guilt, although Joe himself had orchestrated his own passing. Still, their desperate, heartfelt testimonies were never quite enough to counteract the return of evil.

Charlie offered testimony to Joe's life as well. *Freedom* even now toured the museums of the world on an endless pilgrimage of its own, taking Joe's face to the millions who had not looked upon him in life but who still honored him, although perhaps not as deeply as they once had. The gentle, charismatic eyes on Charlie's canvas drew many into the light of salvation, but to those souls already lost to evil, the mystery, the promise, the selfless compassion that still radiated from those painted eyes, meant little or nothing.

Judith's child, when his own pilgrimage of teaching began, would strive to remedy that indifference. Charlie knew this because Joe had said it would be so. Still a toddler, the child was blissfully unaware of the fate that awaited him. He, above all others, had been chosen to carry Joe's true message to the world, and Charlie sometimes watched the boy as he played, wondering if the life Joe had mapped out for the child would one day bring him great happiness or great sadness.

Charlie watched, too, as Judith's guilt drove her ever deeper into a numbing depression that eventually separated her completely from the lives around her. It was an abyss neither Charlie nor the child could find a way to reach down into to offer solace. Judith resided now on a different plane than they—a plane as unreachable as the one Joe had flown to on the day of his ascension, except Judith's plane did not consist of silvery light and love and the peaceful contentment of fond memory. Hers spoke of grief and guilt and dark, impenetrable torment. Charlie could see that torment, that abyss, every time he looked into the vacant green ocean of her empty eyes.

Charlie had done as Joe asked. He had sheltered the woman and child as best he could, erecting iron gates at the entrance to the lane leading to his property to stem the tide of worshipers who still traveled far to reach the shores of the lake. They came to kneel upon the ground where Joe had walked. They came to pray. Charlie would see them now and then, praying at the edge of the water, and he would speak to them kindly, asking them to respect his privacy, and they would always politely leave when their prayers were finished, but soon others would come to take their place. At those times, when strangers prayed by the water, Judith would hide away inside the cabin, trembling in fear. Charlie would hold her hand at such times and speak softly to her, but he knew his words did not reach her. Where her terror and guilt had taken her, Charlie could not follow.

Not once since Joe left them had Charlie touched her as a lover, for Judith's desires, all but the most rudimentary—hunger and a need for sleep—left her forever on the day of Joe's death. She no longer spoke, and her silences sometimes echoed through the cabin like the funereal tolling of a great bell. And at those times when her guilt lay upon her most heavily, Charlie would take her into his arms and whisper consoling words to her, but he suspected that the sound of his voice never entered her ears. As Joe asked him to do, he had pushed away his anger at what she did by the lake that day, and in pushing it away, he found some little peace for himself.

From the day of his birth, the child meant nothing to Judith. Too lost in her own misery to see the beauty of this being she had brought into the world, or the fate that awaited him, she ignored his existence completely. Charlie took the raising of the child into his own hands and, much to his surprise, found great fulfillment in doing so. In memory of the young man who had given him so much, Charlie named the child Joe. And sometimes, when the light was right and memories of old happinesses settled over him, Charlie thought he saw the other Joe in the sparkle of the child's eyes, or heard the other Joe in the chirping laughter on the child's lips.

They became inseparable, him and the child. Wherever he went, he always knew that both Mac and little Joe were trailing along behind him like two shadows, for Mac, too, had accepted the child as his own. Once, when Charlie's attention was elsewhere, he heard a plaintive wail coming from the edge of the lake. Running to investigate, he found Mac tugging a furious Joe by the seat of his pants, away from the shore where Mac had apparently decided the child had wandered too near the water. Charlie had scooped them both in his arms and smothered them each in turn with such admonishment and gratitude that the child never ventured near the lake again, and Mac never again ventured more than two steps away from little Joe.

Charlie's work continued. He painted every day, often late into the night. He seemed to be filled with a well of creativity that, if it had not been emptied daily, would have soon smothered him. Because memories of the young man who had come to him on that summer night so long ago filled every corner of his mind, he painted Joe many times. He remembered every moment of the time they spent together, for upon his death Joe had restored Charlie's memories as he promised. Oddly, with the passing of time, the hour of passion he had spent with Joe seemed of lesser consequence than it once had. Now so many other things about Joe filled his thoughts. The way his hair shone in firelight. The faintest breath of velvet down that shadowed the nape of his neck. The music of his laughter. The gentleness of his eyes. The warmth of his hands, and the soft, caring timbre of his voice when he spoke kind words.

Charlie thought often of his garden and the flowers that still bloomed there every spring. Each dew-laden blossom held a memory for Charlie. Many times, as he passed the flowers along the fence on his way to or from the studio, he would stop and watch their heavy heads sway in the breeze, smell their fragrance sweeten the air around him, and always at those times, memories of Joe would flood through him and he would be happy. He missed Joe, but the fact that Charlie had been blessed to know him at all seemed to be enough to stem his sadness at Joe's absence. Patiently, he waited for the day when he would see Joe again, for not once did he doubt that what Joe had promised would one day come to pass.

Not even the day when Joe left him was a memory that tortured Charlie, for he had seen such happiness on the boy's face when he soared away before him, his wounds healed, his beauty restored, that Charlie knew Joe had gone to a far better place than the one he'd left—a place where he needed to be. He had done all that his father sent him here to do. And more. He had found love for himself and taught love to Charlie. Perhaps that was the greatest of all his miracles. It comforted Charlie to know that Joe was up there, looking down on him, guiding his footsteps even now, watching the child he had placed in Charlie's care, the child who would one day grow to be become a man and fulfill what Joe had foreseen would be his one great task. Charlie still felt Joe's love in every breeze that touched his skin, in every ray of sunlight that warmed his face, in every stroke of paint he placed on canvas. Joe was always with him. Every moment.

Charlie was sorry he never saw the miracle of a handful of Eggos and sausages feeding Joe's thousands. It would have been a fine miracle, he was sure. But somehow that bit of magic was lost in the aftermath of everything else that happened that day upon the ice.

One fall morning, when the air outside was crisp and cool against the skin and the oak leaves in the wood were beginning to brown, Charlie stood inside the studio painting at his easel. At his feet, little Joe painted at his own tiny easel, which Charlie had constructed for him. The child was three years old now and growing like a weed. His painting, Charlie feared, would never find a market, but it was an interesting process to watch and one Charlie never tired of witnessing. With his tiny hand, the child took great pains to create a canvas that his father would be proud of, and occasionally the boy would look up at Charlie to see if he was watching. Today the child was painting what looked to be the figure of a man with a golden helmet around his head.

Joe. Charlie smiled. *He's painting Joe.*

On that day, as the two of them happily created worlds on canvas with brush and paint, Judith walked into the trees surrounding the cabin with a coil of rope in her hands. From those trees, Charlie would never see her living face again. Her guilt and sorrow had taken her at last to a place, a destiny, from which even in her wasted mind she had always known she would not escape.

Her death had little impact on the child. His mother had, after all, been little more than a silent shadow, indifferent to his presence at best, through all the short years of his life. But to Charlie, Judith's death brought forth feelings of his own failure protecting her as Joe had asked. He wept for the woman who had once been his wife, and to his knowledge, he was the only one who did. Where she went upon her death, Charlie would never know.

In the winter of that year, on an evening as beautiful as any he had ever seen, Charlie took the child's hand and led him to the edge of the lake.

As little Joe stooped to dip his fingers in the icy water, Charlie knelt beside him. Looking out across the lake where Joe had once stood at the bow of the boat and laughed as the spray washed over his naked body, Charlie said, "Let me tell you of another boy I once knew. The boy who brought you to me."

"Was he a little boy like me?" the child asked, his eyes as bright as diamonds as he turned from the water to study his father's face.

"No," Charlie said. "He was all grown up. He performed miracles, Joe. He lit the whole world up with his magic."

"I wish he was here now," the child said.

Charlie smiled. "He is, Joe. He will always be here."

And as the winter sun dipped behind the trees, Charlie told the boy many things about the amazing young man who came to him on a summer night that seemed so very long ago, but really wasn't. As he talked, Charlie felt Joe's hand upon his shoulder, heard Joe's laugh again ringing in his ear, while the other Joe, the little Joe, rapt, listened to every word.

EPILOGUE

ONE AUTUMN evening, in his eighty-fifth year of life, Charlie cleaned his brushes and sealed his paints for the very last time. He went to bed an old man and woke up looking as he had at thirty-two, the summer Joe came to him. Once again he was handsome and tall and vibrating with health.

Standing in a white fog as thick and cool as meringue, Charlie looked down at himself and realized he was naked. Grinning, he wiggled his toes. After taking a moment to savor his renewed health and vitality, he reached out with a strong young arm, one he had not wielded for more than five decades, and rapped softly at a wooden door he could not see in the fog but somehow knew was there.

Charlie's grin became a whole lot wider, and he might have even laughed out loud, when Joe threw open the door and pulled him in.

The BOYS on the MOUNTAIN

JOHN INMAN

Jim Brandon has a new house, and boy, is it a pip. Built high on the side of the San Diego mountains by a legendary B-movie actor of the 1930s, Nigel Letters, the house is not only gorgeous, but supposedly haunted. As a writer of horror novels, Jim couldn't be happier.

But after a string of ghostly events sets Jim's teeth on edge and scares the bejesus out of his dog, Jim begins to dig into the house's history. What he finds is enough to creep out anybody. Even Jim. It seems long dead Nigel Letters had a few nasty habits back in his day. And unhappily for Jim, the old bastard still has some tricks up his sleeve.

As Jim welcomes his ex, Michael, and a bevy of old friends for a two-week visit to help christen the new house, he soon realizes his old friends aren't the only visitors who have come to call.

Available at
dsppublications.com

WILLOW MAN
JOHN INMAN

Woody Stiles has sung his country songs in every city on the map. His life is one long road trip in a never-ending quest for fame and fortune. But when his agent books him into a club in his hometown, a place he swore he would never set foot again, Woody comes face to face with a few old demons. One in particular.

With memories of his childhood bombarding him from every angle, Woody must accept the fact that his old enemy, Willow Man, was not just a figment of childish imagination.

With his friends at his side, now all grown up just like he is, Woody goes to battle with the killer that stole his childhood lover. Woody also learns Willow Man has been busy while he was away, destroying even more of Woody's past. And in the midst of all this drama, Woody is stunned to find himself falling in love—something he never thought he would do again.

As kids, Woody and his friends could not stop the killer who lived in the canyon where they played. As adults, they might just have a chance.

Or will they?

Available at
dsppublications.com

JOHN INMAN has been writing fiction since he was old enough to hold a pencil. He and his partner live in beautiful San Diego, California. Together, they share a passion for theater, books, hiking and biking along the trails and canyons of San Diego or, if the mood strikes, simply kicking back with a beer and a movie. John's advice for anyone who wishes to be a writer? "Set time aside to write every day and do it. Don't be afraid to share what you've written. Feedback is important. When a rejection slip comes in, just tear it up and try again. Keep mailing stuff out. Keep writing and rewriting and then rewrite one more time. Every minute of the struggle is worth it in the end, so don't give up. Ever. Remember that publishers are a lot like lovers. Sometimes you have to look a long time to find the one that's right for you."

E-mail: john492@att.net

Facebook: www.facebook.com/john.inman.79

Website: www.johninmanauthor.com

ANGEL
LAURA LEE

MY
DAUGHTER'S
ARMY

GREG HOGBEN

BRANDON WITT
THE
SHATTERED
DOOR

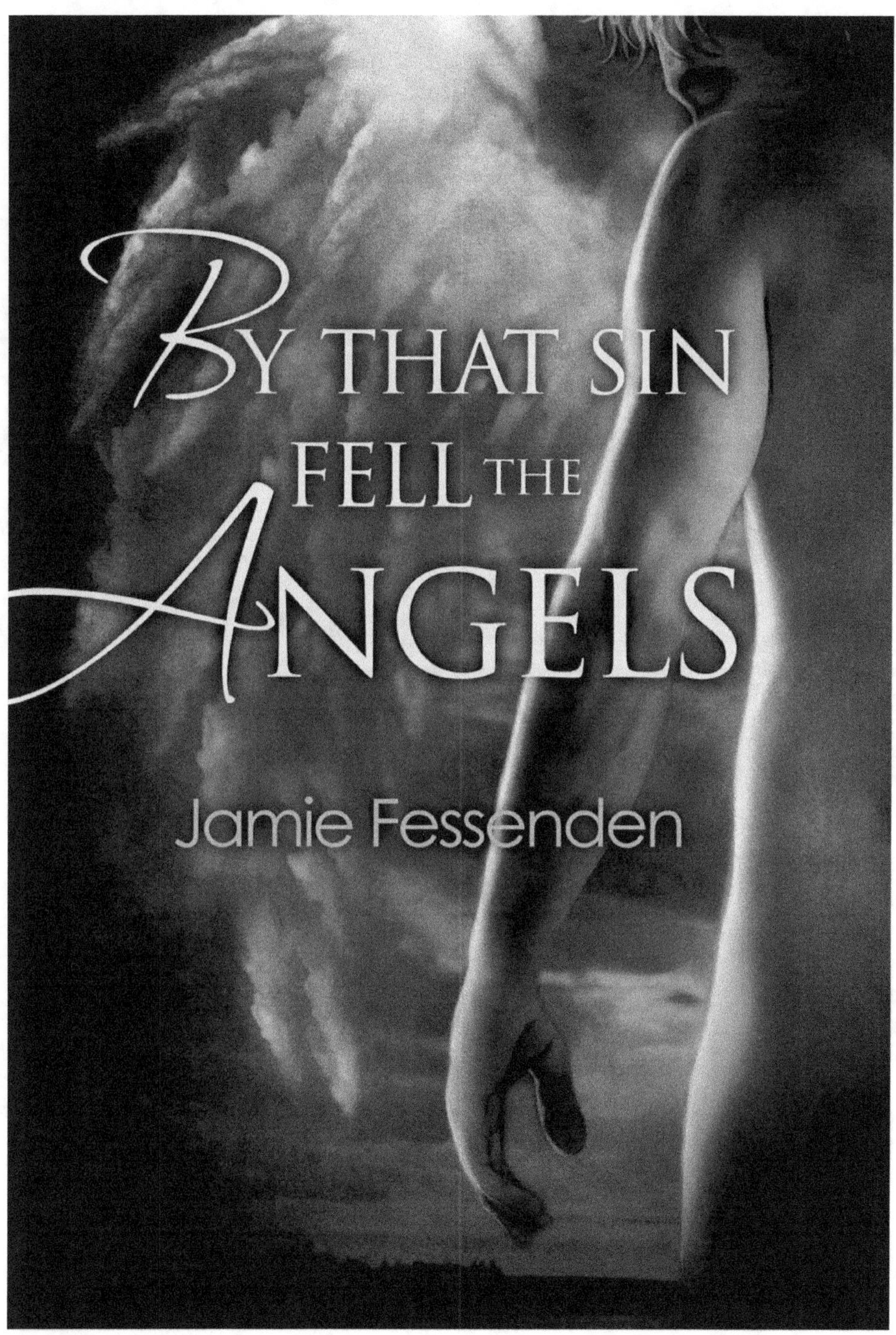

BY THAT SIN
FELL THE
ANGELS
Jamie Fessenden

TRAVELING
LIGHT
LLOYD A. MEEKER

The Falls
A NOVEL BY
JON GARCIA &
MARTY BEAUDET
BASED ON THE
SCREENPLAY BY
JON GARCIA